KILL ME
IF YOU CAN

FRANK LEAN

Secrecy, being an instrument of conspiracy, ought never to be the
system of a regular government.

Essay 'On Publicity'   Jeremy Bentham 1748-1832

1

Monday: Pimpernel Investigations 9 a.m.

Traffic delayed my attempt to cross the road. Rain blurred the windows of Pimpernel Investigations but I could make out a tall, silver-haired figure having an animated conversation with Miss Fothergill, the current secretary cum receptionist. Certainly both were waving their arms to considerable effect. It was impossible to tell if they were having a row or mutually conducting a sound track of the 1812 Overture.

I guessed that Fothergill was trying to give the old guy the brush-off.

I waited impatiently for a gap and then dashed.

I opened the door and entered backwards, folding my umbrella, and turned.

'Oh, Mr Cunane, thank goodness you've arrived,' Fothergill gasped, all hot and flustered. 'I was telling this gentleman that you only take new customers after personal recommendation.'

I was struck dumb.

I've become cautious about accepting commissions from 'walk-ins'. There are so many bloodhounds from the 'media' hoping to make money out of my story that I have to be constantly on the look-out for a set up: phoney Arab sheikhs needing security advice, grief-stricken widows with improbable tales of police negligence, pensioners being persecuted by drug crazed teenagers, etc, etc.

But this was no media sting.

The visitor was the Right Honourable Sir Lewis Greene, one of Her Majesty's senior High Court Judges and without any doubt the most distinguished caller ever to arrive at the office of Pimpernel Investigations.

I gaped at him.

'David, my boy,' he said, striding towards me with his hand extended.

Fothergill looked from me to him, her eyes on stilts.

He gripped my hand and then took my elbow with his left hand as if to make sure that I didn't turn and flee. 'I was explaining to this very charming young lady that my visit is in the nature of an emergency. My

1

purpose in calling on you is absolutely out of the ordinary run of business and I didn't feel able to divulge the details of my problem to her.'

'It's Dave, Uncle Lew … '

'Ah, how well I remember the day you were christened, David for your grandfather and Patrick for your father.'

'And Lewis for you.'

'Indeed, Lewis for me,' he repeated.

His words rapped out like the smack of a judge's gavel.

Sir Lewis Greene is an 'uncle' by courtesy, he's actually my godfather.

'This is Sir Lewis Greene,' I said to Fothergill.

'Oh, I'm so very, very sorry Mr Cunane,' Fothergill said putting her hand over her mouth to cover the pout her full lips were forming. She looked as if she expected the ground to swallow her up, or at least to be peremptorily fired. I suppose that's a fair indication of how things are at Pimpernel Investigations these days.

I was embarrassed by her discomfort.

Fothergill is a tall, slim and attractive young woman. She has what Jan tells me is a layered blonde hairstyle and wears her hair long. When Uncle Lew described her as very charming he wasn't exaggerating. Several of my investigators had asked me who the 'hot-tottie' was and one in particular, Greg Loveland, has managed to find his way round to her side of the reception desk several times. She's repelled him very efficiently so far and I've had no cause to intervene. As long as she doesn't start coming on to me I've no complaints. Neatly dressed in a dark business suit, she raises the tone of the office.

'Not your fault,' I said. 'You can't be expected to know every branch of the Cunane family tree.'

'Indeed, who could know such a tangled thicket?' Sir Lew gallantly seconded.

Fothergill slumped to her seat and composed herself. I think if she'd cried I'd have given her a week's paid leave.

I looked at our visitor with raised eyebrows.

My godfather didn't dispute being on the Cunane family tree because although undocumented, it's almost certain that the Greenes and the Cunanes are related. In one way or another, by pestilence or fratricidal war, the relevant Irish records have been destroyed. It's said that the two families shared a cellar in Liverpool for a while when they arrived in England in the 1840s, washed out of Ireland by the tide of disease and death scouring that country. They'd certainly come from the same village in the west of Ireland, and links with the old country were maintained for generations as the clannish immigrants mostly married newly arrived compatriots.

How often have I been told the story?

Sir Lew Greene attended the same primary school as my father, Paddy, lived in the same street and went to the same church. In every way his background was similar to my father's and they were best friends. Then something happened, a fork in the road of their life together.

A relative left a small fortune to Lewis's mother.

Lewis and his brother were taken out of the parish school and sent to a public school in Yorkshire and then to Cambridge. Dad joined the police and did well but Lewis became a leading QC and then a High Court judge. Somewhere along the line he also became godfather to his friend's son but my contact with him had dwindled to zero over the last few years.

I'm a sheep with a woolly coat of the very blackest hue.

'You'd show me through, Sir Lew,' I said, gesturing towards my office door. Although the headquarters of Pimpernel Investigations isn't palatial there are several offices beyond the reception area as well as a secretarial space where office equipment used for preparing client reports is kept. For some reason Fothergill was the only person present this morning. Probably the weather had caused massive traffic jams.

'Now, David,' Sir Lew said, 'you know I prefer Uncle Lew.'

'OK,' I murmured weakly. There was something in the way he said my name that made me feel like a greedy boy caught with his hand in the biscuit tin. A prisoner under sentence, but what had I done wrong?

Or what had he done wrong?

This was unprecedented: a house-call from the highest echelon of the judiciary. What problem could the redoubtable Sir Lewis Greene have that required my intervention? Did he want to secretly investigate one of his colleagues?

'Perhaps you could bring us some coffee in a few minutes,' I suggested to Fothergill. I wanted to space things out with Uncle Lew. There had to be something very weird going on.

Then it struck me.

Lew had been sent to deliver bad news about my parents.

That fear was dispelled as soon as he entered my room and took a seat.

'Paddy and Eileen are both well?' he asked.

'As far as I know,' I muttered. 'I thought for a minute you were bringing me bad news about them.'

'No,' he said abruptly. 'You may think that what I have to say is bad news but it's not about them.'

I studied him more closely.

Puzzlingly there was no evidence that he'd been rained on like the rest of us and no sign of a coat or umbrella. As usual he was superbly tailored in a dark blue Savile Row suit which fitted his thin and lanky frame to perfection. He had one of those perfectly proportioned slim figures.

Even so, his features hadn't escaped the ravages of age. As he relaxed into his chair I noticed that his hair was thinner than I remembered. Pink scalp now gleamed beneath the silver threads and his face was lined with worry.

'You're looking well,' he commented as if reading my mind, 'unfortunately I can't say the same for myself as I'm sure you're too polite to say.'

'Not at all, sir, you haven't aged a day since I last saw you. But you must be getting close to the big Seven Oh. Don't they retire you then?'

This bright suggestion produced a brief and stillborn smile. White teeth gleamed for a nanosecond. There was something chilly behind his expression that triggered thoughts of 'hanging judges' in my easily stimulated imagination. Unlike many of his colleagues Sir Lew would have donned the black cap with pleasure if asked.

I shivered inwardly.

I desperately wanted to keep the small talk going.

That was preferable to discovering the reason for his visit.

Sleazy private detective and High Court Judge, that pairing didn't come tripping off the tongue. An old-fashioned moralist, Sir Lew had disapproved of my former life style and like my dear parents; he never shirked his duty in letting me know it.

But through all the coldness peripheral contacts were maintained.

I attended his wife Magdalen's funeral but that was years ago. He sent me Christmas and birthday cards of the smallest available dimension. I always found something tasteless to send to him and that was the limit of our relationship until quite recently.

'David, I haven't called on you for polite chit-chat.'

'No.'

'You wouldn't know, because it's secret but for the last few

4

months I've been conducting a high level inquiry on behalf of Her Majesty's Government into the extra-judicial activities of the security services in relation to the terrorist threat to this country. It's known as the EJA Inquiry. There's been much talk of enhanced interrogation techniques lately.'

His words fell across my desk like particles of ice.

'You mean torture?'

'In layman's terms, yes, although those involved bitterly dispute the use of that word. However many other covert methods of garnering information are at issue.'

'Blackmail, bribery and wiretaps?'

'You seem well informed but then you always were a bright lad. Such a pity,' he said with a sigh.

'What's a pity?'

'Nothing.'

I stirred uneasily.

'David there's a great deal about you that I've always admired ...
'

'Go on!'

'Yes, your élan, your coolness, and the way you've picked yourself up and started again after the recent setback.'

'Hmmmmph.'

'Many men in your position would have taken the money and opted for a quiet life but not you. You're a man of style and character. Your father and I were wrong to condemn you as a maverick. I now realise that your resistance to the arrogance of bureaucrats in or out of uniform is entirely admirable.'

'How interesting,' I murmured.

'You're right to be sceptical but I assure you that my admiration is sincere. Could it be something ancestral? After all we share a certain background.'

I stopped myself laughing out loud at this. When I was in prison I had received no visits from Sir Lewis Greene.

Now he was pleading a case.

Why?

My mind raced as I wondered what was coming next.

'I see that you're tiring of my conversation.'

'Not at all, Uncle Lew.'

'Brevity being the soul of wit, I press on. In the course of my inquiries I learned about the activities of a certain individual. I've come to

5

you because I believe that individual's death needs to be expedited in the national interest.'

I felt a sudden sharp surge of anger.

'Let me make sure I've got this right, Uncle Lew,' I said coldly. 'You've come to me because you need advice on how to murder someone?'

He nodded and started to say something else but I waved him to silence. Uncle Lew wanted someone dead. Why didn't he just get in touch with the Underworld and find himself a hit man. Then the hairs on the back of my neck stood up. I realised that that was just what the Right Honourable Sir Lewis Greene thought he was doing now.

'So, Uncle Lew, shall we just pretend that I haven't heard a word you've said and simply stop this interview before we both commit a crime?'

I pushed my chair back and started to stand up but there was a tap on the door and a silent Miss Fothergill entered and served us coffee from a trolley. She placed the cups and saucers, coffee, milk, cream and sugar with the utmost elegance. I subsided and fixed my godfather with my bleakest gaze.

We sipped our coffee in silence. Finally Lew put his cup down.

'Killing isn't murder in this case,' he stated flatly. 'Your past reputation for ruthlessness suggests that you haven't always been so scrupulous. There is such a thing as justifiable homicide.'

'No,' I said, 'whatever you say, you're not getting me to do your dirty work for you.'

He nodded, settled into his chair and fixed me with that special glare judges develop after their first week on the bench.

I glared right back.

'Not a respecter of persons, are you David?'

'Listen Uncle Lew, this is the first time I've had a visit from you in how long?'

'Actually this is my first visit to your office, David.'

'Yes, the first ever visit and ...'

'I attended your wedding reception. That was quite a recent event.'

'You came for five minutes, shook my hand, gave Jan a peck on the cheek, spoke to my father and left.'

'That's an overstatement, I did make an appearance. I'm sure Janine will be a fine wife for you now that you've normalised your relationship with her.'

6

'Our relationship's always been normal.'

'Perhaps I should have said normalised by the standards your parents and I grew up with. In any case, in my circumstances one's social contacts are necessarily limited.'

'You mean you can't risk being seen with a shady character like me.'

'I thought the sterling silver coffee service I gave you and your bride was a fine gift, a peace offering to mark the ending of strained relations.'

'Thank you very much, but it doesn't entitle you to recruit me as an assassin.'

'Dear boy, you don't have to be the one who performs the actual deed. I've come because I know you have contacts and there's no one else I can turn to. I've thought this out more carefully than anything in my entire life. The man I want, I have the details with me.'

'No!' I said sharply, 'there must be no details.'

'But how can you decide unless you know the circumstances?'

He was irritatingly certain that I'd do what he wanted but whatever he'd been reaching for in an inner pocket stayed there.

I ought to have taken him by the scruff of his scrawny judicial neck and thrown him out.

But I couldn't.

Against my better judgement, I couldn't just turn him away.

A stronger beverage than coffee was called for. I opened the desk drawer and took out a bottle of Glenmorangie and uncorked it.

The Right Honourable almost snatched the offered glass from my hand. I'd poured out a good two fingers of the golden liquid but he drained his glass immediately and pushed it across the desk for more.

'My nerves haven't been good lately,' he admitted.

Thankfully he sipped the second glass rather than knocking it back.

'I realise that I'm putting you in a difficult position and if there was any earthly way I could avoid it I would.'

'You don't know what you're asking.'

'So you will consider it?' he asked eagerly.

'I haven't said that.'

I sighed and swallowed a mouthful of whisky.

I hadn't said it but I knew that I was considering it. It was ridiculous. A High Court judge was soliciting murder and I was listening. What could be so threatening to a High Court judge that his thoughts turned to murder?

Was he being blackmailed?

I waited.

Finally he spoke.

'You're humouring me, aren't you? You can't appreciate how embarrassing and out of character this is for me.'

'I'm listening, Uncle Lew. It's not often I find myself being propositioned to kill a total stranger. In fact this is a first for me too.'

'Touché,' he murmured. 'I've been unfair by coming to you.'

'What, just by calling at my office?'

'Yes, I'm afraid that the man in question may be aware of my intentions and by calling at your office I may have put you in danger. My researches may have touched a hidden trip-wire.'

'You could have come here for any reason.'

'The man concerned has a knack of knowing what people are thinking. I've been told that he's always that one step ahead. I took every precaution but he may have followed me here.'

'So I may already be up to my neck in this?'

'You may be.'

'Can't you go to the police? They're bound to take a High Court judge seriously.'

'That's precisely what I can't do. He has many informants in their ranks.'

'What?'

'I'll explain if you'll agree to help me.'

I shook my head. I didn't want explanations. What was the legal term, conspiracy to murder?

'I can't.'

'Why do you think I came to you? I'm at my wit's end. Unless he's stopped, and there's only one way he will be stopped, he'll drag the whole country to ruin. '

The words 'senile dementia' bubbled into my consciousness. I relaxed.

'He's a politician, then?' I asked with a smile. 'Is it the Prime Minister or the Leader of the Opposition you want me to bump off?'

'Don't be flippant. That's always been a failing of yours.'

'Is he or isn't he in politics?'

'Not at the moment. Although in an important position, he's quite obscure. But that may count in his favour. The elites of this country; political, military, religious, civil service, even judicial have been

8

discredited by recent wars and events. The fact that this villain is obscure will work to his advantage. I believe he intends to use another man in the political sphere as his front.'

'And how do you know all this?'

'I told you I'm conducting an official enquiry. The enquiry was intended to be a minor one. It was probably meant to be a white wash job but in the way these things do something unexpected cropped up. A certain person revealed information about the plot, believing I was a party to it. I know that the man I suspect is a ruthless killer.'

'Are you in danger?'

'Possibly.'

'I can get you bodyguards, top men.'

'No, that would confirm his suspicions and place you in needless danger unless you agree to proceed with his disposal at once.'

'So I'm between a rock and hard place?'

'It wouldn't be the first time, would it? Why do you think I came to you? I've heard the rumours?'

'What rumours?'

'Let's just say that there are rumours that various villains who've come up against you have disappeared and that the police have been unable to trace them despite strenuous efforts.'

'That's utter rubbish!'

'Judges gossip, just like everyone else,' he said, sensing that he had me at a disadvantage, 'and, David, I wasn't condemning you. From what I heard those who vanished were thoroughly bad sorts who richly deserved their fate, whatever it was.'

'Just stop it, Lew! From soliciting murder you've now gone to blackmail in one easy move. I'd have thought you'd be aware of the laws of libel and slander.'

'Oh, really, then when I was told that if a certain wealthy man's garden was to be excavated they'll find dead men's bones that was a lie, was it?'

'What wealthy man?' I gasped.

'A wealthy banker called Elsworth who owns a house in an exclusive suburb.'

I felt very hot and then very cold.

The killing of the two thugs who were in the act raping my client Dee Elsworth and killing me had been pure self-defence for what good that would do me if the police investigated.

'That's more rubbish,' I spluttered. My voice sounded weak even to myself.

'Don't worry, David. I mention these events in your past life only to remind you of your own capacities.'

'To blackmail me.'

'Nothing could be further from my mind but you must consider my proposal.'

'Or else?'

'Nothing, nothing, I wouldn't dream of telling anyone what I know. As I said I'm only reminding you of your own capacity.'

'So I'm a professional killer?'

'You've killed before and those two aren't the only ones.'

'God, have you made me your life's work? I've only ever done what I had to do.'

'I've followed your career. I know you're a dangerous man and I need you on my side. The rewards will be considerable.'

'So it's bribery now?'

'No, David, come what may, your future will be bright. I can promise that. You'll be able to leave this business which your father tells me has lost its attraction for you.'

'Very well, let's consider your proposal. The target's so powerful that he has many informants in the police, so sharp that he may already know you mean him harm, and he's a ruthless killer. So nothing could be simpler than getting rid of him. Are you suggesting I invite him to a no-holds-barred cage fighting contest?'

'There must be ways it could be done without alerting him.'

'Oh, were you thinking on the lines of a bomb under his car? Or was it cyanide in his cocktail?'

'Be serious!'

'I am being serious, and may I remind you that whatever you think I've done in the past I'm married and my wife's expecting our baby.'

My scorn seemed to have an effect on the Right Honourable. His face looked more sunken than ever. I almost felt sorry for him.

There was a long pause before he spoke again.

'David, Paddy told me about the baby. Eileen must be delighted.'

'She is.'

'But ... '

'But?'

'I ask you to consider my proposal overnight and if you're still unwilling to help me I want you to put me into contact with someone who can.'

With that he rose from his chair and walked out of my room towards the exit. I was hopeful that if I said no in the morning that would be the end of this farrago.

2

Monday: Pimpernel Investigation 9.30 a.m.

It wasn't the end.

Lew turned to the massive deposit safe, which sits like the Rock of Gibraltar against one wall, opened the upper box and dropped a small black leather notebook into it. He then slammed it shut.

The action of closing the drawer causes the contents to fall into the main safe.

The notebook was what he'd been reaching in his pocket for earlier. He smiled complacently at me.

'That's just in case your answer is yes. You'll be able to go into action immediately.'

'You old bugger!' I whispered. It would take me minutes to open the main safe and stuff the notebook down his throat.

He looked at his watch.

The rain was still slashing down. He wasn't going anywhere. Maybe there was time. The safe key was in my desk but I'd been outwitted. A gleaming silver Rolls Royce Phantom glided to a halt outside.

Lew turned to me.

'I shall expect your call at this time tomorrow. A single word will suffice.'

I opened the outer door for him just as his grey uniformed chauffeur unfurled an umbrella. The Roller must have been circling the block throughout his visit. Was Lew advertising his call deliberately? Why hadn't he slipped into the office wearing an old raincoat?

I cursed silently while Miss Fothergill looked on. By popping the black notebook into the safe the old devil had bushwhacked me. Now if his candidate for extinction perished, there was incriminating evidence in my possession.

I kicked the safe angrily. A pointless act, the pain in my foot was savage.

Chubb, you are more sinned against than sinning, locksmith beloved by screws in Her Majesty's Prisons, maker of burglar-proof safes since the nineteenth century. This deposit safe was one of Chubb's premier products. Insurers guaranteed its contents up to a hundred thousand pounds.

Its presence in the office was down to betrayals I'd suffered at the hands of former staff in bygone days at Pimpernel Investigations.

Now I was betrayed again. I struggled to suppress the surge of self pity.

Rationality returned after a moment.

Lew could only have learned about the thugs I'd shot from Dee Elsworth. She was the only person in the world apart from me who knew that I'd buried those two rapists.

'Is everything all right, Mr Cunane?' Fothergill asked. 'I hope Sir Lew wasn't bringing bad news.'

'No, I'm fine,' I said, straightening up and trying to stand on my injured foot. 'It's just that his visit was unexpected.'

I noticed that she had the office edition of 'Who's Who' open on her desk. I limped back to my room, returned with the key, punched in the combination, opened the steel door and removed the notebook.

I threw it down on my desk and stared at it for a long while as if expecting it to explode.

It was a bomb. If I opened it and learned the name of the man Lew wanted dead my life would be changed irrevocably.

My fingers twitched and crept towards the book. Then I made my mind up.

What right did Lew have to turn my life upside down?

I put the book in a padded envelope, sealed it with yards of Sellotape and took it back to the safe. He could have it back tomorrow.

'Are you sure you're all right Mr Cunane?' Fothergill asked. 'You look as if you've seen a ghost. I could make a cup of tea if you like.'

I made no comment, walked back into my room which suddenly seemed as confining as a prison cell, shut the door and poured another slug of Glenmorangie, a small one this time because I intended driving.

Damn Sir Lew Greene.

As a small child I'd stayed with Lew and his wife quite a number of times. I can still perfectly recall being entertained by two adults who hadn't the slightest notion of how to deal with a small boy. Long intervals of total boredom linger in one's childhood memories.

On one embarrassing occasion I broke a china teacup and hid the pieces behind a sofa. On another I managed to wander off and get lost in their grounds.

The Greenes lived in a huge house that could have accommodated a family of twenty with room to spare. I guess the idea was that having a child around would stimulate Magdalen's fertility. If so it didn't work.

Magdalen Arabella Veronica Anderton-Weldsley came from a far more distinguished lineage than the Greenes or Cunanes, or so she believed. Her family were landed gentry. I'd gleaned from various hints dropped by Paddy and Eileen that her parents were none too pleased when their only surviving child married a descendant of Irish peasants even if he'd been to the same exclusive public school as Magdalen's father and brothers and then to Cambridge. There'd been three older sons besides the much younger Magdalen but two were killed in the Second World War and the third in the auxiliary air force when his Meteor jet crashed into a hillside so the line ended with Magdalen.

The whisky bit into the back of my throat. I shook my head as if trying to wake from a bad dream then I reached for the phone.

A call to Dee Elsworth was out of the question but there was one other possible source of information.

'Dad,' I croaked when I was connected to my father.

'Everything all right, Dave?' he asked cheerily.

'No, everything's not all right,' I snarled.

'No need to bite my head off,' Paddy replied evenly.

'I need to see you at once.'

'And I'm expected to drop everything? I'm tiling the bathroom and your mother's got half the garden dug up. We can't leave here.'

'I'm on my way to you.'

15

'Bloody marvellous, you can give me a hand with the grouting,' he said sarcastically before putting the phone down.

I put away the glasses and the whisky and went into the outer office. It was still raining. The sky was its usual leaden grey colour. 'Who's Who' was back in its place with the reference books. I plucked my umbrella from the stand.

I studied the demure Miss Fothergill for a moment.

There was a problem.

She'd broken a rule I'd set for my staff when I restarted Pimpernel.

She'd shown curiosity about my private affairs and now knew something about my background.

I don't have permanent staff these days, certainly no one on salary who can develop ambitions about replacing me. It's pathetic but that's how I feel. My present 'colleagues' in the investigation game are ex-coppers and the occasional amateur. I pay them per job and I pay well, so there's never a shortage of helpers despite what some coppers still feel about me. I hire specialists as needed. For secretarial staff I rely on an agency.

It's costly but it guarantees anonymity and a degree of secrecy.

My days of jolly banter with staff at Pimpernel Investigations are long over. Miss Fothergill was unusual in that she'd been at her post for three months. Normally I rotate my receptionists more frequently but it was getting to be a drag constantly explaining procedures to new people so she was still with me. Fothergill's tight-lipped manner had ensured her continuity of employment.

'I'll be out for the rest of the day,' I told her. 'I'm expecting the usual reports. Harold Millrace will probably arrive on the last minute, if not later. Anyway, as they come in make them sign for delivery, give them the usual receipt and bung their files in the deposit drawer of the safe. You have your key, don't you?'

'Oh, yes, Mr Cunane,' she said, opening her drawer and brandishing the key. It was the key to the lockable deposit drawer normally kept open during the day, a fact that Sir Lew had just taken advantage of. Fothergill had the key to lock it if she went out for lunch or something. Even if it was left open, the main safe with its massive door was still secure.

Miss Fothergill didn't have the key or combination for that.

Lew's little black book was safe until I had a chance to return it to him.

'Fine,' I said. 'I'll look at them tomorrow. Apart from that, lock up and leave at the normal time.'

'Oh, I could hang on till Mr Millrace comes in if you like,' she said obligingly.

'No, that won't be necessary. It'll serve Millrace right if he has to make two trips and wait a day longer for his cheque.'

'Yes, sir,' she muttered in a discouraged tone.

'If there's anything urgent, you can get in touch on my mobile. Keep yourself busy by filing all the stuff on my desk and sorting the post when it finally arrives.'

She nodded without speaking.

As I walked to the car park I wondered if Fothergill's two little slips, firstly looking Lew up in 'Who's Who' and secondly volunteering for extra duty were enough for me to get rid of her. I decided not. I was the one who'd introduced Lew to her and they'd probably been chatting for quite a while before I came. She'd recovered well and buttoned her lip satisfactorily. That's the big problem with staff in Manchester.

They think they're living in a soap opera and want to know all your business.

Of course my smile free policy goes against the grain. But I'm succeeding in growing a hard shell.

Prison does that for you.

Cunane, man of mystery, that's the image I'm looking for as far as the temps are concerned.

Now Miss Fothergill, whose first name I couldn't recall, knew all about my godfather and she'd seen him foil me with the notebook stunt.

I put thoughts of her behind me as I threaded my grey Ford Mondeo down the narrow lane from the multi-storey and out onto Deansgate. The morning rush was over and I made good time reaching the motorway.

3

Monday: M60 motorway, clockwise section 11 a.m.

I was still thinking about the business when I reached the orbital motorway. I didn't need an economics guru to tell me that the country was in recession. Traffic was noticeably thinner.

Thoughts of Lew Greene's mysterious villain made me study my rear view mirror with care. If there was a tail I couldn't spot it.

Just to be on the safe side I zoomed off the motorway at Worsley and circled the roundabout twice.

Back on the M60 I changed lanes several times. There was definitely no one following me and in any case when I turned off onto the M61 there was nothing to distinguish my Mondeo from the dozens of others driven by salesmen and mid level executives. I approached Bolton on the A666, the road to Hell as my father often jokes, then passed through the old mill town and reached the West Pennine Moors in record time.

My parents' home in a handloom weaver's croft has been entirely rebuilt after the fire that almost destroyed it some years ago. The destruction was a blessing in disguise for Paddy. It's given him the opportunity to deploy his construction skills on a large scale. The only fly in the ointment is that the rundown farm between his house and the main road is as dilapidated as ever. Dogs, cattle, and broken machinery lie about in a scene of chaos. It provides Paddy with something to grumble at.

The cottage is perfectly positioned to catch the maximum daylight although a large oak tree at one side casts shadows that would have been unwelcome to the weavers: built of the local limestone the building merges into the landscape. Where the old weavers once pegged out cloth to bleach in the sun there's a large garden.

I spotted my mother. She was wearing a battered old Barbour

and a shapeless rain hat. She looked like a Russian peasant woman in the bad old days.

The rain was keeping up; drizzle punctuated by heavy downpours, but even so Eileen was swinging a mattock at the unresponsive soil.

I parked the car and hurried towards her. I snatched the tool out of her hand.

'What is it with you two?' I asked angrily. 'Slavery was abolished a long time ago. You're both rolling in money yet you can't let go. You're bashing the soil and he's upstairs robbing a tradesman of a day's work.'

'Oh, don't be so silly Dave,' Eileen said, giving me a peck on the cheek with frozen lips. 'Just think, if we both drop dead from exhaustion, all this will be yours.'

'Don't talk like that!' I said sharply.

'It's better for us to be working like this than toiling on a treadmill in a private gym like you and Jan,' she replied with a smile. 'It keeps us fit and it's productive. I'm putting potatoes in here.'

'The Irish famine was a long time ago,' I muttered but I knew argument was useless.

'Oh, come in and shut up,' she said, 'or at least stop complaining. I don't ask you to give up your many dangerous activities.'

'What?' I exploded. 'You never do anything but that, not that I have any dangerous activities nowadays.'

'How's dear Jan,' she asked, changing the subject. 'That dear sweet girl is trying so hard to be a good wife to you. I wonder if you value her enough.'

This was tough to take from a woman who barely twelve calendar months previously had moved heaven and earth to marry me off to Kate McKenzie, daughter of an old friend of hers. Kate's a good woman. She saved my life. She just isn't the right woman for me.

'Jan's in good health,' I said curtly. With my parents I've learned to take the rough with the smooth.

'And the baby?'

'She went for a scan yesterday. Baby's developing normally.'

'Are you both still resisting the temptation to know whether it's a boy or a girl?'

'Yes,' I said abruptly.

I didn't want to be sidetracked.

'Well, I can see you're in one of your moods,' she said, leading me to the door where we were met by Paddy in white decorator's overalls.

'To what do we owe this honour?' he asked, bowing to me.

'Oh, be careful what you say, he'll bite your head off,' Eileen warned.

'I haven't bitten anyone's head off. I think it's daft for you to be slaving away with a mattock in the teeming rain when the supermarket shelves are groaning with potatoes.'

'They don't taste as good as my own produce,' she shot back. 'I grew some white beetroot that's just delicious with melted cheese.'

'Right, that's it! I'm going,' I said, turning on my heel.

'Hold on, hothead!' Paddy said, gripping my arm. 'You must have the wind up about something or you wouldn't have come up here on a Monday morning. It's not that Hobby Dancer, is it?'

'No, nothing like that, not a call from a serial killer at least. The Right Honourable Sir Lewis Greene has just paid me a visit.'

'My word, what an honour for you,' Paddy said snidely. 'You'd better get your feet under the table and have a cup of tea while you tell us what he's done to ruffle your feathers.'

Eileen busied herself getting out of her peasant gear while Paddy brewed the tea. Then we all sat down at the kitchen table.

'So what was Lew on about?' Paddy asked as he poured out the tea.

I told them about Lew's strange request, confident that it would go no further. I omitted the details of Lew's attempted blackmail but did tell them that he'd referred to my violent past.

Whatever else they are both my parents know how to keep a secret. I sometimes think that I was driven to become an investigator because of the secrecy with which even the most trivial events were shrouded throughout my childhood.

'And he gave you the name?' Paddy asked.

'I told you. It's in a notebook in my safe. I haven't seen it and I don't want to.'

They both stared at me for a while, shifting uncomfortably on their chairs. They didn't seem to have had prior knowledge of Lew's request. If they had they gave no sign. I've never been able to read their faces.

'Do you think it's a practical joke?' Eileen asked eventually.

'No, there never was much joviality in the Greene family,' Paddy retorted. 'Why, when Lew's mum came into that inheritance you'd have thought they'd have had a holiday or a bit of a celebration, but not old Ma Greene, and Lew's just like her. She went straight round to the parish priest and got him to phone that posh school in Yorkshire. Lew and his brother were on their way within the week. Unnatural to send your kids away like, I call it.'

'Go on, Paddy, you old hypocrite. I had to argue you out of sending Dave to the same place,' Eileen rejoined.

She underlined her remark with a nudge that nearly knocked his cup out of his hand.

'What? I've never heard this before.'

'It was just a passing idea,' Paddy muttered awkwardly. I'll swear that he almost blushed. One of his secrets was about to be exposed.

'You sent off for the prospectus and took us for a look round.'

Dim memories of a sightseeing trip to North Yorkshire that included a visit to gloomy school dormitories came flooding back.

'We could have afforded the fees,' he snorted, 'and Dave might have turned out a damn sight better than he has if we'd sent him. He might have been a diplomat or a top civil servant by now.'

'A diplomat,' I sneered. 'Gosh, do you think I might have even got into Parliament? Forget about that. I have a successful detective business,' I said.

'Successful if you don't count the number of times you've been banged up.'

'I've never been convicted of anything,' I said through gritted teeth. 'But if I do what your dear pal Lew Greene wants I'll end up doing life!'

'Yeah, I don't know what Lew's thinking of,' Paddy admitted.

'Poor man, he must be at the end of his tether,' Eileen agreed.

'Poor me, don't you mean?'

'Be fair, Dave, he is your godfather and he's an important man,' Paddy said.

'I hope you're not suggesting that I do his bidding. I came here in the hope that you could use your influence and get him to see sense.'

'And do what?'

'Why, go to the police or the government, of course. If this mystery man's so dangerous they could do something.'

To my surprise Paddy disagreed.

'I don't know about that. Coppers aren't like they were in my day,' he said gloomily. 'Keeping secrets is the last thing some of these young uns care about. If you ask me, it's all this form filling and sending emails. Carpal tunnel syndrome's the major cause of injury on the Force these days. They're lost if they've no one to report to every five minutes. I was only saying to Archie Sinclair the other day, no sooner do they open a sensitive inquiry than you're reading about it in the papers.' The reference to Archie Sinclair made me pull a face. Sinclair was Dad's old boss. A lean faced Scot who'd risen to the giddy height of Assistant Chief Constable. He'd taken the lead in quizzing me about the disappearance of Dee Elsworth's would be rapists.

'OK, so the police are no use, and I can agree with him there …'

'David!' they scolded in unison.

'Just saying … so they're no use *these days* but he could have gone to the government. They'd have had to listen to him. They gave him the job.'

'And if he didn't, what does that tell you?'

'That he's as crazy as a box of broken cream crackers!'

'No, it tells you he couldn't trust anyone except his own family and whether you like it or not that means you.'

'So you think I should go ahead, find him a hit man and let him get on with it?'

'Down to you, son,' he muttered.

'Dave,' Eileen said anxiously, 'you don't know what's troubling

Lew.'

'And I don't want to know.'

'He's known you all your life. I'm sure he wouldn't want to get you in trouble.'

'Then he's got a fine way of going about it. He even left an incriminating document in my safe.'

'Dave, I know you've got the baby coming and everything but you've helped so many people before, some of them a lot less deserving than your Uncle Lew. I just think you should listen to what he has to say.'

'Thanks a bunch, Mum,' I said bitterly.

4

Monday: South bound to Cheshire 12.20 p.m.

Seething, I drove back down Blackburn Road through the run-down terraced streets of Bolton. Mosques, halal butchers, curry parlours and fruit and veg shops selling nothing had replaced the chippies and chapels of old.

I'd been a total fool.

I'd gone to the Pennine Moors expecting that Paddy would tell Lew Greene to book himself a long stay in a celebrity burn-out centre. Instead I'd met a fine display of fence sitting from both of them.

I cursed my weakness.

It was my own fault for running to those two eccentrics like a frightened child. I should have told Sir Lew to bugger off to his face. I ought to go and get that notebook and shove it in his letterbox unread.

He had tried to blackmail me. Why else would he mention the unmarked grave in Dee Elsworth's garden? It was blackmail pure and simple. Was there any tangible proof after all this time? Heck, I'd buried the pair in damp soil with enough quick lime to whitewash half the cottages in Cheshire. There might be no trace of them now.

Might be.

I just didn't know and that lack of certainty paralysed me. Suppose the plods heard the same whispers Lew had tuned into? It wouldn't be long before there were diggers in Dee's garden.

Even so the grave was deep. They might never find it.

But knowing I was the suspect would be enough to keep them going. They'd never give up until they'd excavated every ounce of soil in that garden.

Hearing Paddy's moans over the years about criminals who'd 'got off' had been a good introduction to the mentality of many of the boys in blue. Guilty as hell, that's what a lot of them thought I was, and damn the evidence of my innocence. I'd always be the Manchester Mangler who'd got off on a technicality. Some would jump at the chance to confirm their prejudices.

What was so gut-wrenching about Lew Greene knowing about events at Dee Elsworth's mansion was that it meant that the unwritten agreement I'd had with Dee had been broken. In return for Dee's silence about the killings and they were killings ... I had to face that ... I'd shot two men dead and then buried them ... she'd kept her mouth shut about the fact that I was the father of her twin sons.

We'd buried the two murderous thugs in an extremely deep grave, more like ten feet than six. I was super fit in those days. The work was nerve-wracking and exhausting with a continual fear of discovery. When we'd finished we ended up in Dee's shower room and, then, nature took its course.

My nature, that is.

I was always up for it in those days.

As I still am I suppose, but responsibilities have curbed my lecherous instincts.

I suppose.

Dee only informed me of the consequences of our unplanned tryst when her pregnancy was well established. At the same time she told me she'd no intention of leaving her husband. I'd agreed never to see the twins I fathered. The unspoken bargain was that *all* the happenings of the fatal day were to be consigned to oblivion. My sole memento was an L.S.Lowry painting which Dee gave me and which I still own.

For years after there was a force pulling me to her home. 'Blood calls to blood,' as my old granny would have said if she'd thought of it. How many times had I driven towards the Elsworth mansion hoping for a peek at those boys only to turn away at the last moment? Now Dee must have revealed our secret. Why, oh why? Is it payback time? I wondered how Harold Elsworth would like his sons to undergo a paternity test.

It would break that proud snob's heart, not to mention wrecking two families.

Mentally cringing for having thought it, I rejected the idea. There

26

are never going to be paternity tests. Involvement in messy divorces is definitely not on my agenda.

I was so stressed out and angry that I decided not to return to Manchester but to go and cool off at home. I turned my mobile off.

The motorway exit for central Manchester came up on my left and I drove past. I continued towards Stockport before turning off to join the A34, the highway that leads to the 'Golden Triangle' domain of millionaire footballers and of thousands of the less well off like me.

Thought of home helped to lighten my mood a little. That's the trouble with me; I never stay po-faced for long.

I no longer live in a flat in the fine diverse district of Chorlton-cum-Hardy. Don't get me wrong, diversity's great but you can have too much of a good thing. All the little amenities that had made me comfortable in Chorlton had gradually disappeared; the cheese shop, the barbers, the shoe shop. They all went one after another as if someone was pecking away at my life style. The second hand bookshop had become an Italian deli. Certainly a high end deli was much needed by the high salaried singles flocking to the area but there were already two others and three specialist coffee shops on one short street. Jan and I moved into East Cheshire to an isolated farmhouse on the hills overlooking the Plain.

We sold our separate properties and I got a pot of gold from my libel damages.

When we found our farmhouse it was derelict, partly roofless and waist deep in cow dung but even so it didn't come cheaply. I wasn't the only one with money in the recession. Developers were having fist fights with estate agents to get their hands on ramshackle heaps of stone which could be turned into mini stately homes for Premier League footballers and TV stars.

Luckily, I learned about Topfield Farm from a client who owed me a favour. He was a pal of the eighty-year-old 'gentleman farmer' who wanted to retire and dispose of his properties.

Topfield was never put on the market. One of several small farms which had been amalgamated into a larger unit, the G-F, as we called him, intended it for his son and heir but the son had moved to Australia forty years ago and the building was abandoned to the elements and the cattle.

It fell into ruin apart from the attached barn, which remained in use. Jan and I agreed to an independent valuation and were able to pay cash. The G-F succumbed to Jan's smile and the children's' charm and threw in ten acres of ground adjoining and we moved into the barn and a caravan for six months while the ruin was gutted and renovated to our specifications.

At the time our plans didn't include a nursery but with two spare bedrooms that's not a problem. Eileen's sniping about our private gym is true enough. We have one. The long stone building is L shaped and a drawing room, gym/workshop and garage form the base of the L with our master bedroom above. The long arm of the L includes a small study for the kids to do their homework in, a sitting/family room, oak staircase to the first floor, dining room and finally a massive kitchen that takes up the whole width of the building. With its York stone flagged floor and four-oven AGA the kitchen's the heart of the house. Honestly, I'd never aspired to become an Aga owning property developer but the idea of an Aga appealed to Jan. She made a joke about it but I didn't quarrel with her whim. I'd every reason to please her after she got back together with me. There's a utility room tagged on the end of the building. The property's now worth at least twice or even three times what we shelled out but we've turned down several offers.

Topfield Farm is our place. We're there for keeps.

Set about two hundred yards back from a winding country lane on a small knoll, it has superb views, quite an unusual thing in Cheshire where many properties are screened by dense vegetation, for privacy you know. The barn sits opposite the base of the L with a stone wall creating an enclosed cobbled farmyard where livestock was once mustered.

The only stock today is myself, Jan and her children Jenny and Lloyd, and the dog, Mangler. I was persuaded to buy 'Mangler' when we decided that pregnant Jan wasn't up to looking after the pony Jenny had set her heart on. There's a scheme to turn the barn into a pad for Jan's mum, but that's in the air and depends on the good graces of the Cheshire East planning department.

Every morning when I set out for work I can see faraway

Manchester in the distance. Well, I can see it when the plain isn't smothered in low clouds and rain, which it is about two days out of three. On good days I can see the Beetham Tower and the airport.

Jan believes that the distance we've put between ourselves and the Manchester crime scene has had a soothing effect on my temperament. Certainly we seem to be getting along a lot better. Oil and water, that's Jan and me, attraction of opposites. The first move came in Manchester when she agreed to move back in with me. The children were pining she said. Then she agreed to marriage and the flight to the hills. It was to make things easier with our families she claimed, and now a baby was on the way.

There are lots of reasons why I should forget that Lew Greene is my godfather.

I turned off the A34, took the Handforth Bypass and then the winding lane into the hills, passing signposts with names like Pott Shrigley, Tegg's Nose, Rainow and Wincle. I love driving on those lanes, watching the hedges and overarching trees turn glowing green as the dull colours of winter fade away. Just motoring along them is like a holiday after the streets of Manchester. On one occasion a reddish brown creature, like a salami sausage with tiny legs at each end, ran across my path.

I later discovered that it was a weasel.

The news that such animals actually exist outside the pages of bedtime stories was a revelation. The weasels I'd been dealing with all moved on two legs. I bought nature books and took the kids on walks looking for more.

Today no unusual wildlife crossed my trail.

Finally I drove up the narrow track that leads to Topfield Farm. The sight of the stone buildings usually calms my nerves. The grey limestone sends a message of permanence but now as I got out of the car to open the gate anxieties mounted.

I have no secrets from Jan but in her present state I didn't want to tell her that Lew, someone she was only vaguely aware of, was raking up my past and trying to pressure me into becoming an assassin. The answer to Lew would be 'no' so there was no need to trouble her with his story.

But she is the one person I find it hardest to hide my feelings from.

I parked the Mondeo and swung the heavy five-barred gate back into place with the usual clatter. Jan appeared at the porch door. She was wearing a long short-sleeve print top over black leggings that did nothing to conceal her bump. My heart missed a beat.

'What's happened? Is something the matter?' she asked.

'I'm the boss. I can come home to see my beautiful wife whenever I like.'

'Your beautiful wife is used to seeing you after six and she doesn't like seeing you with that expression on your face. Something's up.'

'Nothing's up.'

'Oh yes, it is. I can tell,' she insisted when I kissed her.

'Where are Jenny and Lloyd?'

'Don't change the subject. You know they're still at school.'

'It's just that Lloyd's left his bike at the end of the lane again. Someone will half inch it.'

'Aren't you always telling us that we're in leafy Cheshire now, not Manchester? The children round here are much more relaxed about their possessions.'

'Relaxed or not, someone will steal that bike. It cost good money.'

I tried to squeeze past her and go into the family room but she held onto me.

'Penny pincher Dave! I'm not letting you inside until you tell me what's upset you.'

'Nothing's upset me except our son's habits.'

Jenny and Lloyd are Jan's children by her first husband but I've legally adopted them and they've changed their names to Cunane. That was another reason for our migration to the hills. We all needed a fresh start.

'Tell me or I'm not letting you in,' she insisted.

Jan has mellowed in a lot of ways, as have I, but there's still plenty of steel in her spine. She held onto me.

As I'd already blurted everything out to Paddy and Eileen there was no point in trying to deceive Jan.

I told her about Sir Lew's request, the notebook and my parents' response.

'Well, he's obviously insane,' she said bluntly. 'Shouldn't we phone the Lord Chancellor's office or something and tell them that their poor old judge has flipped his wig?'

'It's the Ministry of Justice these days and weren't you listening when I told you what he said about my alleged past misdemeanours?'

'That's a bluff. They'd find nothing, assuming that they did dig up half the gardens in Tarn. He didn't have the name did he? There must be a hundred bankers living near the lake at Tarn.'

'He did have the name but it's not only that. There are plenty of people in the Greater Manchester Police Service who'd love to have a crack at me again especially if a judge raised suspicions.'

'I should think they have enough to do with all this terrorism they're always on about without bothering you.'

'Some of them have long memories.'

'Dave, stop being paranoid! You've got good friends in the police. Why, Brendan Cullen practically owes his career to you and he's a detective chief inspector now!'

'I'm not paranoid. There are people out to get me and Brendan's only one man.'

Jack Rix, the copper who'd tried to nail me for the Mangler murders may have been disgraced but he still has his supporters.

'You're in a state and I know you when you get like this. I don't want you going round to the judge's house and doing something we'll both regret like ramming his wig down his throat. All that stuff's in the past. You've got to forget about the Mangler and bloody Dee Elsworth and all that crap about Pimpernel Investigations. Our future's here now.'

'Jan, you know me … '

'I ought to.'

'I've never been one of these people with total recall of every incident in their past life.'

'Who is, Dave?'

'Well, I mean I can remember things when I want to but I'm not trying to. I don't want to be all bitter and twisted even though I have good reason. I'm already forgetting about my so-called colleagues who booted me out of my own business and were happy to see me banged up for something I couldn't possibly have done.'

'I hope you aren't including me with them.'

'No, no, no!'

'Dave, I know I treated you badly but when the kids started demanding to be a family again I knew I had to go the whole hog. It suddenly came to me that if I stayed in journalism the most I could achieve would be a by-line of my own in some supplement of the *Guardian* and the occasional appearance on a panel show when they wanted a hard faced feminist to sneer at.'

'Jan, feminist maybe but hard faced never.'

'Oh, I was getting that way. It hit me like a sledgehammer when I was so wrong about you.'

'Oh …'

'Dave, I know I said it was the kids who wanted you back but it was really me.'

'Yes.'

'I kept waking up in the middle of the night wondering where you were.'

'I was banged up, Jan. I was in the special wing with the nonces.'

'Don't Dave. You can't make me feel guiltier than I feel already.'

'Jan I never blamed you. Have I ever said a word?'

'No, but sometimes you have a look.'

'Jan, I never blamed you. I never will blame you. I blame myself and that cowboy copper Rix for what happened. You only ever wanted me to get off the case.'

'I don't want you off my case,' she said. She pulled me to the sofa, pushed me down and then collapsed on top of me. I suppressed a gasp; never a sylph-like figure, pregnancy hasn't reduced Jan's avoirdupois.

'Dave, you know I never believed you were a serial killer. It was just that you kept on working for that American bitch Ruth Hands.'

'Ruth isn't a bitch. She was a client and she was waiting for me when they let me out of that damned prison.'

'I know. She's wonderful and I'm the bitch who let you down.'

'I never said that. I knew what I was getting myself into. You weren't like those worms plotting behind my back. With you everything was out in the open.'

'I was never jealous of her. I thought she was just exploiting your good nature. That's the trouble with you, Dave. Sometimes you're too nice for your own good. You don't know when to say enough is enough.'

I strained to move my head so that I could look her in the eye.

'Listen my love, nice or nasty; I've already decided not to lift a finger to help Lew. God, if he thinks being Dad's remote relative is enough to involve me in some murder plot he's crazy. Bugger the lot of them. I'll change my name to Smith if I have to. Anyway, let me up now Jan, or you and baby Cunane are going to crush me to death.'

She made no effort to move.

'He did give us a lovely coffee service, Dave, don't forget that,' she said with a laugh.

'Yeah, like it was fashionable back in eighteen hundred.'

Jan put both hands against my chest, pushed herself upright and incidentally expelled the remaining breath from my lungs.

I let out a sigh of relief.

'Well, Dave Cunane, there are some things that never go out of fashion.'

She took me firmly by the hand and led me into the hall and up the stairs to our bedroom.

'Er, Jan,' I said when I saw where things were trending, 'Where are the children?'

'I told you, Dumbo, they're at school. You delivered them, remember? God, that bloody Sir Lew really shaken you up hasn't he? There's plenty of personal time for us.'

'Do you think we ought to?'

'I'm still in the second trimester and I'm as horny as hell.'

'So am I,' I muttered as I lifted off her print top.

Afterwards we lay in each other's arms for a long time, making up unlikely names for our child. Lewis wasn't even suggested, nor was Patrick.

I began to feel a little more normal.

We dozed and the afternoon slipped by.

Eventually we showered and dressed.

'It's the hormones or something,' Jan said. 'I know I should be screaming about bloody Sir Lew Greene but I feel too placid to get worked up. This is just how your little escapades always start.'

'Not this time, love.'

'That's what you say and I know you mean it. Just make sure you don't get involved. Anyway the thought occurs to me that Paddy and Eileen have their reasons for not backing you over Lew. They may not be telling you everything.'

I drew in a sharp breath. Jan has a journalist's keen intuition.

She mistook my response.

'I'm sorry love. My brain's probably addled. Do you think I'm turning into a vegetable?'

'An earth mother, you mean,' I said, giving her bump a friendly pat.

A few minutes later the children clattered into the family room, our peaceful idyll ended and family life resumed. That is, the children switched on the television, quarrelled over choice of channel, raided the kitchen for biscuits, demanded to be fed and then sprawled in awkward postures over the main pieces of furniture and the floor, moving frequently to achieve maximum coverage.

Using the culinary skills honed over my long years of bachelorhood and the immense range of utensils available in our 'dream' kitchen I dished up omelette, chips and beans followed by ice cream.

Afterwards Jan managed to coax Jenny into the study to get on with homework and settled to listen to Lloyd doing his reading. I loaded up the dishwasher.

5

Monday evening

On the surface normal life had resumed but I still felt unsettled. There was a feeling of vertigo as if I was standing on the edge of a precipice that I couldn't shake.

Jan's remark about my parents knowing more than they'd let on had a feel of the truth about it.

There had to be something. Normally they were so protective.

I went into the barn the barn and phoned on my mobile.

Paddy answered.

'Oh, talking, are you? After you stormed out like a bear with a sore behind ...'

'Yeah, yeah, yeah, don't start! You're the one who's always telling me to keep my nose clean and now you want me to help Lew. I want to know the reason why. You must know more than you told me.'

'Eeeeh, you're not so green as you're cabbage looking are you, our David?'

'Oh, come on Dad. Cut out the Les Dawson impersonation. I'm not in the mood.'

'There *was* something we didn't tell you,' he said in his normal voice.

'Go on.'

'Lew's dying. He's been diagnosed with cancer of the pancreas. He's been through all the treatments, radiation, chemotherapy etc, etc. They haven't worked and he's not got long.'

'Oh,' I muttered weakly, 'but even so ... to ask me to ...'

'Shut up David, don't you know that when you speak on a mobile phone you're broadcasting to the world? Lew's health wasn't what I was referring to. As you've figured out there was something else I might as well spill the beans. You know he's very wealthy?'

'Yes.'

'Some time ago, before the bit of bother he came to you about was even on the horizon, he told us he was thinking of changing his will. He was going to leave everything to various charities, church bodies and the like but all these scandals in the church upset him. The estates and properties, especially his late wife's Weldsley lands will be kept in one piece. Death duties will be paid out of his investments so the lands can be handed on in one piece.'

'So?'

'So, Thicko, you're his sole heir. You're going to get the lot. You'll be proper landed gentry, a country squire.'

I like to think it's to my credit that I didn't drop the phone or faint or something. I just said 'No' and grunted.

Paddy resumed after a pause. He detailed the extent of Lew's wealth. It was much greater than I'd ever imagined. Of course, I knew about the big house in Wilmslow and the massive legal fees earned as a barrister but the rest was staggering.

'Yeah, you get the lot, lucky boy. He's left me and your mum a nice sum too and Dee Elsworth gets his porcelain collection but that's it.'

'Dee Elsworth?'

'Yeah, the sly old devil's been carrying on with her for years.'

'The bastard!'

'No, you've got to feel sorry for the poor woman married to that plank of a banker. Lew's tried to get her to leave him for years but she won't. She thinks it'll upset the twins. How, I don't know as Elsworth's out of the country half the time and they're at boarding school. Anyway, it must have been from her that he learned about your adventure.'

'She'd no right.'

'Grow up, Dave. If you'd kept your name out of the newspapers nothing would have come out but Lew happened to mention your name and then she told him she knew you were innocent of the Mangler Murders and that's when it all came out.'

'OK, but I still don't see why you didn't tell me this before.'

'Because if Lew was gentleman enough not to influence you by telling you he was leaving his fortune to you the least your mother and I could do was to say nothing about it.'

'I see,' I muttered.

'Do you? Listen, David whatever you do is up to you …'

'No pressure then?'

'Help him or tell him to shove his money where the sun don't shine, whatever. But you're still our son and don't forget what you were saying about your business. You said it was going down the tubes and David, it's Lew's body that's ill. There's nothing wrong with his mind.'

The phone went dead. Well, at least I now knew what Paddy wanted me to do: help Lew find a hitman and then get out of the PI game.

It was tempting. The recession has turned the PI trade into a dog-eat-dog struggle. There's always someone ready to undercut no matter how low you price a job. The whole industry's too specialised. The free and easy days when I would spend weeks investigating some mystery and righting wrongs are a distant memory. There are firms focusing on every separate branch of investigation. There's even a 'women only' detective agency. My niche, insurance scams and social security fraud is jammed with rivals not least my treacherous former colleagues just across the street. It took a major legal battle to wrest the title 'Pimpernel Investigations' back from them. They wanted to keep the name and the former clients. I got the name back, they have the old office and I'm making inroads on the rest.

I looked around the walls of the barn, white washed by my own hand. There was no answer written up anywhere.

I don't know how I felt at that moment. I was perplexed more than anything. The naked terror came later.

Afterwards for want of something to do I went outside and policed the area. The short track leading to what I now think of as the 'main road', actually the winding country lane connecting us with civilisation, is terminated by a five barred gate. It was wide open. Lloyd loves swinging on it.

I swung it shut and the hinge creaked like someone strangling a cat. I'd been meaning to oil it for some time. I fastened it, not just with the latch but with the steel hoop that folds over the connecting fencepost. We were secure inside our twelve acres. I looked down the lane. It was quiet as evening approached and dusk began to gather. There's not much traffic round here except for the twice daily commutes.

I'd made my mind up. The hesitations of the day were behind me.

The message to Lew would have to be 'no'. I couldn't turn assassin even for him and his fortune and if that meant taking the chance of having my murky past investigated I'd just have to hope the police wouldn't find that grave by the lake. That was a bluff wasn't it, Sir Lew? You'd never land Dee Elsworth in trouble with police and husband.

As for the rest, he'd have to cut me out of his will.

A little glow of self righteousness began to appear on my mental horizon. I told myself I could never live on inherited wealth. OK, there was my parent's property but the way they were going they were likely to outlive me. I could accept that but much of Lew's wealth: the Lancashire farms and the villa in Tuscany were his wife's birthright. She was the survivor of an old landed family. I'd no right to any of that. There was no connection between me and that long line of Weldsleys that could justify it.

It wasn't even like winning on the lottery. A win may be undeserved but you have to buy a ticket and you know it's a chance in a million and that the money's going to good causes.

Even as these righteous thoughts crossed my mind another sneakily popped up behind them: *if it doesn't come to me, who gets it? The Treasury?*

It was wrong. Lew had to be spoken to. OK, a little legacy would be nice but leaving the lot to me was impulsive to the point of insanity. It was the action of a deeply disturbed man.

Don't get me wrong, I'm not a communist. I leave the politics to my beloved wife. I'm just a man making his own way in the world who doesn't want to owe anything to anyone. Independent, that's me.

I collected the children's bikes, guiding each with one hand, kicked a discarded football up to the yard and headed towards the barn. Protecting their bikes against the remote chance of rural crime was the thought that made me pause as I was about to lock the barn door. Despite constant reassuring statements to the contrary crime has got worse, very much worse, even in my life time. Was it so incredible that someone was plotting the highest crime of all, the overthrow of the state? I told myself that it was. There's all the difference in the world between say, drug trafficking and high treason.

But just suppose that Sir Lew wasn't on a one way trip to Fantasy Island.

Damn it to hell, the man was a QC and an Appeal Court judge after all. According to Paddy he wasn't mad, just dying of cancer.

What was it Lew said about a 'tripwire'? Some reference in a document that had made him suspicious but when he researched it further secret alarm bells began ringing, alarms which alerted his mysterious traitor. Just suppose for the sake of argument that the traitor was real and that he was on his way to Topfield Farm.

Nah!

There are probably plenty of traitors in the government machine but were they bold enough to kill a High Court judge? No, Lew's illness must have affected his mind despite what Paddy said.

Still there was nothing to be lost by a little paranoia. I went back to the barn and took certain precautions. In the same mood I slipped in via the backdoor, went quietly to the gun cupboard and took out my shotgun and cartridges. I took them upstairs and hid the unloaded gun under the bed and the cartridges on top of the wardrobe.

Jan and the children were sprawled on the sofa when I got back to the family room. Jan raised her eyebrows questioningly. Even if I'd wanted to keep Paddy's bombshell a secret from her it was pointless to attempt it. I put my finger to my lips and whispered 'later'.

I tried watching television. The news and the Discovery channel are the only things I can bear to watch these days. Children's programmes definitely don't hold my attention. Fortunately, the children were soon yawning. I read a story to Lloyd while he got off. He was always first in bed according to a strict protocol. Twenty minutes later Jan went up with Jenny.

'Well?' she said when she returned.

'Your guess was right. There was something they weren't telling me.'

'Let me guess. He's got a brain tumour and doesn't know what he's saying. They want you to humour him.'

'No. Nothing like that!' I snapped. 'Well, it is a bit like that. He's got pancreatic cancer but according to Paddy, who should know, his mind is perfectly normal.'

'Normal, apart from the fact he's decided to kill someone. Homicidal mania is the term for that.'

'Janine, leave his mind out of it.'

'Out of it? A High Court judge who's as nutty as a fruit cake? I should be phoning the news desk at the Guardian but as he's one of your relations I suppose I have to accept the idea that he's as crazy as a screech owl.'

I shut up, folded my arms and picked up the television control. I started flicking through the fact channels.

'Go on,' she demanded impatiently. 'Tell me the rest.'

'I don't think I should. The news might unbalance you in your present condition.'

I continued to fiddle with the channels.

She pulled off her slipper and cracked me over the leg with it.

'Talk Mister or you sleep in the barn tonight.'

'OK, OK, he's decided to name me in his will. He changed it two months ago.'

She looked at me blankly. Lew Greene hadn't figured largely in my life in recent years, hadn't figured at all. Jan had even less idea of his financial status than I had.

'The coffee set, remember?'

'Of course I remember it. I was tempted to take it on Antiques Road Show and pretend I found it in the attic so I could look shocked when they valued it. Paul Storr, it must be worth plenty unless it's a fake. I asked you about him but you were so tight lipped and grim I thought he must be gaga or something ... the dark secret of the Cunanes. You made it pretty clear you don't like him.'

'It's not that. He's disapproved of me for years and that can turn you off anybody.'

'Yes ... right, I was going to suggest that we sell the coffee set to

40

get the money to do up the barn up for Mum. So, Uncle Fester's loaded is he? What's your share?'

'Jan, he's more than loaded. He's very, very wealthy indeed, up there in the top one or two percent.'

'So, what are we talking about? Give me a ballpark figure; half a million, a million or what?'

'Jan, we're talking about millions, lots of millions and I get the lot. He made his own fortune at the Bar but inherited the Weldsley Estates from his wife; lands all over the country, including London and the Villa Arabella near San Gemignano in Tuscany. He gives a case of the local wine to Paddy and Eileen every year but it never clicked with me, brilliant detective that I am, that he owned the vineyard it was grown in.'

I studied her nervously. What would happen when I told her I was going to turn it all down?

She remained expressionless.

Then she suddenly started roaring with laughter.

'A villa in Tuscany,' she gasped. 'I'd be able to invite all the Guardian bigwigs over when they take their summer hols in Chiantishire. It's unbelievable.'

'I know. Phone Paddy, he'll give you the full run down.'

'No, I don't mean that,' she said. 'I was thinking about the expressions on the faces of certain people at the Guardian if I really did invite them to a grand villa and tell them we owned it. They'd ask if it was purchased with the proceeds of your undiscovered crimes.'

It was a sore point with Jan that several of her former journalist friends had refused to come to our housewarming. They felt Topfield was tainted because it was partly bought with libel damages.

'Jan, if we do ever get our hands on the villa it might just be that I have purchased it with the proceeds of undiscovered crime but it'll never happen. I've decided to turn Lew down. We can't risk what we have here for a crazy adventure.'

She pulled me towards her and kissed me.

'You're right, Dave. Of course you are, but I can't help thinking … and it isn't as if you haven't been involved in wild escapades before.'

'You aren't changing your mind … because I was thinking of

phoning him right away and telling him I can't help him.'

'No, no, you're absolutely right Dave. It's just that it's not every day a girl gets the chance to be a millionaire with villa in Italy. I think we should sleep on it.'

We went up. Early nights have been a feature of Jan's condition.

The children's bedroom doors were open. They were both sleeping peacefully. It was domestic bliss at Topfield Farm and that was the way it was going to stay. Jan noticed the shotgun but calmed down when I told her it was unloaded. Too zonked out to care, she fell asleep as soon as her head hit the pillow. I lay beside her fully clothed. The events of the day were churning over in my mind.

I couldn't wait until morning before I gave Lew my decision. He had to be told. I slipped out of bed, fished around with my feet for my bedroom slippers to avoid switching a light on, slipped them on and went downstairs.

Lew answered almost on the first ring.

'Oh, David, it's you,' he said.

He sounded weak; not at all the confident visitor who'd outwitted me this morning.

'Expecting someone else were you Uncle Lew?'

'Possibly,' he muttered vaguely. 'What is it? Have you come to a decision?'

He was on edge. I swiftly changed my mind. Turning him down flat was too brutal. I had to find a way to let him down gently.

'Listen, Uncle Lew I'd like to come round and see you first thing tomorrow morning. I've been thinking things over and I'd like to talk you again.'

'Are you going to help me?'

'I'd like to talk things through with you.'

Maybe I could persuade him to relay his disturbing finding to the politicians who'd commissioned his enquiry. They'd have to take some action even if it was only to dismiss him. Once the enquiry was out of his hands the danger if there was any danger, must recede. Surely he'd see that.

'Is there any point, David?' he asked. 'I can tell by your tone that you've made your mind up.'

'Uncle Lew, our business isn't the sort of thing that should be discussed on the phone.'

'There is that I suppose. All right, come round if you must. The front door will be unlocked, just come in when you get here.'

I crept back upstairs and undressed by the light from the landing. Janine slept on undisturbed. I fell into a light doze.

I awoke with a shattering jerk as one of the piles of empty cans I'd set up as makeshift booby traps in the yard clattered over. Janine was snoring gently. I got up, crept to the window and peered out from a gap between the curtains. I stood there for five minutes.

'What are you doing Dave?'

'There's someone outside.'

She listened for a moment. There was utter silence, not even the owl which lived in the eaves of our barn was hooting.

'There's nothing,' she said.

'The cans fell over.'

'Probably a prowling badger,' she explained. 'Come back to bed. Sir Lew's set your nerves on edge.'

'Nerves, me? I don't have nerves,' I said, but I slipped back into bed. I hadn't seen any intruders in the yard and I hadn't heard footsteps or curses as I surely would have if that pile of cans had fallen on an intruder.

I lay quietly for a long time and was drowsing when Janine suddenly jerked my arm.

'Did you hear that? It was the outside gate opening. I'd know that sound anywhere.'

She began moving towards the window. Then I heard the unmistakeable noise of a car engine approaching. I pulled her back.

'What the hell! We're not expecting visitors.'

The bedside alarm registered 12:20 a.m.

The farmyard can be illuminated by floodlights which were installed because Lloyd was prone to sleepwalking when we moved to Topfield. As originally installed they were triggered by a motion sensor but our friendly owl foiled that plan by constantly turning them on at all hours of the night.

Now they're controlled by switches, one of which is by my bedside.

I turned the switch on and drew back the curtain.

It was like looking out at a play.

It took an age for my sleepy mind to fit the pieces together and register what I was seeing.

A red Mini Cooper was parked in the farmyard. The passenger door was open and a short, stocky man was stepping out. He had a bottle in his hand and as I gaped he pulled out a lighter and lit a rag attached to the bottle. He ran forward.

I dived back and scrabbled for the gun under my bed.

When I got my act sufficiently together to the extent of opening the window and pointing the still unloaded gun the intruder was on the point of throwing his flaming missile up at us.

'Cartridges!' I screamed to Janine who'd scrambled out of bed and was taking in the lurid scene at my side.

Below me our attacker must have heard my despairing shout. He ignored the gun. I'll swear that he grinned up at me before throwing the petrol bomb.

There was nothing I could do.

The firebomb curved up towards me. I ducked.

Wham!

It went too high. It missed the window and hit the plastic fascia below the roof. By some miracle it didn't break but bounced off at an angle and smashed on the cobbles under our battered old Toyota Land Cruiser. A sheet of flame and thick black smoke enveloped the vehicle.

The bomber himself leaped back, moving away from the flames.

'Thank you, guardian angel,' I thought. Well, my mum believes in them and I must say I've had more than my fair share of luck over the years as well as some bad breaks. In an attack like this the first shot is always the best shot and he'd had his shot. Now it was my turn.

They weren't finished.

The second man, the driver of the Mini Cooper, was out of the car now. He had the Mini's boot open and was holding two bottles. It was impossible to mistake them for anything else but petrol bombs. This killer was tall and thin by contrast with his fellow murderer. He passed one bomb to the short man and set the other down ready for a third attempt. Both were nondescript except that they were wearing suits and had shaven heads which I thought was odd. They had to be ex-military or police.

Janine wrenched my shoulder and pressed two cartridges into my hand.

I frantically broke the gun and loaded.

This time when I poked the gun outside the short bomber had stationed himself some way from the blazing Toyota and was gauging the distance for his second throw as carefully as an Olympic shot-putter.

Shorty put the lighter to the bottle and lit the rag.

There was something calm and professional in his actions. This man had killed before. He wasn't in a panic. There was no undue haste. This time he'd get us. We'd all be incinerated.

I slammed the gun into my shoulder and aimed at him.

I had him over open sights. A half-blind granny could hardly miss at such close range and I'm not a half-blind granny.

One squeeze of the trigger and I'd take his head clean off his shoulders.

Everything was happening very slowly. Seconds seemed to last for decades.

I took first pressure on the trigger, a little more and he'd be dead and we'd be safe.

A fleeting memory of that grave in Dee Elsworth's garden flashed before me. I'm not making it up. I really did remember the last occasion I'd killed men in justifiable self defence. Sir Lew had well and truly refreshed my memory of that part of my biography.

I deflected my aim downwards and fired.

The shotgun blast missed him but pellets must have ricocheted off the cobbles and struck him because he howled and dropped the bomb which exploded at his feet. His legs were instantly encased in flame. Now calm deliberation was replaced by agonised shrieks. The screams went on and on.

The ugly image of a burning man is familiar to everyone from dozens of televised immolations. I watched the reality in horror. For a second I wondered if it would be kinder to shoot him. The man was howling and hopping about in extreme pain. Another careful shot and he'd be out of his misery.

The second man, the long thin character, came to his rescue. He dragged Shorty out of the pool of flame and began beating out the flames on his legs with his jacket.

Beside me Janine had her blood lust up.

'What are you waiting for?' she yelled. 'Shoot them.'

'Get the children,' I shouted, without taking my eyes off the would-be bombers. 'Go to the back door and wait for me.'

She slammed the box of cartridges down on the window sill in front of me.

'Don't let the bastards get away,' were her parting words. 'I'll phone the police.'

'Whatever you do, don't do that!' I screamed but she was gone.

The last thing I needed was the boys in blue turning up. It went without saying that I would be the main target of their suspicions when the questions started.

I'd every intention of allowing the bombers to escape. Having seen the inside of a cell I'd no wish to repeat the experience. This is Cheshire, not America with its wide open spaces where the local sheriffs congratulate householders for defending their lives and property. Here, only the police are licensed to kill.

As I watched the bombers began to make their getaway.

The tall man ripped the flaming clothing off the bomber. He must have burned his own hands badly. Then he lugged the injured man to the Mini Cooper, supporting his weight with his left arm. The high-pitched screams diminished to agonised moans. They were as loud and clear as if the sufferer was in the room with me. From the volume I guessed that he'd survive; at any rate he was moving. I leaned further forward out of the window to track them with the gun in case the tall man decided to pick up the unused firebomb.

My movement attracted his attention. Still holding his partner upright he paused and pulled something out of his trouser pocket.

I knew what it was before the bullet smacked into the window frame where my head had been. I was already on the floor. I hugged the deck for a moment until I heard the sound of an engine revving. Any doubts that I was facing two highly trained killers vanished. The tall guy had fired from the hip. His bullet would have hit me right between the eyes.

When I finally looked out again the Mini Cooper was exiting from our farm track at high speed.

6

When I reached the kitchen Janine was holding Lloyd in her arms while Jenny clung to her side. Both children were half asleep. Janine had had the sense to leave the lights off but the glare from the blaze outside provided more than enough illumination.

'Have they gone?' Janine asked, mouthing her words silently.

I nodded my head.

'Why can't I phone the police or at least the fire brigade?'

'You know why Janine. Think about it.'

She looked distressed as she was well entitled to but I've learned by hard experience that bossing Janine about is counterproductive.

'Are you saying this is down to that bloody relative of yours?'

'It must be. There's no comeback from the detective work I do nowadays. None of the fraudsters who end up in court even know I'm involved.'

'So what Sir Lew told you must be true … There is a conspiracy.'

I shrugged. This wasn't the time for an inquest.

Janine hugged Lloyd fiercely. Both he and Jenny began to wake up.

There had to be some way of protecting Jenny and Lloyd from further damage. Tonight's event could do lasting harm when the knowledge that they'd almost been burned to death sank in.

If they ever learned about it.

Both children are highly imaginative and sensitive. Probably most children are, I only know about these two. When I'd been taken from them before, they'd had nightmares for months. 'Pining' was how Janine described it but it was more than that. They'd needed counselling.

We'd only recently got the better of Lloyd's sleepwalking and he still often comes into our bed.

49

Mangler gave an attention-seeking growl from his basket. Lloyd pulled free from his mother and went to the yellow Labrador. Jenny joined him. The dog rubbed its powerful muzzle along Lloyd's body.

'Dave, what are we going to do?' Janine asked. She pulled me to one side, away from the children.

The move up to the hills has mellowed Janine but there's still a lot of contrariness in her nature. Oil and water, attraction of opposites, that's what it is with us. I recognised the glint in her eye and the firm jut of her jaw.

'I'm not going to start killing people, if that's what you mean. Not for the Right Honourable Sir Lew or all the landed property in England.'

'Thank God,' the devout agnostic whispered, 'but what about us?'

Her blood lust had subsided and I was wise enough not to remind her of it.

'Jenny and Lloyd and Baby Cunane have to go where they'll be safe,' I said quietly, patting her bump, 'and we have to come up with a story that doesn't have them all waking up in the middle of the night screaming.'

She thought about this for a moment. Janine likes to be very open and truthful about everything with the children. I agree up to a point but I think children are children and adults are adults … very unfashionable.

'Dave, if you can make up a story that stops *me* waking up and screaming hit me with it now. To think I wanted to install my mother here,' she said with a strained laugh.

I forced a smile. The mention of her mother gave me a glimmer of an idea.

'Janine, you know your mum wanted us to go up to Colquhuons with her. She hates rattling around in that lodge on her own.'

She nodded.

Colquhuons is a luxurious golf resort on the bonnie, bonnie banks of Loch Lomond. There's an estate of luxurious timeshare lodges in the grounds. Jan's mother owns two weeks of one of the lodges. It's the same two weeks every year, chosen not to clash with the Easter holidays except once in a blue moon. That was fine when the only likely occupants were Janine, her brother, mother and golf-loving father. Now her mother's on her own up there for two weeks every year and she doesn't even play golf. Janine's father is dead and her brother's settled in Canada. Clarissa White, 'Granny Clarrie' to the children, plain Clarrie to her daughter, had implored us to join her but this year the dates meant we'd have had to take the children out of school and Janine wasn't willing to do that even for a single week, let alone two.

'You can tell them you're all going up there now. They love the place ...'

'But it's the middle of the night.'

'You can tell them it's a surprise holiday.'

'I don't know, Dave.'

'You'll all be a lot safer four hundred miles from here.

'OK then, Colquhuons it is,' she said after a moment's thought.

'You tell them about it and I'll say there's been accident with the Land Cruiser. I'd better get outside and put out the fire before the house goes up.'

'But what if the bombers come back?'

'We've got some time, we must have. The shotgun's behind the sofa in the living room. It's not loaded. The shells are here.'

I pressed four cartridges into her hand.

'Don't let me in until I give this knock.'

I rapped on the table three times, then twice more after a pause.

'Tell the kids it's a game.'

'Yes, living with you is a barrel of laughs, isn't it Dave? Laugh a minute!'

I paused on my way to the door, expecting anger after the sarcasm. Instead she gave me a hug and a kiss.

'Try to keep out of trouble,' she warned, 'as if ...'

I gave a silent sigh of relief. Janine accepted that it wasn't any action of mine that had brought danger to our door. I crossed my fingers. How long this favourable mood would last was anyone's guess.

The children and the dog all looked up at me. I gave them a thumbs-up sign and dashed outs

7

Tuesday: 2:25 a.m.

There were two six litre foam fire extinguishers in the barn left over from my house building operations. For once I was grateful for the health and safety regulations.

One was enough to save the Toyota from total destruction. The Land Cruiser has a diesel engine and although there were flames lapping underneath the vehicle the fuel tank hadn't blow up. The main damage was to both offside wheels and the paint work. One tyre was completely burnt through and the vehicle sagged at an odd angle. There was nothing I could do about it for now.

When I'd finished with the foam I looked round the yard.

The remnants of the burned man's clothes lay in a heap. I sorted through them carefully. Every label had been cut out. Not a surprise, I hardly expected to find the owner's name. Nor was there any other clue to identity, wallet, tickets, dry cleaning labels: nothing, but there was one thing which did give me an almighty lift.

There was a Glock nine millimetre automatic pistol in the trouser pocket.

After looking round, half guiltily expecting someone to pop out and ask me what I thought I was doing I put the gun in my pocket. The weight was uncomfortable but just having it brought a feeling of relief.

As for being observed I didn't need to worry. Discharge of firearms and a fire hadn't attracted the slightest attention. The night was still, not even the most distant sounds of traffic disturbed the rural calm. So the only clue to the identity of our would be killers was that they were both smartly suited, drove a red Mini Cooper and one of them was now in urgent need of medical help.

Then I hopped in the Mondeo and after a cautious look around drove to a public call box at a nearby road junction.

I called Paddy.

Eileen answered.

'Dave,' she said breathlessly. 'Is everything all right with Jan?'

'She's fine, Mum. Can you put Dad on?'

'And the baby? Nothing's happened, has it?'

'The baby's fine, so are Janine and the children. It's about Uncle Lew. Please put Dad on.'

'I will if I can wake him. He sleeps like a log with all this DIY he's doing.'

The urge to build runs strongly in us Cunanes. Maybe we'd have been better off if we'd stuck to labouring or maybe steeplejacking, certainly safer.

After a long pause I heard the familiar voice.

'David, what's up?'

'How much has Lew told you about the trouble he's in?'

The question provoked moments of throat clearing from my parent.

I waited.

'What trouble,' he croaked at last. He was maddening.

'The mysterious geezer I told you about this morning Lew claims is trying to seize control of the country.'

Paddy mumbled an indistinct reply.

'So you do know something more than I told you?'

'The answer to that could be yes,' he admitted in a hushed voice. 'Your mother and I have been very worried about Lew for some time.'

'Right, so I'll take it that you know everything he told me and then some. I was hoping it was all a fantasy. What do they call it … pre-senile dementia?'

'No, it's not that. How could he be pre-senile? He's already nearly seventy,' he growled.

'Well, you'd know more about dementia than me, Dad, but it's definitely not a fantasy. I've just chased off two men who were trying to lob petrol bombs into our bedroom.'

'Christ! David, if it's not one thing with you it's another.'

'Bloody hell! This is hardly my fault. He's your flaming

childhood friend. Did he have to drive up to my office in his Roller and advertise that he was calling on my services? He's landed me right in it up to my neck, not to speak of Janine and the kids.'

There was a pause for more throat clearing.

'I'm sorry, you're right. This is down to Lew. Are you sure everyone's OK?'

'Yes, Jan's taking the children away to ...'

'No, don't tell me. I don't want to know. These men, were they street thugs, people from your colourful past?'

'No, they were definitely professionals. They moved as if they'd had training, ex-army or police at a guess.'

'You could be in real trouble. It was the Spook brigade he was investigating. They have unlimited access to all kinds of shady sudden death merchants.'

'Thanks Dad.'

'I told him to go to the Chief Constable but the stubborn fool wouldn't listen.'

'He didn't believe the police could be relied on.'

'I gave him names of men I'd trust with my life but ...'

'Never mind all that Dad, water under the bridge now. I need you to do something for me.'

'What?' he asked.

'Don't worry; it's only a phone call. Phone Lew and if he answers tell him to either get the police to his house pronto or get out of there now. Phone me back on this number.'

I gave him the number of the callbox and then stood waiting anxiously. It's for such moments that cigarettes were invented but like everyone else I've given up long ago. Another prop I could have used was help. Most people have brothers or partners willing to drop everything at a moment's notice and pitch in to help. Me, I have remote cousins posing as Uncles who land me in a sea of trouble.

I was starting to chew my fingernails when the phone rang.

'He's not answering, David. I called his house and his mobile, something's up.'

'Could it be the cancer?'

'He was told to expect a slow death with that. It's something else, something bad. He never goes anywhere without his mobile.'

My heart sank. Lew was dead. Once he'd been seen trying to recruit help he'd sealed his fate. I hadn't had much hope but there'd been a faint chance that his mysterious enemy had decided to silence me first.

I shivered. There was nothing to be gained by grieving for Lew. To survive the next few days I needed to start making my own moves.

'Right Dad, I need you to make another call for me.'

'Why don't you do it yourself, David?'

'You know why. If Lew's mysterious plotter is organised enough to send two men to firebomb me he's organised enough to have my phone and my mobile bugged.'

'And mine.'

'Why would they bother with you? When did you last see him?'

'It was two weeks ago.'

'Yes, and you haven't noticed any petrol bombs flying through your bedroom window, have you? It was normal for you and Lew to meet. Where did you see him?'

'Your mother and I went to his house in Wilmslow. We see him every couple of weeks.'

'So your visit would have been regarded as routine, whereas calling on me … the sleazy, controversial private eye.'

'Yes, I'm so sorry David. I think the best thing you can do is to get out of the country. I can help you with money if you need it.'

'Not needed. Simply phone Brendan Cullen and ask him to get a plod to call round at Lew's house.'

'That lush!'

'Brendan happens to be a DCI on the North West Counter-Terrorism Unit and the only copper who might be willing to do me a favour. For your information he's been sober for years.'

Paddy grumbled some more but I gave him Cullen's number and told him to get Cullen to contact me at seven thirty via the public call box near the bridge over the Irwell about two hundred yards from my office. I have the number for that phone off by heart. My distrust of phones runs very deep. One of the treacherous employees who'd tried to steal my business off me had been a full time electronic eavesdropper in his previous life with the military.

I raced back to Topfield.

Janine had the shotgun at the ready when she answered my 'secret' door knock. The children were upstairs selecting the toys they needed for their surprise holiday.

'Lew isn't answering his phone.'

'So we're either very rich now or in very great danger,' she said.

'I think we can take it that it's the latter. We need to get out right away. Those guys were hitmen and when whoever sent them hears that they failed he's sure to want to try again.'

The packing for the trip to Scotland took less than twenty minutes. That was probably a record for Janine but then knowing that she'd be using the Mondeo probably cramped her style a little. Capacious though the luggage space on a Mondeo is, it could carry less than half of what the Land Cruiser could. Even so I was on the move continuously for the next few minutes, stuffing bags and cases into the car and on the lookout for more visitors all the time.

None came.

I drove out of the farmyard having first scouted the lane on foot. There could have been an ambush round any corner but the sheer number of winding little lanes pushed the odds in our favour. I turned corners at random knowing that as long as I went downhill I'd eventually come out of the hills that rimmed the Cheshire Plain. It was just after one a.m. We left the tangle of minor roads and reached the main Macclesfield to Manchester road. A few more miles and we could be either on the motorway to Scotland or the A34 into central Manchester.

'Stop for a minute,' Janine ordered. 'We need to talk.'

I pulled the car off the road into an alley at the side of a small repair workshop. The tyres crunched noisily over cinders but I didn't stop moving until I was happy that we were completely out of sight of passing traffic. Both children were asleep.

'We need to make some decisions,' Janine announced. 'Are we both going to Scotland and hiding from these people?'

'I've got to see that you're safe.'

'And how long do you think going to Loch Lomond will keep us safe?'

'God knows,' I muttered gloomily, 'it must be safer than here though.'

'Dave if they traced you to Topfield it's not going to take forever for them to trace us to my mum's timeshare lodge in Scotland. It isn't as if we have a long list of safe houses to choose from.'

'Presumably I've now inherited Lew's properties. We could go to the Villa Arabella.'

Janine thought for a moment.

'That won't work. There'll be all sorts of legal fuss before we can move in. You're going to have to find out who these people are and tell them that we're absolutely no threat to them.'

'Yeah, should I put an ad in the personal column of the Times? *Assassins, leave the Cunane family alone.*'

'There must be a way. Leave a message at Topfield where they'll find it. Promise them you'll keep silent.'

'Somehow I think whoever's behind this prefers more permanent methods of ensuring our silence.'

'Dave, this is England!'

'Yes, it is,' I agreed. 'You don't read the crime pages much, do you?'

After a silence I continued.

'There may be another way out of this mess. We both know someone who always has well hidden bolt holes handy.'

'Bob Lane, but Dave you were warned to stay away from him!'

I'd been released from custody, declared to be completely innocent and had won substantial damages from Press and police but Bob's reputation was dodgy. I'd been told by a senior copper, not a friend of mine but an officer who'd served his apprenticeship as a detective under Paddy Cunane and felt that he'd owed him a favour, that some of his colleagues would be watching me like a hawk, hoping to recoup some of their lost reputation by proving that I was a crook. Their preferred method was to catch me in the company of Bob Lane while he performed one of his semi-legal manoeuvres.

Bob never makes a move without a squadron of lawyers in tow but in his world deeds often count for more than the small print in some legislative code.

Don't get me wrong, he's not a major villain or anything near it. It's just that many of the people in the scene he moves in, Manchester clubland and its underside of 'security men' are total nutters. If not scumbags themselves they're often fronting for someone who is.

Drug profits are another thing. Those who make their money that way, not Bob, are always on the lookout for a club they can muscle into to launder their loot. Bob doesn't waste time in the law courts before he ejects them. It's a rough world and the treatment we'd just received: firebombs through the window isn't uncommon so Bob keeps a secret property or two handy so he can lie low if he needs to.

'Janine, how's this for a plan? I'll hide in one of Bob's places and try to contact these killers and convince them I know nothing. It shouldn't be hard because I've no idea who they are. Meanwhile …'

'Meanwhile I go to Scotland.'

'Aye, ye'll be in Scotland afore me.'

'Dave, this isn't a joke!'

Just then Mangler gave a loud growl.

'Someone's coming,' Janine whispered.

I pulled out the Glock and held it on my lap.

We waited in suspense for a few moments and then a fox barked. Mangler bared his teeth but Janine calmed him. The children didn't wake.

Janine put her hand on the gun.

'Where did you get that?'

'One of our visitors left it. I'm just looking after it for him.'

'Dave you fool, you know there are armed police out there just waiting for a chance to shoot you and you go round with a gun.'

'Your idea of leaving a message at Topfield's a good one,' I said, trying to change the subject. 'It's the only point of contact I have with these …'

'Stop it! Give it to me. This thing's going to end up in the deepest part of Loch Lomond.'

'But Janine, it gives us protection. It's only ironmongery.'

'Yes that's what I'll tell the Police Complaints Commission when they approve of the police shooting you because you were carrying an unlicensed firearm. Some good that'll do us!'

I held onto the gun.

'All right, Dave, we'll strike a bargain. Give me the gun and I'll go to Scotland like a good girl and get out of your way while you do whatever you've got to do.'

8

Tuesday: 3.15 a.m.

I phoned Bob's private mobile number from a public call box. I had no idea of his location apart from Manchester.

Janine had dropped me off at the end of Deansgate before heading off towards the M62 and the M6 north. I was disarmed but as Janine well knew Bob Lane has a brother, Clint.

Clint's real name is Vincent Anthony Lane. He was nicknamed Clint by his own father after a film star. No, not Clint Eastwood but Clint Walker who starred in a cowboy series called 'Cheyenne' which capitalised on his massive height. Walker is six foot six, a mere child compared to the height Clint Lane eventually reached, but Lane senior was impressed enough to dub his growing son 'Clint'. The name stuck and is virtually the only legacy any of the family received from their father of whom none of them will speak but who was no longer on the scene when I became acquainted with the Lanes.

In terms of weaponry Clint counts as heavy artillery.

Clint has served as my bodyguard before. In a very special way Clint is equivalent to a whole squad of minders. On one occasion he'd defended me from an angry crowd by swinging a twelve foot long steel scaffolding spar round his head.

Clint's a gentle giant, over seven feet in shoes and socks and built like a main battle tank but his intellectual development hasn't matched his physical. He's not 'care in the community' or anything. Well, he is in a way. That is, he's had some care and still needs it but he functions well in most situations.

Jan has taught him to read: slowly but he does read and what's more he remembers what he's read.

Clint was married to Naomi Carter, who was Jan's nanny when she was still trying to make a go of her journalistic career writing on women's issues for the *Guardian* and other papers. Naomi eventually dumped him saying she wanted more excitement in her life, sad woman. She's now working as a carer in an old folk's home in Nottingham.

To my mind life with Clint had to be more exciting than that.

Clint works on a farm. The constant hard labour, involving lifting awkward animals, bales of hay, and even pulling tractors out of ditches has developed his physique to frightening proportions. He has to have most of his clothes specially made.

The local thug community are in terror of him. Unfortunately those two fire bombers weren't locals. They definitely weren't local knuckle-draggers, not the steroid-crazed types you'd expect at a firebombing party at all. I replayed the attack over and over in my mind.

We'd been very, very lucky.

If things had gone as they'd planned we'd have had no chance. I shivered and not from the night air. Paranoid I may be after being unjustly locked up and finding every man's hand against me but sometimes a touch of it pays off. But for the clattering cans rousing me and the creaking gate alerting Jan we'd be incinerated corpses now and our children with us.

Yes, the killings would be headline news for a day. Some people would be shocked but incendiary attacks are everyday occurrences. I could easily imagine the snide briefings some coppers would give the press ... *'bears all the hallmarks of a gangland killing'*. That's what they'd say before making backhanded references to my many alleged scrapes with the law.

Gangland was just what it wasn't. The way the tall guy had rescued the shorter one at risk of his own neck was completely untypical. A local villain would have saved himself first. Hell, a local villain would have been out of there the instant he spotted me poking the shotgun towards him. Those two were ex-military or ex-police: trained men who knew exactly what they were going to do and came with back-up in the shape of extra fire bombs in case their first try failed.

Clint could supply muscle but was that going to be any use against professional killers?

Accepting Clint's services and taking care of him while he

provided them was the normal price of asking Bob Lane for a favour and I was about to ask him for a biggie. I wanted the use of his current safe house.

The bond between Bob, Clint and me goes back a long way. Bob saved my neck when I was starting out as a PI. He had no particular need to help me then but he did. Why I don't know. Maybe he figured he might need a friend one day or just liked the colour of my bonny blue eyes but help me he did and since then we've exchanged favours more times than I can count.

If Clint has a menacing appearance so does Bob. The man's almost as wide as he's tall and there's very little fat on his solid frame. If his brother's built like the fabled brick shit-house Bob gives the impression that he could walk through the wall of one. He used to be called 'Popeye' by people stupid or brave enough to risk a broken limb. That was back when he ran one of the hardest crews in Manchester. His crew was never openly criminal. Bob made his money fending off the real criminals who were battening on the city's flourishing club scene with little opposition from the police. He was always willing to trade blow for blow with the lowlifes in ways which the likes of Uncle Lew and the top coppers looked down their noses at.

Though he worked on the borderline of legality and may have strayed across it (and who was I to judge him), there's one reason which has kept Bob Lane on the side of the angels.

That reason is the memory of his mother, a tiny little woman, the complete old fashioned 'mum' with her grey hair in a granny bun and a pinafore over her dress. If Clint and Bob could terrify any number of local nuisances and would-be 'hard men' the pair of them lived in equal fear of Mrs Lane. To this day a reminder that his sainted and long dead mother wouldn't approve is enough to quell Clint when he gets above himself and it keeps Bob on the straight and narrow too.

Yeah, I know … get the violin section out. It's corny but true. But for his mother and her memory, Bob and Clint Lane could have been the worst criminals to hit Britain since the Krays.

Bob owns several clubs and is always awake in the wee small hours. It's hard to keep up with what his clubs are called at any particular time but the changes in the drinking regulations have been a godsend to Bob. He's coining it. He's also gone into student haunts in a big way; fancy places with loads of plate glass, abstract art and 'all the lager you can drink for ten quid' nights.

'Mr Lane's executive assistant,' the female voice answered.

'Tammy it's Dave, put Bob on will you?'

Tammy Marsden is Bob's squeeze. She's been with him for some time. A luxuriantly upholstered former lap-dancer, Tammy has expectations and sees Clint as an obstacle in her path to matrimony. However, I sense her intended has doubts. Bob wonders if he'd pass on Clint's handicap to children of his own. I've begun to think that he uses Clint as an excuse for delay. He's heard the relevant medical advice often enough.

I overheard a whispered consultation and then he came on.

'Dave, me old fruit and nut cake, what's troubling you at this hour when an honest businessman such as yourself ought to be clocking up the zeds?'

'So you're admitting that you're a dishonest businessman are you?' I asked.

'What do you mean, dishonest? These are my office hours, besides I'm paying so much tax these days I sometimes think I'm keeping the Royal Navy afloat on my own.'

'Yeah, you are since HMRC caught up with you and what's the Navy these days. Down to their last few cockle boats, aren't they?'

'OK, OK, Sarcasm Boy, what's the prob?'

'The prob, Bob, is that I'm stuck on my tod without wheels. I'm in a call box at the end of Deansgate and I've just had a home visit from some rather nasty gentlemen who wanted to incinerate me.'

There was no sharp intake of breath. That's one of the things I like about Bob.

'Anybody dead?'

'One hurt, one of the opposition that is.'

'And the family?'

'They're all well and now heading for the hills at high speed in my only vehicle. The other's damaged. That's why I need transport that can't be traced to me.'

'You know I only asked if there were any dead first because I trust you to protect your family. I'm looking forward to being Baby Cunane's godfather.'

'Yes.'

'Christ, Dave, I don't know what to say. Do I know any of your playmates?'

'They're definitely not our local scallywags. I've never seen them before. One was burned with his own firebomb.'

'Badly burned?'

'Yes.'

'How sad, I'll put the word out round the local hospitals. They do burns at Wythenshawe don't they?'

'They do but he could be anywhere.'

'So Janine, has she done a moody? I know she doesn't go for the rough stuff.'

'Our separation's only temporary while I get this bother sorted.'

'*Bother* he says. I like it. Someone firebombs your house and its bother. Wheels aren't much of a problem, Dave, but there must be something more I can do.'

'Actually Bob ...'

'Spit it out!'

'I don't know who these people are at all. I have nothing on them, zilch.'

A vision of Lew's notebook sitting in my safe not half a mile away flashed before my eyes. Could I use it to bargain with them?

'So, what's the plan?'

'Find out who they are, I suppose. Well, it's a bit more complicated than that because if I do identify these bastards they'll have no option but to slot me. Janine has this idea that if I convince them that I know nothing and have no hostile intentions they'll lay off.'

'Hmmm, that doesn't sound too likely if they're already trying to wipe your clock. Dave, with you things are always too far gone to be settled with a friendly chat over a cup of tea.'

'Yeah, lovely isn't it? There's more and it gets worse. I believe they've killed a relative of mine and when the police find out they'll be all over the landscape in their size eleven boots.'

'Will they find out?'

'I've already tipped them off.'

'So you'd like somewhere to hide your weary head while you work out if the firebombing was just a friendly warning, like?'

He sounded perplexed.

'Something like that, yes.'

'I can do that for you Dave but make damn sure the house I send you to doesn't get burned down. I've spent a fortune on it and Tammy loves the place.'

'I don't get into these things by choice.'

'This relative, it isn't old Paddy?'

'No.'

I could have said more but there was no point in passing on information which could be fatal.

'Thank God for that. Listen Dave, I'm beginning to wonder if knowing you might be bad for my health. I've got spare wheels here that you can have but the difficulty is getting them to you. I can't leave and I don't trust you with Tammy ... '

'Oh come on, Bob!'

'No, stranger things have happened. Knowing your reputation as a lady's man I wouldn't care to put temptation your way. Back in the day you used to like your women hot and your curries mild.'

'Bob, I'm happily married now.'

'And wasn't Tammy's previous boyfriend the same, until his wife found out, that is.'

I could hear Tammy's protests in the background.

'Right, Dave, I'll get a car to you. The keys of the house will have to wait for a while. I don't have them here.'

I told him where I was.

'There's just one little problem. The only spare hands I've got here belong to your old prison buddy No-Nose Nolan and his oppo, what's his name, the Scouser with the red hair?'

'He's called Lee and he wouldn't thank you for calling him a

Scouser. He's just as much a Mank as you are.'

'Nobody's as Mank as me. Anyway, I use them as a pair of bookends on club security. It's charity really because they're both useless for anything apart from picking up litter. Sorry, rewind that. No-Nose has improved a lot since his illness which is why I give him house room. In fact he's becoming boring, giving me advice on my accounting system the other day he was but I'll let you discover the new No-Nose for yourself. All I'll say is brains can ruin a perfectly good gofer, which is what he was. He's lumbered himself with that Lee, carts him around as if he's his nurse. Lee is bad news and if I let him go, No-Nose will have to go too. Anyway, I'll send them to meet you in Whitworth Street in two cars and they'll leave you one.'

'Thanks a bunch Bob,' I said drawing in my breath. Was I going to get away without Bob's 'big ask' which is what he usually calls taking responsibility for Clint?

I wasn't.

'Dave,' he asked cautiously, 'you don't by any chance need Clint do you? No-Nose can pick him up on the way to you.'

'Bob, I'm not in any danger. Let Clint get his sleep. Just the car, that's all I need. I'm an innocent bystander in all this.'

'I can go with bystander but innocent doesn't sound like you, Dave, or maybe it's the other way round, but if you say so I'll take your word for it. It might be nice if you live to see that baby you're expecting so how about Clint? He can watch your back.'

'I'll be fine, Bob.'

'Go on, man, you need Clint and your Baby does too. I'll tell No-Nose to pick him up. OK?'

He put the phone down before I could reply.

I stepped out of the call box.

There was still plenty of activity along Whitworth Street. Taxis were on the go the whole time, picking people up from the clubs that line the bank of the Rochdale canal. With its footbridges across the canal this small part of Manchester has an exotic feel. It's definitely not Amsterdam or Venice but there's something that draws the crowds. Maybe it's the atmosphere of a big city where drinks and entertainment are on tap 24/7.

The people, drunk and sober, were predominantly young, students blowing their loans.

I looked at my watch. It was well after three.

I briefly considered my options and decided that I didn't have any. Convincing them I didn't know a thing about them was a chance in a million. OK, make that ten million but I had to try.

9

Tuesday: 3.50 a.m.

It began raining heavily while I waited for Bob's soon-to-be redundant bookends.

The streets cleared.

Lights gleamed on the dark waters of the canal. The clubs began shutting their doors.

I shivered in my dark water-proof. It kept the rain off but provided little warmth.

Finally there were two cars, both large and dark, one a BMW estate, the other a Volvo. They entered the street from the Deansgate end and drove slowly.

The drivers were hard to make out but they could only be Bob's gofers.

When I waved him down, Lee stopped and jumped out of the BMW. It was the early hours of the morning but his movements told me he was hyper. I'd never learned his surname. Lee hadn't been a great success at crime. Walking round in scally costume of bright red Lacoste jumpers all the time hadn't helped. He was still in scally gear but he'd apparently learned the value of camouflage. The Rockport boots were still there and the bling: heavy gold chain necklace, sovereign rings on three fingers, and bracelets, but he'd toned down the colour scheme. He was wearing black Reebok full-length trackie bottoms and a black Reebok top with grey inset down the sleeves. A black peaked cap with blue side panels concealed his carroty hair, just a few ginger strands poked out in front of his ears.

Lee stood about five feet two in his boots but that didn't stop him being aggressive to the point of insanity. He always came onto people like a human pit-bull and liked to greet strangers with 'Who're you looking at then?'

Big men crossed the road to get out of his way.

Even in the unnatural glow of the sodium street lights the expression on his face signalled that his combat level was high. His ugly mug wasn't something you wanted to look at even in twilight. Livid spots jostled for lebensraum on his pitted skin.

'How's it hanging, Lee?' I asked just to pull his chain. 'You're looking well. I could take you for a Swiss banker in those dark clothes.'

'Who are you calling a wanker!' he snarled.

There was a twang in his accent that could be taken as Scouse by the uninitiated. I knew he came from Benchhill, Wythenshawe, in Manchester's Deep South.

'Well, it's nice to see you too, Lee,' I said with a smile. 'I'm just being friendly. Would you like a smack on the gob instead?'

'Coming on hard again, are you?'

Last time we'd met he'd been paid to assault me.

'No, just talking to you in a friendly way.'

'I can do without running f**king errands for you, Cunane. You might have got off all them sex murders but in my book you're still a nonce.'

'Hey, you should try for a job with the police Lee. You're wasting your time as Bob Lane's gofer. Yeah, the local Filth want men like you who don't bother their heads about little things like proof and evidence.'

'Are you saying I'm a copper's nark,' he yelped.

He started forward angrily.

'Hang about, Lee!' No-Nose said, emerging from the Volvo and wrapping his arms round his partner in crime. Oddly enough, No-Nose had a book in his hand. I wondered where he'd nicked it. The book shops weren't open yet.

'Mr Cunane's a friend of Bob's. You don't want to mess with him.'

'Get your f**king hands off me,' Lee grunted. 'He said I'm a grass.'

'Sorry about this, Mr C,' No-Nose apologised, tightening his grip. 'What you said is a very sore point with Lee.'

'It's all right, Tony,' I said. 'Let him go and I'll punch his lights out for him.'

His mother and I are the only ones who ever use No-Nose's given name, Tony. I've known him for a long while. He worked as an undercover messenger for Bob when Bob at one time.

'Lee, will you stop pissing about?' No-Nose pleaded.

'Yeah, no hard feelings, Lee,' I said, 'I was only messing with you.'

I held out my hand.

Lee's struggles subsided and No-Nose let him go. He shook my hand and looked away.

'Which car do you want?' he asked.

I walked round both cars, taking my time.

'It's not as if you're buying, Mr C,' No-Nose whispered.

'I fancy the Beamer,' I said to Lee.

'It's too good for the likes of you.'

'Lee!' warned No-Nose 'the big guy's listening to you. This'll all go straight back to Bob.'

The big guy was indeed listening.

Clint was struggling to get out of the back of the BMW. He couldn't work the door handle but he had the window open.

In appearance, apart from his abnormal size, Clint might have been a prosperous farmer from the nineteen thirties, as restored by the National Trust for a Beatrix Potter exhibition. If you ignored the taut skin and bony cheekbones you could say his rosy red and weather beaten complexion was bucolic. His clothes also belonged in an exhibition. A vintage green tweed jacket with massive brown leather buttons covered his upper body. His ensemble was completed by green cord trousers. The corduroy was so thick that it was almost bullet proof, certainly arrow proof.

Clint's dark brown hair is another unusual feature. Like him, it follows an unusual pattern. Thick and wiry, it swirls round his head like an angry sea round a reef, sticking out at odd angles.

'It's all right, Clint. Stay in there,' I said. 'I'm taking this car.'

Clint grinned sheepishly.

'It's nice to see you, Dave; to see you nice.'

'Yeah, it's nice to see you too, Clint,' I said.

Despite earlier misgivings, I meant what I said. I was fond of the big guy. It was just being responsible for him that could get heavy.

He immediately began another struggle against German technology. This time he was trying to get his seat belt back on. It wasn't exactly rocket science but Clint was finding it impossible to secure the belt round his outsized frame.

'If you're going in the BMW, I'll have to come with you,' No-Nose announced. 'You could have had the Volvo on a loan but Bob wants the BMW back by lunchtime. He said something about the airport.'

'Fair enough,' I said, holding my hand out for the keys. 'I just need to go home. There's something I have to do.'

I didn't mention that I might need the speed of the BMW.

Bob's Beamer was a brand new X5M Sport with 355 horse power and white leather interior whereas the Volvo was two years old. It was nice of Bob to give me a choice. Cynically, I guessed at his motive. The offer of a ride in the new car had been necessary to lure Clint out of his bed. The big man was into cars in a big way.

Lee reluctantly passed over the keys. I hopped in and No-Nose joined me. I quickly did a U-turn and headed out of Whitworth Street making for Chester Road and the M60.

As I raced up the ramp onto the motorway in the early light I got my first glimpse of the distant eastern hills. A faint glow of dawn was backlighting the cloud streaked sky over the peaks. The rain had stopped and it looked as if it might stay fine for a while.

I kept my foot down and raced for the intersection that would take me to the A34.

I knew I might be heading back into danger. What would I find at Topfield? Would the bombers have come back and burned down the house for spite? Were they waiting for me? Somehow the coming daylight reassured me. I felt that my mysterious enemy preferred to operate in darkness.

'You're very patient, Mr C.' Tony remarked. 'I'd have been swearing like blue murder with Lee going on like that, but you never seem to do much of that. You never did much effing and jeffing when we were inside and everyone swears there, even the screws and the chaplains.'

'No,' I agreed, deciding to change the subject. 'What is it with you and Lee? You've not come out of the closet, have you?'

'No,' he said, as evenly as if I'd asked him what his shoe size was. 'We're not gay. It's just that Lee needs someone to keep him out of trouble and I seem to be the one.'

'And who keeps you out of trouble, Tony?'

'I'm going straight, honest, Mr C.'

'He is,' Clint chimed in. 'He comes to help me at the farm some days.'

I looked across at the battered face of No-Nose Nolan. The No-Nose bit came from a car accident he'd had as a child and from neglect in getting it fixed. His face was fearsome. He looked as if he'd done fifteen rounds with both Klitschko brothers simultaneously, Vitali and Wladimir taking it in turns to flatten his features. But his face is his fortune to the degree that he has any fortune. His looks made possible a career as a collector for various loan sharks mixed with petty crime. From that he'd graduated to become a minor gofer for Bob Lane.

Scrawny and small as ever, he was looking more prosperous than the last time I saw him. He was wearing a respectable brown leather jacket, blue jeans and newish trainers.

No-Nose is so pathetic that there's something endearing about him. I could understand why Bob extended sympathy to him. He was like one of those three-legged cats that people get attached to. You know you should have had it put to sleep after the accident but you find yourself stumping up for the vet's bills.

I left the A34 and turned onto the Handforth Bypass. If you visit the bypass anytime after midnight during the football season you'll often see one of the local multimillionaire footballers testing his new sports car. It's one of the few straight stretches in the area that isn't booby trapped with speed cameras.

I floored the accelerator and reached a hundred and twenty in a satisfyingly short time.

'Speed limit's seventy, Mr C,' No-nose commented anxiously.

'Who do you think you are, Tony, my wife?' I said, enjoying the moment.

Before No-Nose could reply both of us were startled by a thunderclap of laughter from Clint.

The big guy thought I was incredibly funny.

'No Nose isn't your wife,' he cackled. 'Look at his face. Who'd marry him?'

No-Nose looked at me and shrugged.

I slowed down.

There were tears streaming down Clint's face. He kept on rocking backwards and forwards with laughter.

We drove in silence after that and I kept within the speed limit.

I was grateful for the BMW's four-wheel drive when we reached the hills. Some of the lanes were half flooded. I approached Topfield Farm very carefully. First I drove past the gate slowly and then looped back. I did that twice. There didn't seem to be any men with guns or red Mini-Coopers around. The building was intact. Even so I took my time. I parked in the entrance lane and walked up to the five bar gate ready to run for cover at the first sign of trouble.

It was stupid but then I was crazy to have remained in the country. They could have sniped me like a sitting duck. Luckily my unknown enemies like to do things in a complex way.

There was nothing.

I opened the gate and drove into the yard.

'Do you live here, Mr C?' No-Nose asked wonderingly.

'Yes, I did a lot of the building work myself.'

'Must be worth a fortune, it's the sort of place I used to break into.'

'You can forget that.'

'I told you. I'm as straight as a … as … as one of them giant spirit levels.'

'I'm glad to hear it.'

'Anyway, you've got cameras on it. I never touch a place with cameras.'

'What?'

'Cameras, I've always been careful of them. You can do a job, come out clean as a whistle and then get yourself arrested a week later because you're on Candid Camera. But, like, there are ways you can get round them.'

I'd intended to go straight in, get paper and one of Jenny's marker pens and make a notice proclaiming my ignorance of all events concerning Lew. I knew it was a feeble plan but it offered a slim chance. Janine approved and I told myself that I had to give her idea a try. I intended to offer them Lew's unopened notebook as proof and to leave the office phone number for them to contact me.

But...there are no security cameras at Topfield Farm.

'There's no camera,' I said.

'Yes, there is. Look up there. It's underneath the guttering just below the barn roof. The roof overhangs and you can't see it very well.'

I screwed my eyes up and peered at the place he indicated.

I still couldn't see anything but then there was a gleam of reflected light as clouds shifted.

'Did you forget about it?'

'No, it just wasn't there when I left.'

Clint missed this exchange. He was once again having trouble exiting the BMW.

'Clint, stay where you are,' I said urgently. 'We're out of here.'

If there was danger I'd have to face it alone.

I scratched my head. Why go to the bother of installing a camera?

'Hang about, Mr C,' No-Nose said. 'That camera's focused on the porch door. It's a narrow beam, like. I know the type. It's an Israeli model. We haven't crossed its field of view yet. Whoever put it there doesn't know we're here.'

'Are you sure?'

'Yeah, look at the lens. You'd need one of them big fisheye jobs to get this entire yard and the house front on one screen.'

Hope flared.

I looked back towards the lane. All I could see was a wall of dense foliage with a gap where the curving farm track led to Topfield. There was no movement in the gap and the only sound was the raucous dawn chorus. Unless they had another camera on the lane my arrival must have been unobserved.

I listened for the high pitched sound of an approaching Mini Cooper.

There wasn't a peep, no noise of traffic and no movement.

Meanwhile No-Nose moved closer to the barn wall.

'Yeah, it's one of them spy jobs,' he said when he returned. 'It's really, really small. They mostly use them indoors and hide them in a flower vase or a bookshelf or something.'

He raised his arms to signify a narrow field of view.

'So?'

'So, someone wants to clock you going into your house. I'll check the back.'

He was off before I could stop him, hugging the barn wall under the spy camera and then disappearing behind the kitchen.

Meanwhile, Clint joined the birds and began whistling tunelessly to himself. He returned my stare calmly.

A long moment later No-Nose returned.

'There's another one of the bleeding nuisances stuck on that outhouse thingy you've got round there. It's covering the back porch.'

'You didn't, er … '

'No, of course not, Mr C. What do you take me for?'

'You've been caught before.'

'That was only when someone turned up unexpectedly. Believe me, I know my way round cameras. Only the two, that's all there are.'

I did believe him but where did that get me?

'I could get in the house without showing up on camera and have a look round if you like,' he volunteered. 'It's not illegal because it's your house.'

'Why bother?'

'I could get in easy just to set your mind at rest. I don't need the doors. One of them bedroom windows is open a crack. I can get in there easy and I can see what they've been up to.'

He pointed out the window.

Damn! It was one of the windows of my bedroom, the same one

I'd fired the shotgun from. In the excitement I'd forgotten to fasten it. Still it was too high up to be vulnerable.

'But the camera ...'

'It's just focused on the front door, Boss. No one will see me getting in through the window.'

I thought for a minute. Maybe they'd left a message. I had to know.

I got a ladder out of the barn.

Clint carried the ladder and positioned it below the bedroom.

I've done a lot of ladder work myself and my ascents are always ploddingly slow but No-Nose went up like a monkey on a stick. It took him all of five seconds to open the window and disappear into the bedroom.

Clint hugged himself and grinned with pleasure at being able to help out. I stood alongside him to wait for No-Nose. All sorts of fears crossed my mind. What if the cameras were to give a warning to someone inside the house? Someone waiting with a gun or a knife.

When No-Nose reappeared via the ladder he was white and shaking like a leaf.

'What?'

He clung onto my arm.

'There's a bloody big bomb in the living room. We've got to get out of here.'

Frank Lean

10

Tuesday: Dawn

I backed the BMW down the drive and retreated along the country lane to a lay-by about half a mile away and parked. I left the engine running.

I had difficulty in speaking.

'What was the bomb like?' I finally managed to croak. 'Was it rigged to go off when the door opened?'

'No, it was far more up to date than that. This was state of the art and it was set up by pros.'

'Come on, Tony, how would you know that?'

I left unspoken the thought that No-Nose was just a small time loan shark's runner and unsuccessful housebreaker but he got my drift.

'I just know,' he said.

There was a note of desperation in his voice that carried conviction but I had to be certain.

'It was probably something Lloyd left as a joke and it spooked you.'

'Lloyd's your kid, is he?'

'Yes.'

'Goes on the internet a lot and finds the web sites which show you how to make bombs?'

'He's only five.'

'Well then.'

'Go on, I'm sorry.'

'There was a big wad of grey plastic explosive stuck on your coffee table with a mobile phone on top of it.'

'A phone,' I repeated stupidly. I was sickened. I knew what he was going to say next but I needed to hear him say it.

'Yeah, there was a wire running down from the phone to a

detonator. The bastard who set it up sees you going in on his bloody spy camera, presses speed dial on his phone and then bingo! No more Mr C.'

'Thanks,' I croaked feebly.

'It's a big f**king mother of a bomb, Mr C. There won't be much of your nice house left if it goes off.'

'Listen, there's only one thing to do. You'll have to stay here with Clint while I go back to the house and make sure no one goes in by mistake.'

'Oh, yeah, I stay here with Clint then when I hear a f**king big bang I go to Bob Lane and tell him that I've let his mate get blown into tiny pieces and don't tell me you aren't intending to shift that phone.'

I looked at him sideways.

'Think about it Mr C. The guys that set that bomb can't be far away. Those spy cameras can't send a signal very far. They have to be near. If you go charging up there it's ten to one they'll spot you.'

'And if they see you they'll do nothing?'

'I'll go in and out the same way I did before. They'll never spot me.'

'But they just need a glimpse.'

'Logically, they wouldn't have set up electronic observation if they were also eyeballing the place.'

It was hard to fault his reasoning. If they'd had Topfield under close watch we'd all be dead already. Reasoning? What was I reasoning with No-Nose Nolan for?

'I don't like this, Tony. I'd rather let the house be blown up than have you taking a chance with something you know nothing about.'

He let out a long sigh.

'I haven't told anyone this but I trust you, Mr C.'

'Yes?'

'Last time I was in prison I caught meningitis. They got my mother in and the priest and everything and said I was going to die, that there was irreversible brain damage. But I didn't die.'

'Yeah, I can see that.'

'When I recovered everything was different. My mum says I even talk differently but the thing was I only had to look at something once

80

and I could remember it perfectly. I can do sums in my head too.'

'What's twelve twelves?'

'A hundred and forty four, but I meant harder sums than that.'

'What's five hundred and seventy six times ten thousand and twenty one?'

His eyes closed for no more than a second and then rapped out, 'Five million, seven hundred and seventy two thousand and ninety six.'

I took out my phone and turned on the calculator function. He was right. It took me much longer to find the answer than it did for him to say it.

I had little time to waste on astonishment. I gaped at his battered face for a second. 'What does this have to do with bombs?'

He looked embarrassed.

'I don't like to say where I did it but I've had a good look at several books about bombs, things terrorist groups and anarchists have downloaded from the internet and there's other stuff as well.'

'Yes.'

'The bomb in your house is like one of those IEDs they use against our troops in Afghanistan.'

'IED?'

'Improvised explosive device, it's a NATO acronym.'

'You're serious aren't you?'

'Yeah, it's like my brain's been reconditioned.'

'Reconditioned?'

'You know, like the cars on Discovery Channel. These people buy a heap of junk, like I used to be, and they recondition it. They rebuild it and sell it for thousands of dollars.'

'So your brain's worth thousands of dollars?'

'No, you know what I mean. I can't stop wanting to learn things.'

He patted his jacket pocket. There was a thick paperback book in it. He pulled it out and handed it to me. I read the title in the poor light, *Engineering Mathematics: A Foundation for Electronic, Electrical, Communications and Systems Engineers.*

Full of suspicion, I flicked the book open to check that it wasn't some collection of porn. It contained a mass of diagrams and formulae. I glanced at the information on the back of the book. It said the text was useful up to second year honours degree level.

'Honestly, Mr Cunane, I have to keep reading. It's like a disease. I'm afraid that if I stop my brain will go back to what it was before.'

'God, Tony, your brain really has been reconditioned,' I said, handing back the book. 'It must be turbo charged if you think this is light reading.'

'All right then, I'll be off,' he said.

'Be careful, Einstein.'

'I will be. You keep your ears open for a bang … just joking. It should be easy but I need to be there sharpish. They may decide to put up more cameras.'

He opened the passenger door. I grabbed his arm.

'I can't let you go. I can always rebuild the house but…'

'No, listen, Mr C, I need to do this for myself. I don't want to become a nerd who only knows things in books. I've wasted a lot of time out of my life and now I need to do things, hard things. If there's an anti-handling device on this IED I'll cope with it. Believe me, I'll be perfectly safe.'

He pulled free and began jogging up the lane. His slight figure quickly merged into the long early morning shadows.

Ten minutes later I was parked nearer Topfield Farm waiting to hear whether No-Nose had achieved death or glory. The alternative of phoning the police had occurred to me. I like to tell myself that I'm not that different from a normal citizen.

Lew's warning not to trust the police rang in my ears like the Crack of Doom. Thinking of him brought on a twinge of guilt. I persuaded myself that there could be good reasons why he hadn't answered his phones.

It was hard to believe that just twenty four hours earlier I'd been sleeping in my bed with just a routine Monday morning in front of me. No, that wasn't right; I had the coming baby to look forward to. The ups and downs of family life had become my focus. The days when I would charge around Manchester thinking I was some sort of latter-day Robin Hood were long gone.

Or were they?

I was allowing poor battered No-Nose Nolan to risk his neck and his 'reconditioned brain' to save my property. I'd accepted the flimsiest of evidence that he'd suddenly become a bomb-disposal expert and let him go ahead.

I cursed myself for allowing myself to be taken in. No-Nose had probably got all that stuff about IEDs from films or science fiction books.

I could only put my weakness down to delayed shock about the night's events.

Then the sound of gentle snoring from the back seat penetrated my frantic mind. Clint had mastered the seat belt and was curled up with his feet doubled up across the seat. He took up as much room as three large people. His gaunt face was completely relaxed. He was smiling in his sleep.

Traffic was starting to move as early morning commuters set off to Manchester and the Cheshire towns. No red Mini-Coopers but plenty of four wheeled drives passed us. The intermittent rain had stopped and the clouds were clearing. It was starting to look like a fine day. I was getting eyestrain as I stared up the road towards the bend where No-Nose would appear if he'd survived. There was a thick hawthorn hedge there and a narrow pavement. Horses had recently left their calling cards on the roadway.

Unexpectedly there was a loud rap on the offside window. I almost jumped out of my skin. It was No-Nose. His twisted features were stretched into a wide grin. He resembled a gargoyle after five hundred years of erosion.

'It's OK, Mr C. All clear!' he said. His voice was unnaturally strident in the morning stillness.

11

Tuesday: 6 a.m.

'What did you have to sneak up on me for?' I asked, trying to cover up my surprise.

'Yes,' agreed Clint, chiming in with my complaint. 'Bob says you can give people a heart attack, sneaking up on them.'

Tony's eyebrows shot up. Clint is in the habit of creeping up on his brother.

I got out of the BMW. No-Nose was clutching a bulging plastic carrier bag.

'What's in there?' I asked, suspecting he'd reverted to burglary.

'It's just the doings,' he said offhandedly. 'I've not nicked anything.'

'Sorry,' I muttered.

'Not that you've got much worth nicking, Mr C.'

'For God's sake, Tony, call me Dave. What's in the bag?'

'C4, NATO military explosive, that's what. It's not as powerful as octocellulose.'

'What?'

'Just joking, octocellulose doesn't exist. It's in a science fiction book, four times more powerful than C4.'

I looked at him. So he had been getting ideas out of science fiction books. Maybe the 'reconditioned brain' was a fantasy.

'There's at least four kilograms of C4. They wanted to make sure of you.'

He held the bag open revealing a large lump of off-white coloured plastic explosive. There was also a Nokia phone enclosed in a Ziploc sandwich bag.

'That's not still connected, is it?' I gasped, suddenly distrustful of his bomb disposal expertise.

He put on the gargoyle grin again, switched the bag to his left hand and waved wires and a detonator under my nose.

'Tra-la!' he crowed, holding them up.

'Brilliant,' I muttered, clapping my hands quietly.

Clint joined in noisily. His applause echoed down the lane like a car backfiring. I signalled for silence with a finger on my lips.

'I put the phone in the bag in case there are prints on it, but as these guys are pros I don't expect there are.'

'So what's your brain telling you now?'

'I've an idea where they're hiding.'

'Go on.'

'I came back by a shortcut.'

'There are none.'

'There are. You haven't found them. I came through the hedge because I wanted a look round. There's any number of broken down sheds near your house, Mr C.'

'I know. Call me Dave. I don't like Mr C.'

'Yes, Dave, there are a lot of places where they could hide. I thought if I go back now and keep my eyes open and then you enter the house by the back door they'd set off the bomb and come out of hiding and get lost when it doesn't go off. Then we'll find out who they are.'

'Very logical that new brain of yours, but suppose they just decide to correct their mistake and come out firing sub-machineguns?'

'We'll scarper in that case unless you want to try and take them out with that shotgun you left on your kitchen counter.'

'I was in a hurry,' I mumbled.

I couldn't think of any further objections to his plan even so the situation was unreal. What was I doing, following the instructions of No-Nose Nolan's reconditioned brain?

I must have gaped at him.

'Well?' he prompted. 'We'll have to get a rattle on or they'll be getting jumpy.'

'Why would they do that?'

'Stands to reason, Dave,' he said condescendingly. 'They'd have preferred to set the bomb off in the night and get away without anyone seeing them. The later it gets the more chance there is that someone will get a look at them or they might even get blocked in by traffic on these country lanes.'

'Right,' I said. 'Brain 1, Cunane 0.'

'Give me five minutes.'

I nodded. He handed me the bag. Gingerly, I took the phone out, still in its bag. Even if the bomber had left his prints there was no chance that I'd be able to run them through the police systems.

As No-Nose set off back into the foliage I noticed that his clothes were soaked but the electronics book was now in a plastic sandwich bag off my kitchen counter. He must have been crawling on all fours.

A few moments later I was standing at my back door and feeling through my pockets for the key. I felt as if someone had plastered me onto a giant target. Suppose there was another bomb? These guys believed in back-up … but come to that they couldn't be same guys. One of them was badly injured and the other hurt.

I felt my stomach roll over. These bastards were coming at me in waves. Petrol bombers fail, so send in the plastic explosive guys.

I'd stared at the foliage until my eyes ached but couldn't spot Tony's spy camera. How could it be so obvious to him but not to me? Doubts surfaced again until I remembered that I couldn't see the other camera until he pointed it out. Clint was at my side. He'd refused to stay in the car and I knew him too well to start arguing.

I opened the door and walked into the kitchen. Everything was normal except for the shotgun, which I immediately picked up. As I laid hands on the gun the detonation phone rang.

Red mist descended.

Grabbing up the gun I ran outside. I needed to fight someone. Anger pulsated through my body. People I didn't even know had casually decided to end my life. Somehow this was more vicious and less forgivable than the petrol bombs. With them there'd been a human agent that I could prepare measures against.

Now death was to be delivered at the push of a button.

I scanned the open fields at the back of the property. My gaze flicked from feature to feature; a shed, a cow byre, coloured pony-show jumps with the paint flaking off, a rusting old horse-trailer abandoned in a corner.

Nothing was moving. I was an idiot. As No-Nose would say, it stood to reason that the bombers wouldn't hide in plain sight of the house. Otherwise why would they need spy cameras?

Then I spotted Tony in the corner of an adjacent field. He was down low. He was indicating something beyond my line of sight, nodding his head. He only lacked a wagging tail to be a pointer dog.

I ran to the extreme corner of my land. From this point Topfield Farm and the barn were invisible because of an intervening hedge.

Tony was visible though. He was standing up, waving his arms and pointing.

Diagonally across the adjacent field two people were scrambling through the door of an abandoned hen house. It was big and mounted on wheels, proper poultry farm equipment not something you'd keep in your back garden for half a dozen hens. I could just about make out the killers in the long shadows cast by the trees.

One of the men, and they were both men, was lugging a large suitcase with both hands but the other was unburdened. They were making for a gate, which opened onto the winding tarmac lane.

I completely lost it. If they'd been in range I'd have shot them both but I couldn't. I yelled at them in frustrated rage. Clint began climbing over the fence round the poultry field.

'Bastards!' he yelled.

The one who wasn't carrying anything turned, pulled out a gun and fired a rapid burst.

The sound wasn't loud; pock, pock, pock, pock, just like that, not a frightening sound at all. The gunman was a good two hundred yards away so if he hit us it would be incredible bad luck but I heard the bullets whistle past.

'Get down!' I roared at Clint. Even at long range his size made him vulnerable. Taking no notice of me, Clint vaulted over the fence and began sprinting across the field like an Olympic champion.

'Bastards, bastards!' he screamed.

More bullets whistled above my head and I realised that I was the target, not Clint.

I experienced another spasm of blind rage.

I climbed over the fence and fired, angling the gun like an artillery piece. It was an impossible shot. The gunman and his mate were almost invisible against the deep shadows cast by sycamore trees in that corner of the field. However shotgun pellets spread out at long range and the man with the suitcase seemed to stagger. He may have taken a couple of pellets.

Unfortunately the gun was loaded with number 6 shot which is nasty enough to give a rabbit a bad fright at close range but hardly likely to do much damage to a man at such a distance.

Even so, I believe I discouraged him. Luckily for us he didn't stand his ground. It isn't much fun being fired at and he speeded up his efforts to escape.

As for the other man, he also decided on a quick exit. Whether it was seeing Clint running towards him, waving his arms like a runaway windmill, I'll never know, but he turned to escape. Possibly he thought someone as reckless as Clint must be armed. Anyway when he overtook his partner with the case that guy decided he was carrying excess baggage and dumped his burden.

Both disappeared through the gate.

Ten seconds later Clint reached the hen house.

Before I could stop him he raced on after them only to throw up his hands in disappointment when he reached the gate. The sound of a high performance car accelerating startled birds out of the trees.

'They've gone, the bastards,' he said as I came panting up to him.

'Did you see the car?'

Car identification is an area where Clint excels. He spends hours poring over motor mags and can recite specifications on most cars.

'Red Mini-Cooper.'

'Anything else?'

'Mini-Cooper S, seventeen inch alloy wheels. It costs more than twenty thousand pounds,' he said impressively. I looked back across the fields. By the time I got the BMW on the road they'd be far away.

'At least they've left us a party bag,' Tony shouted.

He was kneeling on the grass next to the discarded case. His fingers were exploring the locks.

'Don't open it!' I warned. 'It might be booby trapped.'

'Nah, they didn't have time for that,' he said confidently. He flicked a small penknife open and quickly jimmied the locks.

Carefully slotted into polystyrene cut-outs was all the equipment needed to blow me or any other target to hell and back. Screens, receivers, aerials, spy cameras, computer, all neatly fitted in detachable trays. There was also a bulky automatic pistol, with a spare magazine alongside it.

'I'll have that,' I said, pulling the gun out.

The pistol was enormous. I have big hands but the grip was huge.

'That'll make a fair sized hole in someone; it's a Desert Eagle, fifty cal,' No-Nose opined.

A glance at the weapon confirmed this.

'Is there anything you don't know, Tony,' I snapped peevishly, regretting my words even as I spoke.

'Not a lot, Dave, but it says it's a Desert Eagle fifty cal here.'

He held up the spare mag on which the words were printed.

'If you're taking that, do you mind if I keep all this gubbins here?'

'Why?'

'I can find a good use for it.'

'Blowing up safes? I thought you were as straight as a spirit level these days.'

'Sorry, I misspoke. I didn't mean the C4. I meant the surveillance gear. Damn useful that is.'

A wave of frustration swept over me.

For a minute there I'd allowed myself to think that we might lay hands on at least one of the men trying to kill me. Then maybe, just maybe, I could have bargained my way out of this mess. That wasn't going to happen now. They were going to keep coming after me until they succeeded. It hadn't escaped me that the latest pair was dressed in suits. Where was there an office full of suit wearing assassins ready for action at a moment's notice? The odds were so far against me that even

90

thinking of escape was fantasy. The red mist of rage that had buoyed me up faded.

I'm not at my best in a muddy field at crack of dawn. My shoes were offering no protection from the rain-sodden grass.

I checked out the hen house.

I was desperate for a clue to their identities.

Naturally it was empty. There wasn't a trace of their presence, no handy till receipts, no tell-tale sweet wrappers, not even a cigarette butt or a lump of chewing gum. If I'd been quicker off the mark or more cunning I might have bagged one of them. But no, I had to go charging across an open field like a maniac and worse, encourage Clint to follow my example.

It was a miracle he hadn't been hit.

I tried to think of the next move.

Fight or flight?

It didn't seem that I had much choice.

A fool's luck, that was the only thing that'd saved me so far. I felt cold sweat on my forehead when I thought about what could have gone wrong.

Without Tony 'No-Nose' Nolan's gift for detecting cameras, I'd now be reduced to atmospheric pollution. Maybe there'd be a few shreds of flesh that a forensic scientist could identify. What was the effect of four kilograms of explosive going off in a confined space? The destruction would have been complete. Not a stone would have been left on a stone.

Four kilograms, there had to be a clue there. Military explosives aren't easily come by.

'Come on,' I ordered, 'back to the house.'

Clint picked up the massive assassination kit with no strain at all and the three of us tramped back to Topfield Farm. Watching him I realised that I hadn't a chance of saving myself, let alone my family, unless I got help.

I needed people to work with me.

'Tony,' I said, making my pitch in a suitably tentative manner, 'how do you fancy hanging around with me for a while? Do you think Bob could spare you?'

'Spare me; I think he'll be glad to see the back of me.'

'Oh? You've been with him practically since he started.'

'Yeah, and that's all that's holding him back but I know. Me and Lee both, he wants rid. I can tell. He's already told me off for reading a book on his time.'

'That's harsh,' I murmured, implying that I'd never be guilty of such a crime against self-improvement.

We squelched on across the field in silence for a while. We reached the boundary of my property and I clambered over the fence.

'Mr C, er Dave,' Tony said when Clint had lifted him over and deposited him next to me. 'Are you serious about me hanging around with you? Working for you might be interesting.'

'Bombs in my living room aren't an everyday occurrence.'

'No, but somebody's out to do you and I don't think they've finished yet. An extra pair of eyes could come in useful.'

'Too right,' I said looking up at the camera on the barn wall, 'but it would only be a temporary job. I've made a rule not to hire permanent staff.'

'I don't mind temporary but there's a condition.'

'What?' I asked cautiously, aware that he had every right to expect my gratitude.

'I'll work for you temporary as long as Lee comes too.'

'Well, we all have our cross to bear. Are you sure?'

'He's not so bad. He's been my mate for a while.'

'He'll have to do what he's told.'

'I'll keep him straight.'

'That's more than anyone else has been able to do.'

'I will,' he insisted.

'What is it with you and Lee? You're not in a civil partnership are you?'

'Mr Cunane!' he said indignantly, 'I told you I'm as straight as one of them giant spirit level thingies and I meant straight in every way. I've had girl friends, lots of them. He's just my best mate.'

'Who's your current girl friend?'

'I'm between relationships at the moment.'

I took that to mean that he and Lee were in the closet and staying there. It was none of my business but I needed to know more.

'Look, Tony, if I'm taking you both on I'm entitled to know the whole story.'

'Do you want the long version or the short version?'

'Short will do. You can save the long one for some dark winter evening when we've nothing else to do.'

'Right, well Lee's dad was the Wythenshawe Telly Man and he was my dad's best mate.'

'Tally Man? In the collection business like you?'

'Telly Man, he used to hang out in this pub in Wythenshawe. This was back in the days when colour tellies were rare and expensive. Everybody wanted one.'

'And didn't want to pay for one?'

'That's right. So my dad heard he'd nicked some gear and went to see him. Telly Man took him to his mother's house. He had tellies stacked up to the ceiling in a back room and he tells my dad to pick one. So he does, only when he got it home it didn't work. They went through another four and none of them worked.'

'So?'

'So, my old man got pretty damned annoyed. He started quizzing Lee's dad and it turned out that the daft bugger had nicked the tellies from a TV repair business and he'd taken the ones waiting to be repaired instead of the ones that were working.'

'Brilliant.'

'Yeah, he wasn't the sharpest knife in the box was the Telly Man but my dad turned him round, gave him a good business plan, like. The pair of them started nicking tellies to order. People would go to the Telly Man and order their telly. He'd tell the punter the price was fifty pounds and then he'd say the telly will be at the back of a certain car park in Wilmslow at six a.m. on Saturday morning and my dad would make sure it was there. He handled the delivery side of the business and the Telly Man took care of supply.'

'I see.'

'But then things went wrong. Telly Man got nicked. He was

sentenced to a year for a first offence and he only had a month left to go when he broke out of prison.'

'The idiot!'

'Well, I said he wasn't sharp but there's worse.'

'Go on.'

'Yeah, well he was on the run and the police caught up with him and he took this family hostage, a family with kids, so instead of a month to serve he got twenty years and ended up in a maximum security prison sharing a cell with this nonce who'd killed two little girls. Not that he was a nonce himself like, just a total wipe out in the brains department.'

'I still don't see why that means you have to be joined at the hip to Lee.'

'It's awkward, I don't like to say Mr Cunane … er … Dave, but I promised my dad before he died.'

'Promised what?' I said irritably.

'That I'd look after Lee. Dad had loads of form and would have got a lot more than twelve months if the Telly Man had grassed him up. Then after he escaped and was banged up with the nonces, Dad was the only one who knew just how stupid the poor guy really was and still believed in him. So he made me promise to keep Lee out of trouble. Dad visited him regular before the poor guy topped himself.'

I studied Tony's sadly broken face. This was the man who was keeping someone else out of trouble. He stared straight back at me.

The story was crazy enough to be believable.

'So there is honour among thieves then?'

'Hah! Some, but it's pretty rare,' Tony agreed. 'There's a lot more stuff went on but that's the bones of it.'

'Just one thing, what's Lee's last name?'

There was no reply.

Tony looked stricken in so far as it was possible for him to have a facial expression.

'Go on, what's his name?'

'Sheerman-Holmes,' he said almost inaudibly, 'but you've not to use it.'

'Why?'

'Because he goes mad if you do.'

'He'll just have to get used to it.'

'No, you don't understand. He really goes mad, foams at the mouth and rolls about on the floor kicking and screaming. Something horrible happened to him when he was a kid and that name sets him off. Please don't say it, Boss … er … Dave. He'll know I told you.'

'Fair enough,' I muttered, wondering why Lee hadn't changed his name if it upset him so much.

'Thanks, Dave.'

'Right, you're hired! I'll consider the bomb disposal job as your aptitude test.'

'Funneeee, Dave!'

I spent the next few minutes negotiating wage rates. There may be honour among thieves but loyalty comes at a price and I wasn't so naive as to believe that this ex-convict with a reconditioned brain would work for the pleasure of my smile and a pat on the head. I made him a generous offer which he accepted.

'Right first job,' I said, 'tidy up the farmyard. Get the big guy to help you and see if you can move the Land Cruiser into the barn on three wheels, then get the hose on all that foam. I'm going for a shower.'

'Right Boss!'

After collecting the C4 from the BMW I went round the back of the house out of sight of my sharp-eyed employee. I opened the shed where Janine keeps her gardening tools and taking a spade quickly dug a hole in the back of a flower bed. I found some empty plastic fertilizer bags and put the C4 and the Desert Eagle in them. Jan had covered the flower bed with a thick layer of mulch. I scraped it back and buried the bags, carefully raking the mulch to make the bed look undisturbed.

The assassination kit was another problem. While they were in the garage I lugged it into Jan's tool shed and covered it up with sacks of compost.

12

Tuesday: 7.30 a.m.

It was seven thirty and I was skulking round the phone box at New Bailey Street on the Salford side of the Irwell waiting for Cullen's call.

Brendan Cullen is one of my oldest friends and the only friend I still have in the police ranks.

That has made our relationship fraught recently.

Various senior officers have tried to have me listed as a person of ill-repute officers are barred from associating with. They failed but they still connect Bren with me to his disadvantage. His face is too much of a reminder of past mistakes for some. They've moved him away from HQ into the Counter-Terrorism unit so they don't have to see him very often.

There was no ring.

I waited for five minutes.

I decided there must be some good reason why he hadn't called.

I turned back along New Bailey Street and walked slowly. I had a lot to think about. Brendan's new home was only a few hundred yards away at Left Bank in Spinningfields. I only had to cross the road and I could be there in minutes. I decided not to. I carried on along New Bailey giving a nod to the statue of Joseph Brotherton, Salford's first MP and an early campaigner against the death penalty. What would he make of the pickle I was in? Things were much simpler in his day with no police force worth mentioning and a virtually unlimited right of self defence.

I crossed the Irwell into Bridge Street and turned into the street called St Mary's Parsonage heading for the bollards at the narrow end of Back Bridge Street which would bring me to my office but when I turned the corner a man jumped out of the shadows, grabbed my arm and plucked me into a doorway.

It was Brendan Cullen.

'Cunane!' he snarled, 'get in here.'

He pressed me against the door. He was seething with anger. He pulled me so close that I was able to focus on the individual bristles of his designer stubble.

'Are you deliberately trying to get me kicked off the job or is this caper just your usual stupidity?' he said.

'What caper?'

'The caper where you got me to send a copper to Sir Lew Greene's door and then inform an involved party by phoning him on an open landline.'

I pulled myself free and pushed him back.

'Involved party? What are you on about?'

'Your father, stupid.'

'So? What's he involved in?'

'The fact that his cousin's been murdered makes him involved.'

'What?'

'Don't tell me you don't know he's been murdered.'

'I didn't know. I guessed after what happened to me … but he was ill, terminal cancer. He could have been in a coma or something.'

'Yeah, 'appen. So what happened to you, sunshine?'

I quickly filled him in. He was as impassive as a Red Indian chief when I told him about the petrol bombs and the high explosive.

'And Sir Lew Greene left you a notebook with the bad guy's name in it? Are you sure you didn't imagine that part?'

'He did.'

'And you haven't looked at it? Unbelievable, except that with you Dave, the wildly improbable is always believable.'

'I told you. My receptionist witnessed him dropping it in the safe.'

'Yeah.'

'It's in a Eurograde level five safe. That means …'

'I know what it means. I'm a policeman, remember.'

Brendan shook he head wearily. He studied me with an expression that was midway between loathing and exasperation. I stared back. His cool Italian suit was showing signs of fatigue, as was he. The

KILL ME IF YOU CAN

days when he was a detective sergeant on the Drug Squad hunting down dealers dressed in a purple shell suit are a very distant memory.

Nowadays he looks every inch the senior copper. The suits are genuine, bought new at Emporio Armani not second-hand at Elite. I wondered if he might run me in. Every relationship has its tipping point and I might have reached mine with Detective Chief Inspector Brendan Cullen. Bren was never wildly ambitious before but now he's remarried to a younger woman he seems much more attached to his career and to his salary than when he was drinking a bottle of whisky a day.

Billy-Jo is Bren's new wife.

She's a good ten years younger than Bren and just as curvaceous as the Jaguar he now drives round in. She's been married before and the Jag's second hand too. It isn't a red 'Morse type' 1960 Mark 2. It's a newish silver XF estate with room for his golf clubs. There's nothing retro about Bren.

Yeah, moving up, is Bren Cullen from the backstreets of Gorton.

'How?' I croaked.

'Are you sure you want to know?'

I nodded.

'I'm sorry Dave, but there's no way to make this nice for you. The old guy was beaten, tortured and then decapitated.'

'Oh God!'

'Yeah, it was bloody gruesome. I've seen some gory messes where the bad boys have been having fun with shotguns and machetes but this one beats the lot. There wasn't a particle of that room that wasn't soaked in blood: walls, ceiling and floor. It was either terrorists or, and this is where you come in, someone who wanted to make it look like terrorists.'

'How do I come in? Are you trying to tell me I had a reason to kill him?'

'It turns out that both you and your father could have been involved because you do have a motive, a bloody big one.'

'What?'

'You have a motive all right, Dave. It was right there in his office. A copy of his will. He changed it recently and made you his sole heir.

You get the lot; the house, the investments, the villa in Tuscany, thousands of acres of prime farm land belonging to his deceased wife's estate at Weldsley and an ice cream with raspberry sauce on top I shouldn't wonder.'

'Listen, Bren, you've got to believe me. The first I knew about that money was last evening when Paddy told me. Bloody hell, I've been on his shit-list for years. I was going to tell the old bugger that I couldn't help him and if he wanted to leave his money to someone else too bad. I couldn't let him buy me.'

'Christ, Dave, spare me the choirboy stuff. I think if he'd offered me that fortune I'd have obliged him.'

'Well, I didn't.'

'Some people might find that hard to believe.'

'It's true. Paddy and Eileen knew he'd changed his will in my favour but they didn't think it was right to tell me until he told me himself. Presumably he'd have told me when I agreed to arrange for his bogeyman to be bumped off.'

'And you'd turn down the chance to go from being the proprietor of a dead-beat detective agency to millionaire landowner in one sweet move? As I say, that's hard to swallow.'

'Bren I was banged up for crime I didn't commit. I won't take the chance of being banged up for killing Lew's bogeyman. You can't spend money in prison.'

He gave me a long searching look then his expression changed to what he probably regarded as a smile but which came out as an ugly leer.

'OK, Dave, *I* believe you but there are lots of coppers who won't, especially as it's you.'

'Thanks.'

'This is what they'll say. Lew Greene called on you yesterday morning, and they already know that, don't even ask me how ... He told you he was cutting you out of his will ...'

'I didn't even know about the will until yesterday evening. He hadn't spoken to me for years.'

'Paddy knew. Whatever he says they won't believe he didn't tell you as soon as he heard.'

100

'Oh, damn.'

'I'm telling you how the suspicious minds of some of my colleagues are putting things together at this very moment, and where you're concerned they're ultra-suspicious ...'

'I'll sue them again. I'll ...'

'Cut the bluster and listen. Lew told you he was disinheriting you so you went round and topped him before he could, simple as that. You knew he was on this EJA Inquiry so you rigged the killing to look like it was done by Islamists.'

'Tell me why Islamists would kill someone who might have been about to deliver a big propaganda boost for their cause?'

'Dave, when did logic ever bother some people where you're concerned? Anyway, we don't know he was about to criticise the Security Services.'

'So I'm in the shit with a bunch of killers and the Fuzz as well?'

He shrugged.

'That's normal for you isn't it, Dave? I needed to have a word to make sure that you get your details straight.'

'Why?'

'You're already up to your armpits in sewage. There's no need for me to jump in it with you.'

'So this is all about you. Thanks mate.'

'Shut up and listen. I'm a lot more use to you as a functioning copper than I would be if I was suspended for associating with a person of dubious reputation. You need all the friends you can get so don't get snarky with me, right?'

I nodded.

'OK, this is your story. You know nothing about what happened to Lew. You don't even know he's dead. Nothing's been released to the Press. They claim it might cause riots, fat chance of that. If they cancelled Coronation Street or shut down Manchester United there might be riots but killing a judge! Anyway, this is my get out ... your old man was worried.

He'd called Sir Lew several times and got no answer. He didn't send you round because he knew you wouldn't be anxious to leave your pregnant wife. He phoned me as a helpful and discreet copper he knew from his days in the police service and I sent a woodentop to check on Sir Lew. The man was one of Her Majesty's senior judges so there was no reason why I shouldn't make enquiries. You weren't involved in any of that, right?'

'Right, but Paddy...'

'He hasn't phoned you or told you anything because I told him not to. He was pretty shaken.'

'He went to Lew's house?'

'Yeah, he was needed to identify the deceased. Fortunately he has a good alibi for himself. He was doing some plastering in a neighbour's house until ten and they reckon Sir Lew was topped in the early evening. We needed him to make the identification because there were no servants there, bloody odd, that. Anyway, my guess is that he intends to clear off for parts unknown with your mother and frankly if I didn't know it would kick off a major manhunt I'd advise you to do the same.'

'Janine and kids have done a midnight flit but I'm not budging.'

'Fine, now you've had the bad news here's the good news.'

'What?'

'The Security Service is all over this investigation. If it had been up to us plain old fashioned rozzers you'd probably have been charged by now, but it isn't.'

'MI5?'

'Yeah, Dave, *M - I - 5*, M for Motherf**kers, I for Idiots and 5 for F**k all! The spook brigade, what part of that don't you understand?'

'I understand none of it.'

'The good part for you Dave is that they go softly, softly: not like us plods in our big boots. It's all highly intellectual, you need a degree in symbionics, or whatever it was that smart arse professor in the *"Da Vinci Code"* had, to even start off at square one with those folk.'

'It's symbology, Bren.'

'There you go. See what I mean? These people are on a high level, like you Dave. Just say nowt to them and make sure you don't drop me in it and you should be fine.'

'If you say so.'

'And for the rest, keep your big yap shut about what Sir Lew told you. He called on you for a friendly visit, right? You talked about cricket, nothing about evil conspiracies.'

'But there is a conspiracy!' I protested.

'And you're going to leave that to the professionals.'

'But it's me this traitor's trying to kill.'

'Then you'll just have to be bloody careful until this gets sorted and believe me it will.'

'Bren! Weren't you listening when I told you? They left a bomb at the farm ... remote control. I might not have the time to wait for your professionals.'

'A bomb,' he muttered rolling his eyes. 'That's all I need, a bomb under my arse.'

'The bomb was for me, not you.'

'Same difference, a known associate of mine gets blown up, so does my career ... criminal association ... '

'Shut up about yourself for a minute.'

'Yeah, sorry, who've you told about the mysterious traitor?'

'Apart from Janine and Paddy you're the only one who knows. Not counting the bombers themselves of course.'

'They must have been amateurs if you defused it.'

'Thanks, Bren. I'll try to get real professionals to kill me next time.'

I didn't bother telling him about Tony Nolan.

'Look, Dave I know this is hard but can you keep the bomb and all that under your hat, as it were, for now? I'm sure that if we get the guys that did the Judge they'll turn out to be the same ones who're trying to do you. Bringing you into this will only complicate things.'

'Complicate them for you, you mean.'

'Precisely,' he agreed.

I pulled the plastic bag containing the detonator phone out of my pocket and handed it to him.

'This is the phone they used as a detonator. It might have prints on it.'

'And if it has they might lead to the Judge's killer? OK, I'll run it if you keep your mouth shut.'

'They're trying very hard to kill me.'

'Dave, you're very good at ducking and diving. You'll just have to carry on dodging and weaving and keeping your mouth firmly shut until there's a lead on the Judge.'

With that he gave me a nudge on the shoulder and left.

I waited a few minutes and then continued on my way.

13

Tuesday: 8 a.m. Pimpernel Investigations Office

They say that a drowning man's entire life flashes before him as he sinks for the third time. I wasn't drowning but Brendan Cullen's news and the sight of the car parked on a double yellow line outside my office produced the same effect.

There were two young men standing by my office door. Both were in dark suits. Both looked lean and fit. Both had briefcases at their feet. Briefcases? Were they accountants?

I didn't see my entire life, just that unhappy part of it when I'd been imprisoned to await trial as a serial rapist and murderer. There's no presumption of innocence in prison. Even the likes of Lee Sheerman-Holmes feel entitled to assert their moral superiority over men in the nonce wing.

For a moment, revulsion and fear got the better of me. I leaned against a wall. One or two passers-by stared, wondering if I was drunk or ill. No one rushed up to offer CPR. I suppose I look too healthy.

I took several deep breaths.

Sanity began to return.

Briefcases? If these guys had briefcases with them maybe they hadn't come to clap me in irons.

I had too much to lose by running away. My life is good now. At least it was until Monday morning. Anyway it was likely that a CCTV operator was already pinpointing my location for the police. I just needed to think for a moment and plan my strategy.

Why was Bren so anxious to ensure that I didn't mention Lew's talk of a conspiracy? I could understand why he didn't want to be associated with me, a sleazy but annoyingly prosperous semi-criminal in the warped minds of his superiors. But my ploy in nominating Paddy, a former detective chief superintendent, as his informant ought to have put him in the clear.

I felt guilty for thinking badly of Bren.

I'd asked to see him and he'd come.

He's a friend. I rescued his career once. He owes me. But the bottom line with Bren is that he has the word 'copper' running through every bone in his body like the lettering in that famous stick of rock. The man is answerable to superiors for some of whom *'private investigator'* is the same thing as *'criminal profiteer'*. Bren needs his job and his lifestyle; the car, nice flat and Billie-Jo.

I walked back to the office.

I passed between the two sentries. Whatever they were, they weren't accountants unless accountants have to be in peak physical condition.

They made no move to stop me.

Tony was calmly officiating at the reception desk. Why not? With the reconstruction of his nose, which should have been done years ago, and a nice suit he'd fit in anywhere. His pale blue eyes had lost the look of blankness and cunning they'd once had. His expression was sharp. I guessed the intelligence had always been there, but was somehow suppressed until disease gave his brain a nasty jog.

'Sorry, Boss. I mean sorry Dave. I couldn't stop her.'

'Stop who?'

'He means stop the lady,' Clint volunteered. 'She went in your office with one of the men. If she'd been a man I wouldn't have let them in, but she's a lady.'

'What's he on about?' I asked, turning to Tony.

'He's right, Dave. They came in mob-handed, three men and a woman. She's a real piece of stuff. Clint would have chucked the men back in the street but he's helpless as a baby with women. I told her you weren't here but she said she'd wait in your office. Went round Clint like a terrier after a rat and just dived in there. She told two of them to wait outside for her.'

'Any identification, search warrants, court orders, minor stuff like that?'

'They just barged in.'

'And now they're going through all the confidential material in my office.'

'Sorry, Dave.'

'Get on the phone to my solicitor.'

My office door opened and a tall, studious looking man in his late fifties poked his head out. He looked suspiciously clever, far too clever. Perhaps it was the rimless glasses precariously balanced on the end of his nose and his raised eyebrows that gave that impression. Hell's teeth! What did I expect? Brendan had said MI5. It stands for military intelligence, doesn't it? Of course the man was intelligent. Did I think they'd send round some dull witted dunderhead with a chip on his shoulder about failing the eleven plus?

He stepped into the reception area.

He was wearing an old brown Huntsman suit in a Prince of Wales check that looked as if he'd inherited it from his father and he peered dispassionately over the rimless specs like an entomologist examining a rare species of beetle he'd found in his net. My vivid imagination immediately supplied a sound track for this scene: it was the sound of cell doors slamming.

I looked at Tony and he gaped back at me open mouthed. He was hearing the same sound track.

I hadn't realised that I'd been shouting at him.

'You won't need a solicitor, Cunane. We're just here for an informal chat,' the entomologist announced.

'You'll find the number under Desailles, Marvin. Tell him to get here fast.'

'This is wasting time, Cunane. You can get a hundred solicitors down here but all they'll tell you is that under the Anti-terrorism, Crime and Security Act 2001 we have the power to study your personal records during a terrorism investigation.'

'Terrorism?'

'We also have the power to ask the Treasury to freeze all your assets and bank accounts.'

'What are you talking about?' I croaked. After two seconds acquaintance the man was bashing me over the head with the law.

He gave me a nasty grin. The killing bottle was open and I was about to be popped into it. They used to put cyanide in the bottles. Now they use nail polish remover but the insects end up just as dead as they ever did: dead and pinned on a display board.

'Come in and talk to us and you'll find out,' he said.

I still hesitated.

'Come into my parlour, said the spider to the fly,' flashed across my mind. I fought down the panic. Only those who've been locked in a cell for months can know the fear of another spell behind bars. It's many times stronger when that loss of liberty was unjust. There's even a technical name for it: *cleisiophobia.* I've only just got over the flashbacks from my last time in clink. A mild dose of PTSD, the therapist said. He wanted me to join a workshop and learn to overcome my phobia. Meditation and repeated exposure to my fear was the suggested treatment. I didn't go when I discovered that his other patients were mostly ex-cons. It's an occupational disease for them.

'Mr Cunane, are you going to talk to us in your own office or do you prefer to be questioned at police headquarters?'

He nodded towards the outer door where the fitness freaks were looking in at us. I don't think they appreciated the danger they were in from Clint.

Then I noticed the bulges under their jackets. They were armed.

I couldn't risk violence with Clint in the room. The big man thought he was bullet proof and I didn't want to see him proved wrong.

'Forget Desailles unless you hear me scream,' I said to Tony. He smiled in relief.

I went in.

'Very funny, Cunane,' the entomologist said.

'I find it keeps me sane, humour I mean.'

'Really?' he muttered.

I reminded myself that I knew nothing about Lew's death. This visit was a complete surprise to me. I had to stay in character.

'Mr Cunane was a bit shy about joining us,'' he announced.

The piece of stuff looked up.

The woman was seated at my desk and had opened the drawers.

108

There was a clink of glass as she rooted around. Unlike her colleague she was fashionably dressed.

'Help yourself, why don't you? Or is it too early for MI5 to start drinking?' I murmured softly, holding back on the resentment.

The entomologist gave the piece of stuff a knowing glance. I could have kicked myself. Letting on that I knew they were MI5 was a mistake. Fortunately, neither of them picked up on how I knew.

'Hah! The fabled Dave Cunane in person,' the Stuff drawled with a smile as warm as a sun-ray lamp, and just as false, 'and as well informed as I was told to expect. I *am* from MI5, Molly Claverhouse. You can call me Molly, if I can call you Dave. This is Harry Hudson-Piggott.'

'I think I can call you anything I like because I'm sure the names you've given me aren't your real names. What is it you call them, "work-names"?'

'I warned you Harry, this guy is really clued up.'

Her beaming smiled remained in place. I wanted to see her scowl.

'No I'm not. I just happen to have read my le Carré, like everyone else.'

'Well, you need to forget all that. That's fiction and le Carré was never with us. He was SIS. We operate in a strictly legal way within parameters laid down by Parliament as Harry has already told you.'

'Like when you burst into my office and start going through the drawers.'

'This is an active terrorism investigation,' Hudson-Piggott said.

'So, I can be laid back about it if you can.'

'Be serious, man!'

Hudson-Piggott began to look aerated but nowhere near coronary thrombosis levels.

'Shush, Harry,' the Stuff said, raising a calming hand to him as if to soothe a naughty child.

Hudson-Piggott didn't turn a hair and I realised I was watching a double act.

Charm continued to ooze out of her face like muck out of a broken sewer.

'We seem to have started on the wrong foot, Mr Cunane, but as

Harry says this is a terrorism investigation. In MI5 we act purely in defence of the realm but speaking of le Carré, have you seen "Tinker, Tailor"? What did you think of it?'

'I preferred the Alec Guinness version. It seemed much more authentic, unlike you and Bill Haydon here.'

'Ouch,' she said, playfully miming a slap on her own wrist. 'At least let's start off on first name terms.'

'Listen, Miss Cleverhouse or whatever your real name is,' I said. 'I'm not going to call you Molly, Holly, Dolly or Polly. Just get out of my chair.'

She leaned back in the seat and clapped her hands.

'Delightful!' she said laughing. 'Actually it's Ms.'

'Ms Cleverhouse, get out of my chair.'

This produced another ripple of laughter.

'Oh dear, you must think I'm awfully rude,' she explained. 'But I can't tell you how fascinating it is to actually meet a Mancunian with the bluntness you Northerners are always boasting about. Most of the men I've met since I came to these desolate regions have been cringing girly-men. I'm the deputy director of our North West office.'

I couldn't restrain a smile at the thought of Brendan Cullen as a cringing girly-man. That smile meant I lost Round One. This cunning secret agent was flattering me for effect. 'Northern' bluntness, that disappeared years ago under the onslaught of PC. All the word 'blunt' suggests now is a warbling singer.

I tried to needle her in another way.

'"*Deputy Director*", that doesn't do anything for me.'

'Oh?'

'Yes, who's the director?'

'Why do you want to know?'

'Come on, Dep, everything's out in the open these days.'

'Why do you want to know?'

'So I'll know who to complain to about your intrusion.'

'He's called Rick Appleyard, but you'll get nowhere with him and as Harry told you we have the right to search anywhere in a terrorist related incident. Mr Appleyard sent us.'

Her innocent, childlike eyes were a shade of hazel. A fringe of short, shaggy blonde hair framed her long face. The impression of youthfulness conveyed by her face was confirmed by her clothes, which were definitely on the casual side for professional dress.

I'm hopeless at guessing women's ages but I put her in her early thirties. She was wearing a dark charcoal jacket with wide lapels, epaulets and pockets. It was of immaculate cut and fit and gave off an understated hint of the military. A black top with matching bootleg trousers covered a slim frame. Co-ordinating with her hazel eyes was a single strand of expensive looking amber beads that dangled down past her waist. A suspicious bulge on her left side suggested that she was armed.

'Like what you see?' she asked.

I did. Another smile.

I was annoyed with myself for liking what I saw.

Round Two to her …

The entomologist decided to sound the gong while she was ahead on points.

'If we can begin,' he said opening a notebook. 'Full name, date and place of birth.'

'Why …'

'It's necessary to establish if you're an alien.'

'Alien! I'm as British as you are …'

'Irish name isn't it? How do I know where you were born? Back end of some bog, no doubt.'

I was ready to hit him.

'Harry, be diplomatic!' Cleverhouse intervened.

They were playing me like a violin. I caved and fed Hudson-Piggott all the details he relentlessly demanded.

'You had a spell in prison.'

'I was never sentenced.'

'But you were in prison.

'On remand and I was completely exonerated.'

'During your prison time did you come into contact with Muslim prisoners?'

'Some.'

'Did you read the Koran or convert to Islam?'

'What?'

'What is your religion?'

'None of your business.'

'Come on Dave,' Cleverhouse chipped in, 'you must realise that many violent extremists converted to Islam while they were inside, Richard Reid the Shoe Bomber, for instance. We have to ask.'

'I'm not a violent extremist or a Muslim but I'm not surprised their numbers are increasing if this is the way you lot carry on.'

'We're talking about terrorism, Cunane, something I find it difficult to be humorous about,' Hudson-Piggott sniffed. 'We should tell him about his relative now.'

Cleverhouse put on a grave face and told me about Sir Lew's death. She laid on the ghoulish details with a trowel: bruises all over his body, finger nails pulled out, head hacked off with a blunt garden tool.

Hudson-Piggott was George Smiley now, not Bill Haydon, watching me like a hawk, gauging every reaction. However, it wasn't difficult to simulate surprise and shock because after the events of the last twenty four hours I was surprised and shocked.

'I need a drink,' I said.

Giving me a sweet smile, Cleverhouse dug out the Glenmorangie and the glasses.

I poured.

'Join me?'

'Too early for me,' she said, 'but Harry?'

'Yes, I'm partial to single malt at any time of the day,' Hudson-Piggott said.

I poured him a dram and we drank together. Seeing him drink made me remember Lew yesterday. Hell, he'd kept his distance in recent years and he didn't approve of my career but he was a relative I'd known since childhood.

What type of sadist tortures a dying man?

My eyes may have moistened I'm not sure. My hand quivered.

'Are you all right?' Cleverhouse asked. 'You've gone very pale.'

'It's shock, that's all,' I muttered, biting back an angry comment.

We sat in respectful silence for a moment and then Hudson-Piggott resumed his questioning.

This time it was all about Sir Lew and his wife Magdalen. Was I aware that Magdalen (and she was always Aunty Magdalen to me, never, horror, Aunty Maggie) owned a considerable estate? I gave what answers I could, mostly honest ones.

'I wasn't aware of things like that. They were never discussed in my childhood.'

'Without doubt you must have known there was a prospect of you inheriting a fortune.'

'When I was young my parents and Sir Lew were anxious for me to have a career in the law. Sir Lew would have found a place for me in chambers. When I set out on my own as a private investigator he was very offended. He told me that mavericks rarely amount to anything. If I ever gave his money a thought, and I repeat I never knew he was so wealthy, I assumed none of it would come my way. For years my contact with him has been limited to Christmas cards, very tiny Christmas cards. I went to Magdalen's funeral six years ago and he came to my wedding last year. That's about it.'

'Surely there's more. Your father has told us that he informed you about Sir Lew's will yesterday evening.'

'So what? Am I supposed to be so greedy that I went round to his house and butchered him immediately? Talk sense.'

'You're asking us to accept that until the last few hours you knew nothing about an inheritance conservatively estimated at upwards of a hundred million.'

I swallowed and took a deep breath. A hundred million, could it be so much?

'I'm not asking you to accept anything. I'm as astonished as you are and I'm sure there's some catch and it'll all go to some cats home or other.'

'Cats home! Into cats was he, Sir Lew?'

'Dogs home then; I've no idea.'

Hudson-Piggott cleared his throat for another go but before he could speak, Cleverclogs intervened.

'The problem is Mr Cunane ... you know we'd both be more comfortable with Dave ...'

'Tell me your real name and I'd let you call me Dave all day long.'

'Yes, and we might question you all day long unless you tell us what's really going on here. You expect us to believe that a relative you've had minimal contact with for years walks in here and ...'

'We talked about cricket and about my parents, just making small talk. It was rather embarrassing really. Then he told me about his cancer and left. That was it.'

'No, that was not it!' she shouted, switching off the charm.

Round Three to me, I win on a knock out.

I got up and walked to the door.

'Where are you going?'

'I thought I'd go for a walk as I didn't invite you here and I don't seem to be under arrest.'

'Stop being stupid and sit down.'

'Is it stupid of me to think you're leading up to suggesting I killed Sir Lew?'

'You had a motive.'

'I was in such a hurry to inherit that I tortured and killed a man with terminal cancer who'd already signed a will in my favour? Now who's being stupid?'

'Put like that it does seem unlikely but you must understand we have to eliminate you before we can be certain this is a terrorist case and not a domestic murder.'

'I suppose so but can I have my desk back?'

'Are you trying to be funny again, Cunane,' Hudson-Piggott asked.

'No, I *really, really* want my desk back.'

Cleverhouse looked at Hudson-Piggott, shrugged and then moved.

Was the whole desk thing some kind of dominance game? Move 178 in the MI5 interrogation handbook?

We changed places.

'Admittedly the idea of you killing Sir Lew is a little off the wall but there are some odd features about your activities that need answers. For instance why were you and those two weirdoes outside in this office well before eight?'

'They're not weirdoes and I'll turn up at my office whenever I like.'

'They're seriously weird. They look like something out of the Brothers Grimm. Is it one of your quaint Northern customs to have a contrasting pair of heavies; Little and Large, Cannon and Ball, Eric and Ernie?'

'Vivid turn of phrase your boss has got,' I said turning to Hudson-Piggott.

'Very well,' she said, 'if that's the way you want to play it.'

'I'm not playing anything with you. You just insulted my friends and I remarked to your underling, the bug-collector here ...'

'Bug-collector!' Hudson-Piggott muttered.

'Yes, you look very like an entomologist of my acquaintance.'

'Can we get on?' Cleverhouse interjected.

'Speed things up if it means you'll leave sooner.'

'Harry.'

'We've been to your home address and there are signs of recent violence there,' the entomologist said.

'What signs?'

'A petrol fire in the farmyard and a bullet hole in one of the bedroom window frames. There were also shotgun and 9 mm cartridge casings in a field adjoining the house.'

I squirmed. In my hurry to get away from Topfield Farm I'd neglected the adjacent field. At least they hadn't found the things I'd buried but that might only be a matter of time. The assassination box was in the shed. As far as I knew it contained nothing illegal. If they found it I could claim it was one of the tools of my trade.

Hudson-Piggott picked up on my discomfort. There was a glint in his eye.

'People sometimes shoot rabbits there,' I said lamely.

'Not with 9 mm semi-automatics, they don't. Also Cunane, your

115

family appear to have disappeared.'

'Yes, very worrying that is, Dave,' Cleverhouse added. 'In view of the possibility of domestic violence we put out a nationwide call for your car and guess what?'

My heart gave a lurch. My too active imagination was already flashing up images of wrecked vehicles and motorway pile-ups.

'What?'

'A vehicle registered to you was recorded crossing the Erskine Bridge over the river Clyde outside Glasgow at five a.m. this morning. The image was blurred but the driver was a woman. She was doing well over ninety miles an hour so the Strathclyde Police want to trace her. They've put a dedicated team on it at our request.'

'So?'

'So your uncle reveals that you are to inherit a fortune, he is brutally killed, your family flee after a violent incident at your farm, you arrive here out of normal hours accompanied by two minders. It's all connected Dave. Don't you see?'

I shook my head.

'What minders?'

'The giant and the little shifty one who misses nothing.'

'They're friends of mine.'

Just then a mobile rang. Hudson-Piggott pulled it out of his suit.

'I'll have to take this, confidential,' he muttered.

He went out and I heard the outer office door shutting.

I started checking the contents of my desk drawers.

'Everything's there,' Cleverhouse said.

'Yeah, I'm sure. It's the additions not the subtractions that worry me.'

She laughed.

'If you're implying that we've bugged this place you're wrong.'

'Am I?'

'Yes, Mr Private Eye, you are. I'll make you a bet that there are more bugs in this place than in a cheap doss-house. But they've not been put here by us. You'd never find our stuff in a hundred years.'

A second later Hudson-Piggott returned.

'Something's come up. We'll have to postpone our interesting chat with Mr Cunane for now,' he said.

Cleverhouse leapt to her feet and they both left.

'Don't go away, Dave,' she said in parting. 'We can track you anywhere you go and I'm *really, really* looking forward to a chat with your wife.'

'She'll only tell you what I've told you.'

She gave a knowing look and left.

Tony nudged me. 'Look at the brief cases,' he whispered.

I watched as the pair of fitness freaks ushered Cleverhouse and Hudson-Piggott into the car.

'They've got submachine guns in them,' Tony said. 'Uzis or MP5s I should think. You can see the handle of that one.'

I'd never seen a pistol grip on the side of a brief case before.

14

Tuesday: open for business

'Tony call the number listed under Electronic Counter Measures in the office phonebook and get them to send someone to sweep this dump for bugs.'

'No need. I can do it myself,' he said eagerly.

'I said, phone!'

'I can do it.'

I was in too much of a hurry to argue. I'd have to phone myself later.

'Well, get on with it then!' I prompted.

I was standing at the office door watching the grey Range Rover bearing the four MI5 operatives disappear into the busy morning traffic.

I waited a moment and scanned the street to see if they'd left a spy to keep an eye on me.

Paranoid? I was entitled to be.

Scanning the street was hopeless.

The pavements were crowded with workers hurrying to beat the 9 a.m. deadline at their offices. There could be any number of people watching us. I'd just have to chance it and make my move before they were ready.

'Clint!' I yelled, 'come with me.'

He roused himself and joined me at the door.

I set off jogging back the way I'd come earlier, towards Bridge Street and the telephone boxes on the other side of the Irwell.

Clint trotted along beside me and when they saw him charging towards them pedestrians gave us a wide berth.

Janine wasn't safe at Colquhuons. The road from the Erskine Bridge went right past the golf resort on the banks of Loch Lomond. The police would scour time-share villages and bed and breakfasts where a family might be hiding. At best I had hours to get them out of there, at worst Janine might already be in custody and that might have been what Harry Hudson-Piggott's urgent call was about.

I had to reach Janine before the police did.

The pair of telephone boxes came in sight. Both were occupied.

I was gearing up to wrench the person off the phone when one of the boxes was suddenly vacated.

I dived in and discovered that I couldn't remember Janine's mobile number off the top of my head. I plucked my dismantled mobile phone out of my inside pocket and fumbled it back together. I'd taken the battery out as a precaution.

As soon as I switched on text and a message came in.

The text was from Janine: *Arr. Safely. How r u?*

There was a voicemail from Paddy. I had no time for that now.

Every second might be vital.

I found Janine's number and started to dial then I paused.

If my mobile was being monitored Janine's probably was as well.

I found Clarrie White's mobile number and dialled that instead.

It rang and rang and rang.

'Dear God, please make her answer,' I prayed silently. Clarrie often forgot to charge her phone or left it out of earshot.

The phone continued to ring. It would go to messages any second.

'Pick it up, you old bugger,' I muttered through clenched teeth.

'Who's an old bugger?' a cockney voice asked.

'Sorry, Clarrie,' I gasped, suddenly short of breath.

'Who're you calling an old bugger, then?'

'Not you my love, someone was trying to get in the phone box.'

'What's going on Dave? Janine's told me what's been happening at the farm. Petrol bombs! I think you should get out of there now.'

'Listen Clarrie, there's worse. You, Janine and the children need to leave Colquhuons in the next ten minutes.'

'Are you saying they're on their way here with their bloody bombs? This is worse than what my mother had to put up with when Hitler bombed Plaistow.'

'Calm down, you're not in physical danger but you need to leave.

Can I talk to Janine?'

I could hear noises off as Janine was called.

'Dave!' Janine said urgently. 'Are you all right?'

'Yes, I'm fine. It's you I'm worried about. I've just had an unpleasant half hour with MI5. I don't know quite what they're up to but ...'

I could hear Clarrie and children all talking at once in the background. Even Mangler was adding to the din.

'Go outside,' I shouted.

She did. The background roar faded.

'Your plan was for me to convince the man who sent those bombers that I know nothing and then back out of things gracefully ...'

'Yes.'

'Well, that's not going to work. They came back to Topfield and left a massive remote controlled bomb in our living room.'

'Oh no! Are you all right? Did they blow the house up?'

'No time to explain now but the house and I are both fine. We defused the bomb.'

'We? Who've you got with you?'

'There's no time for explanations Janine, just listen and do what I say.'

'Yes, Master.'

I had to grin.

'MI5 seem to fancy the idea that I killed Lew.'

'Outrageous!'

'I think they'd prefer it to be me rather than Islamic terrorists or Lew's mystery man, less awkward questions for them that way. Anyway, the police spotted you doing ninety over the Erskine Bridge and ...'

'They're on their way.'

'Yes, MI5 would like to know what happened at Topfield last night. On Bren's advice I've told them nothing and I'd like to keep it that way.'

'So?'

'So get back in the car and get away now. Back towards Glasgow I should think.'

'But what about Mum? I'll never fit her in the Mondeo with the children, Mangler and a ton of luggage.'

'Always practical aren't you?'

'One of us has to be.'

'OK, this is what we'll do. Splash some mud over the Mondeo's number plates and drive to Glasgow Airport. Clarrie will have to follow in her car. Park the cars in the long stay and load your luggage onto trolleys and then go into arrivals and wait near the meeting point. I'll send a man to take you all somewhere else in a different car.'

'Who?'

'It's better if I don't say. He'll make himself known to you.'

She didn't reply.

Although there were many miles between us I detected stiffening at the other end of the line. I knew I was pushing my luck. With the Janine of old there'd have been a flaming row and accusations of child endangerment before now but then she had seen the petrol bombers with her own eyes.

There was a pause of several seconds that felt like hours.

'Jan ...'

'Wait! I'm trying to think.'

'I was only going to say that I'm trying to do what's best for all of us but if you want me to cooperate fully with MI5 and take the risk of being made the scapegoat for their failure to protect Uncle Lew from whoever killed him I will.'

'Stop trying to be so noble Dave and let me think for a minute. I'll tell you one thing. I wasn't doing over ninety on the Erskine Bridge so someone's telling lies. Jenny was wide awake and you know what a phobia she has about us speeding.'

'Yes.'

'So I don't see why I should answer any of their questions about anything. OK, we'll head to Glasgow. Any more orders?'

'Yes, if you get the chance buy several mobiles under false names and give the man I send a couple of them with your numbers. Use your mother's credit card. I won't be able to last a day without speaking to you.'

122

'Me too.'

'Don't forget mobile phones are radios. They'll be listening for us.'

'*Phones are radios,*' she repeated robotically. '*Don't use own credit card.*' I knew she was sending me up but she had to be warned.

'You might have to wait for a few hours at the airport but someone will meet you so get going now.'

'*Yes, lord and master.*'

'Jan ...'

'No, I mean it Dave. I love being ordered about ... well ... just occasionally ... perhaps it's the pregnancy.'

'Yeah, well normally I love arguing with you Jan and then doing what I'm told. Is there anything else?'

'No, we'll be there or we'll be square. Love you.'

'Love you again but bye, I've got to go.'

I put the receiver back into the cradle.

There's probably no bigger control freak in the country than Janine. She likes to plan her movements and everything about her life in the minutest detail. So perhaps it was her pregnancy, or maybe it was witnessing those bombers trying their very best to obliterate us all, but for once Janine was cooperating without major warfare breaking out.

I had to do something else.

I consulted my BlackBerry again.

Suddenly there was a loud rapping on the door of the phone booth. I almost vomited the breakfast I hadn't eaten. I swivelled expecting to see machine guns pointing at me.

A large, fierce looking black lady was gesturing at the phone I'd just picked up again.

I signalled to Clint.

He pushed himself in front of her and smiled angelically.

She looked like a very determined lady but she could see that she'd met her match with Clint. She threw up her arms in disgust and turned away.

I called Barney Beasley, a small time crook in Levenshulme who'd once played a part in a massive benefit fraud involving Irish workers on major construction projects. Beasley was the henchman of the guy who provided the lads with false identities so that they could go on claiming benefits while working all the hours God sent them. Thanks to me he'd been able to avoid being scooped up when the scam unravelled and his mate got nine years. I knew that Beasley was a master of the various methods of leaving England without documentation.

He owed me one but I doubted if he'd see it that way.

One of his many children answered the phone.

'Daaaad!' she bawled, 'someone for you.'

'Who the f**k is it?' I heard him shout in reply.

'Who the f**k are you?' the girl asked. Judging from her voice she might have been ten or so.

'The parish priest.'

I heard her catch her breath for a second.

'Go on, I can tell you're not Father Braden. Who are you really?'

'Tell him it's a friend who remembers the Clarke case.'

I heard the girl relay this message then there was a thunderous and sudden rumble of heavy boots down a staircase.

'You!' Beasley croaked in a harsh Irish accent. 'You have the barefaced gall to call me? You're no f**king friend.'

Beasley was far too fly a bird to drop names on a phone line and I was grateful for that.

'Gall to call? Hell, Barney, next time you get out of bed walk to the window and check there are no bars in front of you. You should thank God that I am your friend or right now you'd be sharing a cell with Jim Clarke. When does he get out by the way?'

'He's got another two years, poor sod,' Beasley said in a more moderate tone. 'His wife's left him you know. Things were never the same between them after a certain person towed away the caravan she was sleeping in and kicked her out on the motorway.'

'I didn't kick her out. She ran off of her own volition.'

'So you say. She says different.'

'I've got a little job that's right up your street. It'll pay well.'

'Get away, you bastard, I wouldn't touch your money.'

'So you'll do it for nothing?'

This produced a rasping laugh from Beasley.

'In a pig's ear I will. What do you want?'

'I want four people transporting to the land of bogs and mists without benefit of papers.'

'Like that, is it? Have the police finally caught up with you?'

'It's not for me and they aren't criminals; two women and two children, oh, and a dog. I just want these people moved without leaving a paper trail. You used to be good at that.'

He laughed again.

'Used to be, hah! When do you want this transport?'

'Today.'

'You don't want f**king much, do you? Today will take some arranging. Give me your number and I'll phone you back in ten.'

I gave him the number. I decided to wait in the phone box. It was one of two and I couldn't afford to miss Beasley's call.

The determined lady had gone away but other people gestured impatiently at me. I'd no idea call boxes were so popular. Perhaps they can't afford mobile tariffs in this part of Salford. I told Clint to pretend he was next in the queue. He put his ugly face on and they sheered away when they saw him.

After fifteen minutes Beasley rang back. That wasn't bad really. It would probably take longer to book a flight out of the country.

'Right, this will cost you,' he said, 'and I want cash on the nail.'

'Sure you do,' I agreed.

'A monkey for me and a carpet for the driver.'

'A carpet?'

'Three hundred, you dickhead.'

'OK.'

Five hundred to Beasley for making a couple of phone calls was outrageous but I'd have paid more. He sensed my eagerness.

'Christ, you're really in a hurry. My man's often done this for a ton.'

'I'd rather pay. That way you might both keep your mouths shut.'

'Whatever you please, but I owe you no favours Cunane. My

man's coming from Felixstowe with a load of Dutch cabbage landing at Dublin docks early tomorrow morning. He has a big sleeping cab in his truck. It might be a squeeze but your refugees, or whatever they are, will have to stay in the cab throughout the crossing. He sails from Bootle tonight. He'll pick your people up at the Burtonwood Services on the M62 at seven p.m. precisely. You don't need his name but the truck is Horan's Supermarkets, Ballinrobe, in County Mayo. It's painted bright green and he'll be looking out for your friends. OK?'

'OK.'

'Then I'll want my money paid up front. Your friends pay the driver: half when they get in, half when they get out.'

'I'll have it with you in an hour or so but listen, Barney if you're thinking of making an anonymous call to Crimestoppers forget it. If there should happen to be a police car within half a mile of Burtonwood Services the boys in blue will be learning the name of Jim Clarke's accomplice.'

'I'm no f**king grass,' he growled.

I hurried out of the phone box and across the bridge back into Manchester.

Before I dismantled my mobile again I listened to Dad's message.

'It's your Dad here.

David, what's happened to your uncle Lew is just terrible. It's been a very bad shock for your mother and me. We knew he was dying but he didn't deserve what was done to him, nobody does. It's too horrible to think of but those responsible should be made to pay. Definitely ... someone should get those bastards. ... I'm sorry I didn't tell you about his will before but he swore us to secrecy and you have to respect a dying man's wishes. At least that's the way I was brought up. Well, whatever, your mum and me are off on our travels. We're taking a short holiday break. It'd be a good idea if you'd do the same because you're working too hard at that damned business of yours but knowing what a stubborn beggar you are I expect you won't. Keep safe. We'll be touring so don't expect us to be in touch for quite a while. Apropos of nothing in particular, your mother wondered if you could pop up to the house and take care of her vegetable patch if you have a moment. Just a spot of weeding which I know you're good at. Start at the last place she was working on. Give our love to Janine and the children. I'm ringing off now.'

I played it again then took the phone apart.

As Brendan had said Dad was on the run.

There was no way on God's earth that Paddy would've agreed to leave for a holiday before his blessed DIY was finished. Eileen often joked that he'd divorce her before he'd give up a job he'd started.

Anyway the timing was all wrong.

The old man must have decided to leg it as soon as he got back to the cottage after identifying Lew. Something had thrown a scare into him and it had to be more than the sight of the severed head of his oldest friend. Dad was the opposite of squeamish.

Had more passed between him and Lew than he'd admitted to? Did he think he knew too much for his own good?

Gardening, he wanted me to do up the garden?

Gardening?

Throughout my childhood there'd been a strict division of labour in the Cunane household. We lived in a semi with a big garden. Paddy did the indoor jobs, the DIY. Eileen did the gardening. That left me as the only surplus labour. My mother battled tirelessly but without success to turn me into a gardener. Even today I struggle to name common flowers: daffodil, daisy, that's about it. Well, maybe one or two more.

When they got a motor mower I did occasionally mow the lawn but only after lengthy financial negotiations. By the time I slouched into action the grass was often knee high.

Eileen eventually gave up asking and got a man to come in once a week.

It was the same with the vegetable patch. When I was little she'd given me my own piece of ground. The truth is I've never had the patience to sit around and wait for things to grow. My weedy patch passed into family legend. Paddy called it my 'nature garden'.

Paddy's roundabout way of passing on information suggested that he feared surveillance.

Was it MI5 that had scared him or was it Lew's mysterious power maniac?

The latter, I guessed.

15

Tuesday: 9.45 a.m.

'Where is she?' I asked as soon as I stepped into the Pimpernel office.

'Where's who, Boss?' Tony replied.

He was sitting at the reception desk looking pleased with himself.

My glare wiped the smile off his face.

'Miss What's her Name Fothergill! What the hell have you done with her? Have you frightened her away?' I asked angrily. I was annoyed with myself. I'd been in such a hurry to get to a public phone that I hadn't warned him that Fothergill would be arriving.

'He frightened her,' Clint commented. 'No-nose's face would frighten anyone.'

'Be quiet!' I snarled, feeling strained.

Clint looked as if I'd slapped him.

I looked at my watch. It was twenty five past nine. In the time she'd been with me Fothergill hadn't been late once. She was on the doorstep before me so often that I'd provided her with a key and the code for the alarm. Why not? Everything confidential was secure in the safe.

I felt a stab of fear.

Had Lew's mysterious killers decided to make a clean sweep of the Pimpernel staff?

'Are you sure she hasn't been here?' I asked.

Tony shook his head in bewilderment.

I studied his face. He had to be lying. That expression of injured innocence on his poor battered mug was part of his criminal tool kit. Fothergill had arrived and there'd been words between them ... after all she didn't know him from Adam ... and she'd cleared off as fast as her legs could take her. Her duties as a temp receptionist didn't include sparring with burglars and that was exactly what Tony Nolan really was,

129

reconditioned brain or not.

'Can I trust you?' I asked doubtfully.

'Yeah, course you can, Dave,' he answered, looking flustered and untrustworthy. 'I found that bug for you. It was sending to a tiny recording receiver in this desk. There was a compact flash card in it and it was switched on.'

'What?' I said blankly. 'That's not possible. MI5 were never alone in this area.'

'Someone planted a bug in your office and it was set to transmit to a miniature digital recorder in this desk,' he explained helpfully.

He indicated the desk he was sitting at. Fothergill's desk as I now thought of it.

'It can't be.'

'See for yourself.'

He stood up and pulled back the chair he was sitting on. I went round the desk, got on my knees and saw for myself.

A small clear plastic object about the size of a packet of twenty king-sized cigarettes was fixed to the underside of the desk, positioned towards the front and on the right hand side for easy access. It was mounted in a fixture which was held in place by small screws. One quick pull and the package could be removed.

I felt as if a hole was opening under my feet. Ever since my false arrest I've been paranoid about treachery, even going to the length of only employing temporary staff who know nothing about the business, and now I was revealed as a complete amateur.

I struggled to my feet and slumped into the chair.

Tony bent down and removed the recorder. He took out the flashcard.

'I knew it had to be somewhere in here when I found this transmitter in your desk.' He dropped a small plastic object in front of me.

'It was attached to your chair.'

'My chair,' I repeated numbly. So was that why Cleverhouse or whatever her name was had made such a game about sitting in my chair?

'MI5 bugged my chair?'

'No Dave, it wasn't them that did this. It was whoever normally sits at this desk.'

'Miss Fothergill.'

'Yeah, there's no doubt about it. The recorder was right where she could get at it. All she had to do was take out the flash card and change the batteries from time to time. You can get up to fifty hours of voice recording on a thirty-two gigabyte card but she probably had a couple of cards and changed them every day.'

I should have known that the silent and helpful Fothergill was too good to be true. Who was she was working for? It could only be Snyder, my former partner. What was she doing? Passing on information about clients so he could underbid me? They must be hard up for work at Snyder's.

Tony put the pieces of equipment on the desk in front of me and I gaped at them.

'So you can trust me, Dave,' Tony prompted as the silence lengthened. 'I know about bugs and bombs and things. That's got no maker's name on it but it's state of the art for commercially obtainable stuff. There are several places in Manchester where you could buy it or you can get it on the Net. It's expensive, not much change out of two grand for that lot, imported from the States.'

I scratched my head in dismay.

'Two grand?'

'Yeah, that's only a ball-park figure. It's the Bang and Olufsen of bugs.'

Ball-park figure ... Bang and Olufsen ... I gaped at Tony.

What had he become?

The idea about Snyder didn't add up. Snyder wasn't doing well enough to pay two grand for a bug or to employ a full time spy. Then I remembered that the bomb was made with American C4 military explosive. American bomb, American bug, where was the sense in that?

My only dubious connection with the States, apart from remote relatives I have there, is through Janine's ex-husband who lives in LA. Henry Talbot's a nasty piece of work and he once tried to snatch Jenny and Lloyd from Jan's custody and smuggle them out of the country but it was inconceivable that he was trying to bomb or bug me. Besides, he'd started a new family in LA.

'Do you think the people bugging you are the ones who planted the bomb at Topfield?' Tony asked. The man had a talent for questions I didn't want to think about.

There had to be a link – American bomb, American bug.

Lost for words I just stared at him. I couldn't work it out. All my assumptions and guesses up to now must be wrong.

It didn't make sense.

'It could be that they're trying to kill you because of something that was said in your office,' Tony surmised. 'I mean I'm not prying but that stands to reason. That bug wasn't there for nothing and it's been there a while.'

He was probably right. It couldn't be a coincidence.

He looked at me with an expression of sympathy. I didn't like that.

'Right, Tony,' I said, 'let's forget about that for now.'

'Is there something I'm not supposed to know about?'

There was such an intelligent expression on his poor battered face that I got the feeling he knew exactly what I'd just been thinking. His transformation was disturbing, Albert Einstein peeping out of a battered boxer's face.

'No Tony, I trust you but there are some things it might be better for you not to know.'

He looked disappointed.

Then it struck me that it definitely wasn't Peter Snyder and his struggling investigation business or any business rival that had bugged me. It could only be the police.

They were hoping to find something incriminating against me.

But why would they? The risks for them were considerable. If I could prove they were bugging me or that Fothergill was undercover police I could sue them from here to breakfast.

I thought for a moment. It wasn't them. Ruthless the Greater Manchester Police might be about protecting their reputation but this bug had nothing to do with them.

132

There was only one way I would find out what had been going on here and that was when I had a chat with Miss Fothergill, but the chat would have to wait. I needed Tony to take the money to Beasley and I needed Lee to drive up to Scotland and round up my nearest and dearest.

'Phone Lee and tell him I want him here as soon as possible,' I said.

'Could be difficult, Dave.'

'In what way?'

'He doesn't usually get up before twelve and he'll have his phone switched off.'

'This is what we're going to do. You're going to take some money to an address in Levenshulme and then you're going to roust Lee out of his pit ... where does he doss by the way?'

'There's a flat over a betting shop that Bob owns a share of. It's in Fallowfield. We kip there.'

'So that's on your way then. Pick Lee up on the way back and I want him here in good condition.'

'Er ... good condition?'

'I don't want him if he's half pissed or stoned out of his mind. Our deal's off in that case Tony.'

His Adam's apple moved convulsively.

'He'll be fine.'

He said it quickly and I sensed he was crossing his fingers. Well, we both had to hope for the best. I needed Lee on the motorway to Scotland. He must be a reasonable driver or Bob would never have let him get behind the wheel of the BMW with his brother in the back.

'He'll be OK to drive?'

'Oh yeah, he'll give Sebastian Vettel a run for his money any day, will Lee.'

'Just as long as he picks up my family safely and brings them back in one piece.'

I went over my plan and then I needed my key to open the safe for the money. Banks are fine but as the MI5 man had informed me, accounts can be frozen. I keep a fighting fund of twenty grand in cash in the safe. I call it the cash float but at the back of my mind I know it's really 'run-away' money if the Voldemorts running the local constabulary decide to use their killing curse on me.

It took me a moment to find the safe key in my desk. I leave it there because even with the key you need the combination to open the safe door and I'm the only one who knows that.

Carefully shielding the door from Tony I fed in the numbers and turned the key in the lock. The door swung open.

The cash box is in a separate compartment at the back. I took it out, checked that the money was in it and put it down. I was about to shut the safe when I took a quick glance at the pile of envelopes and documents lying in the detachable tray under the deposit drawer.

Sir Lew's notebook wasn't there. It should have been there. There'd been material posted by investigators on Monday but under the circumstances I hadn't opened the safe or started work on them.

I pulled out the detachable tray and laid it on the floor then frantically sorted through the documents. Perhaps it had slid inside an open report.

It had to be somewhere.

I tipped the tray upside down, shook it to make sure it was empty and sorted through the documents. The notebook wasn't there. I turned back to the safe. It was capacious but there was nowhere that the notebook could have lodged and remained unseen. A small filing cabinet contained ongoing cases. I pulled it open … nothing. There were account books, the firm's cheque book, VAT receipts and other odds and ends but no notebook.

My heart was pounding.

'Is something wrong, Dave?' Tony asked.

'Something's very bloody wrong,' I said angrily as I checked every single one of the files and envelopes piled on the floor for a second time. Lew's notebook wasn't there and whatever chance I'd ever had of using it to bargain for my life was gone with it.

Then a thought struck me. Had it somehow become jammed in the deposit drawer or even stuck to the metal?

I opened the deposit drawer. I needed a different combination and key. This week's combination was on a scrap of paper in my wallet.

Tony watched me closely. His eyebrows flickered a little when I fished out the paper, read it and turned the dial on the top combination lock. I heard the click of the tumblers, inserted my key and turned it to open the compartment.

For a microsecond hope flared. I'd find the notebook stuck in the mechanism.

There was no way Fothergill or anyone could reach down into the main safe through the letter box. The salesman who talked me into buying the massive Chubb safe had been adamant about that. His pitch had been that it was safe for staff to have access to the upper compartment while the larger, lower section remained completely secure. It was the whole point of the deposit safe.

The door swung fully open.

The top drawer was as empty as an unused grave.

I was in the final stages of a marathon. I was breathing heavily. I could feel the first stirring of a panic attack, an occasional burden since my time in Strangeways. My face filled up with sweat. It was running into my eyes and down the back of my neck.

I tried to wipe it away with the back of my hand.

'Here, use this,' Tony said, going over to the reception counter and picking up the box of 'man-sized' tissues which Fothergill had left there, 'wipe your face.'

He passed me a tissue.

'Hello, what's this?' he said.

He shook the box. It rattled.

He pulled a small rectangular mirror out of it.

'Never mind about that,' I said dismissively. 'It must be Fothergill's.'

'You're sure whatever you're looking for is in the safe?' he asked.

'It was in the safe. I saw it being put in this deposit drawer.'

'And you're the only person who has the combination for the main section?'

'Of course.'

'Shut the door, turn the wheel and then open it again.'

I stared at him. Mutilated though his face was I was becoming

135

familiar with his limited range of facial expressions. This time his features were a complete blank.

'Go on, you said you trust me,' he coaxed. 'Shut the door and carefully shield the combination from me when you open it just like you did when the receptionist was behind you.'

He positioned himself in Fothergill's chair with his back to me.

I closed the door, spun the numbers wheel and re-entered the combination.

I turned the dial: click, click, click, click, click, click. Eventually I heard the sound of the tumblers falling into place. The safe was open.

'The combination is seven three eight oh one nine,' he chanted from the desk. 'It seems like Miss Fothergill …'

'Bloody hell!' I yelped.

'Whatever. Your receptionist knew the combination. It's the oldest trick in the book. Sitting here holding her mirror like this she could see which numbers you were selecting.'

He held the mirror low down in his right hand.

'But I reset the numbers every Friday.'

'Why do you think she keeps this mirror handy?'

'Oh, God … she must have seen me entering the new numbers last thing on Friday.'

I felt sick. My incompetence was revealed again. I had to defend myself.

'She couldn't have opened the safe. She needed the keys as well for that and I keep them in my office during the day or at home when I'm not working.'

'Let me look at them.'

I passed them over. They're long and heavy, not the sort of thing you'd put in your pocket or on a key-chain.

Tony examined them minutely.

'Have you got a magnifying glass?' he asked quietly.

My self esteem hit rock bottom. I went into my office. There was a handlens in my desk. I returned and handed it to him. He'd switched on the light over the reception counter.

He examined the keys with painstaking thoroughness.

136

'Putty,' he said, 'there's traces of putty on these.'

'No,' I croaked.

He misunderstood.

'There is. See this yellowish discolouration, that's putty.'

'Explain.'

'You get a mint tin. They do them at Marks and Spencer. You know: a small flat tin like a spectacle case? They use them for strong mints.'

I nodded, dimly aware of where he was leading me.

'You fill each side of the tin with plumber's putty ...'

'... and then you make an impression of a key which some idiot leaves lying around on top of his desk as he makes a cup of coffee in the kitchen while his receptionist is delivering files to his private office.'

'That's about it, Boss ... er Dave.'

'There must be more to it.'

'Yeah, you need someone to cut the key for you.'

'Some crook?'

He nodded and scratched his head.

'Names, Tony, I need names.'

'There's a few in Manchester who would cut a safe key you. There was a guy called Tommy Portlock who was doing time for it in Strangeways while we were.'

'While *you* were, I was on remand.'

'Yeah, right, well he could do it and he'd probably know most of the guys round here who'd do it, though apart from the key blanks, probably all anyone needs is a good eye, a nice lathe and a few files.'

'Thanks for that.'

'Sorry, Boss,' he muttered.

I needed a stiff drink but I tried to force my mind back onto the reason why I'd opened the safe.

I counted out the cash for Beasley and put it in an envelope.

I didn't attempt to seal the envelope. As my delivery man was watching me there didn't seem much point. I'd said I trusted Tony and I did to the extent that I could trust anyone apart from Janine, Paddy and Bren. I had to know him and his new brain a little better before I was

137

ready for total trust.

I paid him a week's wages in advance plus a hefty bonus. The little guy was valuable.

I made him repeat Beasley's address back to me. I knew it was pointless because Tony claimed total recall of everything but it comforted me and then I sent him on his way.

'Hey, Dave,' he said before he went out, 'have you got a picture of this Fothergill. Portlock might know her or I might, come to that.'

I opened the filing cabinet with the staff records such as they were.

Fothergill's folder was there. I opened it. The passport photo which had been clipped inside was still there. I quickly plucked it out and handed it to Tony.

He studied the picture then handed it back, shaking his head. 'Whoever she is, she's a clever devil.'

'You recognise her?'

'Yeah, I recognise who this is. This is a photo of Adele.'

Hope surging, I stared at him blankly.

'You know, Adele, six Grammies and an Oscar, that Adele.'

16

Tuesday: 12 a.m.

Clint's stomach gave a loud rumble.

It reminded me that I was hungry.

Clint had been sitting patiently all through my humiliating discoveries about Fothergill. I guessed what we'd been saying was all 'symbionics' to him anyway. Sprawled across the small designer sofa which graces my reception area he had his head stuck in a magazine. It was a motoring magazine. I take 'Classic Car' and 'Top Gear' to raise the tone of the place. Clint was labouring with Top Gear. Jeremy Clarkson's mug leered out at me from the cover. Looking at him reminded me about Clint's tactlessness.

I looked at the big man speculatively.

'I'm sorry I shouted at you earlier,' I said.

'That's all right Dave,' he said, with a smile you could toast bread on. 'I could see you were stressed out. Bob says that's why Tammy shouts at me a lot. She gets stressed out all the time so it's all right you shouting. I'm used to it.'

'No, Clint it's not all right. People shouldn't shout at you and I'm really sorry I did.'

'I don't mind.'

'Well, I mind and I'll try not to do it again.'

He fell silent for a moment, his face pensive. Then he said, 'I don't think Bob likes Tammy shouting at me. He shouted back at her one time and he goes out when she does it.'

'Bob doesn't like anyone to hurt your feelings.'

'That's right.'

'Did you know that Tony hurt his face in an accident when he was small?'

'No-Nose,' he frowned.

'No, Clint, Tony Nolan; we've got to call him Tony, not No-Nose.'

'I'll do that Dave,' he said with great seriousness.

'Do you think you could find your way to Brazennose Street,' I asked.

'Yes, it's near the Hidden Gem. I went there with Bob on Mum's anniversary.'

'Yes, that's right. There's a sandwich shop there called Shirley's where they do a terrific monster sandwich. It's a full English breakfast on a big barm cake. Do you think you could bring me one?'

'And what about me?'

'Get whatever you want.'

I offered him money but he pulled a thick wad out of his pocket and then he was out of the door like a shot.

÷

The office got busy for a while. I do my investigations on a sub-contracting basis. The jobs come in from insurance firms and from the DWP. I arrange a price and then farm them out to my self-employed investigators. They're mostly retired coppers or wannabe Sherlocks like me when I was starting up.

They come in. I discuss the job with them. We agree on a price and they go about their business. It's all very hands off and impersonal compared with the old days when I spent weeks on stake-outs or could reckon to have a suit ripped off my back every few months. To tell the truth I'm not completely at home as a bureaucrat but I have a wife and family to support. The highly resented libel damages I won have now mostly evaporated. I spent them on bricks and mortar up at Topfield so I need positive cash flow.

I tell myself that I'm fulfilling a useful function. Snooping is a growth industry in this country and I'm playing my part.

So this morning I forgot my preoccupation with Sir Lew's death and the threat to my family for a few minutes. There were three investigations in my pending tray and I sent three of my snoopers on their way after brief explanations. They know what they're doing.

Meanwhile Clint was in a back office munching his way through a truly enormous concoction accurately titled a 'Bin-Lid'. My mere 'monster' sandwich full of bacon, sausage, black pudding and egg was on a ten inch barm about three inches thick. I was hungry enough but only managed to get through about half before dumping the rest. Although the headquarters of Pimpernel Investigations isn't palatial there are several offices beyond the reception area as well as a secretarial space where office equipment used for preparing client reports is kept. I'd ushered Clint with his magazines and his 'Bin-Lid' into a back room.

Apart from the absence of a receptionist my office appeared normal to a casual observer. Certainly none of the three snoopers made any comment. They were used to my secretive ways and I think they preferred it that way. 'No names, no pack drill,' was what one of them said.

Tony returned with Lee.

Lee's face was bright red as if he'd had his head under a hot shower for ten minutes. The acne scars had faded. He was dressed as I saw him last but had changed his t-shirt.

'Don't start, Boss,' Tony cautioned as he ushered Lee into my office.

A faint but pungent aroma followed them in. I took a deep sniff.

'That's right out of order,' I said. 'I can't have anybody using weed near me. The Fuzz are looking for any excuse to turn this place over. I wouldn't put it past some of them to plant stuff if they got in here so if you're carrying anything you shouldn't be it goes down the toilet now.'

'He's clean, Dave. He just has a tiny little spliff at night to help him sleep. He won't smoke or do anything like that near you.'

'Tiny little spliff' didn't cover it. His outer clothes were perfumed with the stuff.

'Is that right Lee? No dope while you're on the job.'

'Yeah,' he muttered.

'Go on, I want to hear you say it.'

Tony nudged him.

'No dope but I smoke roll ups and I'm not going to give them up,' he said, pulling out a Golden Virginia packet. 'You can't ask me to stop smoking as well. It's inhuman.'

'You could use nicotine patches. They're not inhuman.'

'I've tried them. They don't work.'

I glanced at my watch. Time was pressing.

'OK,' I conceded 'but just make sure your smoke doesn't come anywhere near me.'

He nodded eagerly enough. 'Must want work' crossed my mind.

Whatever Tony had said to him Lee seemed to have lost his aggression. Maybe it was being up so early in the morning. The guy might well be half addled but I needed him.

As with Tony, I paid him his wages in advance and promised him a bonus for a successful job. I'm a true capitalist that way. His eyes lit up when he realised he'd be driving the BMW up to Scotland and back. I gave him instructions about transporting Janine and the family from Glasgow to Burtonwood and handed him a sealed package with two grand in it for Janine. She'd have to buy euros when she reached Ireland. I was taking a risk putting such a sum in Lee's hands but I had to gamble.

It was after ten when Lee left proudly clutching the keys of the BMW. I calculated he'd have time for the round trip. He'd be on motorway almost all the trip

Now I had time for some work of my own.

I decided to make myself presentable, or at least more presentable. I went to the small toilet cum washroom at the back and quickly washed my face. Then I ran an electric razor over my features. I was a little too strenuous, losing flesh as well as whiskers. I slapped on aftershave and did a little dance of pain when it stung. None of this made any difference to my predicament but if I was about to become a customer on some pathologist's slab at least I ought not to look like a vagrant.

The Manchester Office Temp Agency which had supplied me with Fothergill and other temp staff was at 27b Prince Regent Street South, Manchester 2. Before walking round there with Clint for company I installed Tony behind the reception desk with strict instructions to say nothing to investigators returning finished projects to the safe.

'Just nod and smile, they'll think you're just another temp.'

'Well, I am aren't I?'

'Not necessarily Tony, not necessarily if you play your cards right.'

I didn't know what I meant by that but I think at the back of my mind I was already detaching the survival of Pimpernel Investigations from my own survival. Crazy or what?

I needed a picture of Fothergill. They were bound to have one at the Agency.

A walk among ordinary people who weren't trying to shoot me, blow me up or trick me into some elaborate double game was a refreshing prospect but as soon as I got on the street I felt vulnerable. Who wouldn't? There'd been four serious attempts on my life within the last twelve hours if you counted the two separate shootings. What I hoped was that Claverhouse and Hudson-Piggott had set up surveillance on me which would put off potential assassins. Otherwise … OK, possibly hoping for help from MI5 was farfetched but if Lew's traitor did have men on the streets after my blood the presence of MI5 spooks would make them keep their heads down.

Then there was the ever present CCTV. If they were killing to keep the traitor's existence secret appearing on Candid Camera wouldn't be in their interest.

And it was possible that moving around was my best option. They say it's harder to hit a moving target.

All I knew was that I couldn't sit in my office waiting for something to happen. I had to get out there and find out who Fothergill was working for.

We left the office and were walking along Deansgate, Clint still clutching part of his Bin-Lid, when there was a loud explosion close by. I started to throw myself on the pavement but Clint grabbed my arm and said 'Backfire'. He pointed to an old Morgan sports car chugging along across the street. As we watched it was enveloped in blue smoke and there were further loud bangs.

'Bad ignition timing, Dave, gases exploding in the exhaust,' he explained genially, 'common on old sports cars.'

I looked up at him. Had I found another know-all mate?

We turned into Prince Regent Street South, a pedestrian area lined with exclusive shops.

I suppose we were conspicuous and people certainly cleared out of my large companion's way as he ambled along. But I had to balance one thing against another, exposure against security. Even the police would be wary about snatching me off the street with Clint at my side.

The front of Manchester Temp's office was glitzier than Pimpernel's: polished glass and chrome with a neon sign above flashing the word 'JOBS' in two colours. It could be taken as provocative in the current situation but fitted into the surrounding upmarket scene. There were shops selling designer handbags, jewellery, Rolex watches, handmade shoes and other costly items, so why not JOBS?

I tried to do reconnaissance by peering through the window but the view inside was blanked by masses of cards advertising positions at seven pounds – seven pound fifty an hour. It cost me quite a lot more than that to hire them from here: not a bad business if you can get it.

By peeking between the cards I was able to see a little of the interior. It wasn't an 'up-front' place like Pimpernel Investigations with its reception desk as you went in and its charming proprietor a few feet away. This place looked more like a working typing pool. There were four small desks. At two of these young women were being interviewed by older women. There were two unoccupied interviewers one of whom spotted me.

She beckoned me to come inside. There was something commanding about her gesture, as if she was used to being obeyed.

'That lady wants to speak to us,' Clint said helpfully. His face was also jammed against the glass. He could see over the adverts.

'Yeah, but if she offers you a job turn it down. Don't forget you're working for me.'

A beatific smile played across his gaunt features.

'Yes, Dave,' he said, turning to me, 'I won't forget. I'm working for you.'

I rubbed my chin and studied my reflection in the window glass.

There were small red dots on my upper lip where I'd shaved too vigorously. What sort of man cuts himself shaving with an electric razor? I'd be lucky if they offered me a temp spot as a tea boy in a rundown backstreet garage.

Clint pushed the heavy door open.

Several pairs of eyes focused on him.

Fair enough, with his old-fashioned country clothes he did look as if he'd wandered off the set of a movie of a Thomas Hardy novel, playing Diggory Venn in 'The Return of the Native' perhaps, although it wasn't being coloured red from head to foot that made him distinctive.

I guessed that the female interviewers here were on commission just like my investigators, paid by the number of job seekers they placed in temp jobs. Certainly the woman beckoning us forward looked just that bit too eager.

She was tall, big haired, wearing several layers of makeup and her trout-pout smile was overly friendly. She might have been in her forties, fifties or even early sixties. I recognised her type. I'd seen dozens like her. In this little flock she was the bellwether: not male, not castrated and not wearing a bell but certainly a leader and not a person to be trifled with. She wouldn't respond to the Cunane charm.

'If you'll both take seats I can quickly get your details and see if we have anything suitable for you.'

'We're here for information not jobs,' I said. 'Where do you keep your records?'

'We don't give out information,' she said firmly.

I was checking the place out as I spoke. The rear of the room was divided by a glass partition to create a narrow corridor and a larger space. Inside the space two girls were seated at desks bashing away at keyboards, hell for leather. There were electronic timers beside each girl. At the dimly lit end of the corridor was a door marked 'Office'.

That was where I wanted to be.

I strode on past Bighair's desk.

'Hey! You can't just walk down there. You'll disturb the tests,' she protested but I was on my way.

Moving with the speed of a practised line-dancer she blocked my way.

'Clint, give this lady your details,' I said.

The big man obligingly swooped onto a chair at her desk.

That confused her a little.

'Go on, take down his particulars,' I suggested. 'I'm only going to the office to see your boss. I'm one of the dopes who actually employs your temps,' I said, continuing to move forward.

She hovered, plump lips quivering but one of her colleagues must have pressed a panic button because there was movement from the office.

A short, Mediterranean looking man appeared at the head of the passage and placed the flat of his hand on my chest. He had a bald dome like a giant egg nesting in a mat of dense dark hair and an olive complexion. He could have been Greek or Maltese or Turkish, somewhere round there. He was wearing green glasses, a white polo shirt open at the collar, grey slacks and Italian designer moccasins complete with tassels. A wide chest and muscular forearms suggested that he liked working out with weights.

His eyes flicked over me and then focused on Clint. His jaw dropped. He took two paces back towards the darkened area he'd emerged from.

'What's going on?' he barked, pulling out his mobile phone.

A gold tooth glinted in his lower jaw.

'These men are pushing their way in, Mr Gonzi. I offered to interview them to find out their skills but that one demanded to see you.'

He raised the phone.

'I'm calling the police,' he said.

'Terrific,' I said. 'Do it and you can explain to them why the woman you sent me as a temp receptionist turned out to be an expert safe cracker.'

'Robbed Dave blind, she has,' Clint intoned from the desk. His size in relation to the furniture made him look like an adult waiting to be interviewed at an infant school parents' evening.

It was still Clint who held Gonzi's attention, something I was used to on outings with the big man.

146

'Robbed you?'

'Yes, a temp supplied by you has broken into my safe and taken something very valuable,' I said.

'And you are?'

'Dave Cunane, Pimpernel Investigations, and I want some answers or you'll be reading what I think of your agency on the front page of the Manchester Evening News.'

I pulled out my ID and held it in front of his nose. It's not much but a smash and grab man is hardly likely to show ID.

'You must understand that we can't give out information about the workers we place to just anyone who walks in off the street,' Gonzi explained. 'Besides being commercially sensitive that information is restricted because we sometimes get undesirables trying to track down their ex-girlfriends.'

'Do I look like an undesirable?' I asked.

'Shall I get the police?' Bighair said, answering for him.

'No, that won't be necessary Hilda,' Gonzi said. 'Interview the tall gentleman, there must be an opening for him somewhere in the security business. The BBC needs men down at Media City.'

I laughed.

Discomfited by my laughter, she scowled at me and returned to her desk. Clint stared at her hair in open admiration.

I followed Gonzi into his cramped little office, cramped because it was stuffed with filing cabinets.

'I remember you, Mr Cunane,' he said with an ingratiating smile. 'You're one of my best customers. If we offered frequent flyer miles you'd be on your way to Australia right now.'

'If only,' I muttered.

After a little more verbal sparring he pulled out two files. One was marked Pimpernel Investigations and confirmed that I'd paid all charges to date. The other was marked April Fothergill.

'April's always been very satisfactory,' he confided. 'Lots of nice things said about her. I'm sure there must be some misunderstanding.'

'Yeah, a misunderstanding,' I echoed.

He opened the file.

There was a photograph.

April Fothergill was an attractive young black woman.

'That is not the woman who arrived at my office claiming to have come from your agency,' I said.

'Oh, surely,' Gonzi said slapping his bald pate with meaty fingers. 'She must be. I remember asking you if you had any objection to a black receptionist.'

'Why would I object?'

'You know, some people think having a black girl as a receptionist is making a statement … all right at Media City perhaps but not in your average small business not that we're …'

I cut him off.

'Mr Gonzi, my late wife was a black African girl. I'm about as likely to forget some fool asking me if I practise racial discrimination as I am to forget a phone call asking me to play for Manchester United. So don't lie. You didn't phone. What's going on?'

Tiny beads of sweat appeared above Gonzi's bushy eye brows.

'I'm sorry; I must be confusing you with someone else.'

'Yeah, you're confusing me all right. You send me a black girl called Fothergill and she mysteriously turns white before she gets to my office. I think I'd better phone the police, don't you?'

He raised both hands, palms outwards.

'*Pull-eeze*, I'm sure we can find a perfectly innocent explanation without the help of the constabulary.'

'So this has happened before?'

The beads of sweat got bigger. Sweat was trickling into his eyes now. He took the green specs off.

'No, no,' he protested, 'that is, there haven't been allegations of theft before but there have been substitutions.'

'Substitutions?'

'A girl with good qualifications will get a job off us and then sort of … pass the job on to a person who wouldn't have got through our selection process, possibly an illegal immigrant. That must have happened in your case. We have to be particularly careful with Africans.'

'So your Miss Fothergill was an African?'

'I don't think so, but she was black and identity theft is rife among them.'

'The Miss Fothergill who came to me *wasn't* an African, *wasn't* an illegal immigrant and *was* highly skilled at electronic bugging and finding her way into my safe. I think the Equal Opportunities Commission will want to hear about the racial profiling in this firm.'

'Oh, I'm so sorry. My words came out wrong,' he moaned.

'Have you got a head office I can get in touch with about this? They might also want to hear about the action for damages I'll be bringing against them.'

'Oh, my God,' Gonzi groaned. He looked as if he was about to have palpitations. His olive skin had turned distinctly yellow.

'You know all about this, don't you Mr Gonzi? Who approached you?'

'No one approached me. I swear Mr Cunane. I'll swear on my children's lives, anything. Please don't phone head office. I'll lose my job if you bring in the police.'

I studied his face.

The vibes I was getting were that he genuinely didn't know about the Fothergill substitution but that there was something else going on that explained his diversionary lurch into the racist swamps. He was sweating profusely. The front of his polo shirt was now so damp that I could see his dark matted chest hair through it.

'I think someone approached you and gave you a hefty bung to look the other way when they switched identities.'

I took out my phone and put it on my knee. There was a Rolodex on his desk and I began flicking through it. I took out the card for his head office.

'No, for God's sake, don't phone. I'll lose my house, the car, everything … I'm begging you. I'll go on my bended knees.'

'Don't do that. Just tell me about the con you've been pulling.'

He sagged.

'I know nothing about Fothergill, that is, the girl who really is Fothergill not the imposter. I expected her to phone for another job after a week or two. You don't usually keep them for long that's why you're such a good customer ... you keep on paying us a finder's fee for filling same position over and over again.'

'Maybe I like it that way.'

'Yes, well ...'

'Tell me the truth or I phone.'

'Hilda interviews the girls and sometimes we get a really good one, and we do check their identities. They have to bring in their passport or birth certificate. Fothergill really was good.'

'So what was the scam?'

'It's not really a scam. It's a common practice in the recruitment industry.'

'Go on.'

'If a girl's really good ... presentable with excellent skills ... one there'll be no come back on ... we send her out but don't put her on our books. The customer gets an invoice for her wages and the finder's fee but his cheque or money transfer goes to a separate account.'

'You crafty bugger.'

'Mr Cunane, as a fellow businessman I can compensate you very generously for any inconvenience.'

'I bet you can but the bogus Miss Fothergill stole a document that could save someone's life so we're a little beyond compensation. I want the document back. I have to find her.'

Seeing that I wasn't about to phone his bosses Gonzi recovered his cool a little. I decided not to tell him that the life that could be saved was mine.

'I came for information and that's what I'm going to get,' I said.

'Anything, anything,' he muttered.

'What do you know about the original Miss Fothergill?'

'It's all in her file, address, phone number, references and everything.'

'You spoke to her.'

'Hilda did.'

'Get her in here.'

Bighair arrived looking very uncomfortable but after a whispered conversation with Gonzi she spilled the beans. That is, she swore a lot and claimed to know nothing about Fothergill that wasn't in the file.

I used the office photocopier to copy it for myself. I pocketed the photo.

Clint poked his head into the cramped little room. His frame completely blocked the doorway. Gonzi and Bighair stirred and fidgeted at the sight of my companion but were probably too frightened to comment. They got the message that they weren't leaving until I was satisfied.

All I had to do now was search the place. I started on the desk drawers and came up with nothing and then went through the contents of the filing cabinets.

I'd noticed a tiny cross on the spine of the Fothergill file. I extracted all other files with a similar cross.

'That's just a doodle,' Bighair lied.

'Oh yeah, shall we see if your company received their percentage for these people?'

'It's not fair,' Bighair complained, 'we find these people jobs through our local contacts and some investor miles away reaps the benefit.'

'Yeah, life's a bitch. Tell me about it.'

She mistook my meaning.

'It's unfair that these people get rich off our work. We're not cheating them. They get plenty.'

'Foreigners, are they? Black people?'

'Some of them are,' she said defiantly.

'So that's OK then, is it? I don't think the Fraud Squad will agree with you or HMRC. You're not paying any tax on your skim, are you?'

There were at least twenty folders marked with the cross, perhaps thirty. I didn't count but their cut of thirty office temps wages came to quite a tidy sum, tens or even hundreds of thousands when you aggregated it over the years they'd probably been at it.

Bighair folded her arms across her ample chest and fixed me with a Gorgon stare.

I didn't turn to stone.

There were no pictures of the woman I'd known as Fothergill in any of the files.

'OK, we're out of here,' I said.

'Are you turning us in?' Gonzi asked plaintively.

'I ought to, but I'm not a copper. You can return the wages I paid you for the false Fothergill and I want the full amount you've skimmed off the wages I've paid you for all the other temps I've had off you. You have my bank details.'

'But you've been using us for eighteen months.'

'And you've been ripping off your employer for at least that long. I'd better take this.'

I picked up the Rolodex card with the head office details on.

'Oh, f**k,' Bighair said, 'you c***!'

I smiled.

Clint gave her a disapproving stare his mother would have been proud of.

They started arguing furiously as soon as we left.

17

Tuesday: 1 p.m.

When we came out and turned the corner back onto Deansgate it was lunchtime and the street was crowded. It gave some cover from the all seeing CCTV cameras for which I was grateful. Not that Clint didn't stand out like a human light-house however thronged the street was.

I spotted a familiar face among the hundreds bobbing along towards us.

It was Brendan Cullen.

He spotted me at the same time. He raised his hands and gave me a quick signal like a bookie's tic-tac man. As I don't go to the races I had no idea what he meant. I guessed he was indicating that we shouldn't be seen together.

However he dodged out of the crowd and crossed to the Barton Arcade side of the street barely avoiding being crushed in the slow moving traffic. He looked over at me and put a finger on his lips and then on his ear which I took to mean he wanted conversation. Next he mimed drinking a cup of coffee then he turned and set off towards the Market Street end of Deansgate.

I couldn't immediately follow him as the traffic had started to lurch forward. I waited on the kerb. Bren ducked into St Ann Street and I lost sight of him.

Coffee bars in that direction. There were several. I found the anti-terrorist detective in a Starbucks in St Ann's Square. He was carrying a tray towards a seat by the window. He transferred the tray to one hand and beckoned me to come inside with his free hand.

I tried to work out what was going on. This morning it had all been jumping into doorways and secrecy, now we were going public big-time.

Mine not to reason why … I'm not a criminal and to hell with his

153

senior colleagues and their dirty suspicious minds.

I led Clint back across the square to one of the stone seats near the church, asked him to wait and hurried back to Starbucks.

Bren was seated in an armchair near a window with his legs stretched out. He had picked up a paper but now dropped it. There were two cups of latte on the small table beside him. I slumped into the adjoining armchair.

'Let's keep this short and sweet, Dave,' he said.

'Why? Are you afraid I've got a contagious disease?'

'No, I'm just in a hurry. The eleventh floor seems to have accepted that you weren't pulling my strings when I sent that plod round to your Uncle's.'

'Remote cousin and godfather.'

'Whatever, so I'm in the clear on that for now. And actually I'm more comfortable thinking about poor Sir Lew as your uncle.'

'I'm so happy for you.'

'Dave, this isn't a joke. The command team can change their minds like that.'

He snapped his fingers.

I nodded solicitously.

'So?'

'So we've got to make sure that they keep on thinking you're innocent …'

'I am innocent.'

'Those are relative terms, Dave … innocent, guilty; they're a matter of perspective and what people want to believe. We've got to keep them wanting to believe you, not an easy job with your record.'

'I haven't got a record.'

'Not an official one but in the minds of some on the eleventh floor you've got a record as long as Clint Lane's arm and they're the ones who're talking to the spooks … you did well with them by the way. That fancy piece Claverhouse was quite impressed by you.'

'Thanks.'

'But now things are going to another level. They've decided to lift the news embargo on Sir Lew's killing.'

'Sir Lew lived in Cheshire, not under the GMP.'

'Same difference, the murder comes under North West Counter Terrorism.'

'Oh.'

'It's already been on TV and they're not playing down the Islamic aspect ... a policy decision at a higher level than Manchester apparently ...COBRA I think ... someone at the top's scared witless that it'll come back on them if they don't level with the public now.'

'I see.'

'The thing is Dave; my bosses want you to play a major part in the presentation ... vengeful relative calls for action, appeals for information and that sort of stuff. It's all rubbish. You know the script. It's the most repeated play on TV.'

'Yes.'

'Anyway, seeing as your old man has submerged, your name's already been released as Sir Lew's closest available relative. As your friend, I advise you to keep clear. The research shows that sixty per cent of the public always believe the grieving dad or whoever is the actual killer or the kidnapper. So when they try to put you in front of a camera refuse and say you'll issue a statement through your solicitor.'

'You're trying to stage manage me, aren't you?'

'Listen, I'm your friend, the only friend you've got on my side of the fence so don't turn sulky on me. How do you think I met up with you on Deansgate so easily? Man, you're under continuous surveillance, tracked by CCTV as if you had a flashing light on your head. I was ordered to meet you and steer you into a starring role for the news media. By saying "don't do it" I'm disobeying orders. Geddit?'

'I get it. You want to play down my part so there'll be less heat for you about our relationship.'

'Not quite Dave,' he said with a smile. 'I'm still the only one who has the full story about the attempts to kill you ... there've been suggestions that you faked all that stuff at Topfield Farm.'

'What stuff?'

'The burn marks in the farmyard, the bullet hole in the window frame, the cartridge cases in the field.'

'What sort of mind ...'

'Dave, they don't know about the men who attacked you and probably wouldn't believe it if you had it on DVD.'

'But why would I do that to myself?'

'Criminal mastermind, that's you. They don't know what a romantic knight-errant you are. They think that if they eventually charge you for Sir Lew ... and they're still looking for the slightest piece of evidence that puts you at his house ... you'd come up with some cock and bull story about being attacked.'

I jerked back suddenly at this and narrowly avoided kicking over the coffee table.

'I only said *they think* it's a cock and bull story. I believe you,' Bren said quickly as he jerked his arms out to steady the table.

'Oh yes, I'm sure you do.'

'Don't be like that. Anyway you've still got Sir Lew's notebook. There's no way you could have faked that.'

My expression told its own story.

'You haven't got the notebook?'

I nodded.

'Tell me you opened it and found out the name.'

I shook my head.

'Christ, man, you're in lumber now ... I'm in lumber ... they'll want to know why I didn't march you straight round to your safe when you told me about the bloody notebook this morning. I thought ... I don't know what I thought.'

'You thought I was imagining it or making up the story about the mysterious traitor to cover my tracks.'

'No, I always believed you ... well maybe I was a bit suspicious. I am a copper after all. It grinds you down over the years, listening to convincing lie after convincing lie. You get so that you don't believe anything. Ask your Dad about that.'

'I believe you Bren.'

'I never thought you could have killed your uncle, grant me that Dave.'

'Yes.'

'I think I thought you were being a bit economical with the truth and that a better story would come out when you'd got your wits together. I did come at you a bit sudden like.'

'Yeah, you jumped me and got me by the throat.'

He gulped his latte down. I could see he was thinking furiously.

'What happened to the notebook?'

I gave him the bare facts as I knew them about the phony Fothergill. For some reason of pride or shame I didn't mention Tony Nolan's name.

'OK then Dave, panic over; it's not all's well that ends well yet but all is not yet lost. No one apart from you and me knows about this notebook, right?'

I told him about Fothergill's bug.

'Who the f**k is this bitch? I'll tell you one thing; she has nothing to do with MI5 or the police. There's not been a whisper to us about any of this. I bet she's a blackmailer. That's what this is about. Some bastard in the criminal fraternity wants all that money you got in damages and figures this is a good way to get it. You'd pay anything for that notebook, wouldn't you?'

'I don't see how it can be blackmail. I haven't done anything criminal and when Lew dumped the notebook in the safe it was a total surprise to me. Now I'm the intended victim of a conspiracy to murder.'

'But you'd pay to have the notebook back.'

'True, except I haven't got much to pay them with.'

'You have now, or have you completely forgotten that you're now a multi-millionaire? That's vintage Dave Cunane and it's what your friends love about you but I can't bring your phony blackmailing receptionist into the murder enquiry. It would raise all sorts of questions about what we should or shouldn't have done. You should have reported Sir Lew when he propositioned you to be his hitman. I should have reported that it was you who got your old man to ask me to send a copper round to his house.'

'We both did what …'

'… What seemed best at the time? Yes, but that won't stop them sacking me without a pension and banging you up for obstructing an enquiry or worse.'

I let out a long sigh.

It was as if the intensely focused encounter with Bren had suddenly switched off as when Lloyd or Jenny flicked over the programmes on television. I stared out of the window. The sun was trying to peep out from behind the clouds. People were walking around, some casually window shopping, some in a hurry. Clint was still across the square with his head stuck in a magazine. People were talking normally in the cafe. Several had their heads down over laptops and ipads.

No one was looking at us.

'I'm thinking maybe I should do these interviews.'

'No,' he said flatly, shaking his head, 'f**k the bastards or should I say f**k us bastards?'

'Really?'

'The most you should do is to ask when Sir Lew's body's being released to you for burial. Press them on that but get your lawyer to do the pressing. Us coppers hate having our elbows jogged like that. Otherwise KBO, Dave, that's all you can do. Forget about finding this bitch. I think you should keep your head down, keep off the streets and stay away from cameras. The killing of your uncle was a desperate, reckless act. If you'd seen the unbelievable rage that went into it ... ugh, it was bizarre. Whoever did it is coming to the boil. They won't be able to hide for long. I don't want their next stroke to be the butchery of my old mate.'

He leaned over the table and squeezed my arm.

'And another thing, lose the big fellow. He's an absolute giveaway.'

'He'll make anyone think twice about grabbing me.'

Bren got up to go and looking down at me shook his head pityingly.

'You have absolutely no idea of what these people are capable of, have you Dave? Keep safe!'

He left.

I finished my latte and nibbled the biscotti.

They were trying to get me in front of cameras and into the news media. I scratched my head. Was I intended to be the tethered goat? That was how they caught tigers. Was I a victim staked out and waiting for the killers of Sir Lew to creep out of the undergrowth?

Could that be it?

Or was I one of those men the police encourage to appear on TV appeals shortly before they arrest them with a chorus of ten million couch potatoes chanting *'I knew it was him all along.'*

I did know one thing. Bren's theory that the bogus Fothergill was a blackmailer was crap. Whoever heard of a blackmailer who'd leave twenty grand in notes in her victim's safe? I had to find her. She was my only lead.

I trundled out into St Ann's Square and collected Clint. There was a handy call box so I phoned Marvin Desailles at DQW and asked him to come round to the office.

18

Tuesday: 1.20 p.m.

I took my time walking back. For some inexplicable reason I felt good. The rain had stopped. There were chinks of blue showing behind the perpetual cloud cover. We sauntered past Kendall's and then turned the corner into King Street West and took the turn at the Korean restaurant (curried dog a speciality — that's a joke but it is a Korean restaurant) into Butter Lane where my office is situated next to an Indian take away.

I suppose surviving firebombs, bullets and high explosives does something for the metabolism. I don't know what, but I felt good.

Tony Nolan spotted us on the street from his receptionist's desk and opened the door for us. He looked woebegone, a little frayed at the edges but I put that down to his early start of the day.

'OK, Tony it's your lunch break,' I announced genially. 'I want you to go and get a good lunch somewhere and then I'd like you to go to M & S and get yourself a nice dark suit, with shirts and ties and shoes to match.'

'What?' he croaked, his lips pursed in a frown.

'You heard, Tony. We offer a high class service at Pimpernel and I want the employees to look as if they're capable of delivering it.'

'Who's paying for this?'

'I am Tony, bring back the till receipts and I'll refund you. You've got money. Look on this as an upgrade to match the reconditioned brain.'

He showed me his teeth in what I took for a smile.

'Have you come into money, Boss?'

'You could say that Tony but even if I hadn't we have standards here at Pimpernel so you need a suit.'

'Yeah, a suit: it might work for me but I don't think you'll ever get Lee into one.'

'Maybe not,' I agreed. 'We'll regard him as our undercover operative, our link with the mean streets.'

'Yeah, that's Lee all right. Three blokes came and shoved stuff in your safe. They didn't even look at me.'

'Is that a good thing or a bad thing?'

'Good, I suppose. Two of them were ex-coppers.'

'Anyway, it's your lunch break. Take Clint with you, he looks as if he's getting hungry again.'

'Yes, Tony,' Clint said eagerly, 'I found this sandwich place that does bin lids.'

'Bin lids?'

'These great sandwiches Tony. All you can eat on a giant barm cake.'

'*Tony*, since when am I Tony to you?'

'It's not right to call you bad names,' Clint said piously.

The mention of food roused him from the sofa where he'd sprawled as soon as he got in the office. Being so large is a handicap for Clint just as much as if he was severely disabled. Too big for a normal room, he tends to drape himself over whatever seating's available to lessen the impact of his presence. He now bounded up, laid an arm on Tony's shoulder and guided him towards the door.

'I can take you,' Clint continued. 'It's a really good place and there's seats and everything.'

'OK, lead on,' Tony muttered, raising his eyebrows to me as he was hurried out of the office.

I locked the door behind them and put the 'closed' sign up.

I grabbed the phone. 'Real' April Fothergill's number was inoperative. The same with the address as I knew without checking, there was no '21 Sunnyside Villas, Paradise Lane, Moss Side East'. I checked anyway. Zilch! The woman was as much a fraudster as Gonzi and Big Hair. Who'd have thought it? I saved myself the chore of looking up her references. I didn't recognise the name of a single firm she claimed to have worked for. She was as phony as a nine pound note.

I had heavier problems to worry about.

I didn't have long to brood about Brendan Cullen's warning

words before rattling at the door told me that Marvin Desailles had arrived.

A tall black man with a thin face, a beaky hatchet-like nose and long, well-tended locks dangling from under a black and gold Rasta tam over a well cut dark suit; he couldn't be taken for anything other than a member of Manchester's burgeoning black middle class. That didn't mean that he wasn't routinely stopped by the police. The locks and the tam saw to that. Admittedly it was usually young green-horns who stopped him but nevertheless he was stopped even close to the law courts where he plied his trade.

Marvin clings to other island customs in addition to his religion and his headgear. He likes to have a leisurely chat before getting down to practicalities. I owed him the courtesy of listening. Marvin had stuck by me through thick and thin even though his cousin Celeste was one of the main traitors during the attempt to oust me from my detective business.

'Hey, Dave, my bwoy,' he drawled, he likes to come on heavy with the accent and the patois from time to time. It's an affectation. He has a degree in law from Leeds University and he didn't get that by doing Lenny Henry impressions.

'Dave, you goin' to put some work this poor bwoy's way?'

'I am.'

'Jah Bless. It can't come too soon for I-an-I.'

I relayed an edited version of recent events and of Lew's death. I told him that I'd been tipped off that the police would be asking me to put my face on TV to appeal for information.

'An you don' wanna do that?'

'Listen, Lew was a relative, OK, but I only saw him once in a blue moon and he didn't exactly approve of me.'

'Oh, I got lots of relatives like that, mon.'

'Yeah, he died horribly and I'm upset about it but I can't look like someone who's just lost his nearest and dearest. I'll come across as too cool and a million people will decide I killed the poor guy. I think that's what the police want. They'd love to see my face on a wanted poster.'

'You soundin' a teeny bit OTT, there mon.'

'No I'm not. Some of them hate my guts.'

'You know best. So you want me to deal with the Beasts?'

'Beasts Marvin? Don't forget that my old man has been a copper for most of his life.'

'De Babylon, de bacon, de dibbles, call them what you like, mon, but they all smell of frying pig,' he drawled.

'OK,' I said.

'Don't you worry Dave, my mon. The good old firm of DQW will keep them rascals off your back.'

The title DQW which he has engraved on the cards he distributes liberally is a satire against a big Manchester firm with a three letter acronym which had turned him down for a job. He said it stood for 'Drinkwater, Quick and Whittle' which always got a laugh in Manchester pubs. There'd been a complaint to the Law Society so he quickly employed two recent graduates Mark Quinn, and Clarice Woods which enabled him to claim that DQW stood for Desailles, Quinn and Woods although the two partners quickly departed when their brief internships were over.

Marvin is strictly a one man firm and the police detest him because he plays by his rules, not theirs.

It turned out that I hadn't called Marvin a moment too soon because our heart to heart was interrupted by rattling at the door.

It was caused by two uniformed male coppers and two others, a man and a woman. The non-uniform pair were both very well dressed and to my eyes obviously not CID. The sandy haired man wore a dark well-cut suit with a club tie and the woman a navy skirt and matching jacket. She had a thin gold chain round her neck with a crumpled up piece of metal dangling from it. The necklace-wearer was a lot younger than her companion.

The higher ranked uniformed man introduced himself as Chief Superintendent Thornton of the Cheshire police. His partner was Inspector Stott.

'Condolences Mr Cunane, we're sorry for your loss. I understand that regrettably you've already been informed of the circumstances of your relative's murder, quite against procedure that is, but as you're his next of kin we're legally required to notify you officially.'

164

It was Stott who spoke and he sounded peeved.

The young woman coloured up and started to say something but the older man laid his hand on her sleeve and she subsided.

I was grateful that Stott didn't suggest that Lew was my uncle. 'Relative' was as far as I wanted to go and I could have quibbled about the reference to 'next of kin' but I held my tongue.

I waited for him to introduce the suited couple and Stott followed my glance.

'These are two colleagues from another service here to observe,' he said.

'MI5,' I said in a whisper.

He gave a barely detectable nod and curled his lip. I didn't know whether his resentment was because he didn't like spooks or that he regretted missing the chance to grill me himself. I guessed it was the latter.

'Yes, you've answered questions to their satisfaction and there's no forensic evidence to link you to the scene so unless further enquiries reveal something else you're in the clear as far as the Cheshire Constabulary is concerned. However, as the deceased's next of kin we were wondering if you could help us in our enquiries.'

Nice that. A copper practically accuses me and then asks for my help but thanks to Bren I knew that they didn't really want my help.

I was careful to keep my face expressionless and to remain silent.

'Frankly, Mr Cunane, our enquiries are hitting a blank wall at the moment and we wonder if you could assist us by making a televised appeal for information. I can help you with what to say ... basically that as the victim's relative you want justice for him.'

I cleared my throat but Marvin swooped before I could speak.

'Whoa mon!' he said, gripping my elbow and pulling me to one side.

'Who're you?' the Chief Super rasped, possibly as a Cheshire cop he was unfamiliar with Marvin Desailles.

'I is this bwoy's mouthpiece. I is telling him not to go on no television.'

The Caribbean accent was laid on with a trowel.

'It would be very helpful ...' Stott suggested. 'You could appeal to the public for help.'

'No, Mr Cunane wasn't close to de deceased.'

'But he's Sir Lew Greene's next of kin. People will assume he doesn't care about the murder.'

'Gwan! He care plenty, mon! But, he only seen de dead judge three times in de las' fifteen years. He be t'inking he seem cold and unfeeling on de telly. You askin' he to put himself in de frame as de killer. So no telly.'

Marvin began to steer me towards the inner office but Chief Superintendent Thornton wanted to have the last word ... 'Hmmmph ...your client may be unwilling to help us but I don't expect he'll be so unwilling to spend the late Sir Lew's millions. To my mind there's something not right here.'

He favoured me with a resentful scowl.

Marvin was in his face in an instant.

'You be out of order, Mr Babylon. I be reporting you to the PCC for intimidatin' Mr Dave. An another t'ing, Mr Superintendent, when do you be releasing de deadman's body to my client? He be wantin' to arrange de funeral right away. It be his religion.'

Marvin's final comment was news to me and it didn't impress Thornton. 'Not for some time,' he responded dully, 'there are more tests.'

'I be phonin' you every day an if I gets any attitude from you I be reportin' you.'

'Why you ...'

'Cheeky black man, is that what you want to say?' Marvin asked, turning off the accent when he'd got Thornton where he wanted him.

Stott rescued his chief and the four scuttled out of the office.

'Well, Marvin, that went well,' I said, 'now you've made an enemy for life.'

'No, he was already an enemy. I know his sort.'

'You could be right.'

'I am, trust me. Now what are these millions he was yakking about?'

'Er ... I don't want to talk about that.'

'You don't trust your lawyer, is that it Dave?'

'No, it's just that I can't believe I'll ever inherit. I'm sure we'll find that he's fathered five children living in Levenshulme with great expectations or something.'

'Dave, you're a babe in arms. Claimants will start turning up like wasps round a jam jar if you don't grab what's yours straight away. You must let me act for you. I'll get in touch with Sir Lew's lawyer. Have you got a copy of the will?'

'No.'

'What's the lawyer's name?'

'I don't know.'

'You should. If you're the next of kin like the dibble said he should have been in touch already. The Judge's chambers will know. I'll phone them as soon as I get back to my office. Just as a matter of interest how much are we talking about? That dibble was exaggerating to annoy you, right?'

'Actually, it's over a hundred million, well over. Sir Lew was wadded.'

Marvin goggled at me in disbelief and grinned at my joke but when I didn't return his grin he suddenly threw his arms in the air and let out a piercing howl of triumph. Then he linked my arm and we did a crazy dance round the office or rather he did while I stood still.

Suddenly he stopped.

Suspicion crept across his narrow face like a dark shadow.

'It's that cousin of mine; isn't it? You don't want me acting for you.'

'No, Marvin, you must act for me. It's like you said, I *am* a babe in arms.'

'Are you sure about this, Dave?'

'Yeah, why would I want anyone else but you? Who else would I trust?"

'I've done wills and probate work before you know.'

'I'm sure you have.'

'I'll need extra staff; I mean if the estate is as big you say you I'll need to check that every little item Sir Lew owned is passed down to you.

That means staff to check inventories and things. It could take months until we have everything in our hands.'

    'Yes,' I agreed.

    'OK, I'm on my way,' he said.

    He let himself out and departed at speed.

    I felt that I'd committed myself.

19

Tuesday: 2.15 p.m.

I had little time to think about my life's unfolding prospects before Tony and Clint returned. Tony was clutching several Marks and Spencer's bags. I indicated the door of my office and he went in to change. Clint gave me a beaming smile and settled on the sofa with a new stack of car mags he'd bought.

After a few minutes Tony reappeared in his new finery.

'Tra-la!' he crowed, striking a pose.

He did a few turns. The transformation was almost complete. His suit wasn't Savile Row but it was well cut. Like Lew he has that slim frame that clothes hang well on.

I clapped my hands. Clint observed closely, trying to take it all in.

'I haven't looked this pretty since my first Holy Communion. My mum still has the picture of me in my little suit and tie with my hands joined in prayer. Ha, bloody ha!'

Then he looked serious for a moment. His eyes filled up.

'I think that was the last bloody time I've ever wore a suit. My life's all been downhill from then.'

'Oh, come on! What about the reconditioned brain?' I said.

'Yes, your suit's nice, but your nose still isn't right, Tony,' Clint added. 'You've hardly got anything worth calling a nose.'

Tony looked more miserable than ever.

'Yeah, thanks Clint, but maybe we can get his nose fixed,' I interjected, 'and perhaps we can get the docs to do something about you at the same time. Perhaps they could shrink you a bit.'

Clint began laughing but then he suddenly became as solemn as a gravedigger's mate.

You have to be careful what you say to Clint. He can take things too literally.

169

'You know, Dave,' the big man said in what for him was almost a whisper, '*Honey, I Shrunk the Kids* is my favourite film. I watch it over and over. Do you really think they could do something?'

'Yeah, they could chop your bleeding legs off but then I'd probably end up pushing you round in a wheelchair,' Tony said acidly.

'That's enough of that, Tony,' I snapped. Although he was seldom violent and never with friends, the glint that appeared in Clint's eyes was ominous. His next move might be to pitch Tony through the window. 'I didn't want you in a new suit so we could start a misery session. Clint will have to put up with his size but I'm sure they can do something for you.'

'Oh, I won't get my hopes up. I was awarded compensation after my accident, enough money to go private to a top plastic surgeon … 'course my dad spent the lot and after that they never, like bothered getting anything done and then I was making money out of looking like the Hunchback of Notre Dame.'

'Your dad was mean,' Clint said with an untypical hint of satisfaction in his tone.

'No, the bugger was the exact opposite of mean. He spent my compensation on giving his boozing pals the time of their lives. He was the king of Cheetham Hill for about a year.'

'Still, there's always the NHS. Why didn't they take you to see a doctor about it?'

'Reason's bleeding obvious, innit Dave?'

'Is it?'

'Yeah, dad was scared witless they'd ask what had happened to the compensation so he wouldn't let my mum take me anywhere near a hospital.'

'So he *was* mean,' Clint said conclusively.

Just then the morbid discussion was punctuated by the office phone ringing.

I signalled Tony to answer. 'I'm not here if it's someone wanting to murder me,' I instructed. He didn't ask how he'd know that. He just picked up the phone.

'Pimpernel Investigations,' he warbled in a passable Oxford

accent, then 'Oh, it's you, Boss,' in his normal tone and handed the phone to me.

It was Bob Lane.

'Bob, at last,' I said but he cut me off.

'Dave, I'm in a hurry. Can you come to the airport with Clint? I just need a word with you both and I can't do it over the phone. Terminal Two.'

'Ye-es,' I said with a note of hesitation but he wasn't having any of it.

'Terminal Two, a-s-a-p, Dave,' he said and broke the contact.

Thanks to my contrary nature I object to being given orders even by a friend so I took my time and did what I'd been intending to do before he phoned.

I gave Tony instructions for minding the shop. He wouldn't be able to offer new customers competitive quotes on jobs but I gave him the list of our standard charges. He could at least quote those and take down names and send out our brochures. I'd written out cheques for investigators who'd completed assignments, he could give those out and he could post some of the completed reports to clients.

I hastily checked the ones we had. About twenty had come in since since Monday. I selected some and rejected others. Some came in legible and nicely typed on our standard forms but others needed to be edited and polished up before we sent them out. I put the ones needing further work back in my in-tray.

Tony listened carefully as I spoke, 'Yes, Dave; yes Dave,' he repeated over and over so when I finally could think of nothing else to tell him I gave him a verbal test. He had me down word-perfect. The reconditioned brain was still working well.

'Have still you got your own mobile?' I asked.

He replied with a look that suggested I was losing my mind.

'Phone for two taxis from two different companies, if they ask for the destination to tell them they're for clients and you don't know but they'll tip well. Clint and I are going to see Bob at the airport, Terminal Two.'

I then retrieved the photo of the real April Fothergill, the attractive black girl, and put it in my wallet. I reached the outside door before another thought struck. I had an illusion of safety here in my office. So far there hadn't been a repeat of the determined attacks at Topfield Farm. It could be because the police or MI5 had the office under close surveillance but when I left the CCTV zone of central Manchester I'd be out in the jungle again. I might need to run for my life.

I collected my North Face wet weather jacket. It was black and rather battered because I'd worn it during building operations at Topfield. I guessed that was all to the good but I didn't want it as a disguise. I put it on. It has capacious pockets which I now stuffed with the remaining cash from the safe.

The first taxi came.

'Keep him waiting a minute,' I ordered Tony, turning to Clint. 'It's better if you go on your own. Where are we going?'

'Terminal Two,' he grunted, looking up from his magazine.

'Tell your driver to take you through Wythenshawe, not the M56.'

'Wythenshawe, not the M56,' he repeated with eyes fixed on the magazine.

A moment later the second taxi beeped its horn. I dashed out to it, pushing Clint in front of me. Both taxis were parked on the pavement. I crouched down. Clint looked at me with a puzzled frown and took my place in the second cab. I got in the first.

It was a childish manoeuvre but if Crown Prince Franz Ferdinand had changed cars after the first attempt on his life in Sarajevo maybe the First World War wouldn't have happened.

I told my driver to take the M56.

Crazy and full of historical parallels, that's me but we both arrived safely at Terminal Two.

We entered the concourse and mingled with the crowds. There were police all over the place. If there were any lurking assassins surely they'd keep their heads down here. Bob Lane was standing under the meeting point next to a pile of luggage. Tammy was with him. She set her pretty lips in a scowl when she saw Clint.

Clint rushed forward and gave Bob a bear hug.

20

Tuesday: 3.05 p.m.

Clint lifted his heavily built brother at least two feet off the ground.

'Clint!' Tammy squawked disapprovingly. 'There are people watching.'

I thought that was a bit rich as half the men in the concourse had their eyes glued on her. She was wearing a skimpy silver lamé top that did little to hide her mammary abundance, tight black shorts, and silver knee boots with stiletto heels. Her platinum blonde hair, which was piled up on top of her head, could have done service as a landing beacon in a fog.

'Yeah, bro, Let me go!' Bob said.

'Why are you speaking in rhyme?' I asked.

Before he could reply Clint lifted Bob higher, held him at arm's length above his head and then suddenly let him go but caught him and steadied him the instant before he hit the ground. Bob is at least fourteen stone, all muscle and bone, but he landed lightly.

'Rhyme, that's no crime,' he gasped.

'Stop it, Bob!'

'Or you'll shut my gob? … I'm sorry Dave. I think I must have been Shakespeare in another life.'

I had to laugh.

Tammy had watched Clint's performance with a sour look on her face, now she turned to Bob with a 'told you so expression'. I knew what she was thinking. Bob was attached to a freak and he needed to break the bond.

'What it is, Dave,' Bob drawled, 'me and my good lady here are thinking of taking a few days off.'

'Yes.'

'Yes, we're going to Barbados. Check-in opens in five minutes. Bob deserves a break,' Tammy said.

I looked at her hands. There were plenty of rings but not an engagement ring. She noticed my glance.

'We're entitled,' Tammy said, 'and we don't need anyone's approval.'

'Of course you don't,' I agreed.

'The thing is Dave, sorry to spring this on you, but I was hoping ...'

'That I'd keep an eye on Clint.'

'Spot on. What do you say?'

'What can I say, but OK? Hell, this rhyming stuff is catching.'

'Sorry for this, Dave, but do it and I'll be your slave. You can hang onto the Beamer if you like.'

'Till we come back,' Tammy interjected.

'How long are you going for?'

'Just two shakes of a donkey's hind leg,' Bob said. 'We'll be back before you know we've gone.'

'Two weeks and we may take an extra week or so if we like the hotel,' Tammy explained. 'We saw the offer on the internet and it was too good to miss.'

'I see.'

All sorts of objections were churning in my brain but I couldn't bring myself to say anything. Bob studied my face intently.

Tammy pulled his arm.

'Come on, Bob,' she said, 'they're starting to check in now.' With a swivel of her shapely hips, she moved towards the check-in desks.

'Thanks Dave,' Bob said, following her with his eyes.

He waited until she was a few yards away and shielded his mouth with his hand.

'You never know who's listening,' he said in a whisper.

He shook my hand as if in fond farewell and I palmed the key he squeezed into my hand.

'That's the key for 12 Ridley Close, Altrincham. You'll be safe there. There's nothing to connect it to me but for Christ's sake don't wreck the place, Tammy likes it. There are one or two useful things there if you know where to look. You know; safety things, ironmongery, gear like that.'

He gave me a sly wink and touched his finger to his nose.

'Stay there until you're sorted. Anyway, I must go. Clint be good and do exactly what Dave tells you to.'

'I will Bob,' the big man echoed.

With that Bob wheeled his luggage trolley round and headed for the queue. Judging by the size of the cases, he and Tammy were definitely aiming at a lengthy stay.

They were at the head of the queue and it wasn't long before their cases were checked in and they went airside.

'Bye Bob!' Clint roared. The shout clattered round the open spaces. I registered the fact that Clint had no fond farewells for Tammy.

We turned to go.

I felt a twinge of resentment towards Bob but suppressed it. He'd provided me with a bodyguard, two assistants, a car and a safe house. There was also the nudge and wink about ironmongery and safety gear. Short of staying and holding my hand twenty four hours a day there was little more he could do. What happened next was up to me: the secret of the parental cabbage patch or the 'Fothergills', fake and genuine?

The Fothergills, I decided.

We didn't make it to the doors before we were intercepted by a uniformed police inspector. He was backed up by another copper in full paramilitary kit holding an MP5 submachine gun across his chest.

'Excuse me, sir, are you Mr David Cunane?' the inspector asked. His tone was civil not the peremptory bark I'd become used to hearing from our uniformed public guardians so I nodded my head.

'Mr Cunane, I'm sorry to bother you but I have to ask you to come with me to meet someone.'

'What?' I croaked, suspicion flaring in my mind like a volcanic eruption.

'I'm not arresting you, sir. This is purely a courtesy call. Someone wishes to meet you.'

'Who?'

'I honestly don't know but it's important that you meet this person.'

'Can't they phone?'

'They could but your mobile's disconnected.'

'Oh,' I murmured.

'If you'll just come along with us.'

'And see myself on the TV news. Half of these people have their phones set for video already.'

It was true. Tammy's tits and Clint's display had drawn attention to us.

I stood my ground. I was acutely conscious of Clint tensing up alongside me. It only needed one of the coppers to lay a hand on my arm and there'd be bodies flying through the air, policemen's bodies.

Fortunately the inspector was intelligent, either that or he was under strict orders to take a 'softly, softly' approach.

'How about this then, Mr Cunane, the constable and I will go ahead without you? See that code-locked door over there?'

He pointed to a door in the far corner marked 'STAFF ONLY'. It was near the toilets.

'I'll go in and hold it open a fraction. Then you can follow discreetly.'

My inclination was to hop in a taxi and clear off as soon as he was out of sight but I was curious about who wanted to see me. It could hardly be the person who called herself Ms Molly Claverhouse, could it?

'OK, I'll do that but you've got to give me a clue about who wants to see me. Her name's not Molly, is it?'

The inspector looked confused.

'I'm sorry, the person didn't give me a name and discretion was stressed. All I can tell you is that he's a VIP and that the civil police aren't involved in any way except as messengers.'

He must have felt that he'd humbled himself enough because he set off without further explanations. I looked at Clint. There was no answer there. The same bland smile he always gave me played across his gaunt features.

The two police disappeared into the airport infrastructure.

I waited until attention had died down and then followed and Clint fell in behind me.

Once through the door I discovered that the armed constable had gone about his business and only the inspector remained to usher us on through further doors, flights of stairs and corridors. Like the White Rabbit leading Alice into Wonderland he strode ahead quickly and we followed. Eventually we entered the main airport security zone: think cells and interrogation rooms, a fairly grim spot. However we went past it and approached a separate unit with an unmarked door.

The room we entered was bright and pleasantly furnished with pictures on the walls, armchairs and comfortable seats, coffee tables with copies of Cheshire Life, Vogue and the Tatler. The windows gave a view of the runway and there was a coffee machine in a corner. It was like the waiting room in a private hospital or medical practice. There were several doors, again unmarked; probably leading off in my vivid imagination to even more unpleasant cells and interrogation rooms ... soundproofed ones.

'Make yourselves at home, grab a coffee if you like,' the copper said cutting into my fantasy, gesturing to the seats while he entered a door at the far side. His role must have been marginal because he when he emerged a few minutes later he left without giving us another glance.

Somehow I got the impression that it was 'out of sight, out of mind' with him. Were we dangerous to know? I soon found out.

Molly Claverhouse appeared at the inner door. She signalled me with her index finger in a calculatedly offensive way. Was I supposed to be a naughty schoolboy?

'He stays here,' she said coldly, indicating Clint.

'Now wait a minute ...'

'He stays,' she repeated.

'He's not a dog.'

'Really? Whatever he is, he's staying here.'

I cleared my throat, ready to argue but Clint spoke first.

'I'm all right, Dave. I'll read my car mags.'

He still had the four magazines he'd bought earlier, rolled up into a cylinder and gripped in his enormous hand. He settled across three of the low chairs in that typically Clint way of mingling with the furniture I knew well and began studying them intently. Obviously the magazines copiously supplied by whoever ran this facility weren't to his taste.

I followed Claverhouse into the inner office but there were formalities before I got there. The door opened onto a short corridor with windows looking onto the runway on one side and a blank wall on the other. There was a steel door at the end and standing in front of it were two heavies, large muscular ex-service types in blazers and slacks. One had a semi-automatic pistol holstered at his waist, the other held a taser.

The taser man pointed to the wall and grunted 'assume the position' which I did while he frisked me very thoroughly. He then put the taser on a shelf and ran a hand held metal detector from the top of my head to my feet. It produced a bleep at my waist. There was a metal buckle on my belt. I removed it and the keys in my pocket before he cleared me.

'Mobile?' he said.

I shook my head and he looked at me oddly. He gave me back the belt and keys but only after he checked that there was nothing concealed in either.

I was on the point of making a snide comment about not intending to board a plane when I realised they weren't finished. One of the men picked up two heavy steel bars and slotted them into hasps set into reinforced brickwork on either side of the wooden door we'd entered by. He then fixed them in place with padlocks which he locked with a key attached to his belt.

Now even if Clint wanted to come to my rescue he couldn't do it without a JCB or maybe high explosives. Whatever happened, I wasn't walking out of this place in a hurry.

I followed Claverhouse through the steel door into a long, deep room dominated by a heavy mahogany conference table. I stumbled slightly because the floor was raised several inches above the entrance corridor. There was a bank of security monitors mounted above a desk in the far corner on my left. The twelve large screens showed images of the interior and all exterior sides of the terminal. A middle aged, grey haired woman sat at the desk.

My eye was drawn to one screen.

It showed the concourse of Terminal Two.

Unmanned computer work stations took up two sides of the room. On my right there were windows. Heavy curtains blocked the outside view except in the centre. I saw a plane taking off. There was no sound whatever in the room which wasn't surprising because the glass was so thick that the scene outside had a bluish tint. The feeling of oppressive stillness was heightened by the thick carpet on the floor. Our footsteps made no sound. We wafted in to this gathering of spooks like a pair of ghosts. The only noise in the room was the faint hum of air-conditioning.

One of the heavies followed us in and took a seat beside the door which he closed and locked behind him. One of those unusual brief cases with a pistol grip sticking out of the side was propped up against his chair. I was tempted to ask what he was expecting to happen but was sufficiently cowed to remain silent. The upholstered chairs round the table were well spaced out. I guessed the table could accommodate at least twelve. Eight of the places were occupied. I recognised two of the faces. One belonged to Brendan Cullen. He gave no hint of recognition. His lips were closed so tightly that I wondered if he was trying to send me a message. I guessed that he was.

'Keep shtum, Dave.'

The other face I knew was that of the 'entomologist' who called himself Harry Hudson-Piggott. He, at least, gave me a nod. He was seated at the head of the table alongside another man, a solidly built and imposing figure. I looked at the others. They were all men. One was an Asian, probably of Pakistani origin but I suppose he could have been an Afghan. Another man was very definitely black, a black African rather than an Afro-Caribbean. The others were nondescript.

All the men in the room were wearing suits and tending towards their forties or older, not new intake like the two young guys outside the Pimpernel office this morning.

These could all have been gathered from a senior common room in any university in the country, but definitely not from police stations. I was reminded of the days when I worked as a university lecturer ... very brief days. Only the man next to Hudson-Piggott didn't fit that definition. There was something rough and thuggish about him. The shaven head and set of his shoulders suggested that he preferred to settle disputes with his fists rather than academic arguments.

If I'd originally described Hudson-Piggott as an 'entomologist' because he looked at me as if I was a bug on the end of a pin, that impression was heightened by the totally neutral inspection I received from six pairs of eyes.

It resembled a scene from a 'Hornblower' novel where the hero is summoned to a court-martial at the Admiralty. If they were intending to frighten me they were succeeding. I tried to give a casual 'couldn't care less' smile but it turned into a grimace.

The man next to Hudson-Piggott briefly stood up and gestured towards the two vacant seats at the foot of the table. Claverhouse and I sat down.

I was determined to assert myself. I was a citizen of a free country.

'So this is Room 101,' I said. My voice sounded very loud.

The feeble quip produced absolutely no effect, not even a polite chuckle.

'Mr Cunane,' the skin-headed thug at the head of the table said quickly, 'I'm Rick Appleyard and you've formed entirely the wrong impression. We're not here the grill you or confront you with your worst nightmare. We asked you up here because purely by chance Jennifer spotted you down in the concourse.'

He turned with a flourish towards the monitors.

Without taking her eyes off her screens the operator, Jennifer, raised her hand.

'Purely by chance, Mr Bracegirdle, I don't think so. I think the bug you have in my office told you I was coming here and you laid on this reception for me.'

'The name's Appleyard, not Bracegirdle, and you're exaggerating your importance if you think we bugged you. It was pure chance that you turned up just as we were discussing Sir Lewis Greene's murder. It would have been silly not to call you in for a little chat.'

'Sorry about the name mix-up but I have trouble remembering the made-up names you people give yourselves. Have we got a John Benbow or a Horatio Nelson round the table?'

'Mr Cunane, I must say I'm delighted that you live up to your reputation as a comedian. However we're here on serious business and as a member of the organisation set up to keep us all safe from harm I'm hoping that you can cast some light on the terrible events at your uncle's house.'

Hudson-Piggott laid a cautionary hand on his arm and whispered something.

'Sorry, I stand corrected ... your unfortunate *relative's* house. May I extend condolences to you on behalf of all here and of the service which I represent? Sir Lew was once one of our most distinguished auxiliary workers.'

That was news to me but my brain was going into overdrive in an attempt to place the man's accent. I pride myself on my ability to do this but am often wrong. Now I formed a strong impression that this bruiser's clipped tone originated in *Sith Efrika*. The feeling was reinforced by the rough look of him. He could have played tight-head prop for the Springboks. Certainly his head, shaven with greying black hair at the sides, had been well battered at one time and as I inspected more closely I saw that his right ear lobe but not his left had the rugger-bugger's characteristic thickening. Yes, he definitely could have been a tight-head prop, a scrummager and general mauler.

'So can we declare a truce Mr Cunane? I believe you know some of my colleagues but the others are shy about giving out their names.'

'Oh, I'm sure they can make some up. I don't mind,' I said.

This produced an appreciative titter from some of the colleagues. Bren still didn't look at me.

Appleyard then advanced round the table to shake my hand. I risked a peek at Bren out of the corner of my eye. He was giving nothing away.

Appleyard's handshake was extremely firm. He was definitely a prop forward with a grip like a bench vise.

'Now the thing is Mr Cunane, some of my colleagues have formed the opinion that you know a great deal more than you're telling about the sad death of Sir Lew Greene,' he said in a friendly, half apologetic way. 'So even if you hadn't turned up here by chance we'd still have wanted to see you.'

I shook my head, unwilling to utter a denial which certainly would be used against me later. Not for one second did I intend to give away the slightest thing if I could avoid it. From what Hudson-Piggott and Claverhouse had said earlier they didn't appear to know anything about the attempted obliteration of Topfield Farm with C4 explosives. It was best that they remain in ignorance. Anything which underplayed my involvement was good.

'Oh, well perhaps this will go better if I tell you the facts that we've established.'

I shrugged.

Claverhouse administered a painful kick to my left leg.

'Yeah, I suppose so,' I said more to disguise the scream of pain that was welling up in my throat than to show willing.

'OK, well the security camera at the Judge's house appears to show an individual wearing a kufiyah. Unfortunately the camera was smashed before it could give more information. A kufiyah is ...'

'Islamic male headgear usually worn by Arabs.'

'Yes, good, Miss Claverhouse has told us that you're well informed. Watch this and see what you think.'

He pressed buttons on a console in front of him. The lights dimmed, a screen descended on the wall behind him and an overhead projector came on. A few more twiddles at his remote and a video began running. It showed a poorly lit image of the drive leading to Weldsley Park, Lew's grandly named home in Wilmslow, but if you didn't already know was Weldsley you could have taken it for anywhere.

'The killers disabled the external lights before going in,' Appleyard said, anticipating my objection. 'These images have been enhanced to within an inch of their lives. This is the part I want you to take note of.'

A group of blurry figures came closer to the camera. It was hard to make anything out but one of them, the one who disabled the camera, was wearing a kufiyah. That was it: he was wearing a kufiyah, otherwise he was totally nondescript. Not a single feature of his face was visible.

'Disappointing, isn't it?' Appleyard commented, 'but nevertheless a clue as to the identity of those responsible for this appalling crime as is the manner of Sir Lew's death: torture followed by decapitation. We all know that the Tower of London used to be decorated with the heads of the monarch's enemies, but that was in the Tudor era. At the present time decapitation is a signature of Islamic jihad.'

He was wrong but who was I to say. At this point the Asian man seated at Appleyard's right cleared his throat loudly.

'Yes, Yasser,' Appleyard said, 'we all know jihad also means the inner struggle for spiritual purity but in this case I think the decapitation was intended as a message to us.'

He paused and stared at me as if waiting for a response. Was I expected to lead a mob to burn down the nearest mosque? I kept my face blank and strategically placed my leg behind a table support in case Claverhouse felt like using her football skills again.

'Now this is where we require a contribution from you Mr Cunane. It's typical of Islamic fundamentalists to take their revenge, if that is what this killing was, against their victim's whole family ...'

'That's in Iraq or Afghanistan, but this is England,' Yasser intervened.

'And who is to say where these killers may have been trained or where they've come from,' Appleyard countered in a very cold voice. 'I must ask you not to intervene again, Yasser. We're all used to dealing with improbabilities around this table. Every scenario must be evaluated until we decide to reject it.'

This rebuke produced a certain amount of paper sorting and foot shuffling from the others. Yasser concentrated on a thick folder in front of him. I noticed for the first time that the wide table was covered in folders, laptops and photographs except where Claverhouse and I were sitting.

'So this brings us back to you Mr Cunane. There is convincing evidence that some sort of an attempt on your life was made at Topfield

Farm. I can understand that due to your past experiences you may not have wished to involve the police but I assure you that any help you give us in identifying the perpetrators will not be used against you.'

'Well, what do you think I saw?' I hedged.

'Come on, Mr Cunane, there was a bullet in your bedroom window frame at head height. That tells me you were looking out and that someone fired at you. I can promise that if you fired back and hit one of them no action will be taken against you.'

'I didn't fire at anybody.'

'Nevertheless a shotgun was discharged in your farmyard, we have the pellets. There was also an intense petrol fire, your ATV was damaged and there are positive indications that blood was shed on those cobblestones. Come on, man, you can speak freely. Whatever the politicians and lawyers say some of us still believe a man has a right to defend his home. I promise that no action will be taken against you for that.'

'There was an attack but I'm saying no more than that without my lawyer.'

'That would be Mr Marvin Desailles. A most combative solicitor, I believe and we definitely don't want him here holding up our researches. You must grasp the urgency of this matter. These militants may be preparing to strike at the general public. If you could have prevented it and didn't would you like that to be on your conscience?'

He folded his arms and stared at me.

'What do you want me to do?' I asked after a lengthy pause. I was no stranger to emotional blackmail.

'We can set aside the actual incident at your home. Our forensic team have reconstructed that as far as they're able to without your cooperation. What would be tremendously helpful would be if you could identify the men you saw. We know there were four at your uncle's home. Were you attacked by four?'

It seemed easier to go along with him rather than admit anything about the men with the C4.

I nodded. It wasn't a lie, only there were two separate attacks involving two men each.

'I'm impressed that you held them off Mr Cunane but then I'm informed that you have quite a track record for getting out of nasty scrapes. You don't have to be absolutely certain about identifying these guys; a strong suspicion will be enough.'

'OK.'

A series of mug shots was projected onto the screen.

Without exception each one was of an Asian male, some were bearded and some clean-shaven. Some were hardly more than teenagers, others middle-aged. Some wore white skull caps, some kufiyahs, some Afghan hats or turbans. Others were dressed in western clothes.

I watched the first dozen or so, at first saying no as each picture appeared and then merely shaking my head.

'Wait!' I said as they monotonously popped up one after another.

Appleyard paused the pictures and turned to me expectantly.

'All the men I saw were white, not Asian.'

'You can't be certain of that. It was a dark night and look at Yasser here. He certainly qualifies as what our American cousins call a Caucasian, and don't forget some Islamic militants are exactly that … genuine Caucasians … Chechens from the Caucasus. There are also British converts. Carry on looking, please. You've only seen a fraction of the database.'

Every so often Appleyard coaxed me to scrutinise a face more thoroughly.

'Please make very sure it's not this man. We've had him in our sights and a positive identification would enable an arrest and questioning.'

He did this four times. There were four faces above all others that he wanted me to implicate and he pressed me repeatedly but I wouldn't perjure myself. All it needed was a quick nod for each and I could be out of this place but I shook my head instead.

I didn't want to argue the toss with Appleyard but my farmyard had been lit up like a football stadium. He must have known that so what was going on? Those two petrol bombers were white as was the pair in the hen house. I carried on looking. I wondered why Appleyard was retaining his whole team as witnesses to this pointless chore. It must have something to do with his little spat with Yasser. Appleyard wanted to prove something to his team.

Finally, after a frustrating hour Appleyard called a halt. He dismissed everyone except Claverhouse, Hudson-Piggott, Yasser and the armed guard.

'I do hope you're not shielding someone,' he snapped. He brought his face close. His breath was unpleasant, halitosis or something rotten stuck in his teeth.

'My circle of friends among the Islamic extremist community is small to non-existent,' I said.

'Ha, very amusing but the courts have been extremely tough on individuals who've knowingly allowed terrorism to flourish by their obstruction.'

'I'm obstructing nothing and I'd like to go.'

'I'm afraid that's not possible at this time.'

'What?'

'As you probably know the Criminal Justice Act 2003 allows us to hold a terrorist suspect for up to fourteen days subsequently extended to twenty eight days upon reasonable suspicion and if I decide to hold you your aggressive little Rasta lawyer won't be able to do a thing about it.'

'I'm a terrorist suspect now? Are you insane?'

'I'm very far from insane. I'm just going with the evidence; a gun fight at your home, the evidence of military training in the field adjoining it and most of all, your hostile attitude. Suppose instead of being the lucky survivor of an attack by four men you were in fact training for an attack of your own. I think you're a member of an Islamist cell, possibly a sleeper waiting for the call to action. No doubt more evidence will be found in a thorough search of that so-conveniently remote farm of yours. Any judge will agree that we have more than enough.'

Why, oh why did I bury four kilogram's of C4 plastic explosive under Jan's flower bed? It could be my ticket to life imprisonment if this nutter had his way. I tried to row back.

'I've failed to identify the four men you targeted for me and that proves I'm a terrorist? Surely there are other faces to look at? You must have some pictures of white guys. What about Anders Breivik?'

186

'What about him?' he shrieked. 'Breivik has no relevance whatever. I've told you we're looking at Islamic Jihad here.'

'Breivik is a white guy who started shooting innocent people to make some crazy political point.'

So much for appeasement, but my suggestion did seem to cool him a little.

'I'm losing patience with you Cunane. There are strong Islamic indications in this case and I think you recognised some of the faces you were shown but are remaining silent because they're your fellow jihadis. You won't be the first to be radicalised in prison.'

'No, I wasn't radicalised. Sir Lew wasn't close to me but he was family and I want his killers caught. It's just that the men who attacked me weren't among those mug shots.'

He laughed at me. The laugh was all the more sinister for being slightly deranged.

I tried hard not to seem worried but didn't succeed. This guy had leverage over me. I could soon find myself two hundred miles away in London, locked in a cell at Paddington Green police station with four walls, a copy of the Koran and a CCTV camera for company.

Appleyard's eyes were dark brown, almost black and they glittered with spite as he looked at me. All trace of the previous charm had vanished. Such was the intensity of his glare that I took a step back and braced myself.

The expectation of violence was broken when Harry Hudson-Piggott tugged at his boss's elbow. They stepped out of earshot. Hudson-Piggott briefed him about something. He turned to me again.

'Well Cunane, you're in luck. Mr Hudson-Piggott has just informed me that there are in fact more faces for you to look at. They've just come in from Interpol. You'll have to go to our North West regional HQ to look at them. Naturally we don't send such material over the internet so you can only access it there. I suggest that you take a little more care this time. Have another look at the database I've already shown you. Perhaps my warning about our powers might jog your memory.'

21

Tuesday: early evening

All hope of a quick exit from the airport gradually faded.

Clint was brought to join me in the inner office and the door was barred again. Both security guards kept us company. We were fed. I just pecked at my food but Clint kindly cleared my plate for me. The atmosphere in the enclosed room was oppressive although Clint didn't notice it. At one point he even fell asleep.

'What are we waiting for, what's the delay?' I asked the guard for about the tenth time.

'The armoured van won't come any quicker for you asking over and over, sir.'

'But why do we need an armoured van? I could have been to Bury and back on either the bus or the Metrolink by now.'

He raised his eyebrows. 'Civilians' aren't supposed to know that MI5 Regional HQ is on an industrial estate near Bury but I did and in fact it had been mentioned on the local news when MI5 set up regional HQs all over the country. The item was later deleted but not before I'd noticed it.

'We need the van because that's procedure, sir. You're a high value asset who's already been attacked by the opposition so Mr Appleyard couldn't just let you wander about the streets for anyone to take a pop at, could he?' he said wearily.

I grimaced.

'We can't send you in a taxi. Don't you know that half of the taxis round here are driven by IC4 males, some of them recently arrived? Who knows what they get up to?'

'Paranoia,' I grunted. 'You're all mad.'

He raised his eyebrows by way of response which I took as partial agreement.

At half six, by which time I calculated that Jan and the children would be heading for the Irish ferry, there was movement. Claverhouse's two young minders from the morning suddenly appeared, accompanied by the woman herself. They were still in suits and had the brief cases fitted with submachine guns.

Claverhouse signalled us to follow and we walked downstairs through a door and onto the airside. An unwashed white Toyota Hiace van was waiting for us, parked right up against Terminal Two. Entry was by a sliding door on the driver's side. The open door revealed two rows of seats, four places in all. The seats were well padded, firmly anchored and fitted with heavy duty racing style seat belts. The belts were wider than those in normal vehicles and were anchored at six points. The back doors, each with a small window, were closed and bolted.

The van itself, after all the talk of 'armour', didn't look particularly special and Claverhouse must have noticed my disdainful glance. Going by external appearance it could have belonged to a jobbing builder or any tradesman.

'This van is bullet proof, with ram resistant bumpers and forty-millimetre thick windows. It was in use in Dewsbury today hence the delay.'

'You're sure the long wait isn't so that Appleyard can invent some Islamic connections for me? Perhaps he's going to suggest that I've visited a terrorist training camp in Pakistan?'

'Who's delaying things now, Cunane? Why don't you shut up and get in? You sit next to me and your pet monster can spread himself over the two rear seats.'

I turned to relay her order to Clint expecting him to have taken offence. He hadn't. He jumped in joyfully and began rapping the walls, testing their strength.

He examined the complicated seat belts.

'Rated up to 3g, these are, Dave,' he said.

I didn't know what he meant.

'Does he need to bother with that?' Claverhouse said. 'We'll be at our destination before he works out how to put it on.'

'You get a seat belt. Clint gets a seat belt,'

Actually Clint was much more familiar with the racing type harness than I was and didn't need my help. Size was the main problem.

It took a good deal of extending of straps before he could make the harness fit over his massive frame but he did eventually, smiling to himself and checking out the fixings.

Claverhouse turned to me and shook her head.

I strapped myself in next to her. We exchanged sour looks.

Her two minders got in the cab and we set off. She wasn't in the mood for light conversation and neither was I. It was hard to follow the route we were taking. We definitely weren't going the most direct way via the M56 and M60 motorways: more delay and time wasted before I found out how Lee had got on with Jan and the children. They were all probably on the Irish ferry by now. My God, I was beginning to wish I'd joined them.

The tension only began to drain from me when I thought about my family.

A memory from my eventful morning struck me.

When I'd finished burying the C4 explosive under Jan's flower bed, just one of the many stupid things I'd done today, I'd turned back to the house. On the path by the backdoor there were some of Lloyd's little action figures, there were two Ben10s, a Dr Who in an orange space suit and a Power Ranger. Two of the figures had lost arms but one of the Ben10s had four arms so that was all right. Four figures meant two handfuls for a child, perhaps dropped when his fingers relaxed in sleep as Jan carried him to the car in the small hours.

I picked them up and arranged them on a windowsill. The Power Ranger lit up and made a noise. I felt a desperate longing for them all, even for Jan's sharp-tongued mother. When would I see them again?

As long as they were safe it didn't matter what happened to me. It was beginning to seem that I'd escaped the clutches of whatever bunch of loonies was behind Lew's killing only to fall into the almost equally dangerous hands of Rick Appleyard. The motion of the van, the swaying from side to side as we turned what felt like an impossibly large number of corners, gently tranquillised me and I began to drowse. It had been a very long day.

191

The turns were interminable.

I reasoned that we were taking a convoluted route to avoid being followed but it didn't speak well of MI5 if they couldn't guarantee the security of a trip from their branch at the airport to HQ.

What happened next is hard to describe. The word 'suddenly' doesn't convey the full sense of the violence and rapidity of the shocks I felt as the Hiace van was hit time after time on the driver's side, the side I was on. Another vehicle was smashing into us to force us off the road. If I hadn't been secured by the racing harness and the padded headrest I'm sure my neck would have snapped at the very first impact. I felt like a rag doll gripped in the teeth of a massive dog and being shaken to destruction or someone trapped inside a giant tumble-dryer. The armoured sides of our vehicle rang like a bell.

Wham! … Wham! … Wham!

It was like that: one terrific blow after another.

The side smashes stopped. I decided afterwards that there'd been at least three high speed collisions. But now the van, which must have been cruising at anything from fifty to seventy miles an hour, began an up and down motion that tested the seat belts and then almost before my mind could perceive the fact, things began to change from vertical to horizontal.

We were rolling, doing the full three sixty. Once, twice we went over, then I lost count.

My mind registered the sound of screaming. It was Claverhouse and most certainly me, but there was nothing in Clint's *basso profundo* range. I know the sound of his screams. I felt a stab of fear. Was he dead?

We rolled for what felt like ages. Reason told me we were on a steep bank but in my panic it was like the slopes of Everest. We weren't going to stop.

Mercifully, with a final violent jolt we thudded to a halt in that instant.

It was that moment in cartoons where they show the victim sitting with his eyes revolving and little birds tweeting in a circle round his head. This wasn't like that at all.

Total disorientation is the only way I can describe it, certainly no little birds. One moment I was sitting upright trying to make myself comfortable for a nap and thinking about my family. The next moment the world had literally turned upside down.

I was on my side, in total darkness with my head lower than my feet. My body was at a steep angle to the horizontal and I was still lashed into my seat. The 3gs, whatever they were, had proved their worth. My neck was stiff from the violent movement I'd braced against but I could move my head so nothing was broken. My legs were OK too, although they dangled at an odd angle and my knees were throbbing. My eyes ached and I felt a stab of alarm … detached retinas? I felt like someone who'd been forced to undergo the world's most dangerous roller coaster ride for many hours.

My stomach was full of butterflies and I felt sick but the overwhelming feeling was exhilaration.

I was alive. I felt for my watch, not to confirm that it was still working but because it's a sports watch which I use as a timer on bike rides and you can see the time in the dark. I pressed it. The red LED numbers glowed. I hadn't been struck blind. Inconsequentially I registered the time. It was six fifty three. We'd been on the road for less than twenty minutes.

Immediately that thought was interrupted by deep groans coming from behind me.

'Clint,' I managed to croak after clearing my mouth of bile. I was answered by a grunt.

'I'm OK, Dave,' he answered.

He'd made it too. I felt a surge of relief followed by fear. How many more times were we going to face death today?

The darkness was total. The glow from my watch was less than the feeblest candle. Whatever interior lights the van possessed were no longer working. There was a strong smell of petrol. We had to get out of here. I stretched my arm out.

Claverhouse was still there.

'Ms Claverhouse, Molly,' I shouted.

She made a whimpering noise which suggested that she was hurt.

I explored further, my hand travelled over her chest, well protected by the straps and padded buckle and then to her face.

That roused her.

'Get your f**king hand off my face, you f**king arsehole,' she shouted.

'Sorree! I was just checking that you're still alive.'

'I know what you were doing, you dirty bastard,' she snapped.

I was drawing breath for a reply when Clint spoke. Repartee doesn't flow easily when you've just survived a near fatal collision but Clint more than made up for my slowness.

'That was really, really rude!' he shouted at the top of his voice.

There was silence for a second and then Claverhouse and I began laughing simultaneously. I laughed until tears came and she did the same. We laughed from sheer relief at being alive rather than at the ridiculousness of Clint's words which weren't ridiculous at all.

'What she said *was really very, very rude*,' Clint insisted in an injured tone.

'You're quite right, Clint,' Claverhouse agreed, 'we weren't laughing at you and I'm extremely sorry for what I said. I was upset. Mr Cunane, I apologise.'

'Apology accepted but how the hell do we get out of here? The van's resting on the sliding door so we can't leave the way we entered.'

'We'll have to wait for the two Ms to unlock the back door.'

'Unlock?'

'The back doors are fastened with a padlock on the outside.'

'So we can't get out unaided? Brilliant!'

'This is a security van, Cunane. We can't have people slipping out of the back door when they feel like it. We'll just have to wait until the two Ms recover. They may be stunned or something.'

'Two Ms, 3g belts,' Clint said.

'Who are the two M's?'

'Myers and Morgan of course, my security detail, you've already met them. The name's an in joke. They're in front.'

'It may have escaped your notice but this place stinks of petrol and we need to get out now.'

'Yes, can't you rap on the glass or something to get their attention? They may be trying to contact HQ. I'm not getting out of this seat without medical help. I've sprained something badly. I'm sure my spine's damaged.'

I released my belt, tumbled onto the side of the van, now the floor, and hauled myself upright. I banged on the internal partition which separated us from the front compartment. There was no response. I banged harder, still nothing.

I held the light from my watch close to the glass.

All it produced was an eerie red reflection of my own face.

Suddenly there was a stronger light. Clint had a small torch on his key chain. I say small but it was actually of near normal size for anyone else. He passed it to me.

I shone the light through the small observation port into the front cab. Myers and Morgan were still there, still belted into their seats but both thoroughly dead.

The toughened, bullet proof window glass hadn't been strong enough to prevent a section of motorway crash barrier entering their compartment. The unlucky driver's head was smashed to a bleeding pulp with a large section of his brain exposed. The man in the passenger seat had received the full force of the twisted metal through his chest. Yes, I know crash barriers aren't supposed to come loose but then you aren't supposed to hit them with ram resistant bumpers are you? It was a ghoulish sight. Held by their belts at an unnatural angle, blood was draining out of their horrific wounds.

I switched the torch off before I was sick.

'What is it?' Claverhouse asked.

'They won't be helping us.'

'Get me out of this seat. I must see.'

'No, you don't want to do that.'

'Damn you Cunane, help me.'

So I helped her. Spinal injury forgotten, she took a quick peek and turned the torch off.

'Bloody hell, this is your fault,' she said angrily.

I was about to argue when light flooded into our space from the wrecked driver's cab.

'There, I knew someone would come,' Claverhouse said. 'They must have got a message off.'

I shook my head but of course she couldn't see that. Shock can do strange things to people. There was something else.

'Hush, listen,' I ordered.

The light flooding our space seemed to wax and wane as if the source of light was drawing nearer and then going away again. There was an accompanying noise which also grew louder and quieter.

'It's a helicopter!' Clint said.

'Christ, so it is,' Claverhouse agreed. 'It's the police or the air ambulance.'

I looked at my watch again. Astonishingly only three minutes and forty seconds had elapsed since my first look.

'Were the police shadowing the van with a helicopter?'

'Of course they weren't. MI5 is perfectly capable of transporting suspects without their help. Why do you think the van is so ordinary looking?'

'So, unless by a one in a million chance the police just happened to be overhead when we were wrecked, that isn't a police helicopter.'

'Don't be stupid. It must be.'

'The best possible time a police helicopter could get here from a standing start at Barton Aerodrome is something like ten minutes. The same goes for the air ambulance.'

'So what?'

'So, it's the people who've just killed your minders.'

'It was an accident.'

'We were forced off the motorway deliberately, probably by the same people who killed Sir Lew and tried their luck with me or are you saying your men were the world's worst drivers?'

Discussion was terminated when bullets began rattling on the side of van. Someone was firing short bursts from the helicopter. The noise the bullets made as they struck the steel plate was just like someone rapping on a door.

'Oh, hell!' Claverhouse moaned, 'at least we're safe in here.'

'Safe for as long as they don't set our petrol tank on fire, then we'll be roasted like Christmas turkeys,' Clint said contentedly, putting my worst fears into words.

The firing was intermittent with brief pauses while the helicopter shifted its position. I reached the back doors and rattled them. They were firmly shut. The hasp and staple for the padlock were welded onto the van. It was hopeless.

'We need a crowbar, something to lever the doors open,' I said desperately.

'There's nothing like that kept in here,' Claverhouse replied.

I slammed my body against the doors. I was sure there was a slight give but I bounced off the metal and collapsed.

'Not like that, Dave,' Clint corrected. He pulled me upright and squeezing himself between the door and the back of his seat, placed his heels against the door and pushed like a hydraulic ram.

There was a grating noise from the hasp and staple fixings. Clint's strength had stretched them away from the metal holding them but not torn them free. They still held. He stopped pushing. The doors had opened enough for me to put my fingers through but the thick steel shackle of the padlock still held.

Bullets were rattling on the armour plate now. I guessed they were using two submachine guns. It could only be seconds before a spark reached that ruptured petrol tank. I flung myself down beside Clint. My legs weren't as long as his but maybe the extra leverage I could supply would do the trick, Then Claverhouse walked over me and lay on top of me with her heels against the door.

'Altogether,' I screamed.

We heaved. It was the hardest thing I'd ever done.

The staple tore free and the three of us tumbled out of the van. Our escape coincided with a momentary shift in the helicopter's position and we were out of the spotlight.

'Run!' I yelled.

'Like hell,' Claverhouse screamed. She dashed back to the van, fumbled at the passenger door, which she opened with difficulty and pulled out her dead colleague's brief case. A second later, just as the helicopter repositioned itself for another attack she opened fire.

The searchlight winked out but whoever the two gunners were, they knew their business. They fired at the flashes from Claverhouse's weapon. She went down. At the same instant the petrol caught fire. The whole scene was illuminated like the world's worst Guy Fawkes Night. I caught a glimpse of ranks of electricity pylons which told me I was in the Mersey Valley or close to it.

The uprushing flames drove the helicopter away.

I ran forward. There was blood on Claverhouse's forehead. I dragged her away from the burning vehicle. I moved downhill, seeking darkness.

I put a finger on Claverhouse's neck. There was a strong pulse.

'Give her to me,' Clint shouted. He picked her up like a small parcel.

There was bright light from the inferno behind us. Ahead were some trees and then a lake. A lake! Where were we? If the motorway we'd come off was the M60 then this could be one of the water parks which lay beyond the motorway embankment but the puzzle of why we'd been travelling south instead of north was for another time. For now we just had to survive and our chances of that didn't look great.

The helicopter was still somewhere above us. The pilot had dodged back over the motorway when the van blew up. Probably as aware of the pylons as I was, he was hanging back from the valley.

If they had thermal imaging technology on board then we were toast wherever we tried to hide round here. There were no houses, no shelter. Clint and I ran frantically, reaching a cinder track alongside the lake. The searchlight came on. They were searching in the opposite direction on the far side of the blazing van. It was dark down here away from the glare of the motorway. We had a slim chance if we could reach civilisation in the form of streets and houses rather than try to hide in this strip of urban wilderness before they found us. We ran frantically, me gasping at full stretch and Clint loping along easily, quite untroubled by the burden he was carrying.

Suddenly Claverhouse came round.

'Put me down,' she yelled.

Clint stopped and obeyed immediately.

'Keep running, we've no time for this,' I shouted. The helicopter had turned and was now heading for us. Its searchlight was slowly sweeping along the track we were on. In the reflected light I could make out the steelwork of a pylon. The helicopter was threading its way among the obstacles like a sure footed and deadly cat seeking its prey.

'Yes, we have,' she said. She still had the brief case.

'Those bastards killed my team and they're going to pay.'

She opened the case, pulled out the MP5 it contained and loaded another magazine but then she stumbled to her knees. I saw that what I'd taken for a bullet wound was in reality a nasty bruise. She was fighting for consciousness.

'Oh, Christ,' she muttered as she slumped onto the cinder track. Clint grabbed her again but now there was no time to run. The helicopter was on us. Bullets hissed through the air but nowhere near us. Their shooting was wild because they had to steer clear of the immense pylons. I grabbed the MP5 and fired using short bursts more for effect than in the hope of hitting them. The muzzle flash from the weapon must have marked our position like a runway landing light. Without tracer ammunition there was no way to aim accurately in the darkness. Probably none of my bullets hit but the human mind can play strange tricks, at least that pilot's did.

When they were firing at us he'd controlled his machine with surgical steadiness. Now, faced with incoming fire, he weaved and jinked above the lake. He went higher and then made a diving turn possibly looking for a better angle for a strafing run.

The gun gave out a useless click.

All my bravado achieved was to show our exact location in that dark valley.

So this was it. There were no more magazines. We couldn't run far enough. The searchlight swept across the small lake then suddenly all hell broke out. The helicopter was engulfed in flashing lights and sparks. The rotors had hit the high tension cables which were suspended above the artificial lake. It rose, seemed about to escape and then came down like a brick, straight into the lake.

199

We watched in astonishment for a moment. There was something very anticlimactic about it. I'd have preferred to watch the thing burn with the men inside it. A fiery death for them like they'd tried so hard to give me. As it was I could hear shouts and cries for help. My bloodlust cooled. There were survivors.

I was brought back to my own situation when a distant wail of massed sirens grew louder. All traffic had ceased on the motorway. This area was shortly going to be swarming in police. I hurled the MP5 into the lake and the brief case after it.

'That's government property you're destroying,' Claverhouse said.

'Oh, yes, I'm going to wait while your police friends find me with a gun.'

'You're still under … er'

'What? Arrest? I don't think so.'

'Mr Appleyard requires you to look at those photos. He has the legal power to insist that you cooperate. Those men died …'

'Not because of me.'

I watched her patting her clothing. I knew what she was looking for. She'd been wearing a heavy shoulder bag when she got in the van. It had been left behind.

'No gun?' I asked, stepping a little nearer to her.

'I was trying to find my phone.'

'And your gun, but they're in the van aren't they.'

'Don't move a step closer to me. I'm trained in close quarter combat.'

'I'm sorry about your men but I'm not to blame for what happened to them. We're off now if you don't need further help.'

I turned.

'Wait, you bastard.'

'There's gratitude for you Clint,' I said to my companion.

'Arsehole,' she shouted.

We jogged away.

'She's *really* rude, you know,' Clint commented.

22

Tuesday: evening

We made it. We got away from the sirens and reached terraced streets.

My first move was to find a call box. That took us the better part of half an hour.

As soon as I entered the box I remembered that I'd neglected to memorise Tony's mobile number. I phoned the Pimpernel office hoping he'd hung on there. I knew the line was sure to be bugged but it would have to do.

He answered at once.

'Where've you been Boss?' Tony gasped as soon as I spoke. 'It's all happening here. There's been loads more work coming in and I've had to put men on it.'

'Good, good ...'

'And Marvin Desailles has been round. He told me to tell you that everything's going ahead. He gave me a special phone for you to call him on.'

I was glad that Marvin had been discreet with Tony. I wasn't sure that I wanted Tony to know more than he had to.

'And my mate's been on. He phoned from where he delivered the parcels. He wants to know where he's to go with the car.'

'Parcels?'

'Oh, yeah, he delivered them to the right place all. He saw them on their way.'

I breathed a sigh of relief. There'd always been a chance that Lee would take off into the hinterland.

'Listen, Tony, the car ... is it traceable? You know what I mean?'

'Oh, no Dave it's clean. It's ...'

'No, enough information, here's what I want you to do. Shut up the office and then make damn sure no one's following you. I don't care if it takes you all night.'

'Nah, Man City's playing Arsenal. The streets are crowded. I'll have no problem losing a tail. I'll phone my mate from a call box and tell him not to come here.'

'Right and then …'

'Meet up with him and come out to you?'

'Do you know where we'll be going?'

'Yeah, I know the place.'

'We'll be walking. All the pair of you have to do is to make sure no one's tailing you.'

'Easy, peasy,' he said and I put the phone down. God knows how long it would take whoever was tapping the office phone to trace this public callbox. In films and TV programmes they never quite have time but I feared the march of technology had made it instantaneous. I wasn't as confident as Tony. We set off walking down side streets and back alleys until we came to the canal towpath. I prayed that CCTV hadn't reached there yet. Surely there was somewhere still untouched by intruding lenses? Walking anywhere accompanied by Clint was the equivalent of advertising our location. The canal was deserted apart from groups of surly teens smoking and drinking in the shelter of the numerous bridges. They cleared off when they saw Clint coming.

It was true. Looming up out of the darkness, Clint was pretty scary, especially when he smiled and showed his teeth.

Did I feel guilty about shaking off Claverhouse? No, I was well rid of her! The murder of her team was stomach churning but the three hour delay for the 'armoured' van at the airport had given someone time to set up the hit. And how the hell did the killers know what I'd be travelling in? There had to be a leak.

Come to think of it, how had they known I was at the airport seeing off Bob?

My office was bugged to hell and back.

In the circumstances I'd be insane to trust Claverhouse or MI5 again. All that cursing and swearing that got up Clint's nose was due to the fact that she didn't have the means to force us to go with her. Now, having lost us and with two deaths to explain, she'd be on the receiving end of Appleyard's temper and threats.

Thinking it over, I decided that if they did start playing the blame game they would find one person to blame for those deaths ... me. Is that paranoia? No, it isn't. Claverhouse would have to explain to Appleyard. Appleyard would have to explain to his boss and that boss to someone higher and in the end they'd all find it so much more convenient to blame the civilian. I could almost write the scenario for them. The crash on the motorway would be explained as a botched attempt by my men to free me.

Even if I surrendered myself now and managed to convince Appleyard that I had no connection with anything he was sure to spend twenty eight days grilling me in Paddington Green until he was sure he'd squeezed the last little morsel of information out of me.

That wasn't going to happen. MI5 were not going to get their hands on me until the real culprits were found.

After walking for an hour we arrived under a bridge in the centre of Altrincham. The road above was the A56 Manchester Road and I was sure it would be covered by CCTV. As soon as we popped up those lenses would be on us like a hungry cat outside a mouse hole

The operator might not identify me in my black hooded anorak but Clint was unmistakeable.

I could leave him and come back in the Beamer but Clint knew the way to his brother's house. I didn't. If I set off without him it might take me hours to find Bob's hidey-hole, hours during which some busybody was sure to spot him and tell the police that a sinister seven foot tall man was lurking on the canal bank.

It came onto rain heavily.

Pointlessly, I wished Tony Nolan was here with us. He'd be able to snake us round the all-seeing eyes. Alternatively I could dash out on my own and get a taxi to the address but Clint was still the problem. I just couldn't leave him.

In the end there was no choice. I had to hope that my luck would hold.

We emerged onto the wide dual carriageway, ran across six lanes swept by torrential rain and then away from the main road into the nearest residential streets.

Clint led us through the by-ways. It was quite a walk but we passed unnoticed in the dark and rain. At least, I think we did because there was no sudden descent of police cars. Our stroll took us along a wide road and then by a series of turns into the surrounding area. First it was Latimer Avenue, a street of Edwardian detached houses, then along Cranmer with similar houses and finally Ridley Close, a cul-de-sac, consisting of much larger detached houses with big gardens.

I left Clint to shelter under an overhanging tree on Cranmer while I checked out Bob's property on my own. It was fine. There was nothing parked on the street and there were Neighbourhood Watch signs to suggest that the locals were vigilant enough to report prowling gangs of machine gunners.

Bob's property, number twelve, was on the end of the cul-de-sac where the road had been widened into a turning circle. The house had been modernised with plastic windows which detracted from the original Edwardian splendour, but it would be hard for anyone to set up surveillance on the place. There were large trees in the front garden and it was one of only two houses on the short street which had access back and front. A path at the back opened onto a wooded, cinder paved lane bordering a river.

I stood for a while. It was very quiet round here. There were faint sounds of distant traffic and some aircraft noise but that was it. Bob's white Beamer was parked in the drive. There was no noise coming out of it. A pinprick of light told me that it was occupied by a smoker. It had to be Lee.

I tiptoed up to the drive, walked past the BMW and rapped on its door.

Bob flicked his roll-up out onto the drive.

'F**king hell!' he said and swung out of the car with all his familiar truculence. Body language is everything with Lee and now every muscle was tense. He was ready for action. I put my hands up in surrender.

'You didn't need to f**king do that,' he growled. Then he slowly unwound, his body losing all the aggressive stiffness. Perhaps there was some hope for him. At one time he'd have been at my throat already.

'Yeah, sorry, I just wanted to keep you on your toes. There are some really nasty people looking for me, Lee, and working for me might not be a doddle.'

'Do I f**king care? Have I said anything?'

'No, I'm just saying.'

'It's all right, Dave,' Tony said. 'I've filled him in on what's gone down, at least that bit that you've told me about.'

'Yeah, well maybe I'll say more later. I'll have to see.'

'OK. You're paying the wages.'

'Oh, Tony and there I was thinking we have a relationship that goes beyond the pounds and pence.'

'We have. You're a great laugh Dave but you couldn't pay me enough to defuse a bomb for you. No one could.'

'Yeah, Tony Nolan, you're all heart. A diamond geezer if ever there was one.'

Lee gave a short snort at this. The first expression of amusement I'd ever heard from him.

'OK, enough Dave. I defused that bomb because I could, that's all. Maybe it was payback for me taking the piss out of you that time when you were in Strangeways, maybe not, but I'm not sure I'd be as quick to do another one if I didn't know the reason why. That's all I'm saying.'

I raised my eyebrows. So Tony had been meditating about the occasion when he'd spat in my face. That was interesting. Had the reconditioned brain revived his conscience? Defusing a bomb was a nice enough apology.

'Fair enough, all will be revealed. Meanwhile what's happening round here? Where you followed?'

'What do you think? Lee dropped me off at the corner of the main road on the way in. I waited half an hour and there's been nothing coming onto this estate, not even an ice-cream van. I've been in cemeteries that had more action. Bob knew what he was doing when he bought this place. Proper bleeding retirement home, it is.'

'Yeah, well go and find Clint. He's round the corner.'

I opened the door and lit the lights.

Lee followed me in.

'Bright, int it?' he commented mildly.

It was.

Bob changes addresses frequently. As he's supposed to be in the clear with the law I don't know why he does this, but he does. Possibly he fears former associates more than the police or customs. This new address in Ridley Close is a recent move so I could only hope it wasn't on a police database.

I guessed that all Cunane addresses would be watched but what about Sir Lew's many properties if they became available?

I was familiar with some of Bob's other homes. Like them this place had been refitted by an interior designer used to working on Bob's night clubs; clashing colours, gold fittings, chrome and glass everywhere, vases and mirrors too large for a normal house.

What was certain was that Bob Lane had no yearning for the muted pastel shades and understated design currently in vogue. Scandinavian minimalist, ain't him. I'd argued with him but I was wasting my time. For Bob if the cheque that a designer asked him to sign was heavy enough then that meant everything was fine and aesthetics be damned.

Bob is Bob and I value his good points well enough not to care about his judgement in interior decor.

'So how did it go in Scotland, Lee,' I asked.

'Your old lady's a bit of a hard case, int she?'

'What?'

'I found them at the meeting point like you said, dog and all, but I thought she was going to kick my bloody liver out when I said you'd sent me to collect them. You should have given me a note or something. I've had an easier time convincing a copper I was telling the gospel truth than I had with your old lady, and that other one … the mother … for f**k's sake, she's awesome and she talks funny too.'

'She's a cockney, Lee.'

'Cockney, mockney, I don't know but I'd rather be locked up in a cell under Wythenshawe cop shop with three big coppers kicking the shit out of me than try to put one over on that one.'

'Yeah, I know the feeling Lee, so how did you persuade them?'

'I didn't but in the end the old cockney said only Dave Cunane could have sent someone like me to collect his family. A diamond in the rough, that's what she said I was and we got on OK after that.'

Lee looked quite proud as he was telling me this.

'So you got them down to the truck at Burtonwood services.'

'Yeah, I stayed and waved them off.'

'Thanks Lee.'

'It's what you're paying me for, int it? She, I mean your wife, gave me a bag full of mobile phones. They're in the motor. I'll get them.'

Tony returned with Clint after my dialogue with Lee. It was the longest exchange I'd ever had with him without resort to violence. Maybe it was the start of a new era in Cunane/Lee relations … maybe.

Clint clumped into the hall.

He wrinkled his nose.

'Stinks funny in here,' he said.

'That's Tammy's perfume,' Tony explained, 'Gucci "Rush" and you need a gold rush to pay for it.'

'I stink too,' I said, not anxious to start Clint off on a catalogue of complaints about his brother's lover. 'We both reek of petrol, Clint. Point me to a bathroom.'

'There's some upstairs here and there's the Jacuzzi at the back.'

'Upstairs will be fine.'

I followed him upstairs.

'Where?' I asked.

He pointed to a door.

It was the spacious master bedroom, dominated by a king-sized bed with an elaborate carved headboard. The carving was of a naked, busty woman with an elaborate hairdo reclining on her side and extending one hand outwards to the onlooker while the other rested coyly on her private parts. The woman vaguely resembled Tammy Marsden and must have cost a fortune.

It was mildly embarrassing and a little out of character for Bob Lane. Who would even think of such a thing? I looked again. The nipples on the breasts were remarkably prominent. Weird or what, I thought. But then I'd once been battered about the head by one villain's bronze cast of his girlfriend's bosom so maybe such trophies are common in the circles Bob moves in.

My mind boggled.

The decor was equally eye straining. There was heavy embossed wallpaper with big pink flowers and ankle deep carpet also in pink. Paintwork on skirting boards and door frames was in purple as was the upholstery on a large sofa and armchair. Pink and purple, what was Bob thinking of? The door of the large walk-in wardrobe was open giving me a view of racks of women's clothes. A wide dressing table was laden with an impressive selection of beauty aids. Entering this room felt like an invitation to an intimate relationship with dear Tammy and I backed out.

Bob was welcome to the ex-pole dancer as long as he kept her to himself.

'This is Bob and Tammy's room. Isn't there a guest bedroom?'

'No, you stay in here Dave. I'll feel better with you in here.'

'Why is that?'

'I'll just feel better with you in Bob's bed. Dave, I know you wanted to dump me when we were back there at the canal just like some other people do but you didn't. That makes me feel good and if you stay in here I'll be in the next room to you if anything happens in the night.'

I was perplexed at this. I didn't know if I'd be able to cope with spaniel-like devotion from Clint. It was unhealthy.

'Now listen Clint, I'm sure Bob's sorry he couldn't take you on holiday with him ...'

'It's not that Dave. I know he has to be with Tammy like I was with Naomi when I was married. It's just that she hates me and I do silly things when she looks at me. Why can't she be like your Jan? She never makes me feel stupid.'

Normally cheerful at all times, even in circumstances which would make the more imaginative run screaming, Clint's gaunt face bore a hang-dog, miserable look I'd never seen before.

Here was a problem requiring a solution that was beyond the resources of Pimpernel Investigations to supply.

'You're tired, Clint,' I said. 'It's been a long day. Go and clean up, I'll make you a meal and then if you have a good sleep tonight you'll feel better in the morning.'

'Yes, I am tired,' the big man agreed, 'but will you sleep in Bob's bed tonight?

I nodded my head.

He went to his room at once.

I'd already decided to stay in the room and it wasn't fear of starting an argument with Clint that made me agree. I'd spotted a hub charger on the bedside table. As I intended to charge several mobiles that was the decider. There was also the thought that I might not be in this strange house very long.

I looked at myself in a mirror with which the room was well supplied though thankfully not one on the ceiling above the bed. My trousers were ripped at both knees. My eyebrows were scorched from the explosion when I pulled Claverhouse away from the van. Rain had turned the mud I'd collected into something resembling glue that had run and streaked every part of my body. My good shoes were coated with the same stuff.

I was in rags but I'd have to put up with it for now.

I pulled the heavy load of cash out of my pocket and stuffed most of it into the bedside table.

I rinsed my face and hands in the en-suite bathroom and went downstairs and into one of the two reception rooms and poured myself a stiff Glenfiddich at the fully fitted bar. There must have been a couple of grand's worth of drink stacked up against the wall. There was also beer on draught from a keg under the counter.

My next stop was the kitchen. It was less eye aching than Bob and Tammy's bedroom but just as certainly making a statement. In this case the statement was about wealth. It was the complete *'we've made it big'* kitchen made from the amalgamation of two smaller rooms. It had stone floors, green painted cupboards, a granite work top round two walls, a huge double oven in a hooded recess, and a double sink set into a central island cum breakfast counter. This island was made of a solid block of polished teak surrounded by high stools. The space above it was loaded with every possible type and size of cooking utensil.

No expense had been spared.

Crammed with enough equipment to satisfy the most exacting gourmet chef, it wasn't a bad place for two people who to my certain knowledge never cooked a meal if they could avoid it. Bob's culinary skill began and ended with the old fashioned fry-up. Judging from the scene upstairs I guessed that Tammy's life wasn't focused on kitchen skills either.

My appetite directed me to the two outsized American fridge freezers which stood opposite the enormous oven.

Remembering the humble council house on the rough side of the Langley estate which Bob had once shared with his mother, Clint and a sister who died of drug addiction I again wondered what he was thinking of. You could easily cook for twenty people in here, not that Bob or Tammy ever would.

Whenever they entertained they had caterers in or used one of their clubs.

Then a little voice reminded me of my own kitchen at Topfield Farm. We did use it daily but giant kitchens are the besetting sin of the house-converting, upwardly mobile classes. I mentally apologised to Bob.

I rummaged through one of the massive freezers and found a family-sized lasagne which I put in the oven for Clint, then started cooking an eight egg Spanish omelette in a huge frying pan.

Doing a practical task drained away the floodwaters of tension that were building up behind my temples.

I'd just pared the potatoes when a pang of guilt struck. If I'd agreed with Appleyard and identified the men he wanted me to finger then he wouldn't have required me to go to the Bury HQ. I wouldn't have been on the motorway at all and Claverhouse's two Ms would still be alive. I thought about them. Were they a pair of bright young university graduates attracted by the new 'open' MI5 advertising campaign or were they ex-military following a traditional career route? It didn't matter what they were. Now they were dead and it wasn't my fault.

I shook my head angrily.

I returned to my cooking, gently frying the thinly sliced potatoes in extra virgin olive oil.

I get some of my best inspiration in kitchens.

If Bob Lane was Shakespeare in a previous life perhaps I was a famous chef or more likely a kitchen skivvy because it's when I get down to scouring grease off badly burned grills and frying pans that the real stimulation comes. As I added the onions and set the heat to simmer gently I started thinking about the false Miss Fothergill.

I cracked eight eggs into a bowl.

False Fothergill, she'd started with me just over three months ago. Was that when someone began getting nervous about what Sir Lew might be uncovering? The thoroughness of it all was scary, placing an agent on the off chance that Lew might confide in his relation.

No, that didn't make any sense at all. The false Fothergill, hell I couldn't get my head around that. She'd just have to be Miss Fothergill until I caught up with her. Thinking of her as 'False Fothergill' wasn't worth the mental effort. Anyway whoever she was, she hadn't known Sir Lewis Greene from Adam. The very first slip she'd made in her three months of employment was to take down the 'Who's Who' and look him up.

If she was an intelligence operative keeping tabs on Sir Lew's relatives then she'd certainly have been briefed about Sir Lew.

So where did that leave me?

I pondered this as I lightly whisked the eggs. It was difficult to work out the motivation of these spooks. Give me criminals and fraudsters and greed any day.

But there'd been a purpose in Fothergill's actions.

She'd taken Lew's notebook and disappeared into the Manchester scenery.

Just suppose that she was nothing to do with Sir Lew or with his horrific murder. That had to be right. She'd gone to immense trouble to get the job at Pimpernel weeks, if not months, before Lew had even discovered his conspiracy.

So why was she in my office?

There could only be one answer. She was there to find out what I was up to.

So who was interested in me enough to want to listen to the minute and boring details of my office routine? There hadn't been anything the least bit criminal going on, apart from what the people we were reporting on were up to, that is. It was highly unlikely that the tabloid press were after me. They'd had their fingers well and truly burnt over bugging scandals. Nor were the financially-stressed boys in blue any more likely to pay someone to spy on me for three months.

It was crazy.

I added seasoning to the egg mixture, salt and plenty of pepper. I like an omelette to have zing.

Then an inkling of a solution began to arrive.

It was all in the timings. Three months and not a foot wrong by Fothergill. She'd become the perfect receptionist. Then Sir Lew arrives and a) she makes a slip --- looking him up in Who's Who --- and b) she hears us having a row and c) steals the item Lew deposits in the safe, works until the end of the day and then skips for good. She was waiting for proof that I was a criminal, got it when she overheard me arguing with Lew about blackmail and murder and took the notebook as evidence.

Now came the hard part.

Who hated me enough to go to these lengths? There was no one. I've annoyed lots of people but mostly they were the sort who would pay a few quid to boot-boys such as Tony and Lee had once been to hand out a good kicking. I couldn't think of anyone who'd even go to these lengths. The expense alone rules out ninety nine point nine per cent of the people I've helped on their way to prison. One or two of my enemies have ended up in an early grave as Lew reminded me but the chance that their relatives loved them enough to want revenge on me was pretty remote. Well, maybe it's more than one or two but even so I couldn't quite credit it.

I left the kitchen and walked into the hall and stood at the foot of the stairs for a moment.

Bob's interior designer had gone overboard here.

Perhaps he was sending Bob a message? Was he drunk or high on drugs? It was a statement but whatever it meant the clashing colours, oddly focussed lights and glaringly illuminated mirrors gave me eyestrain. Perhaps four kilograms of C4 was the answer to this riot of kitsch.

Clint was on his way downstairs. He raised a hand in salute but continued down into the room with the oversized bar and settled on a massive sofa. Motoring mags were piled up on a glass topped coffee table in front of him. He didn't say anything. Obviously he felt he'd unburdened himself enough for one evening. I told him his meal would take a few minutes longer.

I looked in the other room.

Lee was slumped on an equally large sofa watching football on the wall mounted television. Tony had his head stuck in a book. Neither even looked up.

Back in the kitchen I gave the pan a shake. The potatoes and onions were doing well. I stirred them to make sure they didn't brown, poured the egg mixture into the frying pan and raised the heat. For the next few minutes I carried on getting my omelette right, turning the edge down and making sure the egg mixture was absorbed.

It was ready. I set the table and served three generous portions garnished with salad.

I went into the TV room.

'Grub's up,' I announced.

It took a warning stare from Tony before Lee managed to tear himself away from his viewing.

'What's this,' he asked grumpily.

'Cordon bleu cookery produced by my own fair hand and served with a smile,' I said.

He looked at the table and then he looked at me, 'I don't feel hungry,' he said.

'Yeah,' Tony agreed. 'I thought we might send out for a pizza later.'

'No, you won't be doing that.'

Lee immediately stiffened.

'Why the f**k not?' he growled.

'Because it's likely that there's a large number of coppers and MI5 out there looking for us, that's why the f**k not.'

Tony looked shocked. He didn't say whether it was my language or our predicament that upset him. He sat down abruptly.

'You're eating here and you'll both be staying here until the heat's died down.'

'I didn't sign on for this,' Lee insisted.

'Two MI5 men were murdered a few hours ago. They were driving the van I was in. They were killed by the same people who've tried to kill me several times.'

He considered this and then shrugged, presumably that was as close as he came to saying 'You're right, I'm wrong.'

'Oh … Is there any tomato sauce?' he asked. Was he genuinely indifferent to what I'd said or just thick?

I found the sauce and put it in front of him.

He consented to eat, first picking and then heartily.

While they ate I filled them in on events including the inheritance from Lew. My natural inclination is always to play my cards close to my chest but in this case the deaths of the MI5 men had rattled me. Tony and Lee were likely to meet the same fate as I was if we didn't find out who was behind the killings. The only way we were going to do that was by finding Fothergill and Lew's notebook. So I needed their full cooperation.

'Facebook,' Tony said, 'women that age, they're always on Facebook. That's where you'll find them.'

'Yes, but we don't have the phony Fothergill's real name.'

'It's a hundred to one that this black girl who passed the job onto her knows her or knows someone who knows her. That's how we'll find her.'

'So all we need now is a computer.'

'No problem Dave, Bob's got computers here. I know because I delivered them.'

He led me to a small room next to the lounge. It contained computers, printers, scanners and shelves full of computer books.

'Bob's taking lessons on how to use this but he's a slow learner.

Tammy uses it more than him to order things off eBay.'

He switched the computer on.

'Do you know Bob's password?'

I didn't.

I went out and asked Clint if he knew.

'Judith121179,' he said. 'That's our sister's name and birthday.'

Seconds later Tony was accessing social media. This was an area where I have no expertise at all but he did.

'This'll take some time, Boss. Have you got the photo?'

I handed over the picture of the real April Fothergill.

'The guy at the employment agency said she was African but I guess he meant black. Fothergill doesn't sound very African.'

'No,' he said. He was completely absorbed. I stood by awkwardly. 'Marvin gave me this for you, a prepaid mobile. All you need to do is hit the speed dial,' he said.

'But is it secure?'

'Listen Dave, as this spot of bother is supposed to involve terrorism the super computers at GCHQ are probably on the watch for keywords connected with you ... you know like ...'

'Yeah, I know about Echelon, the spy in the sky.'

'OK, then,' he said and focussed back on the computer screen.

I went and stood by the backdoor and phoned. As I did so I detected the light from Lee's cigarette at the bottom of the garden. He was standing in a small gazebo set near some rain sodden trees.

Talking to Marvin was a strain. He is a master of the art of elliptical conversation but I'm not. He could probably talk for hours without giving a verbal clue to an eavesdropper so I confined my responses to the occasional grunt.

'Yeah, the old guy has done everythin' to make my job easy. I've already made progress. There be no bother with it, bwoy. You a very lucky mon.'

'Is it OK to speak to you?'

'Yes, the phone in your hand calls the one in my hand that be belongin' to my Aunty Velmore. No one goin' to be hackin' her phone. She be in her grave, mon.'

'Oh, I see.'

'Your friendly relative done all de work. I's be robbin' you by chargin' you a fee at all but I will, mon. He even had a statement from two other men in the same line of work as him sayin' he ain't crazy. Mon, that will's copper-plated and cast iron. You'll be getting' what he wanted you to have. De properties have all been valued a couple of months ago by a top accountancy firm and the amount of inheritance tax due estimated. There be money set aside to pay it.'

'Good.'

'Gwarn, is that all you say, "good"? Mon, it's bloody amazing.'

'Right, I'll call you again.' I said and rung off. Realistically, I couldn't quite believe the promises of wealth. I'd be a "very lucky mon" if I was still alive in a few days time.

Lee sauntered up. He reeked of weed.

He spoke before I did.

'Good meal, that was Boss, f**king good. You know it's the first meal someone's actually cooked for me personally since I was a kid. I appreciate it.'

'And I'd appreciate it if you'd keep your promise and not smoke that stuff round here.'

'Just one tiny spliff, that's all. Be human, Boss. I didn't smoke in the house.'

'If the police or customs search this place and find pot that's all they'll need to lock Bob up. What's human about that?'

'Nah.'

'Have you got a bag full of weed on you?'

'No way, I've just got enough for one more spliff. Listen, I smoke them mixed with ordinary tobacco and with a filter tip. I smoke right down to the tip so there's nothing left when I throw it away.'

I nodded and he went inside. The pot seemed to have mellowed him out which was to the good but he could become a liability.

Clint's lasagne was ready. I served it to him. I didn't hang around to watch him eat it.

I tried Jan's number on one of the mobiles she'd given to Lee. There was no answer. I guessed she wasn't answering because the children were asleep.

I texted *'Love to all, am safe D xxx.'*

At a loose end I went to the bar and poured myself another slug of Glenfiddich. I was a spare wheel round here and even if Tony found Fothergill's address I was too tired to do anything about it. I sat in a daze for a while. Too much had happened. Eventually I made a move.

I looked in on Tony. He was beavering away at his keyboard. I asked him how he was doing but he just gave me a blank stare. I lurched towards the door.

'Tomorrow, Dave,' he said, 'I can't find her on Facebook but she may be on some social media site for African immigrants.'

Being human, I was slightly pleased at this first failure by the reconditioned brain. Still it would have been handy if he had located her. I'd have to fall back on traditional methods.

Clint had gone to bed and Lee was stretched out on the sofa, snoring lightly. I wasn't the leader of a scout troop so I decided Tony and Lee could make their own sleeping arrangements. I checked all the doors and windows and looked outside. The house was secure like all Bob Lane's pads. It had top quality burglar alarms and steel reinforced back and front doors. The anachronistic white plastic windows I'd turned my nose up at on arrival were security windows made of toughened polycarbonate. A tiny label proclaimed that they were impact resistant, bullet proof and flame resistant up to one thousand degrees.

Short of using a bulldozer or explosives no one was coming in here quickly.

Rain was lashing down, nothing was stirring and I was exhausted. Fatalistically I decided that sleep came first. If the house was raided during the night there was nothing I could do one way or another. I took the bottle of Glenfiddich upstairs with me.

I took a long shower in the en-suite bathroom and when I returned to the bedroom I found that one of Jan's phones that I'd left plugged into the multicharger had a message.

'Arrived at location. All safe. Staying with driver's mum tonight. I'll phone tomorrow 9 a.m. J xxx'

Pleased that my family was safe I turned the bed down. I

immediately realised that however weary I was I couldn't sleep between Tammy Marsden's purple silk sheets.

I prowled the landing. There was a linen cupboard. I found white cotton sheets, went back to my room and stripped the bed. I looked again at the carving. God! There was no way I could sleep under those twin spheres. Bob must be besotted by her. I fetched a counterpane and draped it over the sculpture. As I tucked the bed sheet in the top of the bed the back of my hand brushed against one of the jutting nipples. There was a slight movement. I recoiled. Knocking the nipple off one of Tammy's tits was bound to be a big no-no with Bob.

I pulled away the counterpane and checked it out. The nipple was intact but it had moved. Disgusted with myself I gently stroked the mammary all over and when I gave a downward flick to the nipple it moved again. Everything else was stationary. Mystified, I half expected the bed to start vibrating or a hidden spotlight to come on but nothing happened.

Pulling back the mattress I examined the carving more carefully. The figure was cut into a thick slab of boxwood which was attached to the bed frame by strong uprights. It looked almost as if it had been made from a plaster cast of Tammy's fair form but it was definitely carved wood. The timber was six inches thick, not a single piece but built up from laminations. I rapped all over it.

The supporting legs gave a solid thunk but the carving was hollow.

I ran my hand along the sides again to see if there was a hidden electrical connection. There wasn't. The sides were completely smooth with no trace of a seam, the back was the same.

I went back to the nipple I'd touched and pressed it again. Once more there was a very slight movement in the seemingly solid carving. I pressed the nipple on the other breast. It moved. Finally I pressed them both at once.

There was an audible click and a hinged panel popped out from the smooth side.

I didn't know whether to be amused or frightened by Bob's ingenuity but this was deadly serious. I pulled away the bedside table and folded the panel down until it was horizontal. Inside the void there was a wire frame mounted on little wheels like the trays in a dishwasher only vertical.

My first thought was drugs. Had Bob lied when he claimed to have no connection with the hard drug trade? Trained to think the worst of people despite my good nature, I was afraid I was about to discover kilograms of heroin or mephedrone. I had to know. Hardly daring to breathe, I pulled the frame. It slid out easily.

Clipped to it was a Glock 17 semi automatic pistol, an Uzi submachine gun and three folded bullet proof jackets, one of them outsized, no doubt to fit Clint. Surprise, shock even, mingled with relief. Bob Lane was a one off.

Thrusting my arm further into the secret compartment I found spare magazines for the Uzi and the Glock and boxes of nine by nineteen millimetre ammo which would fit both weapons. There was enough to withstand a siege. Thinking of all Bob's precautions, the idea of him having 'Bob's last stand' in here didn't seem right. There had to be a bolthole, probably a secret tunnel.

I wondered how Bob rhymed all this out to himself …

> *When the doorbell rings*
> *Squeeze Tammy's things.*
> *If you still hear a racket*
> *Put on your bullet jacket*
> *Grab your semi-auto gun*
> *Then how fast can you run?*

Something like that, but hell, using Tammy's breasts as switches … that was a bit kinky.

I cleaned my prints off everything I'd handled and then, remembering my bargain with Jan, put the frame back as I found it and climbed into bed. The weapons were a last resort. OK, I'd fired at the helicopter. That was on the spur of the moment in the face of imminent death. God, I was confused, but I'd made a promise and I knew I couldn't look my wife in the face if I deliberately armed myself.

219

23

Tuesday night — Wednesday morning

Even if Fothergill, the imposter that is, was now in Australia she'd have left traces in Manchester. I just needed the slightest clue that might lead me to whoever she was working for. If Fothergill was all about me and nothing whatever to do with Sir Lew then whoever sent her had to be local because I'm local.

That was mainly wishful thinking but what else had I to go on?

I went into the large television room where Lee and Tony lay sprawled on sofas. A frowsy stink of tobacco and pot hit me in the face. I looked down at my two employees. They were an unlikely looking pair to pit against the cream of the world's espionage agencies.

Lee had his thumb in his mouth and the self-proclaimed savant, Tony Nolan, had his face jammed into a purple cushion.

Unlikely or not, they were all I had and their very improbability as investigators might be an advantage, that is, if I could keep their noses to the grindstone.

Neither of them was in the habit of rising before midday. That was one of the things that was about to change. I drew back the curtains and flung open the windows. The stinking fog began to dissipate as a powerful draught blew through the room.

'Rise and shine,' I said to Lee, giving his bony shoulder a jerk.

He clicked into a fighting posture at once so the pot hadn't scrambled his brain.

'F**king bastard,' he snarled, taking a swing at me. I easily dodged his wild lunge and pushed him back on the sofa. He rolled off and tumbled at my feet. I put my foot on his neck and pressed him into the floor.

'Listen, Lee,' I growled. 'All this pot you're smoking's making you hyper aggressive. Smoke it inside this house again and I'll break your

221

arm.'

He struggled and I pressed down harder.

Inarticulate groans rose from the floor.

Tony cleared his throat and spoke.

'You can let him up, Mr Cunane ... er ... Dave. It's my fault. I shouldn't have let him smoke in Bob's house but he says he can't sleep without a bit of weed. I'll see he behaves.'

'Yeah, you said that before Tony but I think you like pot yourself.'

'Sorry, Boss ... er ... Dave, but everyone likes a bit of weed after a hard day grafting.'

'No Tony mate, smoke in this house and you're in splints, just like him. Geddit?'

'That's not fair. Everybody smokes it.'

'Maybe, but you're still not listening Tony. I said anyone who smokes weed in this house gets a broken arm. I said nothing about the garden.'

'Yer what?' grunted Lee from below.

'If you must do it, go in the garden down beyond the gazebo.'

'Even if it's raining?' pleaded Tony.

'Yes.'

'You're a hard man, Dave.'

'No, I'm not. I'm too soft for my own good,' I said jerking Lee to his feet. 'I'm not a social worker. If you both want to smoke pot until you don't know what day of the week it is, that's just fine by me. But you do it on your own time. The door's that way if you want to leave.'

For a second I thought Lee was going to but Tony laid a hand on his arm. They stayed. Tony looked sheepish.

'Right, there's breakfast in the kitchen,' I said. 'I'll give you twenty minutes to sort yourselves out.'

I went out and shut the door behind me.

I'd seen that Bob had left the makings of a big fry-up in the fridge and, without Jan at my elbow to disapprove, I reached for the frying pan. To hell with cholesterol! The danger of lead poisoning was more imminent.

222

By the time Tony staggered in, I had a nice pile of bacon, sausages, fried eggs and black pudding to dole out.

'Er … Lee will be along in a minute,' he said as I shared the fried food with him.

I'd almost cleared my plate before the gloomy, tense and spotty face of Lee appeared. He had difficulty processing the idea of a cooked breakfast and it took all Tony's encouragement to get him to eat.

I laid out my idea.

'We've got to find either one of the Fothergills, the fake or the real Fothergill, the black girl.'

Tony looked interested. He made no mention of his failure last night with the computer. Lee's expression was one of glazed incomprehension.

'Lee, if you were on the run, where would you hide?' I asked the question more to see if I could wake him than expecting an answer.

'On the run, Dave? Yeah, I see the one who robbed your safe hiding but what makes you think the black girl's on the run?' Tony said, covering for his mate again.

'She's committed a crime and I guess the False Fothergill has already told her to lie low. Anyway those two crooks at the Temp Agency, Gonzi and Big Haired Hilda, are probably reaching out for her.'

'Why?'

'Because she very likely knows all about their cute little scam, that's why. . . . Lee, I asked you a question: where do you think she'll be hiding?'

He looked at me in panic and scratched his head.

'You know, Lee, like when Beast was after you,' Tony prompted.

'The Beast?' I asked.

'Beast,' Tony corrected. 'He's this bloke in Wythenshawe, armed robber by trade. He has this really savage lurcher. That's why they call him Beast. When Lee crossed him he said he was going to feed Lee to the dog in little pieces.'

'He would have too,' Lee added, 'he's a right f**king c***.'

'Lee, chill with the c-word. You're only allowed to use it if someone's actively trying to kill you, otherwise I go for the arm and it's

223

splint time again.'

He mouthed the word silently.

I pushed my chair back.

'Lee, he means it,' Tony said.

Lee made a sound which could be taken to mean sorry.

'So what did you do when Beast was after your blood?'

'Dunno,' he muttered.

'Come on.'

'Well I dossed on different mates' floors for three weeks until the big bastard got himself arrested for something else.'

'Right, and where did you doss?'

'I just told you, me mates.'

'Where?'

'Wythenshawe, Benchhill mainly. That's where me mates are. People I can trust not to grass me up. I didn't go out for three solid weeks, worse than prison it was.'

'OK, now suppose you were a young black woman about twenty five years of age, no friends and relations around because you've just come from Africa, and you had to go to ground in Manchester. Where would you go?'

Lee scratched his head again.

Tony decided to help him out.

'Dave, she'd go for somewhere she could rent easily and most of the rented property is in Fallowfield and Hulme. Places where the students hang out.'

'Yeah, but she's black,' Lee said. 'She could be in Fallowfield or Hulme but she'd be safer in Moss Side. Anyway there's a lot going down with those students, it's safer in Moss Side.'

He looked uncomfortable and I knew why.

'Some people prey on the students, don't they, Lee? They break into their flats and steal their laptops, mug them on the streets, drag them to cash points and force them to hand over their money and their cash cards.'

'Who do you think you are?' he said nastily. 'I've done my time. I don't need you raking things up.'

'I'm raking it up for a reason. There's a regular little community of muggers in that part of Manchester isn't there? There are so many at it that the police hardly even pretend to be stopping them.'

'So?'

'So you know who some of them are and I want you to use your contacts to find this black girl. It has to be the black girl and not the other one because I can give you a photo of her and you can get copies made. She'll have moved in very recently. She'll be keeping herself to herself and she's most likely on her own. We'll come up with some sort of cover story, rich girl running away from her family or such like.'

'Sounds daft,' Lee muttered.

'OK, so we'll make this real. There's five hundred pounds for whoever spots her and five hundred for you when we reach her. How does that grab you?'

As I watched his eyes lost the glazed look. The light had come on in the Lee brain and there was someone at home. I guessed he was calculating how much weed he could buy for five hundred.

'Yeah, might just work at that,' he agreed.

'Right, get a good breakfast inside you because I want you on this all day and all night until you get a result.'

'Oh, come on Boss, be human. It's only half past seven.'

'Lee, it's because I want to carry on being human that I'm doing this. Five hundred in your pocket for a result, Lee; isn't that enough to get you moving?'

'I guess.'

I turned to Tony.

'Now you've got a hard day ahead of you. I want you to run the office.'

'What?'

'And that's not all. I want you to tell every investigator who comes in a really good sob story about Fothergill going missing and how worried the firm is. There's just a chance she gave one of them a clue about where she hangs out. They are mostly ex-coppers after all and so they're…'

'… really nosy buggers?'

'That's it. I was going to say *trained observers* but nosy will do. Can you talk to ex-coppers?'

'Yes, Dave, I don't think any of them recognise me with the suit and the posh voice.'

'Good, because there's a lot more, I want you to get in touch with a specialised commercial fraud investigation business whose name I'll give you and have the office checked out for fingerprints and bugs.'

'I can do all that myself.'

'No, what I want is a set of Fothergill's prints. I have a friend who may be able to run them.'

'*I* can do that Dave and the bugs as well.'

'I'll admit you found Fothergill's bug but that one was a bit obvious …'

'No, honestly all I need is a bit of stuff. I have a mate who can bring it round, detectors, radio scanners, infrared cameras, phone tap monitors and other stuff. You won't even have to pay. He owes me and he'll lend it to me.'

'You can't scan police radio. It's all encrypted.'

'I know that Dave. I used to be a burglar, remember? I don't want to listen to the bluebottles but to the bugs in your office.'

'Infrared cameras?'

'You take a photo of a wall and if there's a really modern bug you can find it by the heat it gives off. Some of the most ultramodern bugs change frequency rapidly so you can't pick up the signal with a radio receiver or a police scanner. The rapid switching means they give off heat. Even so sometimes you have to spray the wall with liquid nitrogen first to bring up the contrast on the hot spots.'

Once again I was impressed by his expertise. Tony really had changed.

'Who's this friend then?'

'I don't like to say, Dave. He's a very private guy.'

I was about to say that I didn't want his criminal friends all over my office but remembered that I owed him my life. I must have been staring fixedly because he broke into my thoughts…

'It's alright Dave. We'll find the bugs and I know how to lift prints. There'll only be yours and Fothergill's inside the safe, right?'

I nodded.

'And yours, Fothergill's and mine on the desk. So we can find hers by elimination. I can lift them all onto tape. I just need to get latent powder, a brush and some tape.'

'No need, there's a complete fingerprinting kit in the storeroom. We use it when a business suspects an employee of theft.'

'So I'll handle that then?'

'OK, but then there's the business. I'll probably be killed if I go in to work but I'm not shutting up shop.'

'But your inheritance, surely …'

'Surely nothing, I've spent years building up Pimpernel and I'm not letting it slide. You'll have to answer the phone and give out the quotes for jobs. Then investigators want paying for work they've done. I'm up to date with that now but I can't afford any late payments or I'll lose my labour force.'

'Yeah, market forces Dave, law of supply and demand and all that. They have to earn their corn, we all do.'

'Yes Tony, but how am I going to keep in touch with you to tell you what prices to offer or who to put on what job?'

'Suppose I take down all the requests and promise to phone them back tomorrow. You can fill me in on who does what tonight.'

'Yes,' I agreed hesitantly. With delay like that I could see Pimpernel going down the tubes fast. The private investigation business is so competitive that a few days of inattention and you've had it. I'd just have to hope that Tony didn't cause a major catastrophe. Come to think of it, I'd already caused one myself.

'There's one other thing, Tony.'

'Yes,' he said eagerly.

'Clothes, the ones in this house are either for a giant or a human bulldozer. I need some clothes.'

25

Wednesday: Midday

By nine o'clock the wheels were in motion.

Lee and Tony left separately on foot before eight. They'd both promised to use counter-surveillance methods coming and going.

There was a moan from Lee. He complained that his contacts in the 'mugging community' would all still be in their beds until after twelve if not later.

'Fair enough, but I don't want you here,' I said. 'Think of somewhere else to go.'

He screwed his eyes up. I wasn't being nice but then who said I had to be? Did I want to spend what might be my last few hours on this earth in his company?

'He can come with me,' Tony said. 'I'll get some clothes for you and he can bring them back here.'

'OK,' I agreed after a moment's thought, 'but I don't want you hanging round here, Lee.'

'Loosen up Boss, there's some guys I know that's doing community service. The poor sods have to be up early. I can start with them.'

'Nice to see that some muggers actually get caught but good thinking Lee, you're improving.'

'Yeah, well I'll leave your clothes in the gazebo if seeing me is too heavy for you.'

'Don't be like that, Lee. You know I like you really and there's five hundred pounds waiting to prove it when you find the Fothergill woman.'

'Yeah, chill man, but this Fothergill bird, she don't sound like no African to me.'

'Just find her Lee. She may have changed her name but she can't change how she looks.'

'Yeah, maybe, maybe not.'

'Don't leave the stuff in the gazebo. Bang on the back door and I'll take the risk of looking at you. Joke, Lee …'

He nodded and his face was more relaxed than I'd seen it so far. He must need to be insulted and threatened before he felt comfortable with someone. I decided I was making progress with him.

Tony whined a bit at not being allowed to have the Beamer but I didn't want the neighbours to see too much of him and Lee. Anyway I might need it myself. I sent them off down the cinder track.

Before he left I told Tony to write down my instructions but he tapped his forehead and said he could remember what I'd said: the reconditioned brain in action.

When they'd gone my un-reconditioned brain turned to Brendan Cullen and also to my father's message about the vegetable patch. I struggled to come to a decision. To phone, or not to phone, that was the question.

Whatever I did the story seemed to end with me getting a bullet in my head. In the end I decided that if the police were as 'penetrated' as Lew Greene had claimed, Bren might be under very close observation. I couldn't afford to compromise him.

That left the problem of how to retrieve whatever was at Paddy and Eileen's cottage, in the vegetable patch specifically.

I knew my parents were friendly with a local doctor who lived a short way down the lane from them in a converted barn. I'd been introduced to him and his wife but I couldn't remember either of their names.

I knew it was one of those names derived from a trade.

Finally I was reduced to flicking through the telephone directory in the hope that the name might pop up; Slater, Smith, Thatcher, Tyler. It wasn't one of them. It was only when I went into Bob's drinks lounge that something clicked. Tom Brewer: that was the name, Doctor Tom Brewer.

I phoned directory inquiries on an unregistered mobile.

As expected, Tom Brewer wasn't listed but there was a Lindsay Brewer listed on Sheepfold Lane, West Pennine Hills. This was the lane where Paddy and Eileen lived.

I picked up the phone and then put it down. Phoning a stranger made it highly likely that I'd have to use my name, tipping the spy in the sky about my location. Dad should have been called Smith or Jones. Also was it possible that all the phones close to the Brewer's house on Sheepfold Lane were being monitored? I decided it was. In this case a touch of paranoia was more than justified.

Unfortunately the trouble with suspicion is that there's no end to it. A phone call from anywhere in Altrincham might lead the searchers to Bob's house in Ridley Close. It all just depended on how badly the security service or Lew's *certain individual* wanted to find me. The evidence was that one or both of them wanted to very badly indeed.

I shook my head. I had to get a grip. I was damned if I did and damned if I didn't. I couldn't just sit around and wait for Appleyard and Co. to sort things out. Going by the man's witness intimidation tactics they never would.

It was raining so I slung on my black hooded jacket over my ripped trousers and one of Bob's pullovers and left via the back of the house onto the cinder lane. I quickly discovered that the river running to one side was the Bollin, which also flowed near Topfield Farm. I'd no idea where the lane led but in the direction I chose civilisation wasn't far. After a stroll I came to the A538 which led me back into the centre of the small dormitory town. After my experience of looking for a coin operated phone after the helicopter attack I bought a charge card at the main post office and then found a card operated phone at the bus station.

When I rang Brewer's wife, if that's who Lindsay was, answered immediately.

'Er, this is Dave,' I said awkwardly. I was certain that even if all phones in Sheepfold Lane weren't being bugged the word 'Cunane' would be red-flagged by GCHQ. Surely there were millions more Daves in the world than Cunanes?

'I don't know if you remember me but I'm Paddy and Eileen's son. I think we met at a party at their house when Paddy had finished his major restoration but I spoke mainly to your husband Tom.'

'Of course I remember. You're …'

My heart gave a painful throb while I waited for her to drop the fatal surname but she didn't finish the sentence.

'Yes, it's good you've called. We were wondering if we should get in touch with someone about your parents. Hang on, I'll get Tom.'

I drew in a deep breath.

'Tom Brewer, here Dave,' the doctor said a moment later.

'Yes, it's Dave. I'm just a bit worried about my parents. They're not answering the phone.'

'They won't be. I saw them both trundling off on Tuesday morning at sparrow-fart,' he said breezily. 'That Volvo of theirs was loaded to the gunnels as if they were off on a long holiday. They seemed all right, but I thought it was a bit odd as Eileen was supposed to be helping Lindsay mount a local history display for the children at the local primary. Both of them have talked about nothing else for weeks. I wondered if one of your folks was ill.'

'No, they're both fine. You've put my mind at rest. I have this vision of Paddy falling off a ladder and Mum having a stroke or something when she tries to help him.'

'I should think Paddy would be the last man in England to fall off a ladder. Regular steeple-jack he is, some of the things he does on that beloved house of his, and mine too, I might add. He cleared out all our gutters last spring, remarkable for a man of his age. Still, it's unlike Eileen to let Lindsay down like this. Planning it for weeks they were.'

'Sorry, but you know how Paddy is. He probably got an idea into his head of taking a short holiday and decided to clear off without telling anyone.'

'Mmmmm, he's getting old I suppose, though you wouldn't think it if you saw him in action. Probably has his mobile switched off too?'

'Yes.'

'I wouldn't say Paddy's getting Old Timer's Disease or anything – Alzheimer's that is.'

I hate it when people explain their jokes as if I'm an idiot but I made no comment.

'Have you noticed anything out of the ordinary along the lane, people wandering around and having a look at the house and so on?'

This suggestion produced a lengthy pause.

'How do you mean?' Brewer asked eventually. 'You don't think he's in any sort of trouble do you? I know he was a high ranking copper.'

'No, just wondering if they'd locked the house up, and whatnot. You know, wondering if I might have to come up to Sheepfold Lane and secure the place.'

'No one ever comes down here. The local mad farmer puts them off, what with savage dogs and rampaging bulls, it's more than a hiker's life's worth to wander past that farmyard. Your dad and I are always at daggers drawn with Farmer Wilberforce.'

'Yeah, I know all about that. I've had one or two run-ins with that bugger.'

'There is one thing. There's a white van parked at the corner of the lane near Paddy and Eileen's place. I noticed it when I was walking our dogs on Tuesday, but there's no one in it. Probably down to our slovenly farm friends again. Your dad would make Wilberforce shift it if he was around.'

My heart missed a beat again.

I thought about the hen house at Topfield. Was the van relaying a signal from those cute little cameras they were so well equipped with?

'Thanks Tom,' I said, 'you've put my mind at rest. I'll give the old man a piece of my mind for clearing off like this. Thanks again.'

I wiped my fingerprints and then put the receiver down.

I wandered to the nearby railway station and found another BT phone box that took cards and called Jan on the mobile number she'd used last night.

'Dave! I've been waiting for you to call for hours. I hardly slept a wink last night …'

'Worrying will do no one any good.'

'It wasn't that. Junior's kicking like mad. Between you and him my insides are turning to jelly. He's bound to be a footballer. I kept thinking the worst. Are you all right?'

'You know me. Hope springs eternal, etc, etc. I think I'm making some progress with the name and when I do I'll find a solution to all this.

It's not going to be easy or quick and I won't be able to keep in touch as much as I'd like. How're the children and your mum?'

'Oh, we're all coping Dave. It's you I'm worried about. Has there been another you-know-what? You know … bang, bang.'

'No, no,' I lied.

'That's something, maybe they've forgotten about you.'

'Maybe they have, but what about you?'

'We stayed with our driver's mother last night and she just happens to have a holiday cottage, well really more like a farmhouse, to let. It's at …'

'No, don't tell me.'

'I wasn't saying the place. It's near a lake and she lets if for fishing.'

'You should take that up. It'll calm you.'

'They're still after you, aren't they?'

'I told you, I'm OK.'

'I'm coming over. I'll leave the kids with mum.'

'You're not coming because I won't tell you where I am. I can't do anything if I have to worry about you. Listen, I've got to go and I'm hanging up now because it's better to keep things short and sweet. Text me early tomorrow. I love you, love the kids, love your mum and love Man … love our dog.'

She wailed a protest but I gritted my teeth and put the phone down. Call me a cold hearted bastard if you like but the longer we spoke the more chance of detection there was. It was possible that some supercomputer was matching my voice pattern to some previous call they'd recorded.

I wanted to be out of all this.

A call to Barney Beasley and I could be on the next cabbage lorry to the west of Ireland but I knew that the people who were after me wouldn't let up. Distance meant nothing to killers who mounted attacks from helicopters. We might be safe on a remote South Sea island for a while but Ireland meant nothing to them. It was the first place they'd look. Hadn't Harry Hudson-Piggott made a big point about my Irish surname?

I wasn't being paranoid, simply aware and alert. These people really were out to get me.

I wiped the phone and shuffled off back to Ridley Close. It was gloomy and I didn't stand out in my anorak but to be on the safe side I bought an umbrella. As long as it kept raining it would shield me from CCTV cameras.

Lee arrived with my change of clothes. I'd been so pressured that I hadn't given detailed instructions. The large bag with the logo of a posh second hands clothes shop contained a charcoal coloured suit. I looked at the label. It was Austin Reed. Normally I mock the second hand shop. Brendan Cullen was always singing its praises at one time but I've never liked wearing someone else's clothes. Still, beggars can't be choosers. I tried the suit on. It was a good fit. There was also a pair of dark army style camouflage trousers, two denim shirts, a heavy, navy blue pullover and a pair of boots.

'He couldn't guess your shoe size but as your dad was a flatfoot he reckoned you could get your feet into those,' Lee explained with a cheeky grin. 'They're size ten.'

'Thanks,' I said curtly and pointed to the cinder lane.

He left without argument. Actually the boots fit well and as my shoes were soaked and leaking I put them and the camo outfit on.

Now all I had to do was pass the rest of the day until my agents came home. It was hardly James Bond. I used the computer to see if there was anything more on the killings and the helicopter crash. There wasn't. News of any interest to me was in short supply. I spent some time in the gym.

Tony was back first.

He'd located four more bugs but hadn't removed them because he thought it was better to let our listeners think they were undetected.

'Yeah, that way we can run a deception operation, you know like the Double Cross system in World War Two when the British ...'

'Turned all the German agents against their own side, yes, I know. That's very clever Tony but let's hope we don't get too clever for our own good.'

Not at all deflated, he handed me an envelope with fingerprints on tape mounted on backing cards.

'I'm ninety nine percent certain they're hers. They were inside the safe, on the desk and also on the women's sanitary towel thingy in the toilet.'

'That would be her.'

'Yeah,' he said beaming with satisfaction, 'but I haven't told you the best.'

'Go on,' I said. My heart sank. He'd found some way to wreck the firm double quick.

'My friend, the one who's ace at debugging places, well he's also a genius with a computer.'

'Yes,' I said hesitantly. His invisible friend, I thought.

'Well, he penetrated all your rival's office accountancy systems and found what prices they were offering on various jobs, so when the companies rang Pimpernel I was able to answer straight away and undercut the opposition. We're going to have more work than you've had for weeks. The volume of trade we'll be doing will more than make up for the slightly reduced profit margins on the prices I'm offering. Two insurance companies practically bit my hand off.'

'Oh God!' I said burying my head in my hands. 'Don't you think someone will A) find out you've been in their systems and B) smell a rat when Pimpernel suddenly start mopping up all the contracts?'

'I'm not stupid Dave. I quoted the same as others on some jobs, some a bit more and some a bit less and the computer programs all have these backdoors left in by the designers. It's just a matter of knowing where to look for them.'

'And you do?'

'Yes, er I mean my friend does.

'How many of your quotes were less?'

'Enough to give Pimpernel a more healthy balance sheet and I hit Schneider the worst,' he said cunningly.

'Very crafty, you knew I wouldn't mind hitting him.'

He smiled. Peter Schneider is the former employee who's now my main rival.

I thought for a minute and then laughed.

'OK, but be very careful. I don't want to inherit a fortune and then end up in court for computer fraud.'

'No chance Dave. I told you, my friend's a genius. Anyway, don't you think as there's so many bugs it might be that some of your friendly fellow detective agencies are bugging you?'

'It's possible,' I agreed. I didn't like to say that Schneider employed a top ex-military bugging expert who certainly knew how to drill through walls to plant a bug.

'And the other thing?'

'What?'

'The ex-coppers who might know something about our dear former receptionist, you were going to ask them ...'

'Yeah, I did that. She must have been pretty tight lipped with them.'

'That figures.'

'But there was one, Greg Loveland, fancies himself as a bit of a charmer; he said she told him she had a boyfriend who works in the tax office. I'd say he was trying to get into her knickers. She told him the boyfriend's name but he couldn't remember it on the spur of the moment. He says to tell you it'll come to him tonight.'

'It'll come to him when we hand him a fat brown envelope with some notes in, that's what he means.'

'Yeah, that's what I thought. Coppers, they're all bent.'

'Shut it, Tony. My dad's not bent.'

Lee arrived about an hour after Tony. To give him his due he looked exhausted. He'd contacted many of his mates in the 'mugging community' and they were going to contact others. Some had demanded cash in advance so I owed him some. There were no results today but it took time to get such worthy citizens mobilised for action and results might come in at any time in the week ahead.

Tony went out for pizzas and as the meal finished I told my two employees that their work for the day wasn't done. I also gave them both a bonus for work so far and then explained my next little job.

'What about Jaws?' Lee asked. 'Is he coming?'

'Jaws?'

'It's what he calls Clint,' Tony explained.

'Clint isn't coming. He's been working and will need his rest.'

'Good,' Lee grunted, 'he makes me nervous.'

26

Wednesday: 9 p.m. Sheepfold Cottage

As dusk was approaching the three of us climbed into Bob's BMW X5M. We were all kitted out for a walk in the country.

After long and careful thought I'd decided to ask two foreign friends to come along with us, Mr Uzi and Mr Glock. I know what I promised Jan but while I might be prepared to risk my own life by going in without a weapon I felt that I'd no right to risk Lee and Tony. As an afterthought I put the two normal sized bullet proof jackets in the backpack along with the guns.

I'd spent hours poring over an Ordnance Survey map which covered the part of the West Pennine Moors near my Dad's cottage. There's a network of lanes and field paths by which it's possible to approach Sheepfold Lane and Paddy and Eileen's cottage indirectly.

Tony drove and I sat in the back. There'd been a long discussion before we set off. We'd agreed that it would be a solo mission for me. The other two would act as look outs.

Clint stayed at home, getting on making an Airfix model of a four point five litre Bentley in his room.

I tried to socialise with Lee.

'Tell me about this Beast,' I said. 'What did you do to get up his nose and why didn't you go to the Five Oh?'

'Go to the f**king Five Oh?' he repeated swivelling round in his seat and fixing me with an angry glare. 'Do I look as if I'm f**king mad?'

'Actually, Lee, you do look a bit irate,' I said mildly.

I don't know what it was, but there was something about that cropped ginger head studded with livid red pimples like the polka dots on a tart's bikini that roused my spirit of mischief.

'Actually, Boss, I'd be a bit dead now if I started calling the Five Oh every time someone in Benchhill got on my wick.'

'That was quite a good sentence, Lee, no swear words and a touch of irony. You're improving.'

'C***!' he muttered under his breath. 'Here, Nose, stop this f**king car. I want to get out.'

'We're on a motorway, Lee,' Tony replied calmly. 'Why don't you tell Dave about the time you went out with Beast's lurcher?'

There was silence in the high performance vehicle broken only by the sound of Lee grinding his teeth and cursing under his breath.

'It was like this, Dave,' Tony began. 'Beast, his real name's … '

Lee tapped him on the back of the head at this point.

'Well, I'd best not tell you his real name. Beast's a real hard man. Everyone's shit scared of him … '

Lee tapped him again, harder this time.

'Sorry, nearly everyone in Wythenshawe's shit scared of Beast and that includes the Pigs. I reckon he'd even give Clint a hard time because he always fights dirty.'

'Yes, I got that bit,' I said when Tony lapsed into silence. 'Go on, I'm really interested.'

'OK, Lee and some of his mates were in this pub in Benchhill with Beast and they decided to arrange a little test for their lurchers. Mainly it's so Beast can show that his dog's better than anyone else's not that anyone would quarrel with him anyway, but Beast laid it on thick, how wonderful his dog was. There's this place near Sheffield where you can chase hares and things and no one bothers you. So they hire a van and go over there for the day. Beast goes in his own car.'

'We didn't *hire* the f**king van,' Lee corrected.

'Anyway, they're at this field and they have to wait for hours for Beast to arrive and the fun to start but in the end he gets there and they wait a bit more and they finally spot some hares. They all had their dogs, lined up like, Beast along with the rest.

So they let their dogs go.

Beast is drooling, saying his dog will rip a hare to pieces and like I said no one's giving him any arguments.

So off the dogs go, streaking across the field and over this little rise. A few minutes later the dogs trail back. No dead hare but … '

'But Beast's f**king mutt,' Lee broke in, 'the one we're all suppose to be amazed at, comes back last with an empty Coca Cola tin in its mouth and no one says a word. They're all pissing their pants in case Beast loses it. He has a sawn-off in the boot of his car, never goes out without it. So we get back in the van. Beast gets in his car. No one says a word, not a whisper. Then as we're pulling away I shout to him. "Your f**king dog's a wanker," I said. "It's as queer as you are."'

Lee gave a sort of triumphant chuckle at this and then lapsed into silence.

'So?' I said at last.

'On the way home Beast pulls up alongside the van and waves the sawn-off,' Tony said. 'He points at Lee and says you're f**king dead.'

'So we pull off the motorway sudden like and go home round half the side streets in Yorkshire. I had to hide for three weeks with Beast turning the place upside down to find me but he didn't and his reputation's now precisely shit,' Lee explained proudly. 'He's so mad he gets careless and the cops find him with his shooter in the car and he's off for eight years in jail and his mother sends his precious mutt to the glue factory.'

'Showed him a thing or two didn't you?' I said. 'When's he due out.'

'He'll be really old when he does,' Lee said happily. 'Did a screw, didn't he? Put the bugger's eye out so he's in for another ten in Wakefield Jail.'

By this time we were going through Bolton and approaching the road to the West Pennine moors. When we reached the fork in the road I didn't take the direct route to Sheepfold Lane by way of Pennine Road. Instead I took the Turton Road and turned off towards the Pennine Hills Golf Club. According to the map there was a right of way across the golf club leading to Sheepfold Lane.

My parents' cottage stands on one side of a shallow valley. The golf course is on the other slope about two miles away: a series of low, red tiled buildings. I hoped to approach the cottage from the rear where the sloping ground forms my mother's vegetable garden. I wanted to avoid alerting the opposition. I hoped they wouldn't be watching the back way in.

There was a crescent moon and I had a torch but first I had to find the right of way. The 'Public Footpath' sign had been broken, presumably by the golfers. The post was still there though. We only found it and the bramble covered stile that marked the start of the path on our second slow pass along the lane.

It was just before nine. I was more determined to recover Paddy's message than ever. My hopes were high. Did he know who the *'certain individual'* was?

My cunning plan was that Lee would stay with the car, ready to be our getaway driver. Tony Nolan, the reformed burglar, would come with me to within sight of the vegetable patch to point out various dangers like hidden cameras. I had the submachine gun and both bullet proof jackets in a backpack.

We made fair speed across the course although the golf club had made efforts to obscure the right of way by planting quick growing shrubs directly on the path. As we went on I could make out lights at Wilberforce's farm and then the dark outline against a lighter background of the cottage.

The nearer we got the more difficult it became. We had to cross one of Wilberforce's fields and although there were no cattle there were several pieces of rusting agricultural machinery lying about which caused detours.

We stopped about two hundred yards away from my parents' property while Tony gave the old place the once over. The white van was still there. He stared at the house for ten minutes until I began to get impatient.

'Nothing moving, Boss, but I don't like it. There's too many places they could be hiding and why would they leave that van in the lane if they weren't keeping the place under constant surveillance?'

'That's the way they operate Tony. These guys aren't hands on. They're probably half a mile away waiting to see me enter the house on their little screen then … ka-boom! But I'm not going to, am I? I can be in and out of the vegetable patch in a few seconds.'

'I still don't like it. It's too quiet and anyway in this line of work once you suspect someone's waiting for you, even if it's only a one in a hundred chance that they are, you stay clear.'

'Tony, if the Judge gave my dad some hint about who's behind all this shit I'm in it's worth taking a risk to find it. It might take us weeks to track down either one of the Fothergills.'

'Yeah, there is that but if you find his name and still get blown away it won't do you much good will it?'

After more whispered discussion we decided to crawl as far as the edge of the garden so that Tony could inspect the place at closer range.

When we reached the dry stone wall that marked the boundary we crouched behind it. It was dead quiet except for the occasional sound of traffic on the distant road.

'Anything?' I asked after he'd spent another ten minutes staring intently.

'I can't see anything but then I wouldn't, would I?'

'I'm going.'

He gripped my arm. 'I say no,' he said. 'This smells like a trap.'

'I have to go.'

'You still don't trust me, do you?'

'It's not that. I must find the truth. I think Lew left his killer's name for my dad to find.'

'That doesn't compute, Dave. A copper like your dad would have made the name known.'

'Not if it's some really powerful person and he thought he'd be arrested or worse if he opened his mouth. That could be why he legged it so fast. Listen, I've got stuff in here,' I said, slipping the backpack off my shoulders. I pulled out the bullet proof jackets, handing one to him.

'Put it on,' I urged. 'It might give some protection is there is an explosion.'

For a few moments there was the sound of Velcro. There was another noise I couldn't quite make out. I put it down to insects.

'There's this as well,' I said, handing him the Uzi and two spare magazines.

'This is Bob's int it?' he said, holding it very gingerly. 'You know we'll both get five years minimum if it's the police waiting for us?'

'OK, leave it and go back to the car.'

By way of reply he checked the fit of the magazine and then slid back the bolt back and cocked the weapon.

'In for a penny ...' he muttered fatalistically.

A dark cloud cloaked the moon as I prepared to climb over the wall.

We both pulled on the masks I'd improvised from a pair of Tammy's tights. Her perfume lingered on them but they did the job.

There was a light breeze blowing in our faces and carrying faint but pungent odours from the distant farmyard. The joys of country living, I still haven't been able to understand why Paddy and Eileen moved to the country after a life in peaceful suburbs.

I put my foot onto a projecting stone preparing to hoist myself over the wall.

'Wait,' Tony whispered clutching my arm. 'I think I heard something.'

I slumped back to the ground.

I listened intently but there was nothing.

'It's probably an insect,' I said dismissively.

I was about to climb up again when I heard the noise. It was a curious 'plink, plink,' very quiet, barely detectable like large drops of water falling into a water butt. There was a subtle electronic quality to the sound.

We listened again and after an interval the sound was repeated.

'Time the gaps,' Tony whispered to me.

I did, craning my neck to see my watch.

The interval was exactly and unvaryingly fifteen seconds, so it wasn't a natural sound.

'There are people there. They're hiding in the house like I told you,' Tony whispered. 'We'd best be off.'

With a deadening feeling I knew he was right but I had to cling onto something. Paddy had left a message in the vegetable patch. Having made it this far I didn't feel like slinking back to Altrincham without making an attempt.

'What's causing the 'plink plink' sound?' I asked.

'I don't know but it could be some sort of detector, a microwave barrier like radar. You know, it sweeps from side to side in fifteen seconds.'

'But the noise, that's a dead giveaway.'

'You didn't hear it. They'd have got you.'

He was right but that was no comfort.

'Whoever's operating it probably hasn't set it up properly,' he continued. 'They have these small portable T/R sets ...'

'T/R?'

'Transmit and receive. There'll be reflectors to bounce the signal back to the receiver.'

'Oh, yeah,' I said weakly. My mouth tasted as if I'd been drinking acid.

Feeling completely blocked my hand crept to the butt of the Glock pistol that I was wearing on my belt. Should I go over the fence, death or glory style with gun in hand? That thought died swiftly. Killers who planted bombs and used helicopters were hardly likely to be impressed by one man with a Glock. The image of Claverhouse's minders hanging upside down and smashed to pieces in the cab of the 'security van' flooded into my mind.

No, the 'Battle of Mrs Cunane's Vegetable Patch' was never going to happen.

Another sound began reaching my ears, the faint lowing of cattle.

There were cows in a field adjacent to the farm. It wasn't the next field to us, but the next after that and when the clouds cleared for a moment I could see that there were two gates between the cows and us.

'Suppose we let those cows come through here,' I whispered.

'They'll disturb the microwave barrier and set the alarm off. The confusion while they identify what's causing the commotion might give you a few seconds to dig up whatever's hidden, if it's still there, that is.'

'Thanks for the encouragement, Tony.'

'Listen, Dave, I know what you're asking. You want me to let those cows loose but I'm telling you I've never been closer to a cow than the milk they made me drink when I was a kid and I hated the stuff. You should have brought Clint.'

'Should have, would have. Will you do it? You can pick up one of these branches lying around and whack them over the rump with it. They'll soon move.'

'Yeah, and trample me to death. No thanks.'

There was a frustrated silence punctuated only by our heavy breathing for a few moments and then Tony spoke again.

'Why don't you do the cows and I'll go for the message?'

'You're on,' I whispered. I passed him the Glock and took the Uzi off him.

He handed the Glock back.

'It's no use to me, Dave. I need both hands free.'

We both cautiously raised our heads above the level of the wall. There was no volley of shots and after a few minutes the moon provided a glimmer of light. It was extremely hard to see the exact spot where Eileen had been digging, particularly as I was looking from another direction but eventually I made out what I thought was the place. Eileen, or more likely Paddy, had left a fork stuck in the soil at that spot. Eileen was too careful with her tools to leave them lying around.

'Can you see that fork?' I whispered. 'It'll be around there in a tin or a bottle or something.'

'Fork as in knife and fork?'

'No Tony, as in garden fork. You know, the Two Ronnies ... fork handle?'

'Yeah, fork handle.'

'That bit of wood sticking out of the ground is the handle.'

'And what do I do when I get there?' he whispered.

'Use the fork to find it.'

I set off, awkwardly bending low behind the dry stone wall. My knees were giving me hell and my thighs were shrieking about cramp. Maybe Mother Nature was warning me that my days of crawling around in damp fields were drawing to a close. When I reached the empty field I waited until the moon was hidden and then cautiously opened the gate. For once something on Wilberforce's Farm worked well. The gate was well oiled and opened without a sound. Then, keeping as low as I could, I dashed across the field to the gate holding the cattle back.

It also opened easily.

'So far, so good,' I thought.

There was even a handy branch to serve as a cattle prod. I went farther into the field and set to work. There were two more things I didn't know. First, Wilberforce's cattle are always frisky because he doesn't feed them properly and second, several of the cows had recently calved. Their defensive instincts were especially sharp.

I'd hardly laid the stick across the first cow before they were all up and milling about and making frantic noises. Tony's fear of being trampled suddenly seemed very real. I ran for the gate. The cows followed, moving surprisingly swiftly for such ungainly animals. Suddenly it felt as if I was running for my life.

The lowing herd was winding swiftly o'er the lea.

Their motion must have registered on the microwave barrier. I couldn't see Tony and decided he'd panicked at the sight of the runaway herd bearing down on him. He was probably halfway across the golf course.

I turned to follow him and at that precise instant the blinding halogen beams of the white van's headlights shone out from the lane revealing Tony Nolan scrabbling in the vegetable patch. There were shouts from the cottage and then the crack of nine millimetre pistols being fired.

Ignoring the cattle rushing by, I whipped out the Uzi and began firing back. I couldn't see who I was firing at. I just blazed away in the general direction of the van. I got lucky: one of the headlights blinked out.

Tony put up an impressive performance. Although I huddled against the stonework and could hear the zip of bullets going past me Tony didn't fling himself to the ground. Instead he ran towards me, twisting and turning with balletic grace as if he had some avoidance system for bullets.

I don't know whether it was my covering fire or his dodging ability but within seconds he was over the wall and crouching beside me.

'We're done,' he gasped, waving his arm towards the golf course.

'We'll never get across all that open ground.'

Bullets ricocheted off the stones. The way back to Lee was across rising ground offering no cover and they knew exactly where we were.

I was about to agree when circumstances suddenly changed.

With a clattering roar a police helicopter swept overhead. Its searchlight beam played not on us but onto Sheepfold Cottage. There was a blaring noise of police sirens. Their banshee wails counterpointed the roar of the helicopter and the demented bellowing of cattle like an infernal orchestra.

I could barely make out shouted instructions coming from the helicopter.

I raised my eyes an inch above the stonework.

Police cars were jolting down Sheepfold Lane, some coming the long way round past Tom Brewer's barn, others the shorter route through Wilberforce Farm. There were many of them. It was like a copper's motor rally. My mouth dropped open for a minute. This couldn't be for my benefit.

There were three men at the back of the cottage, caught in the overhead beam. They seemed paralysed.

Then my instinct of self-preservation came back to life.

'Come on,' I prompted Tony. 'This is our chance. Let's get among these cattle and across the fields.'

'But it's the police. You said we were up against some sort of private army of rogue security people.'

'OK, you stay and explain yourself if you like, but I'm off.'

I moved and he immediately followed, clinging onto my arm.

The noise and lights maddened the cows but they were no longer running anywhere because there was nowhere for them to go. They were milling about, turning round in circles and tangling with the abandoned machinery. I led Tony through the mêlée using the stick I was still clutching to fend off any that came too close. I couldn't risk taking my eyes away from the cattle for a backward glance at the cottage. We reached the field boundary uninjured by bullet, horn or hoof, and then went on through into the beckoning darkness beyond.

Escape seemed possible.

Then the helicopter began making systematic sweeps over the field we'd just vacated. It was very low but there were no high voltage cables hanging over these fields. It was still some way off scanning the herd of escaped cattle but inevitably the pool of dazzling light started moving towards us. Unlike the attack in the Mersey Valley this bastard was definitely a police helicopter. They certainly had thermal imaging technology on board.

I felt sick. We were certain to be caught. I must get rid of the firearms but between running uphill through muddy ground and looking for the best path back to the BMW I just hadn't time to dump them.

Tony seemed to have gone crazy. Instead of making for the next gate he was veering off at ninety degrees. There was a hollow in the ground there. He flung himself down. I couldn't understand what he was doing.

'Get over here,' he screamed. 'It's our only chance.'

I was torn. It might be better to separate. If I ran on I might reach the next dry stone wall and shelter behind it. However deep his hollow was it wouldn't shelter us from the electronic eye above.

But he'd been right too often for me to desert him. I ran to his position. The helicopter was still the full width of a field away. I reached Tony.

'We've got to get in there. It's our only hope,' he said.

The clouds slid away from the moon and by the faint light I could see a smooth surface entirely filling the dip. It was a dew pond.

'Get in!' Tony yelped. 'I spotted it on our way down.'

Intended for watering the cattle on these upland slopes, like all the equipment on Wilberforce's farm this was in disrepair. The overflow outlet had been allowed to block up and the surface was covered in a nice layer of scum. It might not be much use to the dairy cattle but it would shelter us.

Noise from the engine increased. Holding hands we waded into the pond which was about three feet deep in the centre. God it was cold! I lay down with just my nose above the surface. Almost immediately the area was bathed in light from the helicopter. I submerged into the thick slimy mess. The dazzling beam seemed to hang above us for minutes but it could only have been thirty seconds or so before the searching aircraft flew on.

I came up for air.

The aerial search had moved on into the next field some way beyond our position. I started to climb out but Tony pulled me back.

'Stay here,' he insisted. 'They always do another sweep to be sure they haven't missed anyone. It's standard operating procedure.'

I was shivering violently but I slumped down beside him and sure enough, five minutes later the air-borne coppers swept over us again and once again we escaped. Satisfied that the field was free of hostiles they passed to the other side of Wilberforce's farm. We were free to move.

We plodded uphill in silence. It took a great effort to put one water-logged foot in front of another but I did and we put half a mile between us and the police search.

As we reached the easier going of the golf course it was obvious that the rumpus across the valley hadn't gone unnoticed in the clubhouse. Doors and windows were open, sending long shafts of light across the open ground in front of the building. It only required someone to see us and call the police and we'd be back to dodging that spotlight again.

Moving slowly now, we avoided the illuminated areas and at long last the BMW was in view. Lee was parked in the right direction with the doors open. He'd done this sort of thing before.

27

Wednesday: Car park, Pennine Hills Golf Club 9.50 pm

'What the f**k!' Lee cursed when he saw us.

We were covered in clinging mud and slime from head to foot.

'There's no way you're getting in this car. Bob'll kill me.'

'Oh, come on, he's not as bad as Beast. We'll have it valeted.'

I did take my boots off but I could feel my body slipping into hypothermia and stripping off my soaking clothes would have to wait.

We both got in the back.

'Don't turn the ignition on,' I told Lee. 'Roll down the hill and go into the golf club car park.'

The hill was quite steep and as soon as he released the brake we were moving.

On the way up I'd noticed that there were other four wheel drive cars including BMWs parked in the golf club parking area which was some distance from the club house. The police would almost certainly have someone on the exit road if they knew their business which, judging by the success of their surprise appearance at Sheepfold Cottage, they did. I hoped to slip into the car park and hide amongst similar vehicles until the heat died down.

'We can be away from here in seconds,' Lee snarled. 'The Fuzz'll never keep up with us in this rig.'

He was itching for a high-speed chase.

I wasn't.

'Listen, Steve McQueen, this isn't the Great Escape. We're going to hide in that car park and then slip away from here when everybody else goes home.'

'F**king weird, that's what you are, Boss. And what's with the black mask and the machine gun? Are you in fancy dress as Tom Cruise?'

'Camouflage,' Tony said. 'Do what you're told, Lee. They've got a helicopter so it doesn't matter how fast this car can go. We'll never shake them.'

Lee's words reminded me to stow the weapons and jackets away in the backpack.

We slipped into the car park and parked in the middle of a line of large vehicles. He switched the heater full on and very gradually we thawed out. As we warmed a ripe odour of cow shit filled the interior.

The fuss gradually died down. The golfers closed their doors and windows and went back to their drinking. The helicopter light blinked off but the machine was still somewhere in the area because we could hear it.

As my immediate discomforts eased I had time to think.

It looked as if the regular police were working hand in glove with the opposition. The white van and the waiting men must be Appleyard's MI5 crew. If they were my chances of surviving the week were dramatically reduced. As the idea passed through my mind doubt grew. Would Appleyard's men have opened fire on Tony like that? There'd been no warning. They must have been more of Lew's *certain individual's* men. How many of them had I put down so far? He must have access to an army.

Gradually our breathing returned to normal. Lee and Tony were as alert as feral cats, their heads constantly turning, their eyes and ears seeking the first hint of police.

They didn't arrive. The minutes ticked past, first ten p.m. then ten thirty.

One or two golfers got in their cars and drove away.

'Let's go now,' Lee said impatiently. 'It stinks like a shit house in here.'

'Wait till the club closes and then we'll go,' I said.

'He's right,' Tony said. 'They might be waiting at the bottom of the road. We'll go with the flow. They can't stop everyone.'

'If they get a sniff of you two they'll know you were up to something,' Lee grumbled.

'So we wait until there's less chance of being stopped,' Tony said.

Time passed slowly. There was silence in the car broken only by the occasional scratching sound from Lee as he put in a bit of action with his pimples.

'A spliff would be great now,' he said to Tony.

'Forget it,' I said firmly.

He let out a long sigh.

'You're sad, man, real sad,' he commented, 'boring.'

I didn't reply.

I wondered at his words.

Sad … yes, but boring? Never! On Sunday evening I'd gone to bed as a fully paid up member of the 'reasonably well-off' classes. Now I was a fugitive, coated in filth like a freshly exhumed corpse. I hoped Jan and the children were snugly tucked up in their nice farmhouse in the remotest, most inaccessible corner of the West of Ireland.

'Here,' Tony said, 'I got this. Is it what you wanted?'

He pressed a small screw capped jar into my hand.

I felt faint. Then the blood rushed to my head.

'You got it,' I said numbly. 'I'd given it up for lost. Why didn't you give it to me before?'

'In all the excitement I forgot I'd got it. Right against the fork it was, just under the dirt.'

I held the jar in my hand. I could see there was a piece of paper inside it.

'Well, go on then. Open it. Put me out of my misery,' Tony continued jauntily. 'What's in it that's so important? The name of the next Grand National winner or the winning numbers for the Euro Lottery roll-over?'

I unscrewed the cap, took out a small folded piece of paper, and, shielding the beam of my torch under my coat, I read the message it held.

'David,

I saw the most horrible scene in my life a few hours ago and I've seen some shockers in my time. If there's a hell on earth, that's what those bastards put poor Lew through. He was stretched across a table in his study and they'd tortured him and … well, I'm sure you know by now how they killed him.

It looks as if Lew was able to leave us a clue before he was killed. He must have been tied up with his hands behind his back but he managed to scratch some letters on the table in his study with his ring. It was found when they moved the body. I was present and they didn't want me to see but I did. The letters were M · O · L · O and then the final letter was hard to make out. It could have been a C, an S or even a Z. All the letters were written in capitals. None of the MI5 people or police here had any idea what it means but I'm passing it onto you in the hope that your unconventional eye may see something we can't. They killed him on that table, so the word must have meant something important to him.

Keep safe,
Dad'

My heart sank. I'd been hoping for a name, even an address. I was too stunned to speak.

'Go on,' Tony muttered. 'What does it say? I'm entitled to know.'

'It's some letters which Lew scratched onto the table as they were torturing him. M · O ·L · O· and a fifth letter which could be either a C, an S or a Z.'

'Let me see,' he said impatiently. 'I think I've earned the right.'

'Certainly,' I said passing him the note and the torch.

'I don't think it's an English surname, there's Moloney which is Irish. It's either a code for something or it's an acronym. You know, like FBI or IRA,' he added for Lee's benefit.

'Have you heard of an acronym like that?'

'No, but I know where to look it up. Then again it could be Molos, or Moloc, or Moloz. They all sound like names of places.'

'Or the poor bloke didn't have the time to finish what he was writing,' Lee said. 'Torture, it's inhuman. It would be worth catching the bastard who did it and see how he likes it if we offer him a dose of the same.'

It was dark inside the car but I raised my eyebrows in surprise. There was more to Lee than I'd thought.

'Was he religious?' he continued.

'He was very religious. He disapproved of me for living in sin until I got married.'

'Oh, one of them nutters,' he muttered. 'You know I'm not religious, though my gran was, but if I was tied on a table waiting to be butchered like an animal and I knew there was no way I was going to escape I'd start thinking about religion, God and all that stuff.'

'Yes,' I agreed.

'Hold on,' Tony said urgently. 'Lee, you just reminded me of something. Moloch is a name in the Bible. The bible was one of the first books I read when I came round after the meningitis. If the word he wrote was MOLOC that would be the same.'

'Did you get religion then?' Lee jeered.

'No, no. Well … I did … sort of. Bloody hell, Lee, I nearly died. You just said you'd give it a try if they had you strapped down for torture. They practically had me measured up for a coffin but anyway, this Moloch was a cruel pagan god that the people used to sacrifice children to.'

'Yeah, rubbish, that's all that is. All made up fairy stories.'

'No Lee, there's evidence of child sacrifice in the Middle East. The Carthaginians used to sacrifice their first born sons. They've dug up the bones.'

'That's inhuman,' Lee said.

'It is, but if you were a Middle Eastern terrorist that might be a name you would use for one of your operations.'

Tony cleared his throat as if to add something but then lapsed into silence. We all did.

Eventually the clubhouse revelry came to an end and the golfing fraternity piled into their cars in a rush. There were a lot more people than cars so presumably some of them had stayed sober enough to drive for their friends. They knew that police were lurking at the end of the lane.

We joined the stream and sure enough there was a parked police car when we pulled out onto the main road. We held our collective breaths but the flashing lights didn't come on and we were soon on the motorway to Manchester with Lee driving cautiously.

No one spoke on the rest of the journey.

28

Wednesday 11.30 p.m. — Thursday morning

When we reached 12 Ridley Close, Altrincham, I made Lee and Tony open the garage and clear a space for the X5M and then drove straight in. I'd briefly forgotten my paranoia and didn't check before approaching the house. Things couldn't get any worse, so to hell with it.

I went straight in just as I'd walked into the trap at Sheepfold Cottage or rather sent Tony into it.

Clint was crouched over his model and didn't even look up when I greeted him. I decided not to take offence. He can be like a surly teenager at times.

I went to the bathroom and stripped off without looking at myself in the mirror. Under an intense shower the mud and slime disappeared. I stood under the shower with the temperature on max for a full ten minutes before I began to feel normal again.

I went down and made myself a cup of coffee.

There was no sign of Lee and Tony apart from a pile of Tony's soiled clothing which he'd dumped next to the washing machine. I wasn't intending to play mother for him but I supposed I was under some sort of obligation so I scooped the stuff into the machine and went upstairs to retrieve my own foul smelling rags.

I set the machine on prewash and turned to my coffee cup. It looked lonely sitting on the table by itself so I fortified it with a hefty slug of whisky.

That helped to calm my nerves.

I held my hands in front of my face. There was no tremor but all the same I knew I was badly rattled. It's one thing doing detection: following the *Detective's Handbook* like a good PI and feeling your way to the solution clue by clue. It's quite another thing battering your head against a brick wall while unknown ruffians try to kill you. I'd been counting on finding out the name of the leader of the opposition and all I'd come up with was an obscure biblical reference. For all I knew my ultra-religious godfather had come up with the name of a monster out of sheer terror while they worked him over.

No, that idea was unworthy. Lew was a brave man. The name meant something to him if only I could discover what. I wracked my brain for words to fit in an acronym; Manchester, Mosque, Muslim, Murder. It could be anything and I'd go crazy trying to come up with a solution. My best bet was to stick with what Tony's reconditioned brain had come up with. So MOLOCH from the bible it was.

I had a quick look round the house for a bible. It wasn't the sort of thing I expected Bob and Tammy to have lying around which just shows how mistaken you can be about the people you think you know well. There was a bible prominently displayed on a shelf under a window in the drinks lounge. The book plate announced that it was awarded to Tamsin Marsden for first place in RE. Perhaps Bob had positioned it there to remind her to be nice to Clint. It was well thumbed too.

I got the chapter and verse numbers for Moloch off Google and read through each one carefully.

My conclusions weren't reassuring. Most of the mentions related to evil kings who'd gone to the Valley of Hinnom outside Jerusalem and *passed their sons and daughters through the fire*. By which was meant that they'd sacrificed them to the gods of the Phoenicians and Canaanites; burned them in a fiery furnace while musical instruments were played to drown out the screams … lovely, jubbly! It was one of the ugliest things in the Old Testament. The Valley of Hinnom was also known as *Gehenna* which is appropriately translated as Hell in the King James Bible.

A fairy story made up to frighten old ladies?

I didn't think so. Excavations at the Phoenician settlement of Carthage had uncovered evidence of child sacrifice and the Romans made a great song and dance about Phoenician child sacrifice as an excuse for their own genocide against the Carthaginians.

Why would Lew have devoted his last moment of life to scratching the word Moloch if it was meaningless? Was he telling us that his killers were men who intended to destroy children though fire?

258

Sickeningly, I remembered that they'd attempted to do just that to my family and had nearly roasted me alive in the 'security van'.

Was a terror plot emerging? A plot to murder children by fire?

My mind recoiled. I tried to think of other more mundane explanations of that horrid word.

Suppose Lew had been trying to write the words Molly Claverhouse before he died. Was it possible Paddy had mistaken what must have been a barely legible scrawl? Was Claverhouse the individual Lew feared?

That didn't make sense.

Lew had spoken of a man, not a woman and anyway, Molly Claverhouse had very nearly perished in the van.

I went to the backdoor.

The faint aroma of marijuana wafted up to me. My assistants were communing with the gnomes at the bottom of the garden. I left them to it.

When I looked in to say goodnight Clint had gone to bed without a word. He was sulking because I hadn't taken him on the expedition to the West Pennines.

I went up and slept badly and woke early with a strong feeling of oppression and impending doom.

The events at Sheepfold Cottage spooled through my mind like a silent film.

It was the arrival of the police so promptly which jarred. Were they hand in glove with the enemy? I had to know. If they were, I'd better arrange passage with Barney Beasley's clandestine travel agency. Did he have lorry-drivers going to Brazil or Cuba? Or was the far side of the Moon the only place I'd be safe?

I'd no evidence except for the events last night and the suppression of the facts about the attack on the 'security van'. If the criminal intelligence files were available to MI5 then they must be available to moles in MI5. There was bound to be an open file on Bob Lane which mentioned his habit of frequent changes of address. Couple that with my name and the resources of the police and security service and they might pay a visit at any minute.

I was so jumpy that I took out the Glock pistol I'd tried to arm Tony with last night. I'd slept with it under my pillow. I cleaned it carefully and checked that the action was working. Should I carry the gun round with me during the day?

I decided that it would do me no good at all and put the gun back in the hollow carving. As for the Uzi I cleaned that, reloaded it and replaced it in its hiding place.

I tried to think my way through another day.

I opened the curtains and scanned the street. Once again there were no parked vehicles. I looked at the houses, studying each one carefully. All the ones with a view of Number 12 had their upstairs and downstairs curtains tightly drawn, and no wonder, it was another miserable rainy day.

I wasn't under surveillance.

Lew's killers knew nothing about Bob Lane. I was safe for the moment. I repeated the words to myself like a mantra.

As I went down I passed Clint's room. There was a steady rumble of snoring coming from it. Wouldn't it be nice to be really imperturbable? Not a care in the world beyond getting the latest DS game or model kit, that was Clint. It was a sign of how low I was at that moment that I could be jealous of Clint.

I went into the kitchen and grabbed a quick cup of coffee. It was just after seven a.m. There was no point in rousing the deadly duo, or Clint for that matter. I rummaged through the coats Bob had carelessly piled up in the utility room. Everything of his was either too wide or too short for me. At the bottom of the heap I found an ancient green Barbour jacket complete with attached hood which wouldn't look too bizarre if I folded my arms and gathered it up.

I went out through the backdoor to the cinder lane pocketing up the remains of spliffs on the way. Once away from the shelter of the trees I was pelted by driving rain. It was torrential. I held the hood over my head with one hand and kept the floppy coat closed with the other, telling myself that I looked like a professional gardener on his way to work.

There were other people moving about on foot but they were

preoccupied with fighting off the weather. I attracted no curiosity and made it into the centre of the small town and the phone box I'd used before.

Tom Brewer picked up at once.

'Sorry to call so early Tom, it's Dave again. Are my parents back at the cottage?'

'Dave, the very man I wanted to talk to,' he said in the tones of someone who has momentous news to impart. 'All hell broke loose round here last night. You should have seen it. I haven't enjoyed anything so much since the last time I was at the Cabbage Patch.'

'A proper scrap was it? What about my parents,' I asked anxiously.

'It was better than anything you'll ever see at Twickenham, a real three ringed circus and Paddy will be disappointed to have missed it. Your folks weren't involved in any way, shape or form. I can reassure you on that.'

He obviously wasn't going to be dissuaded from telling me what had happened in his own way so I let him rant on.

'You know I mentioned that white van to you? Parked at the corner? Lindsay and I kept an eye on it for you. Lindsay swore she saw someone moving in the house but I, fool that I am, discounted her suspicions. She's at a certain age you know. But then we saw that someone had moved the van up to the side of the house. I knew it wasn't you or Paddy, so I got in touch with the local gendarmerie. For once they got their thumbs out of their tight little arseholes. They put up a most impressive show, I can tell you.'

'What happened?' I asked impatiently.

'Softly, softly, catchee monkee,' he replied. 'They sent a young man round to my house disguised as a meter reader, gas company van and everything. He told us they suspected cattle rustling.'

'What?'

'Yes, there's been quite a bit of it recently and they suspected the gang was preparing to remove Wilberforce's herd, not that that would have upset me, but the law's the law. We can't have people carrying on as if cattle rustling had never gone out of fashion. The young fellow observed and then they laid on a major operation. We were forbidden to go out, and the Wilberforces were held incommunicado. Heavens, if Old Man Wilberforce had been allowed out he'd have had the whole Wilberforce tribe on the qui vive, there's hundreds of them you know, and they'd have lynched the rustlers when they caught them.'

'The police caught them?'

'Oh yes, the rustlers had the cattle on the move but didn't have time to bring up their cattle truck. The police came down on them like the proverbial ton of bricks: helicopters, cars, vans, dogs, they had the lot. We saw the prisoners being carted off.'

'Prisoners?'

'Yes, there were at least six by my count. Hmm, rewind that … I saw three with my own eyes. Well dressed too, some of them.'

'So it was an exciting night? Is the cottage all right? Do I need to come up?'

'No, it's all secure. One funny thing though, I was just this minute watching the local BBC news expecting to hear about the police triumph but there's been nothing so far. I thought they might have wanted an interview as we're local.'

'You'd think so,' I agreed.

'Anyway, can't hang around chewing the fat with you, old boy, much as I'd like to. I've got patients to see and prescriptions to write.'

'Thanks for your time,' I said hanging up.

I trudged back to Ridley Close through the sheeting rain. I felt a lot happier. Providing Clattergob Tom with an audience was a small price to pay for the knowledge that the boys in blue weren't hand in glove with Mr Big.

Or were they?

Was some local chief inspector even now being reamed out for botching an intelligence service operation?

No, I decided it wasn't possible. To have laid on a helicopter and scores of men the local coppers would have involved higher authority and if the *certain individual's* men had infiltrated the police to that extent then the operation would have been called off before it started.

Moles: that was the answer. There was a mole or two in the police but they weren't in charge.

I was still anxious. There were so many intangibles involved but I felt I was safe for the moment. As I went along the cinder path dodging pools of water and trying to calculate my next move I was more careless than last night.

When I opened the back garden gate and entered the Ridley Close address I wasn't looking left or right and when a burly man leapt out from behind a tree and pinioned me from behind I was taken by surprise. Fear and panic leant me strength and I wriggled in the loosely fitting Barbour like a snake shedding its skin. I dropped to my knees, swinging round low to tackle my assailant. I caught him behind the thighs and pulled him to the ground and, snatching up a jagged piece of white rock from the lawn edge, I raised it to bash his head in.

'Dave, you bloody idiot, it's me,' the man yelled hoarsely.

My rage and fear were so overpowering that I almost continued the downward stroke. I deflected the heavy stone at the last instant missing Brendan Cullen's head by millimetres.

'You're the bloody idiot,' I gasped. 'What's the idea of creeping up on me like this?'

'You're a hard man to get hold of, Cunane,' he said, 'a real slippery customer. Help me up.'

I roughly yanked him to his feet. He wasn't wearing one of his Armani suits but his dark raincoat and jeans were splattered with mud and soil.

'How did you find me?' I demanded. 'Where did you leave your car? Are the rest of your merry men on their way?'

'Questions, questions, let me get my breath.'

'I need to know.'

'Hold on. Don't go into full Cunane panic mode. You're safe. I took precautions. Invite me in for a cup of coffee.'

He tried to smile but the expression on his whiskery face came out more like a scowl. It must have been a nasty moment when the stone was raised over his head.

I let myself into the kitchen and he followed me. There were signs that Clint had made his own breakfast, a large box of cereal was open on the table, six-pint milk bottle left out. Of the other two there was no trace, not even the characteristic stink of marijuana. I was grateful for that. There were some things I didn't want to discuss with Bren.

I filled the kettle and set out two coffee cups without saying a word. There was only instant available which was good enough for me and good enough for my visitor. The kettle boiled and I filled the cups.

'Milk, sugar?' I asked coldly, I knew well enough what he normally took in coffee.

'Haven't you got something stronger to put in it?' he replied. 'It isn't every day I start work by having my head nearly smashed to pieces by a friend.'

Bob's Glenfiddich was on the side. I could have gone upstairs for the Bell's whisky I'd anaesthetised myself with last night but I didn't feel like giving Bren the run of the house.

I poured a stiff slug into both our cups.

'Malt whisky in coffee, purists would take that as an insult to good whisky, Dave,' he said picking his mug and taking an appreciative sip.

'Shall I go and get that rock and bash your head in again?' I asked. 'A) How the hell did you find me and B) can I expect a visit from your esteemed colleagues?'

'The answer to A) is that it was child's play to someone who knows you as well as I do and to B) is, no, you can't.'

'Explain.'

'A call to Bob Lane's club told me he'd suddenly gone on holiday with the titillating Ms Tammy Marsden … and how long do you think that's going to last by the way?'

'It'll last a long time if Tammy's anything to do with it but I'm not sure she'll ever persuade Bob to dump Clint and if she pushes him to choose between them he might just give her her cards.'

'Right, anyway, that's how I found you.'

'The club gave you this address?' I said incredulously.

'No, like I said, I know Bob wouldn't have suddenly gone off without making arrangements for Clint and who would he make the arrangements with … '

264

'Even so … '

'Listen, Dave, there are people down at HQ who think you're the most heartless crim in Manchester but your few friends like me know what a sentimental jerk you really are. I guessed that if Clint was still around he'd be with you. A call to that farm he works at gave me this number. I got the address from that.'

'I suppose it's all round HQ now?'

'Of course not, what do you take me for?'

'A senior officer in the counter-terrorist squad.'

'I am and that's partly why I'm here. The other reason is the shoot-out at your father's place. I had to know that you're all right.'

'I am.'

'Clint?'

'He wasn't there.'

His eyes widened in surprise.

'So who do you have helping you? The dogs tracked at least two men across that golf course. I was sure it was you and Clint and that you were looking for another safe house.'

'Oh, I'd run to Daddy's house to hide from the bad men?'

'So what were you doing there, Dave?'

I looked at him in frustration.

He'd trapped me into saying more than I wanted to.

I explained about Paddy's message.

'That was a pretty wild stunt even for you, stampeding a herd of cattle, but then you always were a cowboy.'

'Thanks Bren. I discovered the word MOLOCH and a fat lot of good it's done me. I'm sure you've already heard all about it.'

His genial expression disappeared. He took a deep gulp of his coffee.

'The old judge's dying clue, eh? I wondered if it was something like that. I saw Paddy getting a good eyeful. I can tell you that that little word has got everybody in a major panic. COBRA's in almost permanent session.'

'Cobra?'

'The Cabinet crisis committee, though they're about as much use as a chocolate fire-guard. This is being dealt with at the highest levels, 10 Downing Street, Brussels and Washington.'

'So?' I muttered, refusing to be impressed. 'What do you think the word means?'

'Moloch was a Middle Eastern pagan idol …'

'Yeah, yeah I know all that. Been there, got the T-shirt.'

'Smart arse! Best opinion is that this gang of fanatics is on the verge of an atrocity involving children. Does the word mean anything special to you? Did Sir Lewis ever talk about it? I believe he was very religious, the house is like a shrine, maybe he thought you'd understand the reference.'

'Oh yeah, my head's never out of a Bible. I've no more idea than you. The only thing that came to me was that he was trying to write the name Molly Claverhouse and that's what came out, MOLOCH, I mean.'

'Oh, that's good Dave. I'm really glad I came round to you. I thought you might be a wildcard on this job, come up with something original, but that really is off the wall.'

'Why? M-O-L and a few squiggles … '

'It wasn't like that Dave. I saw it myself. It was MOLOC written in capitals and as plain as the nose on your face.'

'Oh.'

'Talking of Molly Claverhouse, she wants to see you.'

'No way.'

'Why not? She seems like a perfectly sensible woman. She's a hell of a lot easier to work with than most of her colleagues.'

'She almost got me killed with that so-called security van.'

'That wasn't her fault. Appleyard insisted on it.'

'Oh, did he?'

'Don't start that Dave. I can see the glint in your eye. Appleyard's as much in the dark about this Moloch business as the rest of us.'

'Well, he would want you to think that if he's behind it, wouldn't he?'

'Listen, Dave when things go wrong the first thing these security boys do is check out their own. They've put Appleyard through the wringer and he can account for every second of his time for the last few weeks. He's not your uncle's villain.'

'If you say so.'

'I do say so, so don't go barking up the wrong tree like you usually do. If anyone's under suspicion, Claverhouse is the one. She's been getting some very funny looks. Maybe that's why she wants to see you.'

'That's so typical of you people. She nearly gets killed in three different ways and she comes under suspicion but not her boss who organised the security van.'

'Nobody organised it, Dave. Use of the van is standard procedure.'

'OK, standard procedure, so what about the three guys you boys in blue picked up at Sheepfold Lane. Have any of them spilled the beans?'

'Dave, they were released in the early hours of this morning. They were with the Ministry of Defence security section, a special group recruited mainly from redundant ex-army types to supplement the security service in certain areas.'

'What, guarding barracks and things?'

'No there are certain confidential activities ...'

'Like transporting terror suspects overseas for enhanced interrogation?'

'... certain activities in which it is essential that ministers can honestly deny that MI5 or the SIS has involvement, and Dave, I'm breaking the Official Secrets Act by telling you so much. I'm doing it for Jan's sake so you won't try to go up against these people.'

'But why were they released?'

'Because they were government employees trying to apprehend a terror suspect who escaped when uniforms turned up. Total embarrassment all round. We apologised to them. Don't ask me why. It's above my pay grade as the Yanks say.'

'Right.'

'Now, can I use your loo?'

Before I could speak he was out of his chair, through the door and up the stairs. I heard doors being opened while he checked out the rooms. I was glad that I'd concealed Bob's shooters. Bren will go so far with you but then he turns as awkward as hell. As with most coppers, civilians with guns are the sticking point with him.

'I see the big guy's here,' he said when he came back, 'but who are those two little creeps sleeping on the sofas?'

'Friends of Clint's,' I improvised. 'They came to see him last night.'

'Well, watch yourself, Dave. I'm counting on you to be my wildcard in this game.'

I went to the back door as he left.

The rain had stopped and a pale sun was gleaming through the rain soaked trees.

So Bren had called to make sure that Paddy hadn't left a more serious clue than the word Moloch and I was warned off from further investigation.

But he didn't say anything about finding Fothergill, did he? That was what I intended to next anyway.

29

Thursday: morning and afternoon

Even before Bren reached the end of the garden path I felt my spirits lifting. The sun shone in through the kitchen windows and I felt my appetite returning. Maybe there was light at the end of this particularly murky tunnel. At least I wasn't on my own. If I couldn't find a solution surely all those brain-boxes on the COBRA committee could. Possibly my mood was lightened by Bren's assurance that I was safe in Ridley Close, not that I intended to stay.

Clint emerged from his room. He was dressed in his farm overalls.

His expression showed that he wasn't pleased with the world.

'You didn't take me with you last night,' he accused.

'That's right, Clint. I didn't think you'd want to come.'

'I thought you were my friend, Dave.'

'I am but being friends doesn't mean you have to go everywhere with me.'

'It does if you're in danger and I heard No-Nose telling Lee that he didn't think he was going to make it until you popped up over the wall and started blazing away like James Bond on speed.'

'Clint, I've known you a lot longer than I've known Tony and Lee and believe me, you are my closest and dearest friend.'

The sulky expression relaxed a little but didn't entirely leave the big man's gaunt face.

'Can we go back to the Pimpernel office? I liked it there.'

'No, it's not safe.'

'Is it those bastards who want to get you? I could help. I'm not frightened of them.'

'Clint, you were wonderful at dealing with them but …'

'But I'm too stupid to help.'

'I didn't say that. Things are a bit different now, that's all.'

There was a long silence before he spoke again.

I busied myself by sorting through Bob's mail. I went into the kitchen and Clint followed me.

'I need to go to work, Dave,' he announced.

'Really?'

'Yes, *really*, Dave,' he insisted. 'If you don't need me I'm better off at work.'

'You poor old thing,' I said.

'No, I'm not poor. I've got money,' he said, taking me literally.

'No, I meant that you have to go to work. We can't have you being bored.'

He was on his way in twenty minutes, promising to return about seven, having been fed by the farm. He insisted on giving me the number of his mobile so I wrote it down on a slip of paper and put it in my pocket.

Loyalty to Jan made me feel too guilty for another robust fry-up. Actually I'd used up all the sausage and bacon yesterday. I reached for the muesli. After swallowing as much of the high fibre pap as I could stomach I advanced on the kitchen sink. There were any number of pans and utensils with ingrained grease from yesterday's cholesterol extravaganza. I set to work, whistling to myself. Why I find happiness and mental repose while scraping the embedded remains of a fry up off a metal grill I don't know but I do.

I thought about Molly Claverhouse. What could she want? I thought long and hard and decided that if I never saw her again it would be too soon. I wasn't going to get in touch with her. At the back of my mind there was a hope that if I kept my head down the powerful forces in combat would neutralise each other and then Dave Cunane could emerge into the sunlight again like an early mammalian ancestor peeping out after a battle between dinosaurs.

And what was the battle about?

My conclusion was that someone close to the centre of power was scheming to seize power on the back of a fake terrorist atrocity going by the name of MOLOCH. Others were trying to prevent this by minimising the talk of 'Islamic terrorism'.

If only I knew that wire puller's name.

If only I'd let Lew tell me.

If only … I could be out there now stalking the bastard.

Three quarters of an hour later Tony ambled in when I was stepping back to admire the glittering array of utensils. He was rubbing sleep out of his eyes but he didn't look as if he'd banged himself up with cannabis. There was a hint of purpose in his pale blue eyes that suggested the reconditioned brain was firing on all cylinders.

'Morning, Boss,' he muttered.

'Dave,' I corrected.

'Actually, Dave, I'm more comfortable with Boss,' he said sharply. 'All this "call me Dave" stuff is great if it was just you and me, but it gives Lee the wrong idea. He thinks you're a mate that I'm just tagging along with because I've nothing better to do.'

'Right, Mr Nolan. Am I allowed to call you Tony?'

'Oh, don't take it wrong. I'm just being practical. I want Lee to know he's working for you, that's all.'

He was talking sense but after Clint's little tantrum here was another rebellion. I had to have some come back.

'So, being practical, do you both want contracts of employment? There are some in my desk at the Pimpernel office. Bring a couple back.'

He shuddered at this idea.

'No, we're sound as it is, Boss. I can't be messing with all that kind of shit, tax codes and stuff.'

'Especially as you're drawing benefit while I'm paying you cash,' I added, for the sake of argument.

'Why shouldn't I?' he snapped angrily, his face colouring 'I didn't ask them to give me the money. Shoving it at me they were, job seeker's allowance and this and that. One of these wringing wet social workers wanted to put me on a disability allowance because of the meningitis and the so-called brain damage. Hah! It's the brain damage that's given me another chance in life.'

'OK, Tony,' I said putting my hands up in surrender, 'let's not get political.'

He sounded bitter and he continued grumbling and complaining as if he was addressing a public meeting of the self employed, which in a way I suppose he was.

Anyway, I ignored him and put the kettle on to boil and made us both a cup of tea. He was quoting Friedrich Hayek when I pushed the cup into his hand.

'Who's this Hayek then?' I asked. 'Does he play for Manchester City?'

'He was an Austrian economist, as if you don't know, Boss. He warned of the dangers of the welfare state when it was being set up.'

I smiled benignly.

Tony's transformation into an all-knowing fount of knowledge was surprising but his 'devil take the hindmost' attitude was one I'd come across before in professional criminals. Bob Lane has a touch of it, moderated only by the care he shows for Clint.

'OK, Tony, I give in. You keep whatever's coming to you but don't forget that the main business at Pimpernel Investigations these days is uncovering benefit fraud.'

'As if I'd sit in the office casually chin-wagging with ex-cops about how I make my bread.'

'Speaking of the office, if you get yourself to Altrincham in the next ten minutes you can take a taxi and still open Pimpernel by nine a.m.'

'Slave driver!'

'That's when we open for business, nine a.m. on the dot, and I want that name from Greg Loveland. There's enough cash in the safe to give him a bung but don't go crazy.'

'Oh yeah, we're still on that stuff aren't we?'

'Since my Dad's clue turned out to be totally useless finding the notebook that Fothergill stole is my only way out of this mess.'

'I'm with you but do you want to know something, Dave? I'm not all that sure I want to be out of this mess. I like working at Pimpernel, the suit, the phone calls, the computer and everything. It's the best job I've ever had and I think I could really maximise your turnover.'

'Tony, Pimpernel Investigations having a healthy balance sheet isn't going to do me a scrap of good if someone puts a bullet in my head, is it?'

He looked glum, so I sweetened the pill for him.

'If we find Fothergill and sort out who killed Sir Lew I might need a permanent manager at Pimpernel. I'll have Sir Lew's estate to deal with.'

'I'm on my way,' he said, gulping down his tea.

I'd never seen him move so fast. Talk about incentivised! He was off down the Close in a moment, well turned out in his new suit with his hair gelled and neatly parted.

'*Finding Fothergill*', it sounded like the title of a film starring Michael Caine.

I had difficulty rousing Lee before nine o'clock. The air turned blue with curses but eventually he emerged into daylight. I quickly looked away when he came into the kitchen and I saw the words, 'What the f**k are you looking at?' forming on his thin lips.

Thwarted, he confined himself to a grunt.

Lacking confrontation, the provocative little hooligan subsided onto a chair and allowed himself to be offered toast and coffee and to be briefed on what he was required to do. He was to continue canvassing the 'mugging community' with the photograph of the genuine April Fothergill.

When he left I listened to local radio news for reports of cattle rustling. There wasn't even a whisper about Sheepfold Lane but on TV there were several items of interest on BBC 24 hour news. The Government had raised the terrorist threat level to 'severe' indicating that the Joint Terrorist Analysis Centre within MI5 felt that a terrorist attack on the UK was highly likely. Announcing it, the Home Secretary stated that she had no specific threat in mind but that the step was being taken in light of recent information received in the United States. She denied that the change had anything to do with the murder of Sir Lewis Greene which she said the police were regarding as an '*individual event*' whatever that was. She must have been deliberately lying because to my knowledge MI5 had a video showing at least four men breaking into Lew's house. Whatever that horrific event was, Islamic beheading or robbery gone wrong, it wasn't an *'individual event'*.

Secondly, it was announced that a 'World of Sport' event involving twenty thousand children at the O2 Arena in London had been cancelled without notice due to 'unforeseen events'. The announcer made no connection with the Home Secretary's statement, leaving it to the public to join up the dots.

I did join up the dots and felt very uncomfortable. The information suggested that things were warming up and that I should be out there doing something. A plan to tour 'student digs land'; Withington, Fallowfield, Whalley Range, West Didsbury and see if I could spot Fothergill formed in my mind. She had to eat.

If I could just get the black leather notebook off her I'd have the name of the head of the conspiracy and this whole case could be wound up.

I was torn.

The odds were that heavily armed plotters were still looking for me. If they could go to the length of arranging an ambush at Sheepfold Cottage then they were very likely to have some way of tapping into the all-seeing CCTV system covering every man, woman and child moving on the streets in Central Manchester.

In the end I continued to skulk in Ridley Close. I decided to give it one more day and then maybe the heat would be off me. I texted Jan that I was well and urged her to be patient and not to reply.

'Yes, Lord and Master,' was the reply I received.

For want of something to do I washed the clothes from last night then went into Bob's subterranean gym and ran five miles on his treadmill. After that I took a long soak in his Jacuzzi hoping that some brilliant insight would strike me.

It didn't. Battle of the Dinosaurs and 'don't get crushed' were still the best ideas I could come up with.

Ridley Close was quieter than Southern Cemetery. I sat by the window and watched the elderly neighbours come to life. An old lady delicately pruned her ornamental shrubs, snipping a twig here and a twig there and carrying them to her green bin. A frail couple clutching each other like survivors of a disaster at sea tottered round the corner, went to the end of the Close and back. They were in their late eighties, if not older. A youth delivered an ad mag to every house. A young woman steering a pushchair also tried to control a small girl on a scooter. The postman came and went. Delivery vans arrived and departed. The old lady started on the bushes again. It was infuriating.

I was going insane, not slowly but quickly. I needed action.

Then in the haphazard way things happen they began happening very fast.

I was about to scramble some eggs for my lunch when I heard a faint noise from above. I dashed upstairs. Marvin Desailles phone was buzzing where I'd left it to charge by my bedside.

I snatched it up.

'Hey, Dave my lucky mon,' he said. 'I bin callin' you all morning. You must be the hardest mon in de whole world for a poor lawyer to give good news to.'

'What good news?' I said grumpily.

'It's all going ahead mon, that's what. There'll be no challenges. Your wonderful godfather picked real nice executors for his estate. You know there is this period of time dey call probate while de lucky bwoy like you has to wait until the inheritance is legally cleared, taxes paid and everyt'ing signed, sealed and delivered?'

'Yes, yes, Marvin, I think you told me all that before.'

'No, I dint Dave. You dint give me no time to.'

'Sorry Marvin.'

'Well, the executors are perfectly happy for you to take possession of the estate, live in de houses, use de cars, dig up de lawns, ride de horses etc, etc just as long as you don't try to sell anything off until the probate process is concluded which they don't anticipate will be very long.'

'Which means what?'

'Christ bwoy! You are t'ick. It means you a very rich bwoy! You have access to the bank accounts but can't spend more than ten thousand at a time for now.'

'Oh!'

'Yes, oh, Dave. And it means you can pay me some money. I

need to employ surveyors to see that ever t'ing in Sir Lew's inventories is there. You know how many tractors you suppose to own?'

'Hell no!'

'Well it's plenty, mon, and I need to see you soon at Sir Lew's house in Wilmslow. You need to sign some t'ings.'

'I don't think …'

'Dave, this stuff won't wait. There's folk to be paid, people wanting to know 'bout their futures … Sir Lew's servants, for instance.'

'Servants?' I echoed faintly.

'Yes mon, you got servants now.'

'No, I haven't.'

'Fine! You want me to dismiss them all? I can do that.'

'No, Marvin … for God's sake! I'm up to my eyes in trouble. You've seen the news. The police are trying to imply that Sir Lew's murder was some kind of domestic quarrel involving his family. That kind of narrows down their field of suspects, doesn't it?'

'Mmm, yeah, I see de television but that all *buuuullsheeet* mon, real heavy duty bullshit. If they had the tiniest shred of proof that you done him in they'd have posted an arrest warrant by now. They wantin' to panic you, make you do somet'ing real stupid. Somet'ing to give them a chance to question you again. Now listen, are you listening good, Dave? This your lawyer speakin'. You seem to have a very short attention span these days.'

'I'm listening.'

'There's a very pretty lady sittin' outside my door who says she must see you on a matter of life and death.'

'Jan!'

'No, dis lady from de secret police, Ms Molly Claverhouse?'

'How the bloody hell …' I exploded.

'Dave, dey know I'm your lawyer. They not goan a need be geniuses to know I'm in touch wit' you.'

I took several deep breaths.

'No, I suppose not,' I said, cooling off. Marvin's alternating speech; standard English one second and Jamaican the next was fine for irritating the police but now I found it was getting under my skin.

'What does she want?'

'She won't tell me but she says she won't leave until I let her speak to you.'

Hell bells, would I ever shake the woman off? First through Bren and now through Marvin, she was determined to get her hook into me. I thought for a moment and then picked up one of the unlisted phones Jan had bought for me.

'This is what I'll do,' I told him. 'I'll phone you back in half an hour and give you a number she can call me on.'

'OK, but I must meet you.'

'Yeah, one thing at a time Marvin, I'll get back to you.'

I removed the battery from Marvin's phone and pocketed it. Claverhouse was certainly efficient enough to have just this very minute tracked his call to his Aunty Velmore's mobile and through it to my location. Then I dashed out of the house, got in the BMW and drove first to the M56 and then the M6. Driving fast but staying legal I reached the first southbound service station at Sandbach in well under the half hour. In MacDonald's I ordered a chicken and bacon wrap with a large coffee and put Velmore's mobile back together. I texted the disposable number to Marvin and then dismantled his phone again. Velmore's phone was old and might not have tracking technology or GPS in it but I couldn't take the chance.

The wrap was quite edible and I was hungry. I bit and chewed.

The disposable phone rang before I could swallow more than a couple of bites.

'Cunane, it's me … Molly,' she sounded breathless.

'I didn't think it was the Tooth Fairy.'

'I know we didn't part on the best of terms but I'm putting my job on the line by talking to you.'

'That's fine. I don't want you getting into any trouble.'

I cut her off, put the mobile on the table and took another bite out of my wrap.

It rang again. I waited while it buzzed its way round the tabletop for a full minute then picked it up.

'Wait, Cunane, please don't switch off. There are things I need to explain to you, things you don't know about. My job's on the line unless I bring you onside in this investigation.'

'That's different from what you said a minute ago. You were doing me a favour but now I'm saving your job. I think I'd better wish you good afternoon.'

'No, no,' she wailed.

'I'm listening for exactly another ten seconds, then bye, bye, spy.'

'There are things I can't tell you over a phone. I need to meet you. Listen, we know exactly where your family is. They're in a farmhouse at Lough Gara, County Sligo. I can give you the GPS reference if you want.'

'What?'

'Yes. You've very cleverly put them beyond our official reach but the Scottish police still want to talk to your wife about a serious offence. Motoring offences are extraditable from the Irish Republic. There was a fatal accident at the place where the lady did her speeding. I'm sure the Gardai will cooperate. We're ever so friendly these days.'

'You must be mad or desperate.'

'Desperate, I think. Listen, I'm not threatening your lady or anything and I'm sure all this fuss could be made to go away but ...'

'But you are threatening her ... I get it ... are you still at Marvin Desailles office.'

'Where else?'

'Put him on, but you must stay in his sight at all times. Do you understand?'

'Who do you think I am? Mata Hari?'

'I've no idea who you are. You're certainly a cunning spy but I don't want you getting in touch with anyone, understand? I've absolutely no wish to spend time in Paddington Green looking at Appleyard's ugly mug.'

'As if! It's partly about Appleyard I need to talk.'

'Put Marvin on.'

She called to him.

A moment later I heard the familiar broad tones.

'Lucky mon ...'

'Drop the phony patois Marvin, standard English from now on, please. Things are getting too serious for me to risk any misunderstanding.'

'Yes sir!'

'I want you to take Claverhouse with you for our meeting at Sir Lew's house. I'll see you at the same time, well separately, but I'll see you both there. One hour. Two birds with one stone, and all that.'

'Good thinking, we're on our way.'

'Wait! I want you to check her out first. Strip search her if you have to …'

'Whoa bwoy!'

'She's a bloody spy! She's likely to be carrying all kinds of secret electronic stuff. Make her leave her bag and her gun and whatever else she's wired up with, even her shoes and her hairnet or whatever the hell she's got or there's no meet. Tell her!'

'I'm buzzing for it, man.'

'And Marvin, when you get back sweep your office for bugs. Get a top-line security firm. In fact, have it swept daily while this stuff's going on. Put it on my bill.'

30

Thursday: Afternoon

I drove down to the next interchange switched to the northbound M6 and then after a few miles turned off the motorway towards Congleton. I decided the longer drive would give me time to think but when I reached Wilmslow I discovered a problem.

I wasn't absolutely certain where Lew Greene's house was but didn't like to admit that to Marvin. There was no one else I could call so I wandered the posh streets until I found a quiet road in an exclusive quarter which struck a chord. It was in the right neighbourhood. Certainly every detached house we passed was grander than the one before. Some stood behind immaculate lawns big enough for cricket matches, others were secluded by mature trees or sculpted hedges.

Then there was a bend in the road and round the corner I saw the house I'd known in childhood. I hadn't been there since. I drove past and risked a quick look down the drive. It was Weldsley Park all right and it was as enormous as I remembered it and Marvin's car was already there. I knew I was late but I had things to do before I shoved my head into a possible trap.

I drove round for a few minutes passing the house several times and trying to spot parked cars on surveillance duty or anything else remotely suspicious. The streets were empty. I guessed that this wealthy neighbourhood was regularly patrolled and that parked cars occupied by suspicious looking men would be targeted quickly.

They could have a camera stuck on a tree or something but what the hell. I'd have to risk it.

I found a small petrol station with just four pumps and a small repair shop quite close to the address, I filled the BMW. I might need to drive to Ireland. I asked the woman behind the counter if there was anywhere I could leave my car for an hour or so. She was pretty off-hand but when I said I was moving into the neighbourhood she relented and directed me round the side of the repair shop to a cinder patch facing an empty field which suited me perfectly.

I took out the mobile I was using to contact Jan and phoned her.

'Dave!' she said after the first ring. She must have had the phone in her hand. I cursed myself for causing anxiety at this time in her life but Jan is Jan. She's a tough cookie. She has to be.

'Hi love, I'm just about to visit one of our new mansions and there are some things we need to discuss …'

'What are you on about Dave? Have you been drinking?'

'No, I'm sitting close to Weldsley Park which Marvin Desailles informs me we can now inhabit if we wish …'

'And what about these people who're trying to make me a widow? Will they be waiting there to disinhabit you?'

'No,' I said firmly, 'there's no such word as disinhabit and I've already checked the house and Marvin's waiting for me there. The thing is, he's with someone.' There was no point in discussing the gunplay at Sheepfold Cottage with her.

'Who?'

Jan's always direct.

'An MI5 person.'

'Dave, I know you too well. By 'person' you mean she's a woman. Describe her in detail.'

'Jan, there isn't time for this.'

'More suspicious still, describe her or I'm on the next plane to Manchester to see for myself.'

'OK, OK, No-Nose Nolan, remember him? Describes her as a 'fancy piece' and I suppose she is … a tall hazel eyed blonde in her thirties … deputy director of MI5 in North West England.'

'So you have noticed her then. I bet you can tell me her bra size.'

'Jan, just drop it. The bloody woman's threatening us, you in particular. She knows exactly where you are.'

'Go on.'

'You know the Erskine Bridge speeding story, well they've embroidered that.'

I related the details of Claverhouse's attempt at blackmail.

There was silence for a moment. I didn't expect hysterics but prepared myself for abuse.

Jan spoke after a long pause. She was calm.

'Well, they're a bunch of liars, that's all I can say. Nothing happened on that road, certainly no fatal crash. And if you're expecting me to up sticks and do another quick getaway in a truck you can have another think and do you want to know why?'

'Yes.'

'I told you that the driver of the cabbage lorry brought us to his mother's house on the night we arrived … Mary Doyle, that's her name, our landlady here and one of the nicest women I've met in ages … well her other son Patrick is a sergeant in the Garda Siochana and what's more he's the only copper for many miles around. So if I'm to be arrested he'll be bound to hear it first. I'll have a chat with Mary, did I mention that she reads the Guardian On-line, and I'm sure she'll help us when she learns that the British security services are conspiring to arrest a pregnant woman on trumped up charges. So just you tell your fancy piece to try pulling her little stunt and see where it gets her. We're all just settling in here.'

Jan sounded as strong willed as ever but I detected a faint hint of tearfulness in her last sentence.

'Good stuff. I hated the idea of you moving again. Tell me how everything's going.'

'The children were mad with excitement about cramming into the cabbage lorry, Mum not so much. It was a real adventure for them.'

'But you're all settling in now.'

'Yes, Mum's taken Jenny and Lloyd and Mangler for a walk round the lake to give me a break.'

'You're sure you're all right, the baby …'

'Stop worrying, Dave. Ireland has excellent maternity services. Everything's as it should be. I did a spot of sightseeing yesterday and there were gravestones in the local cemetery dedicated to … er … people with the same name as you, but spelt with an extra "n". Jenny spotted the first one and she's been like a dog with two tails since. I found a local historian and he said there are a lot of people with your name round here so I feel quite at home. I could stay a month discovering long lost relatives.'

'Small world,' I muttered, 'but you are coming back aren't you?'

'I can't wait but make sure that MI5 woman isn't within twenty miles of me or I might not be able to control myself.'

We talked for a few more minutes and then I set off for Weldsley on foot. It might be useful to preserve the anonymity of my transport for a while longer. As the mansion loomed ahead, and that's what it was … a mini-stately home … a gentleman's residence or whatever jargon estate agents use to describe a stonking big house with about twelve bedrooms … I was certain that I'd never live here. Not for the first time I wondered what had been on Lew Greene's mind when he moved here. Children I suppose, at least ten, knowing his religious inclinations but there were none or rather, now there was me: the Heir of Weldsley.

A man was waiting for me at the imposing entrance gates.

I recognised Lew's chauffeur from the fatal Monday morning.

'Mr Cunane, sir,' he said reverentially. 'It's so terrible what happened to your uncle. We were expecting you here before now.'

'We?' I asked. I didn't feel it was the right moment to correct him about my exact relationship to Sir Lew.

'There's me, my wife, Janet, and the Zamoras, the Filipino couple who used to look after Sir Lew and cook for us all and of course Harry Bradshaw our gardener cum handyman. We're all anxious to know what you want us to do and if you'll be keeping us on, sir.'

He gestured towards the group gathered around the entrance quite a way down the drive.

What got to me in this exchange was that final little word 'sir'.

This guy meant it in a quite different way than the half contemptuous grunt I was used to in shops or at the barber. I usually got a curt 'mate' in those places if I was lucky. He was for real and I had a sudden feeling that he'd be on his knees and holding his hands out in feudal allegiance to me in another instant.

'Listen, er … Mr … '

'Kelly, Peter Kelly, sir.'

'Yes, Mr Kelly, the reason I'm here is that I've come to meet my lawyer and sign some documents.'

'Oh yes, he told us that. He's in his car with your wife. I invited him into the house but he preferred to wait for you. We were hoping you'd come today and inspect the house and possibly eat a meal here.'

'I'm sure inspection isn't necessary, Mr Kelly, and to reverse a classic phrase that's no lady and she isn't my wife.'

'Oh, I'm so sorry, I assumed she was Mrs Cunane.' he half turned to look at the couple in the car. There was a curious expression on his face.

'Mr Cunane, your late uncle remarked on the unusual nature of some of your activities on the day I drove him to your office,' he said quietly.

'Did he? Did he say anything else?' I asked eagerly.

'No sir. Sir Lew never discussed private business or family with me. He talked of household matters. I was his general factotum as well as his chauffeur. I served as a butler if he was entertaining his legal guests and did anything else he wanted doing. Religion or football was what he generally talked to me about, but there was one thing. He arranged for us all to stay in a hotel at Grasmere on the night he was killed. Hardly a coincidence was it, sir? And I think he was expecting a member of his family to deal with those who killed him.'

'I intend to.'

'Good, but you will come inside and let me introduce you to Weldsley Court and Sir, please call me Peter. Sir Lew always did.'

I experienced an odd twinge; the strange feeling an Englishman gets when his sensitive class prejudices are given a twist. I was the one who was always insisting on being called Dave. I could hardly insist that Kelly start calling me Dave. He'd be outraged.

'Peter,' I said quietly, 'I need to have a long talk with you about this and that. I will come inside and I must tell you this isn't the first time I've been at Weldsley so no introduction is necessary but I must have a chat with that woman and then my lawyer so perhaps you and your colleagues could wait inside for a few minutes.'

He looked baffled. First Marvin had refused to enter and then me. He must have been wondering what was going on. Well, it was too bad. He controlled his developing frown and gave me a smile.

'Very well, sir, we'll expect you shortly.'

I watched him walk back to the house. The little group dispersed. Marvin and Claverhouse were getting out of the car and coming towards me. I was still barely inside the drive.

I hadn't felt so uncomfortable since appearing in a school nativity play as a shepherd. All I needed now to be really welcomed as the new squire of Weldsley was a troupe of bucolic blonde maidens strewing rose-petals in my path.

'No, get back in the car, Marvin,' I said. 'I'll talk to Ms Claverhouse in private.'

'You're sure you don't need legal advice?' he asked.

'I'm sure.'

He shrugged expressively and turned round.

'If you want to be useful go inside and tell them I'm not sacking anyone.'

He waved his fingers and went in the house.

'Welcome to the manor, my lord,' Claverhouse said.

'Cut the crap, Claverhouse.'

'Ooh, how sharp and alliterative and Northern you are Dave. We could almost be in one of your wonderful Manchester soap operas.'

'It's Cunane to you and I'll give you a few minutes but before we start your threat about my wife won't wash. She's ready to fight you in every court in Ireland.'

'Oh well, it got you here didn't it? I expected you'd tell me to f**k off on the phone but you can't blame a girl for trying, can you? I'm desperate to talk to you.'

'Can you manage talking and walking at the same time? I'm uncomfortable standing here like the bull's eye on a target.'

She nodded and we set off towards the path which led to the main garden. It was situated on the far side of the house. As we wandered behind trees out of sight of the house I had a quick stab of nerves. Perhaps I should have brought a gun.

'Dave, and I am going to call you that whatever you say, did you

286

watch the Home Sec doing her stuff for peace and harmony?'

I grunted agreement. The wide lawn we were approaching was certainly big enough for a helicopter and was unimpeded by power cables.

'The line they're taking is that your relative couldn't possibly have been beheaded by Islamic jihadis. They want to play down any suggestion of a threat because if they admitted it they'd have to do something about it. You saw the video. Those men were jihadis.'

'The ones here might have been,' I said cautiously, 'but the men who attacked me definitely weren't.'

I wasn't going to mention my part in last night's escapade at Sheepfold Cottage. Bren knew about it but there was no reason that Claverhouse should be told I was involved. She certainly must have been informed that the men arrested and released at the scene were from the new MoD group.

I felt another stab of nerves. I was positively queasy. Suppose this bloody woman was a double agent? Was she running with MI5 and hunting for Lew's *certain individual* at the same time? That was the game her lot played, running with the hare and hunting with the hounds.

We walked on towards a very pleasant formal rose garden which hadn't been here last time I visited.

'Rick Appleyard wants you to think about this … as they won't accept that your uncle was killed by jihadis it then becomes convenient for the appeasers and cowards in Whitehall that he was killed by someone else, in particular, by you. They're treating your lack of cooperation as an admission of guilt. Rick can extract you from this predicament if you will state in public that jihadis killed Sir Lew. He's got a tame TV producer all set up to organise an interview. What do you think?'

I couldn't say what I really thought … that every second I spent in her company put me in danger.

I played for time.

'I don't know. I need some time. I don't like identifying people I'm not certain about.'

'That won't happen. Rick will be perfectly happy with a general statement that the men who came for you *could* have been Islamic militants, no more than that. He'll deal with what happened to Sir Lew. It's all a matter of giving things the right spin.'

My *head* was spinning.

Why were they so desperate to pitch the whole thing onto the Islamic community? She and Appleyard had to be working for Lew's mystery plotters.

'I can see you're still undecided,' she said. 'Here's Rick's phone number and mine.' She handed me a slip of paper. 'Call either one of us. You have a few hours to decide but after that the deal's off and you must take the consequences.'

'OK,' I said struggling to keep the relief out of my voice.

'I'm out of here,' she said, turning to go. 'It's nice to see how the other half live.'

With that she was off at a fast pace. I followed more slowly. She left via the main gates and strode off down the main road.

31

Thursday: afternoon

I entered through the kitchen door at the side the house, the tradesman's entrance. I owned the house and didn't feel like going through all the bowing and scraping that Peter Kelly had taken a fancy to. Sir Lew was a High Court judge, maybe that ceremony had been appropriate for him but I was only a 'sleazy' private detective and the expectations of my 'servants' were churning me up in ways I could do without.

The kitchen was large and suited to the size of the house but not at all excessive. It was also completely the domain of the 'staff'. I couldn't imagine Lew ever coming in here to eat his breakfast. I approved of it.

Beyond the kitchen there was a small breakfast room. It revived awkward memories of Aunty Magdalen trying to come up with a menu that I'd deign to eat. I'd been a faddy child. Yes, I certainly didn't need to be introduced to Weldsley. That had all happened long ago but was still a painful memory.

I could hear Marvin's bray in the distance. He was holding forth in correct English and standing in the entrance hall with the staff gathered around him when I sprang out of the dining room like a jack in the box.

There was complete silence. Marvin shut up in mid oration, a first for him.

Kelly spoke. His eyebrows were struggling to meet his receding hairline.

'Sir! You've taken us by surprise. We were gathering here to meet you at the entrance of your new home.'

He clapped his hands and the other four joined in with him. It wasn't a rapturous ovation but it was more than a polite greeting.

Now I was the one surprised and I blushed: a first for Dave Cunane. Was I supposed to make a speech? All I knew was that I wasn't going to. I was here for information about who had killed my godfather and was still trying to kill me and everything else was rubbish. I guessed that Marvin had just relayed my 'no-dismissal' offer and that the assurance that they still had jobs was responsible for the warmth.

'Now, Mr Kelly … yes I know it's Peter, Peter,' I said as he started to protest, 'but you must allow me a little formality. I'm very familiar with this house. I roamed every corner of it as a child.'

'Lady Magdalen often spoke of you,' the woman by Kelly's side piped up obsequiously.

Kelly introduced his wife, Janet, to me.

She was a small, well-rounded woman in her fifties. Her uncompromisingly grey hair was done up in a bob. She had rosy cheeks and was wearing a green pinafore over a blue dress. A crucifix dangled on a gold chain round her neck. I detected a certain chill beneath the surface warmth. Was she the iron hand in Peter Kelly's velvet glove?

'Pleased to meet you, sir,' she said in a broad Lancashire accent. She bent her head as she greeted me. 'I could tell that Lady Magdalen had been very fond of you, sir.'

I decided I could do without people bowing to me as I replied 'Not so fond after I broke one of her china cups and hid the bits behind a chair.'

'Boys will be boys. I'm sure she understood.'

'Talking of boys,' Marvin Desailles interjected, 'this boy here has to sign some things for me. If you could show me …'

'Yes, yes,' Kelly agreed. 'I'll show you both through to somewhere more private.'

I shook hands all round and then Kelly led us led into the imposing hallway dominated by large dark religious pictures in the style of Rembrandt that I remembered well. I looked around. It was a gloomy place and the religious paintings did nothing for it.

There was something missing, police tape.

'Is the room where Sir Lew was killed sealed off?' I asked.

'No sir, a team came on Wednesday and spent all that day and yesterday cleaning the house up. They had steam cleaners and all kinds of chemicals and they removed every trace of what happened down to the tiniest dot. Apparently it was a blood bath in Sir Lew's study but we never saw it, thank God.'

'Surprising,' I commented.

'Yes, we thought they were trying to pretend that nothing had happened.'

'But they had SOCOs here, you know crime scene investigators?'

'Oh yes, the men and women in white coats, but they were leaving when we came back to the house on Tuesday evening.'

He led us into the well remembered breakfast room. Marvin put his briefcase on the table and quickly pulled out several imposing legal forms which I signed without reading.

'It's just a formality Dave, as your uncle didn't die intestate. This gives me the right to do searches in his papers.'

I noticed that Kelly frowned during this exchange.

'Now I must be on my way Dave, er ... Mr Cunane. I need to see to that thing you told me about. I can let myself out,' he said as Kelly moved to escort him.

'Is there anything else I can help you with, sir?' Kelly asked.

'I wonder if we could go into Sir Lew's study for a chat, Peter.'

He nodded and gestured to the door. Again I got the impression that something didn't sit too well with him. Did he secretly resent having to show me round his old master's home? I followed him to the study. It was the one room in the house I'd never been in before. As a child I'd been made to understand that it was Uncle Lew's inner sanctum where he wasn't to be disturbed.

Like the rest of this gloomy house it was dark, panelled in oak and crammed with bookcases extending from floor to ceiling. A full sized replica of Salvador Dali's 'Christ of Saint John of the Cross' was displayed on one wall. The looming figure might be all very well in a Glasgow art gallery but here it was too much. There was also an ancient looking crucifix with an exquisite ivory figure of Christ on the open roll top desk. The religious atmosphere felt oppressive to me. The head of a particularly severe order of monks or nuns would have been at home.

There was a faint smell of disinfectant but otherwise nothing to suggest that Lew had been bloodily tortured and decapitated in here.

I went to the long table. I knew from glimpses in my childhood that this was where Lew arranged his books and papers when studying for a case. No one was allowed in the room for fear that anything was displaced.

Its surface was smooth and unblemished. I drew my hand over it. There were no scratches.

'They had a French polisher in, sir. I saw his van.'

'Sit down, Peter,' I said as he continued to hover at my side.

'Yes, sir,' he said.

'Oh man, I don't want any more 'sirs' from you.'

'But, sir … '

'Peter, I'm a private detective. I've been involved in some very nasty cases but to my mind I've always come up smelling of roses. Your late boss, Sir Lew, may have thought differently. He kept his distance from me in the last few years.'

'He made you his heir.'

His expression had changed. No longer the willing flunky, he looked sour, almost hostile.

With a sudden insight I guessed why: he'd been expecting something for himself in Lew's will.

'As far as I'm concerned he could have left it all to the Cat's Home.'

'Oh, you've inherited it all right. Sir Lew's solicitor was round here asking if we knew where you were. He couldn't get in touch with you at your office or your home.'

'OK, I'm Uncle Lew's heir. I'll treat the staff here as he would have wanted me to but you've got to drop all this 'sirring'. In my job I'm more used to knuckle sandwiches than pats on the back.'

'Yes sir.'

'No sir, call me sir again and I'll slot you … Joke, Peter.'

'As you say,' he muttered.

Curiously, having been ordered to cast off convention his whole body seemed to relax. He slumped into his chair and stretched his legs out.

'There's a problem, Peter.'

'Yes, Sir Lew said you often had problems to solve.'

'This problem is that some important people prefer to believe that Sir Lew wasn't executed by Islamic terrorists while some hardliners in MI5 are demanding that I say he was. If I don't agree with them the important people will say I'm the prime suspect. If I go against the other lot they'll make my life difficult in other ways. So you see what the problem is?'

'Yes, between them they've got your privates in a nutcracker.'

'Precisely, Peter. Now you're talking my language. Being a detective I have my own suspect who's neither an Islamic terrorist nor, of course, me.'

'I see sir,' he said infuriatingly.

'I think a particular man I've come across knows what happened to Lew and I believe he's been in this house to threaten Lew.'

I described Appleyard's distinctive appearance and speech without mentioning his name. Appleyard was probably a cover-name.

'Has he been round here?'

Kelly took his time answering.

'No, I've never seen anyone answering that description.'

'What about the woman who was in the car with my lawyer, the one you thought was my wife?'

'No, I've never seen her before today. She's not the type you'd forget in a hurry.'

My heart sank.

'I can think of only one person connected with the secret game that came here and that was Mr Pickering, but it couldn't be him. He'd never harm Sir Lew. He was the son of Sir Lew's oldest friend.'

'Tell me about him,' I said eagerly. At last I had a name.

'No, sir, I don't care to. Sir Lew was close to him.'

'Peter, don't you know that that's what traitors do? They don't go round in black hats like villains in a pantomime.'

'I do know what a traitor is but Mr Pickering isn't one or a murderer either. That's impossible.'

It was beginning to look as if I'd hit another of the brick walls this case was so well supplied with.

'Can you at least tell me when Mr Pickering was here?'

'He was here on the Friday before Sir Lew's death, a nice gentleman. We thought he'd be staying for the weekend but he returned to London.'

'Do you know why he was here?'

'It was something to do with the Inquiry Sir Lew was involved in. He and Sir Lew left the house and went to the far end of the garden and talked for hours.'

'Do you know what they talked about?'

'Oh, if I did know I wouldn't care to say. Sir Lew was always very discreet and he expected discretion from me.'

'Peter, Sir Lew, a kindly man whom I've known since childhood was cruelly tortured and murdered in this room. Would you like me to tell you the details?'

He shuddered and involuntarily put a hand to his throat.

'You must have some idea of what they were talking about,' I persisted. 'Were they laughing and joking, arguing or what?'

'No, er … Mr Cunane, Sir Lew was always a serious man. They both seemed down in the mouth, Mr Pickering more than he usually was.'

'Pickering's been here at other times?'

'Yes, he was a frequent visitor. Sir Lew knew his father well.'

'So Pickering's his real name?'

'Of course, Mr Cunane, but I don't think I should say any more.'

'Why not, don't you know that the people who murdered Sir Lew are still out there?'

'We had a call from London, someone important. He reminded us that we have to stick to the story they put in the newspapers that a passing madman killed Sir Lew. There's a political party trying to stir up trouble … '

'The BfB?'

He nodded.

'And we were warned to stick to the official story if the press came sniffing round.'

'Peter, I'm not the BfB or the press.'

'No, you're not.'

I decided to try Jan's approach for getting the children to take medicine. She bribes them with sweeties.

'What age are you, Peter?' I asked.

This produced a resentful look but he answered after a moment's consideration.

'I'm sixty four but what ... '

'Bear with me, Peter,' I interrupted, holding my hand up, 'and your dear wife?'

'She'll be fifty nine in August if it's any of your business.'

'So if this awful thing hadn't happened to Sir Lew you were going to carry on working for him until you both dropped, were you?'

'Oh no, there's a lovely cottage in the Trough of Bowland. It's adjoining the Duke of Westminster's lands but belongs to us; er ... I mean it belongs to you. Sir Lew used to rent it out as a holiday let but ... '

'You'd like it as a retirement home?'

'Sir Lew as good as promised it.'

'But there's nothing in the will?'

'No,' he admitted, with a sad shake of his head.

'I don't see any problem with an ex-employee taking a cottage from the estate at a reduced rent,' I said, gazing at him frankly and marvelling at my own chutzpah. 'I'll tell Mr Desailles to prepare the papers. I take it you have a pension coming from the estate?'

He nodded.

'We'll have to see if there's a possibility of enhancing it.'

After that the story came out quick and fast.

Sir Lew had become a legal consultant to the SIS when he was a rising young barrister. His main contact was Alban Pickering's father, Arnold Pickering. Lew and Arnold had been at the same school, surprise, surprise. Arnold later rose to high rank in the service just as Lew did in the legal profession.

When the Government needed to launch an Inquiry to fend off allegations that it had supported torture what could be more natural than that it should turn to Sir Lew to conduct the Inquiry, a man who understood the problems of intelligence gathering?

All went smoothly for a while.

Kelly spoke of Sir Lew's journeys up and down the country, the many meetings in London. Lew's temperament seemed benign, all was going well. Then there came a special meeting in the week before Lew was killed.

It was held in the vast car park of the Bluewater Shopping Centre in Kent. Kelly didn't see whoever Lew met but he did see that his boss was in a towering rage when he got back in the Roller.

After that nothing went well. According to Kelly, Lew had hardly slept or had a meal in the days before his death. He seemed alternately angry or depressed.

I didn't need to be a genius to work out that Lew had learned something unpleasant at Bluewater. What was it: that torture was being sanctioned by one section of the service?

Alban Pickering had been summoned to explain.

He'd been at Weldsley Park on the Friday afternoon following the Bluewater meeting on the Wednesday.

Had his masters given him the mission of persuading Lew to keep his mouth shut? Had he failed in that? Was it on that Friday that Lew learned about the MOLOCH operation and the name of the chief conspirator?

I could imagine Pickering trying to explain to Lew why MOLOCH was necessary.

Perhaps he'd raked up religious causes, trying to enlist the devout Christian against the Muslims. That seemed a bit off the wall. True, Lew was devout enough but he was no supporter of religious wars. More likely Pickering had appealed to Lew's feelings of solidarity, the need for an old Secret Service hand to stand firm with his colleagues.

If that was the scenario whoever tasked Pickering had misjudged the target. Lew Greene was the last man on earth to overthrow the constitutional and legal set-up in this country.

Even so, there was a gap to explain.

If Lew had learned about the plot on the Friday why did he wait until Monday morning before taking action?

I asked Kelly what Lew had done on the rest of the weekend

before his death.

'He didn't seem as agitated as he was before Mr Pickering's visit.'

'Not agitated?'

'Yes, he slept well on Friday night and got up early. He wanted to go for a very long walk up in the hills. I think it's called the Gritstone Trail. I dropped him off at the start and picked him up at Tegg's Nose. There was a strong wind but he said it had blown the cobwebs out of his mind. I got the impression he'd come to a decision. He went to church on Sunday and then spent a lot of time in here. I think he was writing something because he asked Janet to borrow her pen because his had run out. Then on Monday I took him to your office. He came back here and bundled us all off to Grasmere. That's how he came to be on his own when he died.'

'He didn't die, Peter. He was murdered.'

'Yes sir,' he said stubbornly.

I didn't correct him.

'Were there any visitors after Mr Pickering?'

He looked uncomfortable and made no reply.

'Come on Peter, this isn't the third degree. I asked a simple question.'

Kelly made no reply again. He looked down at his hands.

I stood up and walked round the room for a moment. The books on the shelves were mainly legal texts with a sprinkling of history and theology.

'You've been threatened haven't you?' I asked. 'You weren't just asked to stick to the story of the madman killing Sir Lew, you were told to keep quiet about whoever visited him on Sunday.'

He grunted in a way that I took to be affirmative.

'Peter, there's an undercover war going on,' I said. 'They're keeping it out of the media, that's why you were threatened and why the clean up squad came here. Do you understand?'

He nodded.

'They said they'd kill Janet if I told anyone about Sir Lew's visitors. They didn't seem to know that Mr Pickering had been here.'

I tried to absorb this information before speaking again.

'Who were the visitors on Sunday?' I asked after a moment.

'It was late, after nine o'clock. There were two of them. One was tall and thin, a very gentlemanly type … I heard Sir Lew ask him what name he was using so I knew it was Secret Service business.'

'What name did he say?'

'Appleyard.'

My heart gave a lurch.

I repeated my previous description of the man I knew as Appleyard, even venturing to imitate his accent.

'That wasn't him. This man was slighter taller than you and a few years younger than me and very well spoken. There was no accent.'

'OK, you said there were two men.'

'The other one was much smaller and foxy looking, with dark eyes. He looked like an ex-soldier. I didn't get his name. They were only with Sir Lew for a few minutes. They left without much ceremony and showed themselves out.'

'Have you any idea what was said?'

'No, but they weren't friendly. Usually Sir Lew would show a guest to the front door but these two just slunk out.'

'Thanks,' I said, 'is there any whisky in here, I need a drink after that.'

Kelly breathed a sigh of relief.

'This way, sir,' he said deliberately, leading me out of the study into a conservatory overlooking the vast rear lawn.

Kelly opened a cupboard revealing a connoisseur's collection of malt whiskies.

'I'll try that one,' I said, indicating a bottle of seventeen-year old malt.

Kelly poured a healthy dram into a crystal glass with a tulip shape. I knew it was a specialist 'whisky nosing' glass.

'Spring water, sir?' he asked.

'Yes, Peter and I'll let you carry on calling me sir if you'll join me in a glass.'

He did.

'Sir Lew loved the Balvenie,' he commented.

It was like nectar. I resisted the vulgar urge to take a full bottle back with me. We Cunanes may be lowborn but we know the right thing to do.

'I'll see you get the papers about the cottage and the pension enhancement early next week. Mr Desailles will probably have something for you to sign.'

I showed myself out.

My excursion into the feudal world of Sir Lew and Lady Magdalen Arabella Veronica Anderton-Weldsley Greene had been short but not very sweet. I was better suited to the world I knew. Kelly was as loyal as the day is long to Lew but it was painfully clear that he trusted me about as far as he could throw me. I'm afraid the feeling was mutual. I guessed that if Lew's security service pals asked him for info about me Kelly would sing like the proverbial cage bird.

Early retirement to the cottage of his dreams was the best outcome for both of us.

32

Thursday: 5 p.m.

I drove back to Ridley Close by an indirect route, stopping several times to see if I was being tailed. If I was, I couldn't detect it but then if it was MI5 I probably wouldn't.

I was embroiled in action as soon as I turned into the Close.

The old lady from across the road who'd been clipping her ornamental shrubs so assiduously this morning threw herself into the path of the BMW. She was still clutching her secateurs very firmly.

'He's been trying to break into your house. I saw him, he's been round the back and he's tried the windows and he's banged on the door enough to wake the dead. I didn't phone the police because I know Mr Lane wouldn't like that.'

'Who is it?'

At the sound of raised voices the culprit emerged. He poked his head round the side of the house. It was Lee. He waved and gave me a sheepish grin. For a moment he looked like a normal 'young adult'.

I subsided.

'I know him. It's all right, Mrs …'

'Cunningham.'

'He's OK.'

'Are you sure? He looks very dodgy to me and he smokes that substance. I can smell it from here. I know you're all right because you look after Mr Lane's brother. You're his carer, aren't you?'

'You could say that, Mrs Cunningham.'

'I knew you worked for Mr Lane when I saw you driving his car.'

I cleared my throat noisily.

'Mr Lane's told me not to phone the police if I see anything going on. He said not to bother with them but to get in touch with one of his men. Well, he's right isn't he? The police they have these days couldn't organise a … Oh, I'm sorry! I see I'm holding you up. Anyway, as long as you're happy it's all right. And if you're in touch with Mr L let him know I was keeping an eye out. He's always so generous to me.'

'OK, I'll tell him. Thanks.'

I peeled myself away and parked the car in the drive. Then a thought struck me.

I got out and went back.

'Mrs Cunningham, if you do see anyone creeping around who looks as if he shouldn't be here will you give me a bell on this number? Mr L's away.'

I gave her the number of the unlisted mobile and I wrote it down on a fifty pound note.

She smiled gratefully.

'Oooh, that's naughty, writing on good money, you shouldn't do that,' she said, quickly tucking the note in her purse. 'What name shall I say?'

I looked at her blankly.

'If someone else answers and I want you?'

'Just ask for Mr Topfield and if you do see anything the same terms apply as with Mr Lane.'

I returned to number Twelve.

'Inside, you,' I said to Lee.

He pulled a face but complied.

'Don't start on me,' he said.

'Lee, if you're thinking of taking up a criminal career you can forget it. Smoking dope on a posh residential street where you aren't known will get you arrested any day of the week.'

He looked at me.

His pale blue eyes were expressionless and if he hadn't been such a weedy runt a nervous person could have been quite frightened by that stare. His lips twitched and I mentally recited the swear words he was about to come out with.

'I came back early because I found that bitch you're looking for,' he said in a dead flat tone. 'I tried phoning you but your f**king mobile's turned off.'

'Where is she?'

'That's a problem. A toe-rag called Lamar Dushawn Bell found her. She's in Moss Side but he won't say exactly where. He wants more than five hundred.'

It crossed my mind that it was Lee who wanted more than five hundred but I had to go along with him.

'How do you know this Lamar isn't pulling a fast one?'

'That's just what I said to him, Boss. He's a dodgy bastard but he showed me this.'

He took out his mobile phone and held it under my nose.

I took it from him.

It was a latest model with a very large screen. I'd seen Lee playing with it.

The rectangular image showed a woman coming out of a door onto a street. The number of the door was obscured.

It was April Fothergill, that is to say the real April Fothergill, the young black woman with good office skills who'd been referred to the Pimpernel receptionist job by Mr Greasy Gonzi's agency.

There was no mistake. I compared the excellent image with the photo she'd supplied to the agency. It was her. Her face seemed to be registering shock.

'It's Fothergill, int it?' Lee continued. 'This guy called Lamar Dushawn Bell spotted her. He wants his money.'

'How did Lamar get so close to her? He must have been practically touching her.'

'No Boss,' Tony said pityingly. 'Lamar's a total nerd. He has this top-line phone with a twelve megapixel camera and video capture and he's fitted it with an add-on zoom lens. The guy's a walking TV studio. He can film anything.'

'So why's he out mugging students?'

'He has to pay for his f**king phone, doesn't he?' Lee said gruffly.

I could have argued with his logic if I'd had all day but I didn't.

'So this is from a video?'

'Yeah, he videoed her and she didn't like it. She practically knocked him off his bike and kicked him a couple of times. She tried to snatch the phone. That's why he wants more money … he says he dint know he was gettin' mixed up with no gangs.'

'Gangs?' I repeated. Once again there was that feeling that I was hitting my head against a brick wall.

'He says she's linked up with the Snare Drum crowd.'

The Snare Drum crowd had been involved in a war with a rival group called the Pepper Pot mob … Yes, not a joke. There'd been shootings, long prison terms and for some time a lull in violence for which the police took the credit but was more down to exhaustion by the gangs rather than fear of the law. If the original April Fothergill was tied up with the Drums then opening that can of worms was the last thing I wanted to do.

'I'll go to six hundred if he can send me that video straight away, otherwise tell him to forget it. We don't want to get involved.'

I waited for Lee to announce that he also wanted more money but to my surprise all he did was phone Lamar with my offer.

There was a lengthy discussion but in the end Lee took down Lamar's bank details. I agreed to transfer two hundred by internet banking and the rest when I'd received the video.

I accessed my bank account, agreeably surprised to find that Gonzi had paid me three thousand pounds in compensation. Appleyard's threat to freeze my assets had been an empty threat. Nothing was frozen and Lamar's money went straight through as we both had the same bank.

Lamar sent his video to Lee.

He'd obligingly filmed the street name: Austin Redfearn Close, just off Claremont Road. I knew it well. He'd captured a view of April arriving, getting out of a red Porsche Boxster, waving goodbye to the driver, a hard looking man with an elaborate blond cornrow 'do' and then walking up to her front door. She must have sensed that she was being observed because she turned and made a run at the cameraman. The image swung up and down as Lamar fought her off and then he was away, cycling out of Austin Redfearn as fast as he could.

I transferred the remaining four hundred.

Lee spoke on the phone again.

'Thanks Boss, Lamar's off on his travels. The guy in the car is

Shaka Higgings and you don't want to mess with him. He's a mean dude and he's put quite a few people in intensive care.'

'Damn it to hell. The first decent lead I get and I find she's shacked up with a major criminal. Six hundred pounds to find her and we daren't get in touch.'

'Best not, Boss. He's worse than Beast, that guy.'

In frustration I poured myself a small glass of malt whisky. I drank it too quickly and it burned my throat.

Lee was fiddling with something in his jacket pocket.

'All right, Lee you've earned it but go right to the bottom of the garden this time. We don't want Mrs Cunningham saying we're setting up a crack house.'

He was off like a shot. I was impressed that he hadn't even mentioned the five hundred I'd promised him. Perhaps he was too addled to remember.

I tried to think of a way to reach 'black' April Fothergill without starting a major riot.

In the end light dawned.

I took out Aunty Velmore's phone, prayed that it was still secure, reassembled it and called Marvin and sent him on his way. It took some prodding before he agreed that the gangster's woman was a witness to a crime against me and that he had enough credit in the world Higgings moved in to have a chance of reaching her.

I barely had time for self satisfaction before Lee was back.

'It's Tony, he just called.'

He passed me his mobile.

'Osman Ahmed Gullet,' Tony announced. 'Somali immigrant, he works for the Probation Service.'

'What?'

'This is your guy, your thieving receptionist's boyfriend. He's Somali and he's quite recent in the country.'

'But he works for the probation service?'

It sounded unlikely but who was I to say?

'Yeah, he's an interpreter or something but Dave, the best yet. I beat Loveland down to two hundred for the name and he has a mate high up in the Probation Service who gave him Gullet's address. He threw that in for free.'

'Wonders will never cease.'

'Yeah, but I had to promise to keep him well supplied with cushy jobs. He's off to Thailand this summer and he wants plenty of spending money.'

'I wonder why?'

'You know why. He's quite a lad is our Greg.'

'Yes, anyway, the address of this Gullet is?'

'No, you've got that wrong Boss. You'd address the man as Mr Ahmed Gullet. Ahmed Gullet is his surname. Osman is his birth name and he probably has another name that he's known by among the Somali people, like a nickname.'

'Thanks for the info Tony, but the address is?'

'Just saying Boss, 15 Layborn Road, Levenshulme. It's off Matthews Lane which is … '

'Off Stockport Road, yes I know. Listen Tony, I'm getting a bit nervous about using Bob's car. I need fresh wheels but not stolen ones. Do you know anyone who could lend you a clean car for a couple of days?'

'Yeah, it'll cost you though. I can use some of the money I saved for you by beating down Loveland's price.'

'Do that, shut the office and get yourself round here. And Tony, do you still have that clever friend with the bug detectors, the portable ones?'

'Yes,' he said hesitantly, 'they're all portable. They wouldn't be any use otherwise.'

'Yeah, well borrow one off him and bring it with you. And Tony, buy half a dozen pre-pay phones in different shops.'

'Will do, Boss. The price of freedom in the 'surveillance state' is paranoia. Who said that Dave?'

'I've no idea but I'm sure you'll tell me.'

'Me, I just made it up.'

'OK, Mastermind, get a move on.'

He gave a crazed cackle and cut the call.

I allowed myself to wonder if the 'reconditioned brain' was collapsing under the strain.

I handed Lee his phone.

*

An hour later the Velmore phone rang.

'Marvin?'

'Don't Marvin me, man. It's Mr Desailles to you in future.'

There was no trace of humour in Marvin's voice.

'What's happened?'

'What's happened, he asks. What hasn't happened would be more like it.'

'Tell me.'

'I go to the lady's address, all nice and polite and no sooner do I get my backside on her nice tan leather sofa than that maniac Higgings appears and puts a gun to my head.'

'The bastard.'

'I don't know anything about his parents but I do know he threatened to prevent me having more children and I believed him. Man, he's foaming at the mouth because you sent someone round to bother his lady. The boy Lamar gave him your name when Higgings caught up with him.'

'Is Lamar all right?'

'Yes, he spilled the beans to Higgings out of his bedroom window but it's me you should be worried about. He roughed me up bad, Dave. He ripped up my tam and cut off one of my locks with his blade.'

'Are you still in one piece?'

'Just about, he ruined my suit and that's going to cost you, Dave.'

'Did you find anything out?'

'Nothing good. When they threatened me I told them that swapping identities is illegal and they thought that was very funny. Her name isn't Lakesha Uhura anyway. She's really April Fothergill, and just for spite she rang the woman you're looking for, the phony receptionist, and told her that you were after her. She'll be in the wind now, man.'

'Oh,' I said nervously. 'Marvin, … er … Mr Desailles, do I need to look for a new lawyer?'

'Whaaaat! And me give up the best client I've ever had? No way, but I am going to charge you for a new suit and tam.'

'Fine by me.'

'And Dave, me bwoy, I didn't mean that about calling me Marvin. I just lost my cool there for a bit. That Shaka Higgings, that pervert! Next time the bacon feel his collar let him dare to come crawling to my door asking for the best black lawyer in town. We'll see who needs a decent haircut then.'

33

Thursday: 6.30 p.m.

Tony had got hold of a three year old Golf. It was black, which is a good colour for surveillance work. I'd decided to also take the BMW with me and asked him to check it out for bugs or trackers. I expected his 'portable' full spectrum device would be quite a sizeable piece of kit but the black plastic gadget he took from an inside pocket was no larger than an old mobile brick with two aerial prongs.

'You're clean, Boss,' he announced after walking round the car.

For good measure I sent him into every room in the house.

''Nothing, Dave,' he said, 'no transmissions whatever.'

'So why don't I feel secure?'

'This detector is the best on the market ...'

'So where did you get it? And don't tell me a mysterious friend lent it to you.'

He started fiddling with his fingers as if he was playing on an invisible keyboard.

'Best if you don't know, Dave.'

'A loyal employee has no secrets from his boss.'

His battered face furrowed as he put the re-wired brain into top gear. Finally he resolved his problem. It took him a minute.

'It was in that box we found at your place. I took it.'

'You light fingered little ...'

'Dave, it was too good to waste and I put it to good use, didn't I?'

I stared at him. He was right and maybe I was wrong. He was the future of private detection and I was the past.

He took my silence as an invitation to make a plea ... 'I think we should go back to Topfield and retrieve that whole box of tricks. There was a complete video surveillance kit for four operators.'

'What, you saw that in the few seconds I let you look?'

'I knew what I was looking at. There are these pocket cameras and they're wired to a lens which you wear as a button on your shirt. The camera transmits whatever it's focused on to the other three units and if you have Android on your mobile you get a split screen with four images. It's like doing surveillance with an extra three sets of eyes.'

'OK, maybe we'll try it but for now we've got to get to ourselves to Layborn Road Levenshulme before my ex-receptionist does another runner.'

I was banking on her waiting until her boyfriend arrived home from work. He knocked off at 5.30 p.m. I'd no proof but I was hoping that 'real' Fothergill, 'white' Fothergill, the notebook thief ... whatever I was supposed to call the damned woman ... would be linking up with Osman Ahmed Gullet before she made a move. That was my hunch based on years of old-fashioned non-electronic detective experience. Fothergill's sort never runs without the boyfriend if they can help it and on her previous form she wasn't the type to panic.

If I was wrong and she went solo I'd still have a chance to find out where she was from Ahmed Gullet. Maybe Tony's cameras and bugs would come in handy for that but meanwhile it was back to tried and trusted methods. I intended to confront Fothergill and get Lew's notebook back.

Tony and I set off in the Golf leaving Lee with instructions to bring along Clint in the BMW when he arrived from work. If the big guy was tired from lifting horses or pulling tractors out of ditches or whatever it was he'd been up to, that was too bad. I didn't need any more sulks. Communication would be through the sterile charged mobiles I had upstairs. The ones Tony had brought with him would also have to be charged. Maybe it was paranoia but then my enemies had been one step ahead throughout. It was time I put myself out in front.

We reached Levenshulme by 6.15.

By pure luck we were in time to see a tall, slender black man dressed in 'smart casual' western clothes turn into the street as we parked in a spot on Matthews Lane where we had a view of Layborn.

'He's Somali,' Tony said.

'How can you tell?'

'I just can. They're different from other black Africans.'

'Where's he going?'

The man turned into a house on the odd numbered side. By counting down we worked out that it was number fifteen.

I'd no way of being certain this guy was Osman but I said 'bingo' to myself. This was the best progress so far.

Our position on Matthews Lane wasn't good. We were on double yellows. Layborn Road itself was impossible. Two rows of terraced houses faced each across a narrow street, and every house had at least one car. There were no spaces, not that I fancied sitting in full view of so many windows. They'd think I was a bailiff if not the police. Sightlines from the park on the other side of Matthews Lane were tricky as dusk gathered and anyway there was another cross lane at the end of Layborn, not to mention a back alley. This was the sort of job where MI5 would use twenty men. I had Tony now and Lee when he finally arrived. I didn't include Clint, he'd probably be exhausted.

I sent Tony down the street. He returned in ten minutes.

'I got a peek into fifteen. The front door and the front window are wide open. There's Somali music blaring out. It's a party or something.'

Out of curiosity I opened the window. There was music.

'How do you know that's Somali music?' I asked, anxious to explore the limits of the reconditioned brain. Perhaps he knew where the tune was on the Somali charts.

'I don't but it's loud and repetitive and non-European and the house is full of Somalis and they're all jogging up and down to it.'

'Logical,' I muttered, 'but did you see Fothergill?'

'I don't know her, Dave. There were women but they were wearing Islamic kit.'

'Hijabs?'

'No, not veils; they were in long dresses, long sleeves, very modest stuff. I saw a few faces but I could only risk a quick squint. I don't want my throat cut.'

'Not a good idea.'

'A couple of them could have been white girls. That house is crammed with people, standing room only.'

I felt fury mounting.

'Hell and damnation! If only Fothergill and Osman were by themselves. As it is we'll have to wait until she makes a move and we're in the world's worst place to see which way she jumps.'

'So what do we do?' he asked.

I said nothing.

I didn't like to tell him that we were waiting until Clint got here and then I was going to storm Osman Ahmed Gullet's house. Fothergill was a thief and she owed me some answers as well as Lew's notebook.

Door kicking had been a speciality of my early days.

There was a long pause.

Then I became aware Tony was staring intently at the side of my head. Perhaps my fangs were showing.

'There is another way, Dave,' he said calmly.

'Go on,' I said, straining to be tolerant.

'I noticed that there's an empty house with a 'For Rent' sign three doors down on the other side from fifteen. I can break in round the back and then observe from upstairs.'

'It'll be alarmed. You'll have the whole street out after you.'

'Trust me, I won't.'

Light finally dawned in my un-reconditioned brain.

'You didn't happen to palm any of those spy cameras from the Topfield box did you?'

'As it happens, Dave, I did. They were like the *full spectrum, portable bug detector*, too good for a man in my line of work to leave lying around. I've got them here.'

He had a small rucksack in which I'd seen him stuff a flask of coffee and some biscuits before we set out. He took it off the back seat, rummaged around and plucked out a handful of miniature gizmos with lens attached on wires.

'Tra-la!' he crowed.

'You little bugger,' I said.

He laughed triumphantly.

'Great Tony, but can I remind you that your current line of work is as a temporary manager of a detective agency?'

'So? ... We've got to move with the times. You said yourself that bloody Schneider, our main competitor, has a top ex-military electronic expert working for him.'

There was no more to be said.

Half an hour later, we were unobtrusively parked in the entrance of a school two hundred yards away from the Layborn Road address. We were receiving good pictures of the front and back of Osman Ahmed Gullet's home. More and more people were arriving and entering the terraced house.

What the hell were they up to?

Some of the visitors were heavily bearded and were wearing long white robes.

I felt I was getting into deep waters.

The surveillance was proceeding satisfactorily. Lee was on his way with Clint, pausing only at one of the many MacDonald's in this part of Manchester to pick up half dozen or so Big Macs for Clint's evening snack. So why was I still full of gloom and foreboding?

It was the Islamic angle.

I'd discounted Appleyard's crazy Islamic terrorism riff mostly because the men who'd attacked me were very definitely white Brits. But Levenshulme has often figured in arrests of Islamic militants. One white British convert had even run a stall on Levenshulme market trying to recruit young men for the 'holy war'. The Levenshulme situation was one of the reasons why they'd set up regional branches of MI5, wasn't it?

Fothergill couldn't be caught up in all that, could she?

If she was an undercover holy warrior what was she doing in my office? But then I never had come up with *any* plausible reason for her being there and doing what she did.

Islamic terrorism might be it.

I catch her looking up Uncle Lew's in Who's Who and that same evening he's killed jihadi style. Yes, I'd already been through all that. English nobility used to get their heads chopped off at one time but we aren't living in the Middle Ages now, are we? There *have* been cases of completely non-religious killers decapitating their victims, haven't there? Maniacs of course ...

313

I was confused.

Up to this moment I'd speculated that Lew's murder was part of a 'false flag' operation by some bunch of loonies on the margins of the secret world. The MOLOCH scenario fitted that.

Now I was beginning to have doubts that the flag was false. I could have been wrong.

I ought to phone Brendan Cullen.

Yet I hesitated. Bren said they'd already discounted Fothergill. There could be any number of reasons for the gathering in Layborn Road and I'd look like a total fool if they raided the address and found nothing more provocative than someone blowing out candles on a birthday cake.

Lee finally arrived. He passed in burgers to us. I was hungry.

I came to a decision. Door kicking was off tonight. We'd watch and wait. There'd be an opportunity. Fothergill must have taken Lakesha William's tip-off seriously. OK, she'd gone to ground among a huge party of Somalis. It wasn't ideal but I could wait her out.

'What am I going to do with Jaws, Boss?' Lee asked. 'Shall I take him back home?'

Clint was doing his familiar performance of struggling with his seat belt. Bob really ought to buy a car designed for the XXX man. I got out and helped him unravel the belt.

'Stay where you are, Clint. You'll never get into a VW Golf.'

'It has four doors.'

'Clint, if you do jam yourself into it we'll need the Fire Brigade to cut you free.'

'It's only a one point two litre, not even a GTi and it's got standard wheels. It's low spec, Dave.'

'Yeah, not what a guy like you wants to be seen in. Stay in the Beamer and get some sleep. There'll be a job for you in the early hours of the morning.'

His gaunt features formed an enormous grin. I helped him to arrange his ungainly limbs in the back of the BMW. Being with him was twenty four hour parenting but I didn't mind. I waited until he was still.

'So what the hell's going on then?' Lee asked.

'Not a lot,' I said.

'I'm entitled to know. If we get picked up by the police I'll get done for whatever they do you for.'

'Lee, there's no reason for us to get done.'

'Oh yeah, well why are you spying on them and why are you carrying a gun? Are you expecting another shoot out like Wednesday night because you can count me out.'

'Gun?'

'It's in your belt behind your back. I saw it when you tucked Jaws up for beddie-byes.'

'He's right Dave. We didn't sign up for this,' Tony confirmed.

'The gun is insurance and for your protection as much as mine. You wouldn't be here if I hadn't had the Uzi on Wednesday.'

'Maybe not, but still Dave … I'm not suicidal like these hard guys who go around with guns. When they tangle with the cops they either end up dead or doing thirty years which is the same thing as far as I'm concerned.'

'Yeah, look at Beast. Even his own mother won't visit him,' Lee added. 'I'm walking away. I don't want to be banged up in the next cell to that bastard.'

'Wait! I'll unload the gun but how the hell am I going to control that mob in Layborn Road unless they think I'm armed?'

There was a brief debate between my employees before they accepted my offer.

I unloaded the Glock and handed the bullets to Tony. He put them in the glove compartment of the BMW.

'So who are we up against?' he asked when he got back in. 'I thought we were just finding this Fothergill woman?'

'We are but you can see with your own eyes that she's mixed up with people who could be the Islamic militants who killed Sir Lew Greene.'

'How do you make that out?' Tony asked.

'I wasn't ready to believe that Lew's killers were Islamics. You saw with your own eyes that those two who rigged the bomb were white guys and so were the earlier two.'

'Yeah, they weren't shouting *Allahu akbar*.'

Lee frowned as he followed his friend's argument.

'I didn't think she was a suspect before but Fothergill met Lew on the day he was killed. She checked him out in Who's Who and probably found out his address. Then she stole information he'd left for me and ...'

'... she disappears, your Uncle's murdered, she shacks up with her Muslim boyfriend and turns up wearing Islamic costume among a bunch of Somalis who just might be celebrating your uncle's murder.'

'So ...'

'That bitch!' Lee exclaimed, 'she's a f**king turncoat. Give me the gun; I'll fill her in myself.'

'Calm down, Lee, calm down,' I said in a Liverpool accent.

They both laughed politely.

'I don't know that's the right explanation of what Fothergill's been up to but it's possible,' I said.

There was silence for a while and then I sent Lee down Layborn Road to see what vibes he could pick up. It was possibly a mistake but Tony had been once and might rouse suspicions on a second trip so it had to be Lee. I wanted a feel about what was going on at 15 Layborn Road that electronics couldn't supply.

'It's a f**king wedding reception,' Lee said when he got back in the car twenty five minutes later. 'The neighbours are all going ape-shit. There's weird music and men dancing with each other in the back street. They've been at it all day and yesterday. One old guy said he'd called the police and a lot of f**king good that did. A copper told him to be tolerant of cultural differences or they'd do him for racism. And I'll tell you another thing, you know these Mozzies aren't supposed to drink?'

I nodded, astounded at his flow of words.

'Well, some of them are drunk out of their skulls and others are as high as kites on these leaves that they're chewing ...'

'It's khat,' said Know-all Nolan.

'No, they're not eating f**king cats! That's the Chinese, int it? They're doped, going round giggling at each other like a right bunch o'noodles. One of them wanted to dance with me but I showed him where to go.'

'Did you see Fothergill?'

316

'No women. The old guy I spoke to said they're all upstairs. They never have a party with men and women in the same room. Unnatural, int it?'

Lee's account confirmed what I was seeing with the spy cameras.

We settled down to wait. Things calmed down in Layborn Road and by midnight men were drifting away from the party. Fothergill didn't show her face. I'd heard of men wearing the burka as a disguise … but Islamic women dressing as men? That was a no-no. So Fothergill was still there *if* she'd ever been there, and *if* she'd not left Manchester as soon as Lakesha Uhura tipped her off.

There were too many ifs for comfort. If only Tony could have got a camera or a microphone *inside* the house.

The whole foray into Levenshulme had too many ifs but it clearly states in the Private Detective's Handbook that you follow your clues until you've eliminated all possibilities. Then what remains is the truth. I comforted myself that wherever Fothergill was Osman Ahmed Gullet was close by.

We took turns for short naps, two of us studying the receiving set while one dozed. Clint slept on peacefully.

After almost eight hours of squinting at a small screen the action started shortly after two. Three women, all wearing hijabs of various sizes and colours and up to eight men emerged onto the street. The women were also wearing ankle length coats: one coat was a light shade and the other two black or navy. They stood talking for a while then three taxis showed up at once and they all split up and began piling into them.

I started the car.

'Not this clapped-out heap,' Lee snarled. 'Get in the Beamer.'

He was right.

As we transferred I peered at the image on Tony's phone.

It was no use. It was impossible to see the hidden faces. My instinct told me that the woman who'd called herself April Fothergill would be in the lighter coat. That was probably some kind of residual racism … white woman – light coat … nonsense really but I had to pick one and she was the right height and general build.

'Can't you focus on this one?' I asked, tapping the image I hoped was Fothergill.

'You can,' he said, demonstrating the zoom function just as the woman climbed into the taxi. I noted that my target was carrying a heavy hold-all. It had to be Fothergill making a run for it. Three males got in the taxi with her and they were the first away.

'Lee, follow that cab and that isn't a joke.'

'Yes, Boss,' he grunted.

'How can you be sure it's her?' Tony challenged. 'They all look the same in those jilbabs.'

'Jilbabs?' I repeated.

'Yeah, the long coats are called jilbabs.'

It was the early hours of the morning and I was tired and uncertain and Tony's gift was grating on my nerves.

'Is it those men, Dave?' Clint said from the back.

'Some men and they could be bad guys, Jaws,' Lee answered. 'Just the sort you like to take apart. Why don't you sit back and enjoy the ride.'

Clint took no offence. When I turned to look at him he was smiling.

'Big joke,' he said. 'He means the man not the shark, Dave. Is there anything to drink?'

Tony fished in his rucksack and passed him a large carton of orange juice.

We followed the taxi onto Stockport Road. It turned towards the town centre but soon veered off left following Dickenson Road, Platt Lane and then Lloyd Street into the heart of Moss Side. Travelling painfully slowly the cab dropped off first one man and then another. It was now nearly three.

The cab pulled into the kerb to drop off its last fares near where Marvin had his encounter with Shaka Higgings. Was Fothergill one of Lakesha's neighbours?

'Lots of Somalis live round here, Boss,' Lee warned.

We watched a Somali man and a cloaked woman pay the driver and go towards a house.

'Drive past them very slowly,' I ordered.

'I'm not thick,' Lee protested.

As we crawled to within earshot of them they both turned towards us. Even in the yellow sodium street light it was obvious that the woman in the pale jilbab was black.

'So now what?' Lee asked as he accelerated away.

34

Friday: 2.00 – 3.00 a.m.

I was desperate. How could I be so wrong?

'Say they're leaving town, Fothergill and the boyfriend I mean, and they haven't got a car. Where do they go at this time of night?'

'Piccadilly Station,' Tony piped up like a school swot. This time I wasn't annoyed. I just prayed that he was right.

When we reached Piccadilly I left Lee and the now drowsing Clint in the car while Tony and I raced inside.

There were still trains arriving and a few people moving about but the first London train from Piccadilly wasn't until six a.m. London because it had to be a Somali fugitive's first choice of hiding place. Three hours of waiting would seem like an eternity to someone on the run.

We walked through the all night shops to make sure they weren't hiding somewhere. We couldn't find them.

Time was passing and I felt that Fothergill was slipping through my fingers again.

It was possible they were in a 24/7 cafe down in Piccadilly or Oldham Square but I hadn't the resources to check everything.

'Have you noticed the fares?' Tony asked as I stood panting under the destination display on the main concourse. 'It's more than a hundred quid to London.'

'I didn't pay her enough to make her rich.'

That left buses.

'They'll not be going on a bus,' Lee opined when we got back in the car. 'Who goes on a bus these days?'

'Not everyone's as good at nicking cars as you are,' I snapped.

Chorlton Street bus station was lit up like a Dutch brothel but nothing was happening inside. A few people and cars were gathered in the street outside waiting for arrivals or departures. I ran up and down both sides of the street looking in cars and doorways.

There was no sign of Fothergill.

To cap everything it started raining heavily.

I enquired at the ticket kiosk. Sweat was running into my eyes.

'There's a bus due in from Aberdeen and a military bus going to Aldershot, that's all we've got in the next hour.'

'I'm looking for this couple, she's English and he's a Somali man. It's delicate, she's running away,' I gasped.

'Nobody like that been here, mate,' the man said dismissively. What would he have done if I'd said the girl was twelve years old: another shrug? I might have hit him if he wasn't in a Perspex booth.

My disappointment must have been almost out of control because he took pity on me.

'Try the other bus station,' he suggested. 'Shudehill's busier than this place these days.'

'Have you got a timetable or anything,' I pleaded. 'They're heading for London.'

He shook his head. My hunger for violence surged again.

Instead I shoved a twenty pound note over the counter.

'Like that is it?' he said, 'life and death? We're National and I'm not supposed to give out stuff about rival companies but seeing as you're so friendly ...'

He pocketed the note, turned and went round the back for a moment.

'There's a Preston to London Megabus leaving Shudehill Interchange at four a.m.' he said when he came back.

It was now just after three forty five.

We made it to Shudehill by three fifty. Switching drivers, Tony circled the block in the BMW while Lee and I dashed into the bus depot.

The blue London-bound bus had just pulled in from Preston. The driver was lifting up the luggage hatch for the line of passengers.

I scanned the crowd.

There were two figures in black burkas standing with their backs to me, one tall and the other shorter.

It could only be Fothergill and her partner. They must have

changed to trick me.

I advanced into the queue and grabbed the shorter person by the arm and spun her round.

The woman's face was completely veiled in black. There was a narrow gap for vision and a pair of thick specs poked out of that. Behind the specs was a pair of very dark eyes. I glanced down at the woman's feet. She was wearing sandals without socks. Her skin was brown.

Her companion was heavily built and pregnant and also had specs in her letterbox.

They both started to wail. It wasn't a loud sound, just thin and persistent and I guessed they could keep it up for hours.

I whipped out my private detective's ID, the one with the photo and the Pimpernel Investigations logo and flashed it at them. It looks nothing like a police warrant card but I didn't let them look at it for long.

'Sorry, police, mistake,' I babbled.

At the mention of the word police the wailing suddenly stopped. The pregnant one was holding a white plastic bag, which she held protectively to her bosom. Our eyes met for a moment and then she lowered her head and pressed forward to stow her suitcase in the luggage compartment.

None of the other passengers, who included several Muslims, made any fuss on their behalf. It was so early in the morning that I think a lot of them were asleep on their feet.

Lee grabbed my arm and pulled me away.

'Nice one, Boss,' he said gleefully, 'for your next trick try grabbing someone really feisty like a couple of nuns. We'd better clear off before the Filth arrives. That driver saw you.'

I've experienced some bitter moments. Having a cell door slammed in my face and being told I was a nonce were among them, but this was special. If I couldn't pin down Lew's killer it wasn't just my life in jeopardy.

We began to walk away. At that moment a taxi drew up in the street outside and a couple got out and began running to the bus.

I pulled Lee behind a pillar.

I hardly dared to breathe in case the sound frightened them

away.

It was Fothergill and her Somali pal and they weren't wearing Islamic costumes. Fothergill was in blue jeans and a dark jacket. There was a white baseball cap on her head. She was still the same trim, neat person I'd had such confidence in at the Pimpernel office. Osman was in a leather jacket and denim jeans. The only Islamic touch was the white crocheted cotton cap on his head. Both were wearing small rucksacks and carrying plastic bags in their hands.

I let them pass us and then jumped out and shoved the Glock into Osman's back.

'Going somewhere, Miss Fothergill?' I asked.

'Mr Cunane!' she said in sudden fright, dropping her hand luggage. Even under the artificial lights I could see the colour drain out of her face. I let her glimpse the Glock while still covering Osman. I've seen enough fear in people's faces to know that my former receptionist was expecting me to kill her. Her face and body were screwed up as she waited for my bullet.

Suddenly, what should have been a moment of triumph was the very opposite.

I felt sick.

The Somali somehow sensed my moment of weakness; his free right hand moved towards his jacket.

'Don't Osman,' I said 'or you'll get a taste of what Lew Greene got.'

'That wasn't us. It wasn't our fault,' the interpreter blustered in heavily accented English. His hand was still moving to his inside pocket.

I jammed the gun even harder into his back.

'I'll shoot,' I warned.

'Yeah, do, Boss,' Lee advised. 'Give him what his mates gave your uncle. Shoot the bastard.'

'Do what he says, Osman,' Fothergill gasped. She reached her hand out to the Somali and clutched his arm.

I could feel the tension in Osman's body. All his muscles were coiled for action. I got ready to deck him with the gun. There was no way Fothergill was walking away from me again.

324

Then Osman exhaled slowly and the stress went out of him. He muttered something in Somali.

'Check him out, Lee,' I ordered.

Lee pushed Fothergill out of the way, pulled Osman's arm down to his side and then thrust his hand into the jacket.

'Nice,' he said, pulling out a large curved knife. He then twisted Osman and, pulling the scabbard off him, sheathed the curved blade.

'You can get five years for carrying that thing around,' I commented oddly. I was so relieved at disarming him without bloodshed that I might have said anything. I slipped the Glock under my belt behind my back.

'You're not the police. You're only private,' he spluttered.

'I'm the man who's telling you what to do,' I said. 'You're booked on that coach aren't you?'

'We both are,' Fothergill said quietly, finding her voice again although her face still had a deathly pallor.

'Well, Osman's catching the bus; but not you Miss Fothergill. You've got something that belongs to me.'

'You're not letting him go,' Lee protested. 'Your uncle's dead because of this piece of shit.'

'You heard him, I'm not the police. I can't arrest him and I don't want to shoot him but I want rid. He's going on that bus if he doesn't want me to take him on a visit to MI5.'

Fothergill and Osman stared at each other for a moment. It would be nice to say that a look of love and longing passed between them but it didn't. The only impression I got was of frantic calculation by two desperate and not very involved people. The last passengers were filing onto the bus. The driver checked his booking roster and looked around.

'Go!' Fothergill urged. 'I'll text you.'

I wasn't convinced by her nobility. The woman had a stage career ahead of her.

All I wanted from her was my stolen property and some information.

I realised that I had no idea what was going on in her head.

Osman bent forward and gave her a hasty peck on the cheek and then dived onto the bus.

We stood for three more minutes until the bus pulled out of the Interchange punctually at 4 a.m.. Osman was in a seat at the back. There was no particular expression on his dark face as the bus slid past us and no wave for Fothergill.

She, however, had tears in her eyes.

'Next stop London,' Lee announced.

I came down from the adrenaline rush and suddenly felt tired at the prospect of what lay ahead.

I wasn't ready to trust dear, sweet Miss Fothergill not to have all kinds of secret equipment stowed beneath her so-normal exterior. Still, if she did have hidden knives or guns I was stymied. I couldn't search her in the middle of a bus station or anywhere else for that matter.

She appeared to be on the point of fainting, a brilliant actress. The quick look of calculation that passed between her and the Somali gave the lie to this emotional scene.

We each took an arm and escorted her out to the street. I realised that what I was doing could be called kidnapping.

Tony completed his circuit in the BMW and pulled in opposite us. He gestured to me with his hands. I realised that he was signalling that there wasn't room for Fothergill, Clint and a third person in the back. Opening the door, Clint sprang out onto the pavement, followed by Tony holding out the car keys to Lee.

Fothergill looked at Clint and flinched.

'This proves you're a criminal,' she said.

'What are you on about?' I asked.

'You're a filthy murdering criminal and this is your gang,' she said.

'Get in the car,' I ordered.

'What, so you can kill me?'

'Clint, pick her up. Tony go round to the other side, she'll sit between us.'

Clint did as he was told, inserted the terrified woman into the rear middle seat and then took the front seat.

Lee did a u-turn and headed out of the city centre.

'You cold hearted maniac,' she said. 'Where are you taking me? I've a right to know if you're going to kill me.'

'Cold hearted, that's good from the piece of work who methodically spied on me for weeks. We're going to somewhere that's convenient to ask you a few questions. Now, get your head down and shut up.'

I yanked her baseball cap down over her eyes and made sure she wasn't looking out.

I watched her closely. Her breathing came back to normal but her lips continued to tremble and she gave a convincing impression of someone who was surprised at still being alive.

The drive back to Ridley Close seemed to go on forever. The shop fronts and buildings along our route through Sale were becoming as familiar to me as the path to my own front door. A faint predawn light was illuminating the trees when we turned into Ridley Close.

My problems began when Lee drove into the dark space of the garage.

The prisoner let out a little shriek.

'This is where you're going to kill me, isn't it?' she gasped.

'No,' I said sharply.

'You are. You're a murderer. I heard you say it.'

'Get her out of the car,' I ordered, speaking more harshly than I intended because I was anxious to prevent her rousing the neighbourhood by screaming her silly head off.

She wouldn't get out of the car. She struggled and when Lee leaned forward to get his arm round her she gave him a bloody nose with her elbow. He recoiled, cursing.

Clint reached in with his long arms and hauled her out. She lashed out and kicked with all her strength but his long arms held her still. The struggle seemed to revive her.

'You've no right to do this,' she sobbed when the big man carried her close to his chest like a struggling infant.

'And you've got the right to spy and steal, have you?' I snarled, when we installed her in the kitchen. She seemed especially terrified of Clint so I sent him out.

327

I made her sit down while Lee and Tony stood guard over her but she'd got her nerve back and I wanted to keep her off balance.

I took a deep breath.

'Watch her,' I ordered and went upstairs to the bathroom in my room. My jeans and t-shirt felt frowsty and my whole body was sticky with dried sweat. I stripped and shaved carefully then took a long shower running the water as hot as I could bear it.

I'd noticed previously that Bob favoured Calvin Klein toiletries and had the full range in large quantities and now I liberally applied men's all-over body wash and shampoo. Then I slapped on the after shave and eau de cologne. When I left that bathroom I was a clean and fresh man.

My choice of clothes was not extensive. I'd renovated the black leather shoes which had been ruined during the escape along the canal bank and I had the charcoal Austin Reed suit. There was also a pair of clean jeans and a fresh t-shirt.

Fothergill was expecting to be confronted by a gangster. It might help to refute that image of me she was cultivating if I was formally dressed. So Austin Reed it was. I had a reasonable shirt and rooted through Bob's wardrobe for a wearable tie.

I brushed my hair carefully and examined the result in Tammy's full length mirror. Yes, Dave Cunane was back, the old charmer. All I had to do now was get to the bottom of what was going on in my former receptionist's confused mind.

Simple.

It was after 5 a.m. when I went downstairs and the atmosphere in the kitchen had subtly changed. Tony now seemed more like Fothergill's companion than her captor. Lee still looked hostile.

'Have you been talking to her?' I asked.

'It was nothing,' Tony said quickly. I could tell he was lying.

'She's a liar and a thief and you need to be careful with the likes of her.'

'Is it lying and stealing to collect evidence about a criminal?' she yelled. 'Anyway, you're going to kill me whatever I say.'

'Bitch!' Lee snarled, removing the bloody handkerchief he'd

clamped over his face for a moment. She'd really done a job on his nose. 'We let your freaky friend with the big knife go but someone's going to pay for what you've done.'

He brandished the knife he'd taken off Osman and mimed cutting his throat. What with the dried blood all over his mug and neck and the crazed expression it was a convincing act.

Fothergill slumped forward.

Tears began forming in her eyes.

I wasn't impressed.

'I told him not to bring that with him but Somali men don't feel dressed unless they're carrying a knife.' she said in a quavering voice.

She gave Lee a look of supplication then put her head in her hands and began sobbing bitterly. Her body shook.

Clever actress or frightened woman, I knew what my theory was, but her melodramatics had an immediate effect on Lee.

His bloodthirsty fury evaporated.

First he hid the dagger behind his back and as the heart wringing sobs showed no sign of abating, he put it in a cupboard. Then he held his hands up in front of Fothergill to show he had no evil intent.

Brilliant, one pout from those pretty lips and he's a no-show.

Trust me to employ the one thug in Manchester with severe qualms about threatening people, even people who richly deserved to be threatened.

'That's enough, Lee,' I said. 'Wash your face.'

Whether Fothergill was watching through her fingers or genuinely recovering from her fright I don't know but the sobbing and heaving subsided.

'I can't do this, Boss,' Lee whispered in my ear. 'It's inhuman. If you're going to chain her up in the cellar and beat her up you'll have to do it without me.'

'Wash your face,' I repeated, pushing him away. He grabbed a wet cloth off the sink and stood by the back door wiping his face.

I followed him.

'When we were at Shudehill, Lee, you wanted me to shoot this woman's boyfriend in cold blood so don't come over all gooey on me now.'

'That was different. He's a killer and he has it coming.'

'Different because he's a bloke and she's a fit looking woman?'

He shrugged and I turned away from him.

Tony had also beaten a retreat. He was now sitting at the kitchen island, with his head in a book and pretending to tune out the scene around him.

That left me.

'All right, *Miss Fothergill*, or whoever you are, don't phone us, we'll phone you if you've got the part in our soap opera,' I said sarcastically. 'I don't buy all this. You tricked me and bugged me for three months. You're no sob sister and I'm no killer. All I want from you is the truth. Give it me and you can go on your way. We'll start with your real name.'

'That's none of your business.'

'The sooner you give me the truth the quicker we can finish this little drama you're enjoying so much.'

She shook her head and shut her lips.

Clint came in at that precise moment, pretending that he needed a drink of water. Actually he'd heard me coming downstairs and was just being nosy. In his obliging way with women, he turned and smiled warmly at Fothergill. She started trembling. No pouting for Clint. There's nothing sinister about Clint's smile, quite the reverse, but all those teeth in that gaunt face broke her resolve.

'Pauline Milner,' she said in a low voice.

'Why did you pull your stunt with Lakesha Uhura and the Office Temp Agency?'

'She had the right qualifications for a job with you. I didn't.'

'You mean you're unqualified for office work?'

'No, I'm overqualified. I have a good degree in business studies and I'm doing an MBA. That crummy Agency wouldn't have sent me out on routine work.'

That rang true. She'd certainly been in a class of her own as a receptionist.

'Why did you want a job in my office apart from the obvious

reason that you're a spy?'

'I'm not a spy.'

'You had an electronic recorder under your desk and a bug in my office.'

'Oh, that!'

'Yes!'

She thought for a moment.

'I do occasional part time work for a firm of solicitors, GKY. They had an important client who wanted to check up on what you were up to. They arranged for Lakesha to get the job and switch with me. She was well paid for a few hours of her time and she gave me a quick course on being a receptionist. I was shown what to do with the recorder and I delivered the information to their office. I never listened to any of it myself so I don't know your filthy secrets and you don't need to kill me. I was told to keep very quiet and not be inquisitive so you'd have no excuse to fire me and it worked. I kept my eyes to myself and said nothing and you didn't fire me. In fact I think you mistook me for a piece of furniture.'

'The one thing I didn't mistake you for was a spy.'

She was seated, I was standing and I was tired and the Glock was digging a hole in the base of my spine. I pulled the gun out.

Fothergill/Milner jumped in fright.

'Sorry,' I said. 'It isn't loaded.'

I pointed at the ceiling and pulled the trigger. Click.

It didn't make any difference. Her eyes were bulging with terror.

'He isn't a killer,' Tony volunteered. 'He's a genuine private detective.'

'That's what you think,' she said bitterly. 'I know differently.'

My patience was wearing very thin.

'Who was the mystery client?'

'They wouldn't tell me but I found out his name when you murdered him.'

'Are you mental?'

'It was that old man who came to your office on Monday. I recognised his voice because he spoke to me on the phone at GKY when I took the job. It was such a cultured voice, one you wouldn't forget. I wouldn't have taken the job if he hadn't reassured me that it was all quite above board. He sounded very distinguished. He said he needed to confirm something about you for a most important reason and that what I was doing wasn't strictly illegal but he couldn't explain. It was obvious to me that he wanted to break some sort of hold you had over him.'

I struggled to grasp what she was saying.

'You think I killed Sir Lew Greene?'

'That's exactly what you did.'

'He was my godfather and my cousin,' I protested weakly. This was turning into a nightmare.

'Did you think for a moment I was taken in by that little act you both put on for my benefit? As if he was your godfather, it's ridiculous. How could a man like that be connected to a crook like you? I looked him up in Who's Who and there was no mention of any Cunanes. You were blackmailing him and that notebook he left in the safe was the proof.'

There was whisky on the counter. I found a glass, poured myself a slug and downed it in one. I was shaken.

35

Friday: early hours

I pulled up a chair and sat down opposite Fothergill/Milner at the small kitchen table. I may have been scowling. If I was, it was only to be expected. This woman had shared my office for months and all that time she'd believed I was a dangerous criminal.

As for charming the truth out of her I might as well have tried to charm a hungry tiger out of eating me. The only time she'd opened up was when she thought poor soft Clint was going to knock nine bells out of her.

I looked into her blue eyes. She stared back defiantly.

'Sir Lew Greene really was my godfather,' I rasped. 'Have I to go and get the photos of my christening?'

She shook her head.

'It would just be more lies.'

'Where's the notebook you stole?'

'You'll kill me if I tell you.'

'For the last time I'm not a killer but you are a thief and don't think I don't know how you found the safe combination.'

'Lakesha showed me how to do that,' she said without a blush. 'She'd seen the safe through your window and she said no-one who hadn't got plenty to hide would have something like that. It was just as well because that was where you put the notebook you were using to blackmail poor Sir Lew.'

'Blackmail? You really are mental. I've already told you Lew was my godfather. There's nothing I could possibly have blackmailed him about even if I'd wanted to.'

'You were blackmailing him,' she said triumphantly. 'I heard you shouting about it. Those walls are thin. You said you used blackmail, bribery and wiretaps and then you said you'd gone on to blackmail in one easy move. I wrote it down, one easy move. It stuck in my mind. And I definitely heard you say you were a professional killer.'

This time the civilised veneer came right off. I slammed my hands down on the table top.

'I said *he'd* gone on to blackmail in one easy move,' I roared, '*He* wanted me to kill someone.'

Fothergill jumped in fright and let out a little whimper. I knew she was acting but Lee sidled up to the table. Before he could open his mouth to accuse me of crimes against humanity I pointed to the back door. He moved away.

'Like the nasty little Keyhole Kate you are, you got the story back to front. I don't want to upset my chivalrous young friend over there but I'm getting seriously pissed off with you.'

She gave another little whimper of pretended fear.

'Where's the notebook you stole on Monday?' I asked. It was hard to grasp that all this kicked off less than a week ago.

'If I tell you what's to stop you killing me? That notebook's the only thing that's keeping me alive because you know if it's found it'll prove you're a blackmailer and killer.'

I felt as if I'd been kicked in the stomach. Lee was right. If we went on like this I'd end up slapping her around in sheer frustration.

I stepped across to the hall and summoned Clint, my ultimate sanction. If it hadn't been so serious it would have been funny. She apparently believed that Clint, friend of animals and protector of women, was capable of wringing her neck.

He came in quickly. I could see he was still peeved about being excluded.

'Clint, I want you to stand in this doorway like one of the Queen's soldiers on guard at Buckingham Palace.'

'Yes, Dave,' he said with a smile as wide as the Atlantic on his gaunt face.

'No one is to leave this room. Not her,' I said, pointing, 'not Tony and not Lee: no-one is to leave. Do you understand?'

'Yes, Dave, that's easy.'

'Whatever they say you don't let them go out. It's dangerous out there. Those bad men may be waiting.'

He nodded and folded his arms across his chest.

'You can count on me, Dave.'

'I knew I could. I'll be in the garden so no one will go out that way either.'

I went to the backdoor and took a gulp of cool morning air. I stood for some minutes practicing deep breathing. When my pulse returned to normal I turned to face them.

Lee and Tony looked like a pair of actors who'd just found themselves in leading roles in the world's very worst play. Fothergill/Milner was cowering with her head in her hands like one of Henry the Eighth's wives waiting for the axe to fall.

'This has got to end, one way or another,' I said in a sepulchral voice. 'This is what we'll do.'

My assistants exchanged frightened stares as if I was about to order them to dig a mass grave.

'You two seem to be on the same wavelength as this lunatic. I'll give you some time to talk sense into her head. You've got to convince her that she's completely wrong about me. I am not a blackmailer and murderer. I've never killed anyone except in self defence which is what put some completely wrong ideas in Sir Lew's head. Lee, please lend me some tobacco and Rizla papers. I'm going out for a smoke and when I come back I want to know where that notebook is or I can't be responsible for the consequences.'

The soft-hearted little scally began fumbling in his pockets. In the end he made two roll-ups for me. As I left Tony looked at me and nodded his head. A flash of that scary intellect appeared on his face.

'Fifteen minutes,' I said and slammed the door shut as I went out.

It was years since I'd smoked but it's like riding a bicycle. The mild Virginia smoke slid into my lungs and I tried to relax by thinking of my children sleeping peacefully at Lough Gara. I was tempted to phone Jan but a call in the early hours was sure to send her to the airport for the next plane to Manchester, not a good idea.

Instead I sent a text to Marvin on Aunty Velmore's phone asking him to check if charges for the spying operation appeared on Lew's accounts from GKY, the giant law firm he'd also chosen to transact his will. There had to be a paper trail and it would be nice to know if I was still paying to be spied on.

If I was, Marvin could refuse payment on grounds of illegality and dob them in to the Law Society if he liked.

Thank you very much Uncle Lew.

My anger flared. This was 'déjà vu all over again'. Hadn't I once before paid wages to a bunch of employees who were betraying me? I tried to swim back against the tide of self-pity but it was hard. People laugh at post traumatic stress but it's real.

I went in.

Clint was still at attention by the kitchen door. Fothergill/Milner, Lee and Tony were seated at the table drinking coffee, all very matey.

'It's all right, Dave,' Tony said quickly. 'Pauline knows she got it all wrong about you and that's your Uncle Lew's fault.'

'Yeah, he gave her the wrong slant on things,' Lee seconded. 'I think he was really checking you out, Boss.'

'It could be,' I agreed. 'That explains the spying but not why she stole the notebook.'

'It's like this,' Tony explained, 'thinking the worst of you and the best of him when she heard all that about murder and blackmail she naturally thought it was you saying it.'

'Can't she speak for herself?'

'What he's saying is right,' Milner said in a low voice. 'I did think it was you but now, after what Tony's said I think I might have jumped to conclusions.'

'Thanks a bunch! Why did you take the notebook?'

'When you came out and caught me with Who's Who open at Sir Lew's entry I was terrified. I thought you'd found me out and after what I'd heard I was sure you'd want to kill me. I almost ran then but that would have raised your suspicions so I waited until the end of the day. I had to hide from you. I'd met a friend at a salsa dancing class at Boxers Night Club.'

'Osman,' I muttered.

Boxers is one of Bob Lane's clubs.

'Yes, he'd already suggested that I move in with him. Osman knows all about hiding. He came here on a student visa ... '

'But he's overstayed and now he's an illegal immigrant?' I interjected. 'So if you marry him he has a chance of legal status?'

She pursed her lips and nodded.

His illegal status would explain why he hadn't screamed for the police when we collared him at Shudehill Interchange.

'Then we heard that you were paying people to find me so Osman got the Islamic costume from a friend and I wore it when I had to go out but you still found me.'

'But it was more than Islamic costume wasn't it? Are you an Islamic jihadi?'

She laughed.

'You've got it all wrong. My parents are Methodists and I still go to church.'

'Good for you but you were hanging out with a bunch of Islamic militants when we found you.'

'They're not militants; they're just ordinary Somali Muslims. They were celebrating Osman's cousin's wedding to another cousin. It's a clan thing. The wedding was the day before yesterday but the celebrations go on for days. They'll probably still be at it next week. Osman doesn't really approve of the traditional ways.'

'Go on.'

'Osman isn't as deep into Islam as they are. He hasn't been to mosque since he arrived in England.'

'That would be why he was wearing an Islamic crocheted hat and carrying a ruddy big dagger when we met him, would it?'

'The knife was to protect me and he wears the hat, the kufi, to convince his uncle Mansuur that he's still a loyal Muslim. He's been dependent on Mansuur since he overstayed his visa.'

'OK, let's skip Osman's life history. Where's the notebook you stole?'

'Yeah, er, Boss,' Tony broke in, 'we've been talking about that. Pauline still isn't absolutely certain that you have her best interests at heart.'

'That's right Tony, victims of robbery rarely think well of thieves. You should know that.'

'There's no need to be sarcastic, Dave. Pauline's admitted that she hid the notebook in your office.'

'Sounds likely!'

'She doesn't have it on her. We made her turn out all her bags and everything. So I believe her.'

'And I should entrust the lives of my children to your judgement Tony?'

'You've already trusted your own life to it,' he said.

There was no answer to that.

'The deal is this. If you allow us to take her to the office she'll show us where the notebook is and then we'll let her go and bring back the notebook.'

'Nice! The minute you're out of this house she'll cut loose and tell the police she's been kidnapped. She's got you just where she wants you. I'm coming with you.'

'Dave, a word in private please,' Tony said pushing back his chair and advancing towards me. He put his arm on my shoulder and steered me to the backdoor. Was I now under the control of the reconditioned brain?

'Listen,' he said in a low voice, 'I know it's rubbish but Pauline really believes that if she gets in that car with you she'll be making her last journey. She thinks you'll shoot her in the head when you get the book.'

'That is rubbish.'

'Dave, it's not what I believe. It's what she believes. You were really cold to her when she worked with you and she's convinced herself that if not actually a killer you could be.'

I seethed. I wanted that notebook so badly that I was almost ready to kill for it, almost but not quite.

I turned to face 'Pauline Milner', an identity that was as dissonant as the note a cracked bell to me.

'All right, luvvie,' I said in a fruity Manchester accent, 'I'm considering the plan my friends have come up with. You see they

338

sympathise with criminals because they're ex-criminals themselves. I don't and I've never been a criminal so you need to convince me that you won't be down at the cop shop screaming kidnap as soon as these two let you go.'

'I won't go to the police because Osman will lose any chance of gaining UK residence if they find he's been involved in theft. Let me go and you'll get your precious notebook back. Anyway, I couldn't lead the police to you because I don't know where this house is.'

Two reasons: one so-so and one good. It was true that she hadn't seen much on the journey to Altrincham.

I looked at her. It was the same expressionless face I'd seen across the reception desk at Pimpernel for weeks. What was she: a mistaken fool or a master spy? Whatever she was, she was a lot cooler than she'd been earlier.

My hunger to have that notebook in my hand was intense and it was true that I'd already entrusted my life to Tony Nolan and his reconditioned brain. Still, there was always Bob's cellar. I could demand that she tell them where the notebook was stashed and lock her in there until her two admirers brought the book back. The drawback was that I'd lose whatever trust and credit I currently had with Tony and Lee.

I didn't need a reconditioned brain to work that one out.

'OK, I agree to your arrangement Tony, but with one modification. Clint goes with you and if she doesn't hand over the notebook he brings her back.'

We all looked at Clint, whose eyes gleamed with satisfaction.

Tony then turned to Lee who nodded his head. To my satisfaction neither consulted 'Pauline'.

'OK by me, Boss,' Lee agreed.

'And Miss Fothergill, and you'll always be Miss Fothergill to me, you can look on this trip to the suburbs as a belated leaving 'do' from Pimpernel Investigations. I don't want to see you again and just to make sure that you don't know where this house is do you mind wearing your hijab over your face as a blindfold? It's not that I don't trust you but you know what they say... once bitten, twice shy?'

'You don't need to be like that, Mr Cunane,' she said cattily, 'spying on you was your own relative's idea so maybe he thought there was no smoke without fire?'

'Hmmm, I suppose one proverb deserves another but just get out of here before I change my mind.'

I put her phone down on the table in front of her giving the battery to Lee.

'She gets the battery when you kiss her goodbye.'

They left quickly but before departure I made sure Clint understood his part and I also retrieved the bullets for the Glock.

When they'd gone I made myself a cup of coffee. It was the last thing I needed because I was already wired but it seemed like the thing to do. I went into one of the reception rooms and sat back on the sofa. My mind was buzzing. What was I going to do when I learned the name of Lew's mystery plotter? I'd have to give the book to Claverhouse and Appleyard but it was hard to trust them. Brendan Cullen yes, but it was impossible to know which side of the fence Claverhouse and Appleyard were really on.

No, I'd have to play it the way Lew had originally wanted. He didn't trust anyone official. He'd wanted me to be his avenging angel and had gone to a lot of trouble to make sure he had the right man. I guessed that Lew was one of those people who know how to get rich and stay rich. He'd married a rich woman and never spent a penny since or made an investment without thorough research. How long had he known he might need me, 'a man capable of drastic measures' as he believed? Or had he only started investigating me when he decided to entrust me with his massive fortune? Whatever the reason was he'd enmeshed me in his web.

There was also the thought that the old prude probably stuck a pretty young woman in my office to see if I'd given up my bed-hopping ways.

So when the notebook arrived I'd have the mystery plotter's name: Joe Bloggs for the sake of argument. Then I was supposed to set myself up as judge, jury and executioner and kill Mr J Bloggs? I didn't think so. The best I could hope for now was to make a deal with Joseph Bloggs Esquire: immunity in return for my silence.

Was such immunity even remotely possible?

Joe Bloggs was powerful, might even be on the point of achieving supreme power. Wouldn't he squash me like a bug as soon as I came into his range? The best solution for Jan and the children might be if I picked up the Glock and blew my brains out.

No, that wouldn't happen.

I took the Glock and put it into Bob's rucksack and after a moment's thought went upstairs for the Uzi and the bullet proof jackets and packed them as well. Things were getting lively and I might need them in a hurry. It was better to be safe than sorry. Always careful not to offend my tender minder assistants I put the rucksack away in a cupboard.

I would try to lie low and keep out of things; maybe slip off to Ireland and take the family to the Italian villa. Everything might blow over. How could an individual be expected to influence events on this scale?

It was too much and I must have fallen asleep at that point.

When I came to the Aunty Velmore phone was ringing.

Time had passed and my sidekicks hadn't returned. It was nearly eight a.m. Something must have gone wrong. That cunning woman had tricked them. I should never have let her go.

The phone rang insistently.

I picked it up.

'Dave, I got your text,' Marvin said throatily.

'Marvin, I'm so sorry. I texted you because I didn't want to wake you up early.'

'Man, I sleep with the phone right next to me. You woke up Cissy and she kick me out of bed.'

Cissy, aka Cecilia Roebuck, is Marvin's partner.

'So I'm up and I t'ink I might as well go down to the office right there and then an take a look and there it is. GKY is charging the estate for special business research. It started with at an initial cost of three and a half grand and is marked "continuing" at five hundred a week for the last three months. I've already queried this and the man at GKY came over all vague on me ... he don' know what it is, some private research they're doing for Sir Lew.'

'Spying on me, that's what the research is.'

I filled him in on the details.

'Dave, you know GKY are the guys who complained to the Law Society 'bout me after I started calling my business DQW for a laugh. The word on them is that GKY stands for Go Kill Yourself and they don' like a one man firm taking the piss out of them.'

'So now you'll be able to get your own back.'

'Best not Dave, they employ hundreds of people and I'm still one man. They'd wear me down.'

'OK, but you can tell them we're challenging that part of their bill and tell them exactly why.'

'I'd like to do that Dave but as your lawyer I must advise you that it's better to pay up and shut up. A big firm like GKY will just drag you through the courts with appeals and delays and you'll end up paying much more than what they're charging for your uncle's little game and I guess they don't feel they owe you any favours after you let me take the Weldsley Estate business away from them.'

'Well ...'

'Listen Dave, mon, accentuate de positive. This girl was clever enough to get two people to pay her wages for the same work and then to hide in plain sight but you got her. You're like a terrier Dave, once you get your teeth in you don' let go.'

'Thanks for the advice Marvin. Do what you think best about GKY.'

'Do you want me to come and look at the notebook wit' you? Be a witness, like.'

'Marvin, these people have already tried to kill me four times because they thought I'd had a look at it. It wouldn't be healthy for you to take a peek.'

'Go on.'

'No. I'm not going to cause Cissy a load of grief by getting you killed. I feel bad enough about what Shaka Higgins did to you.'

He laughed and closed the call.

36

Friday: 8.10 a.m.

I heard the car pull up outside.

Clint, Tony and Lee were in it and Tony was holding up a sealed envelope.

They'd got the notebook.

They rushed into the house.

'We put her on the eight o'clock London train,' Tony started.

'Forget about her,' I snapped. 'She's not important now.'

'Tony and Lee paid for her ticket,' Clint said.

'Hey, Jaws, zip it up,' Lee warned.

My heart had already started pounding but before ripping the notebook out of the envelope I remembered what I'd said to Marvin about the danger of knowing too much. My associates had gathered round to share any discovery.

'Guys, it's better if I do this alone,' I said, 'then if you need to deny that you know anything you can be convincing.'

'You're wrong, Dave, if we get to the stage where we're denying things it'll already be too late,' Tony said. 'Knowing things might help us live a little longer. We're all in this together or we're out. Just say the word and we'll go.'

'Damn right,' muttered Lee.

I decided to make no further noble but pointless statements of the bleeding obvious.

The envelope was exactly the same as I'd left it on Monday when I'd swathed it in three yards of Sellotape. It didn't appear to have been opened.

'Where was it?'

'You know the office has a suspended ceiling?' Tony said.

'I should, I had it installed.'

'Pauline just went into the office, climbed on the desk, pushed up a ceiling tile and pulled this out. We'd have found it if we'd searched but we didn't even look.'

'Why would you? But has it been tampered with since Monday?'

'Let me make sure,' Tony insisted.

Reluctantly I parted company with the envelope.

He examined it under a strong light.

'This hasn't been opened, Dave. See the outer layer of paper covering the padded envelope?'

'Yes.'

'It's thin and tears easily. It's layered for security reasons. These envelopes are used for high value goods; passports, cash, jewellery and stuff. If you stick it up with extra Sellotape like you did, then you'll tear the outer skin when you take the tape off and you can see if it's been tampered with. This hasn't. There's no way anyone could remove all this Sellotape without ripping the paper and I can see where you wrote Private and Confidential and signed it in your handwriting so it's the same envelope.'

He was convincing but MI5 have the resources to swap the envelope and copy the handwriting but as I couldn't imagine why they would bother I kept my mouth shut. I found a sharp knife, slashed the tape and pulled out the notebook.

It appeared to be the same notebook I'd handled on Monday: small, about four and a half inches by three and bound in luxurious black leather. The letters LG were embossed in gold on the top right hand corner.

Scarcely daring to breathe I opened it.

Tony stood behind me, observing intently over my right shoulder. It was annoying but he wanted to be in this for keeps so what could I say?

Lee and Clint had already started to look for something to eat.

The first few pages were a disappointment.

'They'll be passwords,' Tony commented, 'Neladgam43, wife's name and year of her birth and the others are more of the same; how very, very careless of you, Uncle Lew.'

344

'Runs in the family,' I muttered, thinking of the ease with which Fothergill/Milner had cracked my security.

I turned the page over.

There were names of Manchester and London churches with times attached.

'Mass times,' Tony explained.

'Yes, he was a very pious man, Uncle Lew, but that didn't stop him sharing another man's wife,' I said sourly.

'Dave, your uncle's left you millions and you sound as if you don't like him.'

'Listen Tony, when I went to bed on Sunday evening I was a happy man, with a family and my own business ...'

'A struggling business.'

'Whatever! But compared to now I hadn't a care in the world and that's down to dear old Uncle Lew.'

'Come on, Dave, things were worse when you were banged up with the nonces in Strangeways.'

'Maybe,' I conceded.

I repressed the memory of Tony spitting in my face. He gave me a very serious look so perhaps he was remembering the same event.

I turned more pages over. They were filled with appointments, shopping lists, addresses, every kind of mundane detail that a busy man might need to note down and they were in no kind of order and gave away nothing about his enquiries. I remembered that Lew was under sentence of death from cancer when he wrote all this. His filing system involved putting a line through the appointments he'd completed. Last week's appointment at the Bluewater Shopping Centre, Hithe, Kent was listed but the name of the appointee wasn't.

If I had a month I could retrace his movements and perhaps come up whatever had led him to the existence of the plot but I didn't have a month.

It wasn't until the very last few pages that I found what I was looking for.

My heart was already beating fast, now it almost jumped out of my chest because across the top of the page was the name <u>M.O.Lochhead</u>

and Sons, Ltd, underlined. Underneath it this was written:

'David,

Should you decide to do what I will ask tomorrow, you will need to contact Margaret Pickering, the wife of my very dear friend, Alban Pickering. If you ask the code question I will write below she will reply with the code phrase listed here. She will then do a further check by asking you a question only you can answer. She very likely will take further precautions and only then will she give you Alban's current location, phone number etc.

It is essential you follow these procedures correctly and are word perfect or she will not respond. This may all seem childish to you but following just such procedure has saved many lives in the past.

Alban is a close friend and the son of a close friend. I trust him with my life, such as it is. He is as concerned as I am by the gravity of the plot against our dear country and would, himself, dearly like to take the measure I will propose to you. However he is watched day and night and the slightest diversion from routine on his part will lead not only to his death but the death of his family.

You are our only chance of success: a resourceful man with a capacity for violence whose ability is unknown to our enemy.

Alban will give you the name and also provide you with the equipment you will need for your task. I'm afraid the game is up for me. The man visited me this evening (Sunday). He came to gloat.

If I'd been armed I'd have killed him but I wasn't and his guard was alert. He went under the name of Rick Appleyard which is only a work name. Alban knows who the creature really is but despite all my pleading he won't give me the name but has decided on one last attempt at persuasion for the good of the service. I can only hope he succeeds. If he does Alban will order you to stand down. If he fails he will name the man to you and give you all the support he can. The rest is up to you.

I can only stress again that without this individual at the helm this plot cannot succeed.

One further thing.

The man calling himself Appleyard is arrogant and like many criminals thinks no-one is as clever as himself. I asked him for a number I could phone if I changed my mind about cooperating and he told his bodyguard, a former soldier *whom he addressed as Lansdale, to give him a piece of paper. The bodyguard had a small notepad from which he tore a sheet. Appleyard then wrote down a mobile phone number which, as I'm sure he knew very well, does not exist. However on tracing over the paper with a pencil I found that the following had been previously written on the pad.*

Technetium-99m now complete ... Caesium-137 material still arriving ... 8.5 metric tons R/W now available ... dump at M.O.Lochhead and Sons Ltd w/h ... X-day Saturday asr ... wind ... strong breeze 25-30 mph westerly

I believe this gives clues about the method they will use to implement their plot and the timing. I have relayed this information to Alban so he may be able to clarify the meaning. I'm sure the name M.O.Lochhead is significant.

Margaret Pickering can be reached on 0298 2906826. She will answer with her full name. You will say "Mrs Pickering I'm calling on behalf of the Green Energy Solar Panel Company. Do you know the Government is helping us to offer you a very good deal on solar panels?"

She will say "No thank you. The way the climate is now I don't think solar panels are any use to me. Please don't phone again.'

If satisfied she will then call your number, using a secure phone. She will ask a special question. If you answer correctly she will give you the information you need about Alban.

David, whatever choice you make I wish you the best of everything and I apologise for ever doubting you and believing the worst. Quite by chance my friend Mrs Elsworth revealed your true nature to me. I believe you will be a worthy custodian of my late wife's inheritance,

With fondest regards,

Lew

I was stunned. I hardly noticed when Tony plucked the notebook from my fingers. I'd been pinning so much on having a name, a person I could plead my case with.

Tony disappeared into the computer room.

I looked at my watch. It was nine o'clock. If the cloak for my call to Margaret Pickering was to pose as a cold-caller now was the time to for it. I dashed upstairs for the anonymous mobiles Tony had delivered

347

yesterday. They were fully charged. It took me a moment to note down the numbers then I went down, grabbed the notebook back off Tony who'd already scribbled down the info and called Margaret Pickering's number.

She picked up at once.

'Margaret Pickering.'

I intoned Lew's pass phrase into the phone. I said each word carefully and deliberately, avoiding any slip.

There was a pause of several seconds before she replied. My heart was in my mouth, and then she came back with the correct answer. Her words were not spoken with the polished, upper class diction I'd been expecting. This lady sounded a lot like Granny Clarrie, an East Ender. I broke the call and put the phone down. It rang immediately.

'What did the boy hide behind the sofa?'

It took me a second or two to gather my wits. It wasn't what I'd been expecting. Lew, Aunty Magdalen, Weldsley ... then my brain made the link.

'He hid a broken china cup.'

'Yes, that's what I've got here. Now listen, have you got another mobile, if you have one call me on this number. I don't want to make things easy for them.'

As soon as I muttered yes, she ended the call.

I phoned her on a second unregistered phone.

'Sorry for the telephone games, but they're necessary,' she said when she replied. 'You're the judge's special man, aren't you?'

'Yes,' I said cautiously.

'I'm going out of my mind with worry about my husband. I'm supposed to put you in touch with him but when I call the number he left me I just get nothing. His phone's switched off, which never happens with him. Something's wrong. He's never out of touch.'

Her anxiety transmitted itself to me and magnified a hundred times in my mind but I struggled to keep a grip.

'There could be any number of explanations.'

'No, it's bad. I know it. I've been half expecting it since he opposed that monster's plan.'

348

'Do you know the man's name?'

'No, er … my husband would never tell me. He said they knew he didn't tell his wife things and that would save my life if anything happened to him.'

'Tell me what he did after he received the judge's news on Sunday.'

'That's what's caused this! He dashed off back up north.'

'Where? I think you can say … our phones are secure.'

'Secure, that's a joke. There is some warehouse up there, in Corrieland, you know … in a big city. He had to check it before confronting the swine who's doing these things and trying to get him to stop. I argued with him but he said he had to take a chance for the good of the service and now look what's happened. I'm now a widow for the good of the service.'

'We don't know what's happened but you've given me an idea and I'll try to track him down.'

'He's dead! I know it.'

'You can't be certain of that. Give me the number just in case.'

She said it quickly and I made her repeat it.

'It's no use. I'm certain he's dead. Listen if you have a wife and children don't be like … like my poor, loyal, flag-saluting chump of a husband. Put them first. Get on a plane to America or Australia. Whatever happens here won't affect them.'

'I'm committed and I have to go on.'

'Brave, are you? It's better to be alive if you ask me. My husband only wanted to use you as a last resort but first the judge has gone and now him. You are the last resort whoever you are. I hope to God you're as good and as lucky as I was told you are.'

The phone went dead.

Tony came back to me as I was removing the battery.

'Have you got the name?'

'No.'

'Well, you'll want to hear what the bastard's up to. I know the whole thing.'

'Go on,' I said sceptically.

'Geiger counters, Dave. What do they do?' he asked breezily.

'I've no time for this.'

'Yes you have if you want to understand the cunning plan these people have come up with. They measure radiation.'

'Yes,' I agreed. I was annoyed. I needed a minute to think about what Margaret Pickering had told me but Tony wasn't going to let me have it.

'What were people shit scared of at Windscale, Chernobyl, Three Mile Island, Fukushima and loads of other nuclear accidents? Radiation, that's what and fear of radiation panics people.'

'Right.'

'Particles, that's how you get the radiation to the people … carried on the breeze, in this case at thirty miles an hour. They're going to spread a cloud of radioactive particles by burning a dump of radioactive waste.'

I thought for a moment but I realised he had to be right.

'But it's insane. Who'd want to live in a country after it had been contaminated?'

'That's the cunning bit. I said it was a cunning plan. Technetium-99m is used in nuclear medicine. It decays almost immediately which is why they use it. If you burned a big pile of waste containing microscopic traces of it the smoke would register on a Geiger counter but it wouldn't do any harm.'

'OK.'

'Now if you want a panic you salt the area round the bonfire with some Caesium-137. That's really lethal stuff. The balloon would go up if the Government thought a cloud of Caesium was drifting across the country. They'd have to start mass evacuations of millions of people, move them down south or up to Scotland.'

'Are you sure?'

'Why do you think your uncle was trying to write M.O. Lochhead under his body while they tortured him? They must have let him in on the secret and he knew that if anyone went to that warehouse they'd discover the whole gigantic con trick.'

'I must phone Brendan.'

'Wait, there's another thing. They're hoping the cloud will blow east over Rochdale, Oldham, Bradford and all the rest of West Yorkshire. Those are places where there are a lot of Muslims.'

'That's too complicated for my limited brain.'

'No, think about it. You said this Appleyard guy was mustard to blame the Muslims for your Uncle Lew ... doesn't like Muslims, right?'

'Yes.'

'Well, now he's got half the Muslim population in the country on the move. What could be easier than to put them in camps and deport them after blaming the whole thing on them? How's that for a plot, Dave?'

I looked at him for a moment. His eyes were gleaming with intelligence if that's possible. Tony could be really dangerous if he put his reconditioned brain to it.

I phoned Brendan Cullen, there was no reply. I phoned Claverhouse and again she wasn't answering. I tried Pickering's number with the same result. I suddenly felt as if the collar of my shirt was trying to strangle me. I pulled it loose. Pickering, Cullen, Claverhouse and were unavailable. It was impossible. Something bad was happening. In despair I phoned Rick Appleyard's number. It too was unavailable. I phoned Appleyard because if he really was the villain I could do something to him if he let me get within arm's length. I wasn't convinced of his guilt. As described by Peter Kelly, Lew's visitor was nothing like Appleyard.

I was on the point of phoning the GMP when the house phone rang.

I picked it up.

'Is that Mr Lane's carer?' a quavering voice enquired. 'It's Mrs Cunningham here. There are men in black creeping up on your house. They've got the road shut off ...'

The line went dead. It had been cut.

I sprinted into the kitchen.

'Lee, get the car out of the garage and drive over the lawn and through the rose bed to the gazebo,' I ordered while retrieving the rucksack from the cupboard.

He looked at me as if I'd gone mad.

'Do it now!' I screamed.

He moved.

'Tony, Clint, we're being raided, into the cellar now!'

Tony dashed out of the computer room. He had two books in his hand. Clint already had the cellar door open and we went down the steps like rabbits with a fox on their tails. An explosion rattled through the house. That would be the front door being blown in. Finding the cellar entrance might take them a minute or two longer. We had a chance. Clint knew what to do. He opened the secret passage door and thrust Tony through it. I followed. Clint squeezed himself in behind me.

37

Friday: 9.25 a.m.

It took us just seconds to reach the end of the escape tunnel. There were no sounds behind us.

Clint heaved up the manhole cover just as Lee stopped the BMW in exactly the right spot. Not much of it was visible from the street side of the house because the brick-built, double garage blocked the view. There was a path between the garage and the house.

We weren't a second too soon.

I could hear shouts and radio chatter from the front of the house.

I jumped into the car next to Lee. I'd have preferred to drive but out of the corner of my eye I caught a glimpse of a figure in black military combat fatigues with a black hood or balaclava of the type worn by Formula One racing car drivers crossing the gap between house and garage. He didn't look in our direction but the man following him did.

He knelt, aimed an automatic weapon and opened fire at once. No caution, no warning: these weren't police.

A bullet hit the inside of the door as I was slamming it shut and another shattered the passenger side mirror. As luck would have it Tony and Clint got in at the other side and were completely shielded by the garage.

Lee accelerated across the lawns, crunching through rose bushes and then smashing through the hedge and fence at the back. A bullet hit the rear window. It must have traversed the interior diagonally and exited through Lee's open window without hitting anything else or anybody. In seconds we were out onto the cinder lane jolting over potholes that threatened to ram our heads through the BMW's roof. In another moment we were zooming through a maze of side streets.

A glance in the mirror showed no pursuit but I couldn't expect it to be far behind. There were very visible tracks across the lawns. They may have lost vital seconds connecting with their transport but I couldn't count on it.

Using the glowing screen of the BMW's GPS navigation device as guidance I directed Lee onto the main A538 and then turned left instead of back towards Manchester. We'd be picked up immediately on the wide straight commuter roads into the city.

The main objective now was to get away from the hit squad targeting Ridley Close. Who were they? They could only be the mysterious MoD team that obeyed Mr Big. Distance had to be my main priority.

Lee was straining at the bit for a car chase but I kept reminding him about speed limits. Mr Big had his contacts in the civil police so reports of a car chase might get his attention.

We drove carefully through Hale and Hale Barns until we reached the motorway intersection, a complex junction involving two separate roundabouts. On my orders Lee drove slowly round the first roundabout. If we were being tailed they were very far behind.

'Could they have put a tracker on the car,' I asked.

'There's no signal of any sort from this car,' Tony stated flatly, holding up his bug detector, 'but they could be tracking us by satellite or even with a drone.'

'Would they go to such lengths? This is Manchester not Afghanistan.'

'Dave, those were real bullets they were firing. If they think you've rumbled their plot they'd go to any lengths. Ask yourself how they found Ridley Close? They must have triangulated phone calls you've received. Have you used any phone more than twice?'

I thought for a second.

'Aunty Velmore.'

'Who's she?'

'It's what I call the phone Marvin gave me.'

He held out his hand.

I felt through the numerous mobiles in my pockets and fished it out.

'Dave!' he accused, 'this isn't even switched off! And it's got

GPS.'

He flung it out of the window.

'Pull in somewhere,' he said to Lee. We pulled up at the side of the road leading towards Wilmslow.

I hung my head. Days of meticulously following procedure and then I'd neglected it with a phone that was bound to be suspect.

'So they'll be on us in minutes?' I muttered.

'If they're following us visually and by that phone they could be. They'll be able to identify this car from above.'

'Drive on,' I told Lee.

The route ahead took us into the tunnel under the runways of Manchester Airport. It wasn't a long tunnel but we made the most of it by crawling along at five miles an hour and ignoring the angry horns of the cars behind us. We emerged on the road passing Lindow Moss and pulled into the nature reserve. The trees were in lush foliage and after a ten minute wait I decided that if we were being observed from above they'd lost us.

As we cruised along the tree shrouded lanes of Wilmslow my confidence grew. Then it was on to Weldsley Park for a change of car. We left the BMW under a yew in a corner of the drive.

'Mr Cunane, what can I do for you?' Peter Kelly asked genially.

'I need one of the cars.'

'There's the Rolls. I'll be happy to drive you anywhere you like.'

'Have you got anything else?'

'Sir Lew used his Ford Focus when he was going to church or the shops or anywhere by himself. The Rolls was mainly for court days ... '

The question of why the hell he'd parked it outside my office on Monday occurred to me. Maybe he'd feared that if he came in on public transport they'd have bumped him off before he ever reached Pimpernel Investigations. Or could it be that he thought that unless I was targeted I wouldn't do his bidding. Who knew?

'... and then there's the estate car. The long wheel base Land Rover that your uncle uses when we visit the farms on the estate,' he continued, unconsciously slipping into the present tense.

'They'll do. I'll take them both,' I said abruptly. There wasn't time to worry about his sensitivities.

To his credit Kelly obeyed without even a Jeeves-like rolling of the eyes.

While we waited I phoned Margaret Pickering on a previously unused phone. There was no reply. That could be ominous or it could simply be that she was out at the shops.

Lee took the opportunity to study the BMW. Inspection revealed that apart from the bullet holes in the passenger door and the rear window there were several dents and deep scratches on the front and sides of the formerly immaculate vehicle. He was aghast.

'It wasn't my fault. I only did what you told me.'

'Don't worry, Lee.'

'Worry? He'll rip my f**king head off. Bob loves that car more than he loves Tammy.'

Kelly arrived in a black, highly polished two year old Ford Focus. He got out and looked at the Beamer. He raised one eyebrow fractionally.

'This is minor damage. I can have this fixed at the main dealer's today and back to you as good as new in a couple of days.'

'Minor damage? That's a f**king bullet hole.'

'Young man, there's a code of honour among us chauffeurs. If the dealer makes any sort of fuss he knows he'll lose the custom of every other chauffeur in a hundred mile radius. As I say, the damage is minor and it's fixable. I shall say this was an accidental discharge by a lawfully armed individual. Such things are not uncommon.'

'There you go, Lee, there's nothing to worry about. You and Tony take the Ford.'

Kelly showed no unwillingness about handing over the keys of his deceased master's car to Lee who despite the minor improvements I'd detected still looked the very image of a young scally.

Kelly set off again and Lee watched him go.

'Helpful old bugger, int he?'

'It's his job, Lee. He's a servant.'

Lee laughed out loud at the ridiculousness of that answer.

'Do you own this place?' he asked distrustfully. He thought I was involving him in some complicated scam.

'That's what they tell me.'

'Right,' he said with a barking laugh, 'and I own f**king Wythenshawe Hall, not.'

Further jollity was cut short by the deep roar of the V8 engine of the long wheel-base Land Rover Defender that hurtled round the corner of the house and slammed to a stop in front of me. It was painted navy blue with a coat of arms on each of the front doors and the words 'Weldsley Estates' underneath. From a distance it could be taken for a police vehicle.

'It's fully fuelled and serviced, sir,' Kelly said. 'I can arrange for it to be picked up wherever you want to drop it. My number's in the glove compartment.'

'Thanks,' I muttered.

I told Clint to come with me in the Land Rover and Lee and Tony to follow us. Then I set off to Topfield Farm.

'Will those men be there?' Clint asked as we rounded the last curve in the road before the farm.

'No, they can't be everywhere at once,' I said hopefully.

Driving along the familiar lanes brought on a risky feeling of normality. I needed to keep reminding myself that danger could be waiting round the next bend and sure enough when we reached Topfield Farm it was.

Brendan Cullen's silver Jaguar XF estate was parked outside the house.

The man himself waved to us as we approached.

As soon as the Ford stopped behind me Tony dashed to the barn door.

'Can I?' he asked.

I nodded and he disappeared into the barn. I knew exactly what he wanted. Meanwhile Bren came to the Land Rover and opened my door. He punched my shoulder. I stepped out and shook his hand as it seemed like an occasion to congratulate myself that I'd managed to survive so far.

'Dave, you dodgy bugger, where were you? I've been waiting here for hours.' Bren said.

'Why?' I asked. I was completely mystified.

He looked haggard. The well groomed look he'd been cultivating since his promotion to the Counter Terrorist Squad had vanished. He hadn't shaved for two days and his suit looked as if he'd slept in it.

'Why not, didn't you get my message? I was sure you'd want to head back home when you were told that the heat was off and anyway I need to talk to you.'

'Hold on. What do you mean about the heat being off?'

He stared at me perplexedly.

'Rick Appleyard should have phoned you first thing this morning to tell you that you're no longer a person of interest in the Sir Lewis Greene investigation. Four Somalis were arrested at Sparkbrook in Birmingham late last night. They had the knife they used to kill your uncle and a video of the killing which they were about to put on the internet.'

'He didn't phone and there was nothing about arrests in Sparkbrook on the news. In fact there was no mention of Sir Lewis Greene at all. That's old news.'

I felt cold. The sun was shining but I felt very cold.

'Bren, how would Appleyard be able to phone me?'

'Oh, I gave him the Ridley Close number. I'd have phoned you myself but I'd no chance to get to an outside callbox. I wanted you to get the good news as soon as possible. I couldn't phone because I had other things on my mind just then such as being suspended for a breach of professional confidence and anyway I wanted to keep our connection off the radar.'

'What!'

'Yeah, suspended, that's me. Twenty years service and now I'm suspended on the say-so of some freaky spook from London. I'm supposed to be leaking stuff to the *Sun*. Need the money to maintain my lifestyle, don't I,' he said rubbing fingers and thumb together.

'Bren, nothing you've said so far makes any sense. We've just dodged out of Ridley Close seconds ahead of a raid by a squad of paramilitaries who looked very like our friends from Wilberforce's farm. They were firing live ammo and were shooting to kill.'

'That's right, parted Clint's hair for him, they did,' Lee said.

He led Clint in front of Bren and made him bend to reveal a faint crease where a bullet had passed close to the big man's skull.

I felt weak at the knees. A fraction lower and the bullet would have taken off the top Clint's head. It was typical of Clint not to tell me himself. He probably thought I'd pack him off to his farm.

'Good, isn't it Dave?' Clint said evasively, 'Bob always says they're only goals when they hit the back of the net.'

I turned to apologise for almost getting him killed but Lee shook his head at me.

'Yeah, that's right Jaws,' he said, taking Clint's arm and patting his hand. 'They only count when they're in the back of the net.'

Clint beamed a gratified smile. He was delighted by the attention.

Brendan Cullen had looked ropy before but now whatever colour remained in his face drained away. For a moment he swayed in shock. But he was made of stern stuff and quickly rallied.

'Dave, I swear that when Rick Appleyard told me that about the militants in Birmingham he was telling the truth. I know you don't like him but he was straight with me. A copper gets a bad feeling when people are lying to him and I'm certain he was telling me what he believed was God's honest truth.'

There was an uncomfortable pause, drawn out longer than a few seconds.

I trust Bren's instincts but my instinct of self preservation is stronger than my trust. Kick it around as much as you like but there was no getting away from the bad news that Brendan Cullen had given away my location and that soon after men arrived at that location to kill me.

It was Tony who broke the awkward silence. He emerged from the barn with bulging pockets and a carrier bag full of stuff …

'Dave, we've been here about five minutes and if I was thinking of springing an ambush I'd do it just about now.'

He was right. We weren't followed but Bren could have been.

'Back in the cars,' I shouted.

Encumbered though Tony was, he and Lee moved to the Ford with the speed of experienced escapees, Clint more slowly. I was left

359

facing Bren. He looked anguished.

'For Christ's sake, Dave, say you trust me.'

'With my life, Bren, with my life; but you weren't the one who dreamed up that fairy story about four Somalis. They didn't suspend you for leaking to the press. They suspended you so you'd lead them to me. You were being played, whether it was by Appleyard or someone else is what I need to find out.'

'Yes,' he gasped.

'Follow us.'

I dashed to the Land Rover and he got behind the wheel of his silver Jag.

We rapidly backed out to the lane and formed a convoy heading towards Bollington. It didn't make much sense to go back by the way we'd come. My Land Rover was about three hundred yards from the house and cresting the hill that gives Topfield its name when there was a thunderous explosion. The ground shook and the road moved enough to toss the heavy Land Rover into the air. It fell back onto its rugged suspension with a jolt.

I felt as if I'd been stabbed through the heart. After such a blast, there wouldn't have been much left of Topfield Farm or of us if we'd all been standing in front of it. Six months of back-breaking labour, that's what Topfield Farm had cost me: that and the even harder struggle before for my liberty and a normal family life.

What would I tell Jan?

The thought of her and the children gave me a surge of strength. Jan was tough enough for both of us. We'd pull through this as we've pulled through everything else.

I needed to put some distance between myself and the ruin of my home.

I drove on winding lanes towards Bollington and from there down the 'Silk Road' to Macclesfield. I didn't stop in the market town but turned onto the Buxton Road. I followed its tortuous curves, scenes of innumerable motor cycle fatalities, until I reached the summit and then the car park of the Cat and Fiddle pub. Steering the Land Rover round those bends was demanding and took my mind off the near disaster at

Topfield but I didn't stop thinking.

'What is this, Dave, a scenic tour of Cheshire?' Bren complained when we gathered by the Land Rover.

The Cat and Fiddle is the second highest pub in England at nearly seventeen hundred feet above the Peak District on the Cheshire/Derbyshire border.

'Yeah, shouldn't we be heading for the Channel Tunnel or somewhere?' Lee whined.

'No, we damn well should not,' I snapped. 'It's one man who's behind all this. He's manipulating the Security Services with lies about Islamic terrorists but he's not going to manipulate me out of this country. Lee, if you've had enough take the Ford and head for Wythenshawe. I'm sure your friends will hide you until the radiation starts.'

'Chill Boss, I'm no coward,' Lee protested. 'I wouldn't be here if I was.'

'Sorry, Lee, all this running away is getting to me as well, but what I said is right. It's just one man who's setting this up. I came here because we can see the road for miles in both directions so we'll know if they're coming for us by road and if they go for an airstrike we've always got the pub to shelter in.'

'Thinking ahead, Boss,' Tony muttered, 'I like it.'

We instinctively glanced at the pub. Built of limestone with thick walls for protection against hard winters, it resembles a bomb shelter.

There was nothing on the road and the sky was clear.

Bren began talking.

'OK, up to last night it pressure, pressure, pressure. COBRA was in nonstop session and the planning for a major civil disaster was going full steam ahead. Say what you like about the Civil Service but there are contingency plans for almost everything including an invasion by men from Mars. Whether terrorists had taken a school hostage like they did at Beslan or blown up a stadium full of kiddies they have the response written down just waiting to be issued. Sir Garret McGarrigle, the Cabinet Secretary, was in constant contact with the incident room ...'

'Where is it?' I interjected.

'You've been in it. It's at Manchester Airport. It's the nearest fully-secured, comms centre to Sir Lew's house. Bury was always a mistake for MI5. The top bods from London can be in and out of the airport in no time. That was part of the trouble. They didn't trust Appleyard to handle the Manchester end. Once there were suspicions raised about him and his deputy, Claverhouse, they shipped other people in from London.'

'Suspicions?'

'That's the way things work in Spookworld: if you can't blame someone when things go wrong on your patch you're in the shit. Appleyard had two things going wrong: a trusted Judge getting decapitated by terrorists and two of his own guys getting terminated. The system is that he gets the blame until he could prove himself innocent.'

'Maybe they're right.'

'No, I believe him but think what you like,' he said with a shrug. 'The result was to put us all under a cloud. The men on the spot were suspect so DG came up with another plan.'

'DG?'

'The Director General of MI5, Sir Freddy Jones.'

'That's not really his name?'

'It is and will you shut up for a minute?'

'OK, but get to the point where they raided Ridley Close.'

'I was never at that point,' he said bitterly. 'They kicked me out before then, remember?'

'Go on.'

'Jones hasn't got an endless supply of trusted agents he can pull in. London's stretched as it is. So he recalled a shed load of retired officers, "reclaimed assets" he calls them. Talk about Dad's Army, half are on Zimmer frames and the rest have sticks but McGarrigle and Jones reckon they're trustworthy and they began converging on Manchester just as fast as their invalid buggies could get them there. Some of these guys date from an era when ordinary police were expected to approach the Security Service on bended knees. Their idea of co-operation is to ask you to make them a cup of tea while they get on with the serious work.'

'Tough!'

'It bloody well was. The big idea was that a terror strike against children was imminent ...'

'MOLOCH.'

'That's right, these guys are all well schooled in the Old Testament and they had us shutting down or investigating every public event involving more than thirty children right down to kiddies dance displays. They were on the point of shutting the schools. That is until they nabbed the Birmingham cell. Then it was ...panic over ... start the blame game.'

'Bren, there is an attack but it's nothing to do with an Old Testament god and it's very much not over.'

38

Friday: 11.00 a.m.

'What?'

'Lew's word, the clue he spent the last seconds of his life scratching out, wasn't MOLOCH it was M.O.Lochhead and the bastard behind all this has used the suggestion about the Old Testament god to divert your whole team from discovering that fact.'

He looked unconvinced.

'Nice one Dave, so who's this Lochhead?'

'It's not a person but the name of a company,' Tony said, 'at least according to this.'

He held up his iPhone.

'I Googled Manchester warehouses and here it is … M.O.Lochhead and Sons, established 1945, warehousing. They have a warehouse near Oldham Road.'

Bren still wasn't jumping for joy.

I took out Lew's notebook.

'It's all in here. I found the woman claiming to be April Fothergill and got Lew's notebook off her. The name Lew wanted to give me was M.O.Lochhead. He never knew who the head of the conspiracy was, at least not until the bastard murdered him.'

'Dave, I don't believe this. They've got the guys in Sparkbrook for the terrorist plot but nothing's ever simple with you is it? First there's a mysterious Mr Big with his name in a missing notebook and now it's a warehouse company in a sleazy part of Manchester.'

'Sleazy part of Manchester, weren't you born in Gorton?'

'So what? The Moloch enquiry has closed down apart from those involved in nailing the bent coppers who leaked to the press,' he said bitterly.

'Bren, there's a lot more evidence if you can stop feeling sorry for yourself and listen. It's all here in the notebook. Lew told a guy called Alban Pickering, a high up in the Secret Service about this …'

'Did you say Alban Pickering?'

'Yes.'

'He's been on a watch list to be arrested since last Thursday.'

'Why?'

'He's suspected of being too close to the Islamic militants and of being the one who facilitated the MOLOCH boys. He worked for MI6 in Kenya and the Horn of Africa and they think he went native.'

'Suspected? Suspected by the same people who think you're bent? Who are they?'

'Dave, they don't consult me about these things. High ups.'

'Well, they're wrong. Alban Pickering was a trusted friend of my godfather. He was checking this warehouse out on Monday morning and his wife hasn't heard from him since.'

'He's probably been picked up. They don't always tell the next of kin immediately.'

'You're so stupid! Do you think I just invented the story about the paramilitaries who came round to Ridley Close and started shooting as soon as they saw me?'

'Now you mention it you've been known to exaggerate before now. Admit it. They were probably guys from MI5 who wanted your slant on how Jeremy Myers and Idwal Morgan came to a sticky end. They still have a theory that Clint here somehow used his strength to force the security van off the motorway.'

'Ridiculous!'

'No, it's not. The back of that van had been forced open by someone of abnormal strength.'

'What about Claverhouse? She was there.'

'Claverhouse … Shmaverhouse! I told you, she and Appleyard are about to be shat upon from a great height.

'It's all in here Bren, read it!' I said thrusting the notebook at him.

He gave me an odd look but went to his car and began studying the notebook.

At one point he took out a mobile and phoned someone.

'Dave, what if he's phoned that hit squad?' Tony asked.

'I trust him with my life.'

'What about our lives?' Lee growled.

'Them too.'

Bren got out of his Jag. He took a blue LED light strip with the word POLICE from the back of the car and clamped it on the roof. When he plugged it in it started flashing. So did Bren, transformed from the defeated and harassed individual I'd met at Topfield: energised, determined.

'Right, they stay here,' he said, pointing at my three companions. 'This is a job for professionals. That means me and my lads. The bastards sent them home, same as me.'

'Surely you can get official help?'

'No, I told you, I'm suspended, a pariah.'

'There must be some way.'

'Dave, there's no point me trying to get help from the Counter-Terrorism Unit. The boss there, Detective Chief Superintendent Blenkinsop, is the one who suspended me and HQ isn't taking calls from me.'

'Give him the new information.'

'He won't believe me. I'm not sure I believe it myself.'

I realised then what Bren's game plan was. He intended to break the case himself and take the credit.

'Do you believe it?'

'Yeah, I don't think even you would forge the stuff in this notebook. So it's down to me … Caesium-137. You can come, Dave, as everyone seems so anxious to meet you.'

'Oh, thanks.'

He was running at maximum revs and missed my sarcasm.

'My lads will get together and meet us at the Lochhead warehouse then we'll see who sorts this thing out: the police or Sir Freddy Jones' pensioners.'

'Wait a minute,' I said grabbing his arm. 'Not so fast. I want that notebook back.'

'Police evidence, Dave and also my insurance policy if this thing goes pear shaped.'

'Well, you might say thanks,' I said hotly. 'You were telling me I was delusional a few minutes ago.'

'Thanks.'

'You've got your "lads" I want mine,' I said, still holding onto his arm.

Clint picked up the bad vibes and came and stood beside me.

'They're civilians, two of them ex-cons, and one … well I don't know what Clint is.'

'What they are Bren, is the team which has cracked this case. It's not over yet and if you think I'm going to let you ditch them for the greater glory of Brendan Cullen and the GMP you can think again.'

Clint moved to stand between Bren and the Jag.

Bren surrendered.

He put his arms up.

'All right, they can come but you'll have to ditch the Land Rover. I need to be at the M.O.Lochhead warehouse in half an hour and that thing will never keep up.'

There was a glint in his eye.

I knew him well enough to know what he was thinking. Once he was on the main roads he'd leave the trio in the Ford Focus well behind. He didn't know Lee.

'You come in my car, Dave. The big guy goes with the others.'

'OK,' I said.

'Not OK,' shouted Tony Nolan. 'You're not thinking. How did they know to set that bomb off?'

I looked at Bren. He shook his head.

Tony took out his bug detector and walked slowly round the Jag.

It began pinging when he came to the offside rear wheel, then furiously when he reached the back He moved the detector up and down and put his hand under the tailgate.

'Open it,' he demanded.

Bren pressed his key and the lock clicked open. Tony lifted the tailgate up and passed his detector over the interior floor covering.

'Here we go,' he said, lifting up the carpet.

Attached to the metal floor was a small square object.

'That would be a GPS tracker,' Tony crowed, 'and they must have manned the hen house at Topfield as soon as you parked the Jag. All they were waiting for was for us to turn up. They probably had the bomb fused for delayed action to give them a chance to get away before it blew.'

Bren tossed the tracker onto the ground and raised his heel to crush it.

'No, put it on the Land Rover and then they'll think we're still here,' I said.

Seconds later I was in the Jag, siren blaring and all lights flashing, and Bren was racing away from the Cat and Fiddle in the direction of Buxton. As I expected, he was driving like a would-be suicide, of whom plenty have come to grief on this road. Fortunately, we'd already traversed the most dangerous section.

Bren kept looking in his mirror.

'What the hell,' he said.

I turned.

The Ford Focus was gaining on us.

'Yes, Bren,' I lied, 'Lee's a part time rally driver. He does stunt driving for TV companies.'

He grunted to himself and accelerated.

'Liar,' he muttered. 'He's a bloody get-away driver for Bob Lane, that's what he is. The closest that little no-hoper's ever been to a TV company is when his Dad got sent down for stealing TVs. I checked him out after I saw him at Bob's hidey-hole.'

'He's good though.'

Lee was now tailgating us, quite an experience at over a hundred miles an hour on narrow roads. Where was that 3g seatbelt when I needed it?

We were through Buxton and on the A6 into Manchester in a very short time. The Jag ate up the miles and Lee kept pace with us. We went through speed traps but weren't stopped. The flashing lights, I supposed. We jumped lights, cut through road works, and raced down the wrong side of the busy Stockport section of the A6 but we approached Oldham Road in less than twenty five minutes.

We turned into the industrial area.

It was deserted. There were no houses, only derelict businesses and no one on the streets. We went round one bend and then another before coming to a stop in a street where the pavements had been wrecked by heavy trucks and the road was pitted and scarred by vehicle tracks.

Probably the place was jammed with traffic in prosperous times but in this recession it was desolate and almost sinister. The place looked ripe for a full-blown ambush. We were lost. There was no sign of M.O.Lochhead's warehouse.

Tony leaned out of the window of the Ford pointing at his mobile.

'GPS again,' Bren muttered, 'the bloody techno-freak.'

Tony pointed to the next corner.

Bren drove round it cautiously and parked alongside an industrial unit. It wasn't what I'd been expecting a warehouse to look like but the word 'Lochhead' was visible on the building. Secured behind a chain link fence and razor wire it was a large modern looking structure, a steel and aluminium construction which could only be a few years old.

A sign on the corner announced 'Unit to Let' with the name of a Manchester commercial estate agent underneath.

The single entrance was a work of art. It consisted of a massive automated steel gate on a track. To ensure closure someone had threaded a heavy chain round and round the gate and the upright retainer. The chain was fastened with an outsized padlock. We slowly drove round the block with the Ford tailing us. When we'd completed the circuit for a second time Bren parked in the entrance. Lee parked alongside.

Beyond the gates there was a marshalling area and turning space the size of two football pitches. We gazed through the gate at the unit beyond. Our drive-by hadn't provoked a response. The place looked abandoned. The attached car-park was empty.

'We're going to need a bolt cutter to cut that chain. We might as well wait until my mates get here, Bren concluded.

'No need,' Tony said. 'I can get us in.'

'Past that massive padlock?' Bren asked sceptically.

'I can,' he repeated. 'Size isn't everything.'

'He can,' Lee seconded.

Tony fumbled in his jacket and extracted a thick wallet, which he opened in to reveal a set of lock picks.

'We might as well let him try,' I said.

A second later Tony was at the gates.

Bren and I joined him. Lee stayed in the car with Clint. I was alert for any sign of movement, but the air was tranquil, with just the faintest breeze stirring piles of litter into motion. A scrap of paper blew against my foot. I picked it up. It was a National Health Service bandage wrapper.

We were a long way from a hospital.

As if on cue, the distant wail of an ambulance siren reached me as I studied the wrapper. It was the only disturbing sound. There was no bird song. Here in this post-industrial wasteland we were the only living things. There weren't even dogs or cats.

I could hear Tony grunting to himself as he fiddled with his picks.

'We're in,' he said turning to me with a triumphant smile on his battered features. He held up the heavy padlock in his hand. 'Cheap Chinese rubbish,' he announced.

We joined him to unravel the chain and push the heavy gate open. To my surprise it slid open very easily. It was oiled and obviously in regular use. There were no windows in the warehouse structure but attached to it there was a dingy looking temporary office unit. If we were being observed it had to be from there.

Being shot at and almost bombed can have the effect of making a person jumpy and I almost leapt out of my skin when another vehicle drove up suddenly. It was a private ambulance, like the ones used for conveying corpses to undertakers. There were three men crammed in its cab.

'My team,' Bren exclaimed quickly enough to prevent me making a run for it.

The men joined Brendan. All of them were casually dressed in leather jackets or fleeces but all three had guns in their hands.

'Get in the Ford,' Bren ordered Tony. 'You wait in the Jag, Dave.'

I didn't like the way he spoke to me but he raised his hands to push me so I moved.

'This is no place for civilians,' he said slowly. 'I mean it Dave. You can stay in the Jag and phone HQ if anything happens to us but it's down to my team now. Those three must leave.'

Tony retreated to the car and Lee backed out and drove round the corner.

'Lennon, you come with me. Smithy and Temple you cover us from behind the van.'

The ambulace/van was now in the spot vacated by Lee.

Lennon was about six foot four and appeared to have muscles on his muscles. He might even give Clint a run for his money. He was wearing a navy blue Berghaus fleece and jeans and sporting a villainous moustache.

Smith and Temple took up firing positions behind the ambulance.

Lennon wasn't happy. He unzipped his fleece just enough to reveal a bullet proof jacket.

'With respect sir, you aren't armed and you aren't wearing a jacket. You should stay in the car and let Smithy come with me.'

'No, we'll do it like I said. I've left a message for the Cabinet Secretary and when he phones back I want to have a result.'

'Death or glory, is that it sir?'

'No, the place looks deserted. I have to find out if it is. That's routine police work, Detective Sergeant or would you prefer that we hang about until the Zimmer Brigade are all over us? If there is a dirty bomb in there, guess who'll get the credit for finding it if we wait.'

'OK, Boss,' the burly henchman agreed.

I got out of the car and approached the pair.

Bren ignored me.

'Hang on,' I said grabbing Bren's arm. 'You're betting there's no-one there but they probably left guards for the bomb … armed guards.'

'This is a police operation now, Dave,' he said curtly, fending me off.

'Oh, yeah, you and three men in an ambulance make a big police operation. Where's the rest of the squad?'

'This is it. D/S Lennon couldn't reach the other three.'

'Well, I'm coming with you,' I said.

'Dave, I'm trying to save you for that pregnant wife of yours. Getting suspended will probably spoil my beautiful relationship with Billy-Jo, so I thought one of us might as well come out of this with his marriage intact.'

'Stuff that,' I said.

He shook his head but made no further argument when I set off with him.

'I'm coming,' Clint said from behind me. He still had his heavy tweed jacket on but he looked twice as thick round the circumference as normal, a regular Michelin man. Tony caught my glance.

'Lee put him in his bullet proof,' he said.

'Thank God one of us has some sense but what about the ironmongery? Bren will arrest us all for sure ...'

'In the boot.'

I breathed a sigh of relief.

Tony and Lee followed us, with Lee in the rear.

'Dear God, what is this?' Bren muttered when he looked over his shoulder, 'The Magnificent Seven?'

'Eight, you mean.'

'I only count seven, your two little pals count as halves.'

'Don't sneer, Cullen,' I said, 'my lads are magnificent.'

'Magnificent idiots, that's what they are.'

I laughed and he punched my arm.

'Let's do this thing,' he said and began to run.

We reached the unit. Close up it was even more imposing than seen from the street. It was like a jumbo jet hangar that someone had picked up off an airfield and dumped in the backstreets. There were a series of four concertina gates each ten metres high and separated by tall steel columns. I knew they were ten metres because that was written above them alongside a speed limit sign for two mph. There were traffic lights fixed up there too.

Proportionate to the gates the structure itself was large. The steel clad building went on above the gates for another ten metres. There was an enormous volume of space inside.

Each concertina shutter was operated by motors or chains inside the warehouse and high and wide enough for heavy trucks. Presumably trucks came in one side and went out another when they'd dumped their load.

There were handgrips where the folding shutters joined in the middle but no locks Tony could pick. Bren and Smithy grabbed one side while Clint took the other. They tried to heave the gates apart. Nothing happened.

Bren banged on the shutter and shouted 'Police'. He was joined by Lennon and Smith. There was no response from inside.

A newspaper was trapped under the shutter.

Bren ripped it free and looked at the date.

'This is Thursday's 'Evening News'. The place is in use.'

I could see that he was desperately eager to find the dirty bomb and save his career. Nothing was going to stop him getting in now.

Apart from the folding shutters, the only access to the entire structure was through a single door in the front of the office. The temporary office itself looked flimsy enough to tear down with our bare hands but precautions had been taken against that. Heavy steel bars protected the small windows alongside the door. There was razor wire all over the roof and the corners were reinforced with angle iron.

That single door was a high security steel fixture set in a steel frame with six locking points and a tamper proof lock.

'Well that's it for now,' Bren said. 'We need a locksmith.'

'Or a tank,' agreed Lennon.

'I can do it,' Tony said eagerly, taking out his picklocks again. 'I've seen a cut-out diagram of that lock in a catalogue.'

'And how did you manage to get hold of such a catalogue? Distribution of diagrams of high security locks must be restricted,' the policeman demanded.

'Oh, it was … er … never mind,' Tony gabbled. He waved his

hands loosely to indicate the impossibility of further explanation. 'I've seen it and I can crack it. It was on page seventy eight of the catalogue.'

'Nice to see where you recruit your staff, Dave,' Bren said, turning to me. 'Are you running the Strangeways Rehabilitation Programme?'

'Tony's special, he's got a reconditioned brain.'

Bren looked at me out of the side of his face but made no effort to stop Tony getting to work. He had nothing more to lose.

'This doesn't make sense,' Tony commented as he went to work with his picks. 'They have a rubbish Chinese lock on the outside gate and a state of the art lock on here. There must be some other way of opening those folding shutters, perhaps with a remote.'

I looked at the area above the shutters. Apart from the traffic lights and the signs there was nothing up there, no sign of a receiver for signals from a remote. My faith in Tony's powers decreased.

I didn't expect him to succeed.

Behind me Bren had taken out his phone and started up a muted conversation.

'Yes, Sir Garret,' he was saying, 'this might be the real MOLOCH. I believe the Sparkbrook arrests are a blind alley. It's a warehouse belonging to M.O.Lochhead and Sons Limited. Moloch … yes sir … It's a huge warehouse … completely deserted … We think there might be a large dirty bomb in here … We have a locksmith working to get us in … It could be some time … Cunane's with me … There are eight of us … We're armed … Thank you, sir. Yes, I'll cooperate fully with the MI5 team …'

He broke the call and turned to his men with his thumb up.

'Reinstated,' he said to me.

I raised my eyebrows and made a mental note to demand a letter of thanks from the Chief Constable for preserving the reputation of the GMP. Bren shrugged, put his phone away and raised his left hand. His fingers were crossed.

Tony frowned and concentrated. Beads of sweat formed on his hairline but after several minutes and after placing more picks into the lock it clicked open.

'I've read all the standard works on locksmithing,' Tony said apologetically. 'They're restricted but you can get them if you know where to look. This looks very fancy but it's just your standard five-lever mortice.'

Bren looked at me with an 'I told you so' expression and opened the door.

'They may have all sorts of electronic back up alarms,' Tony warned. 'There could be booby traps.'

'Bugger that,' Bren said. I knew it really was death or glory for him.

He dived inside, closely followed by Smithy and then by me.

Through an unlocked side door we stepped into a cavernous dark space. Unless they were troglodytes used to living in dark spaces there was no one inside except us.

Bren took out a small torch but it was like trying to illuminate a cathedral with a single candle.

'Can you hear something?' he said to me.

We stood in silence.

There was a faint droning sound coming from the dark space at the back of the warehouse. There was something sinister about the sound. I felt the hairs rise on the back of my neck.

'It's the bloody bomb.' Bren said. 'The bastards have left it to go off. That's why there's no-one here.'

'Bombs are supposed to tick,' I muttered but he ignored me.

'Lights, we need lights,' he said desperately.

'There must be a manual way to open those shutters,' Tony whispered. 'They'd need it if there was a power cut.'

He slipped away from my side and was joined by Clint. There was a sound of metal being moved and then Clint managed to force one side of the nearest shutter open a few inches. Smithy and Lennon ran to join him. They struggled but couldn't manage to open it further.

'It's motorised and the brake or whatever is pushing against us,' Lennon gasped to his boss.

Nevertheless the narrow shaft of light he'd helped to create revealed a control box mounted at waist height on the wall next to the door we'd come in by. It was secured by a padlock. Unfortunately the rest of the space beyond the entrance remained in deep gloom. Nothing was glowing in the dark but remembering the reference to highly radioactive Caesium 137 I didn't fancy copying Bren's heroics any further. Nor did he, there was no way anyone was going into that darkness which could be concealing any number of radioactive devices.

Bren strode over to the control box and rattled it. The heavy steel door covering the controls didn't budge. In his frustration he launched a high kick at it and immediately recoiled.

'Hell and damnation,' he cursed, 'we're going to have to wait for lights and a generator unless ... '

'Car headlights,' I suggested.

'I need to preserve the scene,' Bren said. 'It's bad enough having all you lot trampling about. Still, if you could get a headlight up to that slit we'd at least see what's making the buzzing sound.'

'No, I can do the lock,' Tony said eagerly.

'In a pig's ear, you can,' Bren snapped. 'Nobody's going to get into that box without a thermal lance.'

'I can do it,' Tony insisted.

The lock was a big single dial combination padlock with numbers 0 to 99 on the dial. It had been well used but was immune to Tony's pick locking skills.

'For this type you need to put six numbers in for six cams in the right order then it opens,' Tony explained. 'That's why it's so big. You turn clockwise for the first and then anticlockwise for the next and so on.'

'Getting the sequence at random will take you at least a week,' Bren said with an edge of contempt in his voice. 'There must be millions of combinations.'

'No, there's tolerance built into these. Say the first number is 99, yeah, well, the cam would open at 98 or 0 as well as 99 and on top of that if it's been used a lot like this one the metal will be worn where the cams drop. I can do it.'

'Be my guest,' Bren said.

Tony contorted himself around the box until he had his ear against the back of the padlock. Then he started twisting the dial clockwise round and round, quickly at first and then slowly.

'Twenty three,' he said, 'somebody write it down.'

Bren whipped out a notebook.

Tony started again anticlockwise this time.

'Seven.'

It took hardly more time than Bren needed to write them down for Tony to get all six numbers. The lock clicked open when he entered them. Bren opened the door and threw a lever to switch on the internal lights.

'Christ! Maybe you are a genius,' he muttered to Tony.

Powerful fluorescent lights came on overhead in sequence with a flutter of sound. Flick, flick, flick, running from the entrance shutter to the rear the lights came on progressively, illuminating section after section.

There was a collective in-drawing of breath.

The place was empty. There were no vehicles, no people and most definitely of all, no massive bomb.

I didn't know whether to be relieved or disappointed.

The next thing I noticed was the litter. There was lots of it; newspapers, flattened pizza boxes, food wrappers, and empty drink cans carpeted the asphalt floor.

They all looked as if they'd been dumped just yesterday. Dozens of people had been here very recently.

A platform ran all round the interior, its height convenient for loading. A couple of fork-lift trucks indicated that that had been its purpose. Above the platform there were storage gantries. Whatever had been stored or collected here there was now no sign of it.

My eye was drawn to the far end of the lengthy building. Massive green and black flags had been draped over the wall. Beneath them there was a low table with indistinct objects on it. The buzzing sound appeared to be coming from there.

There was a smell of diesel and petrol and dust but mixed with those scents there was something else, something rank and rotten.

We spread out and advanced to the rear of the warehouse. As we neared the table we saw what was causing the droning sound.

A cloud of bluebottles buzzed nauseatingly into the air.

378

The object they'd been settled on was a bloody and raw human head.

The entire table top was layered in coagulated blood. As I watched I saw movement. It was seething with maggots. I winced. The human body contains ten pints of blood and someone had spilled all of it on that table top.

Under the table there was a headless body, the neck open and gaping towards us, the white bone of the vertebra clearly visible. Maggots were wriggling about in the inner spaces. Lying alongside was a curved Islamic scimitar. Copies of the Koran and posters with Arabic or Urdu writing were scattered about the area.

I recognised the bearded mug of Osama bin Laden on a large poster.

My companions drew back but Bren took a few steps forward and looked closely at the severed head.

'It's Alban Pickering,' he said, 'I recognise him from the photo they put out. Right, out of here you lot. We've disturbed the scene enough. Smithy, get the SOCOs up here. Warn them the place might be as radioactive as hell.'

'They collected the hospital waste here and shifted it yesterday probably to where they're going to start this radioactive bonfire.' I said.

Bren's disappointment was tangible.

'Yes,' he agreed, 'nice to see that one of us is still thinking like a detective,' he said, clapping me on the shoulder as we reached daylight. 'I don't suppose you know where?'

I shook my head.

With a grim expression on his face he took out his phone to relay the bad news to London. I left him to it. Police sirens were screaming in the distance.

39

Friday: 2.15 p.m.

Our constabulary friends gathered for a powwow outside the open warehouse. There was considerable head shaking and I guessed some dispute. All four used their phones to speak to third parties. Then quite suddenly they were done.

Weirdly and simultaneously Bren, Lennon, Temple and Smith put away their phones, stopped talking to each other and began staring across at us.

'Uh, oh!' Lee said. He was tensed for flight with his car keys in his hand.

'Keep *caaaalm*, Lee,' I said in my best mock-Scouse, 'keep *caaaalm*. They're not going to arrest you.'

Neither Lee nor Tony thought my stab at comedy was funny enough for a laugh. They watched Bren approach in grim silence.

Bren reached us. He put an arm round my shoulder and drew me apart from Tony, Lee and Clint.

'Er, Dave ...'

'Yes, Bren.'

'You know that I love you like a brother?'

'Never doubted it.'

'And you heard me mention your name to the Cabinet Secretary?'

'I did, Bren. I was gratified.'

'Sure you don't mean grafittified? You know ... had stuff written all over your property by your little friends? Lee got his first ASBO for that.'

'No Bren, I was gratified and, whatever those two were, they aren't vandals now.'

'*Gratified*, nice word; anyway back to the real world. If there had been a dirty bomb here and we could draw a line under this MOLOCH business, I've no doubt Sir Garrett would put you down for an MBE to show you how *gratified* he is ...'

'... and an OBE or even a CBE for you.'

'Yes indeed, whereas, in actual fact ...'

'No medals but he has reinstated you.'

'Correct. He's ordered me to be reinstated. This isn't ...'

'This isn't likely to *gratify* your bosses, who aren't very *gratified* with themselves for the way they've behaved. They were too quick to act and now they've got egg all over their faces '

'True. I doubt that I'm on the Cop of the Month list down at HQ but we've found out what happened to poor Pickering and that has to count as a partial result so they can't shitcan me again, at least not straight away, but you and your playmates ...'

'Are inconveniences that are better out of the way ... is that it?'

'Yes, I'd be highly *gratified* if you'd remove yourselves pronto!'

'Enough said. Can I have Lew's notebook back?'

'No, I already told you, I need it.'

'OK.'

I rejoined my 'playmates'.

'He wants us out before the Top Cops arrive,' I said.

Tony and Lee didn't need an invitation to leave before a visit by high ranking coppers. They headed for the gate and were round the corner to where the Ford was parked at a swift trot. Life had taught them the value of making themselves scarce.

Clint was different. There was much more of him to vanish and he didn't run much at the best of times.

'It's not fair, Dave,' he grumbled. 'They would never have found that man's body if it wasn't for you.'

'That's right, but it's not something I want the credit for.'

'It was those men who fired at us who did that to him, wasn't it Dave?'

'I think so.'

It was quite a stroll to the entrance. The sirens sounded nearer but there was no way I was going to run.

'Shall I put the chain and padlock back and lock them in?' Clint asked when we reached the gate. He picked them up.

'It's not DCI Cullen's fault,' I said. 'He's just doing his job.'

'All right, Dave,' he agreed, pausing at the screech of wheels as several vehicles raced round the corner towards us.

They slammed to an emergency stop right in front of us, three of them: large windowless black vans without police decals. OK, I'd seen Bren's men roll up in a private ambulance and so I was slower off the mark than I should have been.

Unfortunately, they weren't.

The doors swung open and a swarm of armed men in black coveralls and balaclavas poured onto the street. They were carrying sub-machine guns. Clint was quicker than me. He hurled the heavy padlock, knocking one of them over and swung the chain, bringing three down. I was surrounded, pummelled and dragged down. Clint continued to struggle. They couldn't control him.

'Lose him!' someone ordered.

One of the goons stepped in front of Clint. The others scrambled clear. Clint had the chain raised above his head in both hands for another swing. The goon aimed and fired a burst into Clint's chest. Clint sank onto his knees, moaning. He struggled to get to his feet, still holding the chain. The killer skipped behind Clint, kicked him so hard that he fell flat on his face and calmly and deliberately fired another burst into the big man's back.

All this happened inside the space of a very few seconds. I wasn't timing it but they were professional. Four of them picked me up and I caught a glimpse of Bren and his men running forward with pistols ready. Then there was a rattle of automatic fire from the hostiles. Before I could crane my neck to see the effect I was clouted over the head with the butt of a gun.

The lights went out.

*

When I came round my face and the right side of my jaw were in agony. I was on my back. I tried to explore my facial injury and discovered that my hands were fastened behind my back with plastic handcuffs. I also discovered that my whole body was one mass of aches and that I was in darkness.

I groaned loudly.

That was a mistake.

The door of the garden shed into which I'd been flung was thrown open and two of the thugs in black coveralls and balaclavas dragged me out. I struggled to focus my eyes in the bright sunshine. Appropriately enough I found myself looking at a neatly maintained garden, lawn, borders, overhanging trees … the lot. I didn't get long to admire it.

'Wake him up!' someone out of my line of sight ordered.

At once the pair holding me let go and I fell face down onto a gravel path.

They began kicking me. I felt one of my ribs go. The pain was agonising. I yelped.

'Not that way! I need him able to talk,' the voice shouted.

The kicking stopped and one of the two cursed in a foreign language. Jan and I had honeymooned on the Dalmatian coast and the words sounded familiar from that time. I was in too much pain to recollect what was spoken there.

'You tell these idiots what I want,' the tormentor's voice said, speaking to another person.

'*Voda*, we need *voda*,' a woman's voice said. I knew her voice but the mental effort needed to recall who she was was beyond me at that moment.

Seconds later I heard a bucket being filled from a tap. It seemed to take forever. The pain went on. My face and jaw throbbed. I knew I was bleeding where my face had struck the sharp gravel.

Then I was grabbed by the hair and turned onto my back and very cold water was poured onto my face. I coughed and spluttered and struggled for breath but one had his foot on my chest and I couldn't turn away. Strangely enough I felt better after the drenching and my mental reflexes began functioning.

Clint was dead. Bren and his mates were probably dead as well.

I'd allowed myself to become a prisoner and the woman who knew Serbo-Croat was Molly Claverhouse. I assumed the tormentor was charming Rick Appleyard who'd so conveniently 'forgotten' to warn me a few hours earlier that the hunt for me was off but had remembered to send his snatch-squad to Ridley Close.

I understood that I was very close to death.

Regret, not fear was the dominant emotion in my mind. Regret that I'd got Clint killed. If only I'd sent him ahead with Lee and Tony he'd have been round the corner in the Ford when the killers arrived but I had to let him play the bodyguard.

Regret that I would never see Jan and the children again.

Regret that my unborn child would never know me.

'Get him on his knees,' the tormentor directed.

I was wrenched upright and propped up on each side. Now I faced the man giving the orders. He was tall and slim but like the others was wearing a balaclava. Irrelevantly, I remembered what the name of the material their masks and coveralls were made from was. It was Nomex, a fireproof fibre used by Special Forces and firemen. The slim man couldn't be Rick Appleyard. He definitely wasn't a rugger-bugger and his speech was unaccented, educated English.

A thought about his identity stirred in the back of my mind but it was the person standing next to him who had all my attention.

Molly Claverhouse stared back at me.

I gazed at her intently. In the old days of capital punishment, which have never really gone away for some of us, the prisoner in the death cell always got a look at his executioner when the genial Pierrepoint popped in to measure him for the drop. I felt her cold hazel eyes were measuring me up for mine.

She was wearing a dark grey Paul Smith trouser suit in pure wool. I knew that because I'd been with Jan when she priced one. She also wore a pink butterfly print blouse and black patent leather shoes with a medium heel.

She gave me a strange look and shook her head very slightly. There was a message for me there but I was in too much pain to interpret it. I wanted to speak, to call her names but my lips were too sore to waste my breath on her.

'So Cunane, I understand you've been trying very hard to uncover my identity. It seems a shame to deny you that pleasure now that you'll have so little time to enjoy it but I will preserve my anonymity a while longer. Accept my condolences for the death of your large friend.'

I didn't answer, partly because my mouth was so sore and partly because conversation was inappropriate.

'What? No jokes Mr Cunane? I shall have to see if I can loosen your tongue because I want the answers to some questions.'

My mind was working slowly but it was still working, just about. Of those who'd recently chided me for my sense of humour one stood out. Harry Hudson-Piggott, the 'bug-hunter', a man I'd assumed was Claverhouse's subordinate: wrongly assumed. How could I have been so blind? He was the one pulling their strings not the other way around.

'No jokes for you Hudson-Piggott,' I grunted.

'Ah, thank you so much for confirming that you are fully back with us, Mr C. I was beginning to be afraid that my contractors had kicked you completely senseless. It can happen you know.'

'Bastard!'

'Ah, defiance, an admirable trait but what I require from you is compliance. I assume that as an intelligent man you've already worked out what your fate will be?'

'You're a killer. You'll do what killers do.'

'Yes, but now I'm tidying up. The amount of killing involved in that depends on what you tell me.'

I may have given an uncomprehending grunt. I knew it wouldn't have mattered to him if I'd begged and pleaded for my life. He was as determined to have the last word as he was to kill me.

'Yes, Cunane, we are on the eve of great events, major changes in the course of world history. An essential ingredient in the success of these changes is that the back story is absolutely unimpeachable. For instance, how many would have followed Churchill in 1940 if some newspaper had come up with irrefutable evidence that he'd been in secret talks with Hitler for years? Damn few!'

He pulled the Nomex hood off. As he fiddled about getting his rimless specs back on there was that cold, ultra-clever look on his face that had reminded me of an entomologist collecting insects. Why hadn't I twigged his role earlier?

It crossed my mind that the longer I kept him talking the longer I'd delay whatever horrors he had in mind for me.

'Did he?' I asked.

'What,' he sneered.

'Churchill, did he have secret talks with Hitler?'

'Of course not, you fool. I merely invented that as an example of how important getting the back story straight is. In the present case there can never be the slightest hint that Islamic terrorists weren't responsible for such prior measures as the killings of Greene and Pickering and of course tomorrow's event.'

'Oh, how dense of me.'

'Right, this is what we'll do. I'll ask you a question and if you fail to answer to my satisfaction then you'll be compelled to answer.'

'Is the word torture too blunt for you?'

'I prefer the milder term. It makes little difference but fewer eyebrows are raised at the word compulsion. Unfortunately even such a harmless word alerted your late relative to my activities thus ensuring his demise.'

I couldn't follow what he was saying and in his cold clinical way he noticed.

'A gentle smack on the face, I think,' he said to one the henchmen holding me on my knees.

The burly thug holding my right arm's idea of a slap went far beyond what the teachers of my childhood would have considered acceptable. My head rang and I flickered in and out of consciousness.

'Cunane, Cunane,' Hudson-Piggott shouted into my face, 'tune in please. I need your full attention.'

I spat out a mouthful of blood.

'Good, good, full consciousness returning, is it? I think you're scoring at least thirteen on the Glasgow Coma Scale. First question, did the judge know my identity when he visited you on Monday?'

'You tortured him to death that night. You should know the

answer to that.'

'I'm asking you, Cunane. He was refractory, the old fool, and I had other purposes for him. I repeat and I'll only do this once, did the judge divulge my identity when he visited you on Monday?'

I didn't speak.

I was picked up bodily and hauled to a small concrete lined garden pond.

'So handy,' Hudson-Piggott commented.

They positioned me over the edge of the steep-sided pond. The water was deep.

One of the men grabbed my hair and shoved my head under water. I struggled but he was very strong. I was held down. I didn't immediately fight for air. Part of me hoped that this was just a cruel game, but it wasn't. I began to experience oxygen starvation. My brain felt as if it was bursting. My heart laboured. They had to let me up now but they didn't. I felt consciousness slipping away. I ceased struggling. The water was like a comforting blanket. The reflective surface danced before my dying eyes.

Then they dragged me up.

I began to gasp convulsively. I was aware again. I moaned pitifully.

'Answer the question.'

There was no point in resisting. I couldn't face the water again. Let him shoot me; that would at least end my troubles quickly.

'No, of course not,' I gasped. 'He'd have gone to the Government if he'd been able to name you.'

'A lie, I think, but no matter. If there was no name given why did he visit you on Monday?'

I tried to think of an answer. I was slow.

They had me over the pond again. I tried to gabble something but my words came out as gibberish and my head was in the water again before I could say anything sensible.

This time, though I knew what to expect, the sensation of being unable to breathe was almost unbearable. They'd pushed me under just as I was attempting to catch a breath. My mouth, nostrils and airway filled with water. I struggled to expel it from my windpipe but the coughing reflex was incredibly painful. Once again just as I was fading they yanked me out and flung me on the lawn. I lay on my back gasping like a stranded fish.

'Speak,' Hudson-Piggott said, prodding me with the toe of his boot. He allowed me to recover.

'I'm a detective. He asked me to find out who you were. I was his last resort.'

I held back about Lew's plan to use me as an assassin.

'Detectives need clues. What clues did Greene leave you? Why did you take so long before you revealed what MOLOCH really meant?'

'I didn't know what it meant. He did leave clues but it took me days to put them together and come up with the truth.'

'Hmmm, I suspect that coming up with the truth is something you rarely do Cunane. Is that why you went to your parents' cottage: to recover a clue?'

I was confused. If I said no I'd be back under the water. If I said yes I'd be condemning Paddy and Eileen to death.

'There was no clue. My father doesn't trust phones and he left a message to apologise for not telling me about Sir Lew's legacy earlier.'

He laughed. It wasn't a cruel Bond-villain type laugh; just a normal sound of amusement.

'How noble of you to attempt to protect your parents but it will do them no good. Do you expect me to accept that you risked life and limb for such a feeble reason?'

'It's true.'

'Another of your lies … there was detailed information about my plans in your mother's vegetable patch which you sat on for a whole day until you passed it on to the unfortunate DCI Cullen this morning.'

'Unfortunate? Why is he unfortunate?'

'You are the one answering questions here. Who else did you tell besides Cullen and Appleyard?'

'Appleyard, what do you mean? I only spoke to him on one occasion and you were present. You know exactly what I told him.'

He gave his henchmen a nod and my head was under water

again.

This time I was already weakened when they shoved me under and I quickly felt myself slipping away from the pain and the struggle for air. The water was so comforting. If only they'd let me surrender to it there'd be an end to questions. I swallowed water.

I was very dazed when they pulled me out and it took them some time to rouse me.

'Appleyard?' Hudson-Piggott said.

'I told him what I knew,' I said weakly.

'About the warehouse and Pickering?'

I cleared my throat. I didn't answer. The men grabbed me again.

'Did you tell Appleyard? Answer or this time they'll hold you under until you drown.'

I nodded my head. I couldn't face the water again.

'As I thought!' Hudson-Piggott said to Claverhouse triumphantly. 'We'll round up Cunane's employees, friends and relatives later. They're small fry but I want Rick here now. Phone him,' he ordered.

'Is this necessary? Surely you can deal with Rick under the discipline of the service when the present operation is concluded,' she argued.

'Is it necessary?' he repeated. 'Are you suggesting that I leave Appleyard free to talk to whoever he pleases? Do you think there's the slightest chance of Sir Freddy Jones listening to Cunane's ex-convict friends or to his wife or even his ex-bobby father? No, there isn't a cat in hell's chance but will he listen to Appleyard? Of course he will and I can't take any risks when we're on the brink of success. Phone him and tell him to get himself here now.'

'Yes sir,' Claverhouse said quietly taking out her phone.

40

Friday: 5 p.m.

They left me lying on the grass. Time passed slowly. Hudson-Piggott and Claverhouse had a prolonged conversation which mainly consisted of him doing a lot of talking and striking poses. Several times Hudson-Piggott put both hands behind his back and thrust his chest forward. It reminded me of someone trying to imitate a duck but I guessed he thought it made him look important. The world has become used to the characteristic poses of many evil men, was this to be a nightmare for the twenty first?

The lawn was cold and gradually I began to shiver, moderately at first and then convulsively. My lungs were full of water. I kept on coughing and it felt as if I would expire right there in the beautiful garden without further intervention from Hudson-Piggott.

Claverhouse came over to me. I may have been on the ground for as long as half an hour.

She put her hand on my forehead.

'Try to hold on,' she whispered, 'we'll be safe soon.'

She turned towards Hudson-Piggott.

'If you want this bastard alive for tomorrow you'd better get him under cover. He'll die of pneumonia if you don't.'

'Do as she says,' Hudson-Piggott ordered.

I felt intense relief at the prospect of living a little longer. My treatment by Hudson-Piggott so far had led me to expect summary execution when the questioning was over. I was needed for something tomorrow.

I was picked up and then just as suddenly dropped. At least it was the lawn this time not the gravel. Even so, the breath was knocked out of my lungs. I fell awkwardly but I was facing Hudson-Piggott and had a grandstand view of what happened next.

Rick Appleyard was bundled into the garden escorted by Nomex clad heavies.

'What is it, Boss? You didn't have to send Lansdale for me. And who are these guys?' he asked.

'What is it, Boss,' Hudson-Piggott repeated. 'What is it, Boss? What it is my dear Rick, is that you're a damned traitor and you've been found out.'

'What! No! I'm no traitor.'

'You are,' Hudson-Piggott insisted.

Then he pulled out a semi-automatic pistol and shot Appleyard between the eyes. The MI5 man died instantly and crumpled onto the lawn.

I must have gaped in shock because Hudson-Piggott caught a glimpse of my expression.

'You'll get yours tomorrow Cunane,' he mocked.

Claverhouse started heaving. She bent to her knees trying to suppress her sobs.

'For God's sake, pull yourself together woman!' Hudson-Piggott snarled. 'Did you think we could save this country from itself without a few casualties? I thought Rick was my man but he was playing a double game and now he's paid the price. Let his fate be a good lesson to you.'

Claverhouse straightened up and took several deep breaths.

'Yes sir,' she gasped. 'It's just that that was such a shock. I've worked with Rick for a long while but I can now see that he had to go.'

'I'm glad you do see it that way,' Hudson-Piggott said, holstering his gun. 'You know I'm trying to reach our great goal with as little bloodshed as possible but we can't take the risk of letting people like Rick hang around. He wanted to keep a foot in both camps but that isn't possible now. You do know that, don't you?'

'Oh, yes sir,' Claverhouse said respectfully, 'I do.'

'Right, well, organise the removal of this rubbish from the lawn. They can both go into the garden shed until tomorrow. Make sure that one's really secure,' he said pointing to me with his foot.

He left the lawn and went into the house.

Claverhouse turned to the assembled mercenaries or hired

assassins or whatever they were and began issuing orders as if things were perfectly normal.

They went to Rick's corpse first. One of them began fumbling with his jacket pockets, feeling for his wallet.

'None of that!' Claverhouse yelled, pulling out her own gun. 'He must be left undisturbed. His death has to look like a political killing not some common robbery but you'd better let me have his gun.'

The man who'd been about to rob the corpse now yanked the jacket off the dead man's shoulders, revealing his pistol in its shoulder holster. He gingerly handed it over to Claverhouse on the finger of one hand as if expecting her to shoot him.

'The body must be left undisturbed. Do you understand? If you're thinking of creeping back for his wallet forget it.'

'Da, gospodo!' the thug replied, stepping back and bowing submissively.

Other men came forward. They started to drag the body across the lawn.

Claverhouse went crazy.

'Nijedan! Nijedan!' she screamed. 'No! Carry the body, don't drag it.'

She pushed the men away and mimed lifting. She had Appleyard's pistol in her hand and looked furious enough to use it.

They got the message.

Six of them carefully picked up the body under Claverhouse's unrelenting supervision and gently laid it on a paved surface in front of the garden shed. This was well to the rear of the extensive lawn and was quite old and of conventional design with a door and window on one side and a sloping, felt covered roof.

They came back for me.

I was kicked and dragged without ceremony and dumped next to the unfortunate Appleyard.

I could see inside the shed. It was well stocked with plastic sacks of fertiliser and compost. There were tools on racks and a lawn mower. It was raised quite high above the damp soil on a brick plinth which gave me a glimmer of hope. If I could prise up a floorboard then escape was possible.

A glance at the number of black clad guards made my heart sink again. They were swarming round the shed. Some went inside and cleared a space. Claverhouse indicated what she wanted them to do. She spoke their language. They pushed two pallets of compost sacks close together to form a bier. They lifted the corpse onto it and arranged the arms and legs like practised undertakers. The thought struck me that they'd had plenty of experience in laying out corpses.

Then it was my turn.

As before, I got a lot less consideration. They picked me up and dropped me on a pile of dirty old sacking that the gardener probably used as frost protection for precious plants. It broke my fall but I landed on the side with the broken rib and let out a groan.

One of the men muttered something to the others and they laughed.

'Get back while I check he's still tied up,' Claverhouse ordered her henchmen, waving the gun by way of translation. They withdrew a short distance and she bent over me, obscuring the view from outside with her back.

'There's a knife in a pocket on the inside of Rick's belt,' she whispered. 'It's your only chance.'

I went rigid with shock.

'Can you sit up while I check your cuffs? They have to believe I'm hurting you.'

She grabbed my hair roughly and pulled me upright. I moved with her and let out a convincing cry of pain. She checked that my hands were still fastened.

'The cuffs will have to stay on for now but I'll fasten your feet loosely so you can slip your foot out when you have to.'

'What . . .'

'No, there's no time . . . listen. Tomorrow you'll be taken to the bomb site. You have to be alive for a reason or you'd be dead by now. It'll be Hudson-Piggott's man, Lansdale, who'll kill you. He's the one who butchered your uncle. He likes doing that sort of thing but you'll have to surprise him and get away to tell the true story. Do you understand?'

'But you . . .'

'I'm working for the Government. I was Harry's traitor, not poor Rick.'

'But . . .'

'No more talk. Those bloody contractors are watching me like hawks.'

It was true. When she finished fastening my feet and stood up they were arranged in a semi-circle round the doorway and were watching intently.

She stood over Appleyard's body for a moment, then bent over it and closed the eyelids. Her shoulders were shaking.

She left, slamming the door shut behind her.

I wasn't alone though. From time to time I heard noises from outside. I slowly mulled over the word she'd used to describe the men: contractors. A band of mercenaries employed by some front company and hired out to anyone who needed dirty work doing.

I waited until it was pitch dark before I made my move. I couldn't remember if there was a moon but it was completely obscured by clouds if there was. No light reached me. My chest was aching and my broken rib and battered head were throbbing and I was in no mood for heroics but what they say about 'animal spirits' is true. My instinct for survival completely overwhelmed any urge to surrender to my fate.

Despite what Claverhouse had said, the bonds round my ankles felt very tight but I managed to first slip my shoes off and then with great and painful effort to pull my right foot out of the loop.

I got my legs under my body and slowly raised myself until my eyes were level with the lower edge of the dirty glass window which was visible as a lesser blackness against a greater. In the inky darkness outside I couldn't see any sign of the guards not even as dim shapes but I knew were there. Perhaps they weren't at the rear of the shed which led off to a vegetable garden and a large greenhouse and I could loosen the boards and slip out that way.

I was about to stand up when a light flared outside. One man was lighting another's cigarette and then his own.

I froze in position. They must be able to see my head.

I waited. Seconds passed and then more seconds and they didn't come. They'd lost their night vision. The window was filthy and being closer to it than they were I could see out better than they could see in. I relaxed and then with infinite caution and slowness stood up.

My senses were hyper alert.

There was a sound of someone clearing his throat in front of the hut and then a slight squelching noise as a booted foot changed position on the damp ground. I began forming the theory that there were three guards on the hut; two at the front, and one at the back waiting to pounce if I tried to tackle the men in front . . . crafty!

I turned, facing the door and window and feeling for the corpse behind my back. I didn't know exactly where I was standing in relation to the body. My fingers were stiff and numb from the tightly bound cuffs.

I touched something but there was no feeling in my fingers. I couldn't tell what it was. I desperately worked my fingers to restore circulation.

Finally my hands came back to life.

At first I felt nothing but the smooth surface of the compost bags until I reached his face. I recoiled. There was still some warmth. I told myself it felt warm because my hands were so cold. I moved back. Slowly, careful to avoid any sudden motion that might alert them, I inched along until I felt the buckle of Appleyard's belt. I traced the edge with my fingers. It fitted the body very closely.

I tried to slide my fingers under the edge but there was no gap. Either the body had already begun to swell in decomposition, unlikely because the temperature was just above freezing, or the late Rick had been a very fit man. It was the latter. Rick had been built like a young oak tree.

I gently depressed the belt until I found part of it that didn't flex under my fingers. This must be it, I thought. The knife's here. I rammed my fingers under the belt at that point. To my horror the corpse emitted a sound, an expiration of air like a sigh.

I nearly fainted.

Was Appleyard still alive?

It was impossible. He'd been shot at point blank range. I'd seen the neat hole between his eyes, eyes that had rolled back into the head when his body was carried, eyes that Claverhouse had closed.

I shivered. It was damned cold and I come from a family where lots of tales had been told about ghosties and ghoulies.

'Trapped wind,' I said to myself and pressed on.

There was a zip on the inside of the belt. I opened it and took out a metal object. It was a short naked blade, edged along two thirds of its length. I gripped the handle in my left hand while repositioning the belt and jacket with my right. I could only hope the corpse looked undisturbed. I took back all the bad things I'd ever thought about poor Appleyard.

I huddled down on my sacks.

Should I cut myself free now? That required a bit of thought. I didn't want to be discovered prematurely.

In the end I cut the plastic round my left wrist only. They'd allowed me to keep my watch and I was able to loop the severed ends round my watch strap so that it looked as if I was still secured as long as I clamped my wrists together. The knife went into the top of the sock on my right leg. I decided to put one shoe on and leave the other off because it was easier to free my feet that way. The plastic hung loosely round my left leg and I slipped my unshod foot through it. To a casual glance I was securely fastened but now I could free my feet almost as quickly as I could my hands. I couldn't be sure that it would be Claverhouse who inspected my fastening when they came to move me to the dirty bomb site.

My mind roved over the events of the day: the killing of my friends, Appleyard's death and Claverhouse's actions. Could I be sure that she wasn't trying to subtly manoeuvre me into doing exactly what she wanted before this Lansdale killed me? Lansdale, small, foxy looking with dark eyes, an ex-soldier: that was how Peter Kelly had described him.

At least I was forewarned against him and I owed him the information he'd carelessly passed to Lew on that scrap of paper. Yes, I owed him for that and I also owed him a very painful death if I could deliver it.

Thinking on those lines led me back to Claverhouse's words. I was being kept alive for a reason. Could it be that Hudson-Piggott had me in mind as the one who'd scatter the Caesium 137 round the fake 'dirty' bomb?

Thoughts of escape through the floorboards were crushed by the constant sounds of movement outside the hut. I'd never make it. I decided my best move was to feign weakness until it came to knife play with Lansdale.

I was moved before dawn.

I hadn't slept but the sacks had given me some insulation against the biting cold of the floor and I felt less tense and strained than when they'd thrown me down.

I was hungry and thirsty but I had hope now.

Fortunately they were in a hurry and they didn't check that I was still securely tied up. The missing shoe was ignored and I was wrapped in the same sacking that I'd lain on and thrown in the back of a van. To my horror ropes were tied round the sacking completely cocooning me.

The journey we took was a short one.

41

Saturday: Dawn

I couldn't see out but I could tell that the van was moving slowly along a deeply rutted lane, turning frequently and slowing almost to a stop at times. There was no other traffic. The jolting motion hurt my ribs and I had to fight to stay centred. If I was fated to die today I'd rather go out fighting than whining and whimpering like a whipped dog.

Not that I'd ever witnessed a dog being whipped in pet loving England but I could imagine it. That picture of cruelty refocused me onto my own situation.

The van lurched to a stop and I heard them taking Rick Appleyard's body out. There was an overwhelming stench of rubber: rubber tyres. It was strong enough to make me gag.

After a protracted interval I was also taken out and laid on the cold ground. The smell of rubber was overpowering. I was in some sort of enclosed space entirely surrounded by rubber tyres. There were fragments of metal on the ground: nothing useful, just bits of bolts and wire. I could move them by scraping my fingers. I heard the van drive away leaving me in the killing ground.

My doubts and fears surged. Claverhouse was playing a cruel joke on me.

I'd arrived at the real MOLOCH this time, the cruel furnace where children were sacrificed. When they started their radioactive bonfire I'd be in the middle of it.

I tried to work out where I was.

It had to be some kind of recycling area where old vehicles were ground into tiny particles of metal and tyres were salvaged. I struggled to get free. My foot came out of the plastic shackle but I couldn't make any headway against the sacking. Whoever had cocooned me had taken his time and done it thoroughly.

But there had to be a way. I couldn't allow myself to be turned into roasted meat. I freed my hands and was trying desperately to reach the knife in my sock when I felt a sharp kick.

'Wait, you fool!' Claverhouse whispered close to my ear. 'You'll get your chance soon.'

I gasped with relief. She was here and she was still on my side.

I stopped struggling and lay quietly, taking very shallow breaths. It was all right for Claverhouse to tell me to wait but the sacking was thick and I wasn't getting much air. I fought to stay awake and relaxed and ready for action.

I'd just started on this when the binding ropes were removed and I was gripped by several hands and rolled over until I was face down. I waited but there no further attention was given to me so I took my chance to grab the blade and hide it in my sleeve. I could have been lying in the middle of a circle of observers but I had to risk it. Then I heard booted feet crunching over rough ground close by. I clamped my hands behind my back just in time.

The sacking was pulled off me.

My handcuffs wouldn't have stood a second of inspection but they weren't looking. Something else had their attention. I struggled to get onto my back and was helped by a contractor's booted foot. He forced me back down when I tried to sit up.

I screwed up my eyes and craned my head forwards to see where I was. The stench of rubber was now joined by the smell of oil. As far as I could tell with my insect's eye view I was lying at the base of an immense pyramid of rubber. Not rubber tyres but ground up rubber: product of an immense shredding machine which towered nearby. Large though it was, the pyramids it had produced were even bigger. Conveyor belts had carried the shredded material upwards onto the conical heaps. They were shut down now.

Someone had just drenched the base of the cone near me in oil. One of Hudson-Piggott's thugs clumped past carrying a jerry can in each hand.

'Dave!' a familiar mocking voice called out as if seeing me was something Molly Claverhouse had been looking forward to all day.

400

'I didn't think we parted company on the right terms last time so I wanted to see you again,' she continued.

'Get on with it,' another voice snapped. 'I'm still not convinced any of this is necessary.'

My sight was coming back.

The man who spoke was Hudson-Piggott. He was now dressed in a full body radiation suit with an air pack on his back not in black Nomex. He held the face mask under his left arm with one hand and his pistol in the other.

Alongside him was a shorter figure I guessed was Lansdale, also wearing full radiation kit. Claverhouse too; she was in radiation kit, though hers was somehow different.

'Right Cunane,' Hudson-Piggott started, 'decision time. You're looking at a choice …'

'Oh, I thought I was looking at a bunch of bloody traitors,' I snarled, expecting anything, a bullet in the head, a sudden dousing with oil, any cruel death they could inflict.

It was foolish of me to speak. My words earned me a kick and a warning look from Claverhouse but not a bullet.

Like a teacher correcting a dim schoolboy Hudson-Piggott tutted mildly. He spoke with a cultivated upper class voice.

'Actually, we're a bunch of patriots, Cunane, but you wouldn't understand that being Irish.'

'You toffee nosed get!' I snarled, imminence of death bringing out all my prejudices. 'I understand that you're a sadistic killer.'

'Hmmm, you've still got life in you then. Perhaps we should just throw the sacking back over you and forget about you.'

'Sir, we must stick to the plan,' Claverhouse interjected.

'Cunane, I'm in two minds about your disposal. There are two ways: one slow and one quick. The quick route involves the Sergeant here, a man who's known for his brisk methods with troublemakers.'

'A man who's a murdering little rat, you mean,' I muttered.

Hudson-Piggott reacted to my comment by drawing back his lips and revealing long teeth. He whinnied like one of Jenny's ponies.

'Eck, eck, eck,' he went. 'He wants to break your nasty neck and leave you here so it looks as if you lit this inferno. You'll be wearing Islamic rig and clutching a copy of the Koran in your sweaty little palm.'

He bent over me and turned my head to the left so that I could see a portable torch kit with its oxy and acetylene tanks lying on the ground. There was a pile of clothing next to it, also a heap of splintered wood against the base of the cone.

My stomach gave a lurch but I tried to be defiant.

'You're a total nut job, aren't you,' I said, 'a bloody psychopath.'

He let out that annoying whinny again.

'Eck, eck, eck, not at all Cunane. I often think I'm the only sane man in a mad world.'

'That's a sure sign of insanity!'

'Hmmm, as you persist in your stupid defiance I'm inclined to take your answer as no and let Sergeant Lansdale get on with things. However, thanks to you, we're running late. So if you won't cooperate I'll have your family dealt with by the Sergeant. You have a choice, it's up to you.'

Lansdale loomed over me. I could see the clouds and hear birds in the distance. The wind was blowing fiercely and the clouds were scudding across the sky. Lansdale raised his eyebrows expectantly. I swear he was licking his lips at the prospect of breaking my neck.

Claverhouse stood to one side. She looked very strained and though she didn't speak I felt that her hazel eyes were imploring me. I noticed that she didn't appear to have a weapon. Both Hudson-Piggott and Lansdale were wearing shoulder holsters over the NBC suits.

'What's this choice then?' I muttered.

'OK, you do exactly what we tell you. You'll still die but your family will survive. On the other hand, if you inconvenience us Sergeant Lansdale will kill you now and we'll deal with your family later. By 'deal' I mean that they will disappear. There's a remote possibility that your children may be taken for adoption but I wouldn't count on that in the chaos of the regime-change which is coming.'

It wasn't remotely funny but I found myself laughing. It was my nerves I suppose. His crazy idea of choice was no choice.

'I choose the first option,' I said.

'Comical to the last, eh Cunane? I admire constancy in a man, a quality the unfortunate Rick Appleyard lacked. In consideration I'll explain to you why your death will not be in vain.'

He assumed that odd duck-like posture that I'd seen before. Lecturing mode, I guessed.

'Boss, we haven't got all day,' Lansdale complained. 'This bastard has already caused us to bring the operation forward. Let me do him now.'

'No,' Hudson-Piggott said sharply. 'It will be better for our back story if the authorities find Mr Cunane's radiation burned body near our little blaze and I shouldn't imagine you want to deal with the radioactive material yourself, do you Sergeant? Our contractor friends are terrified of it.'

Lansdale shook his head and swore under his breath.

'No, I didn't imagine you would,' Hudson-Piggott said. 'All right, Cunane thanks to various incentives we've been offering the recycling industry this is the biggest pile of waste rubber ever assembled in this country. As you can see these massive cones are attractively garlanded in white material round their summits. From a distance they resemble the Alps, only the 'snow' is low-level radioactive waste from hospitals. Feeble stuff, but potent enough to make our smoke column radioactive but harmless.'

'Brilliant!'

'Isn't it? Your part, Cunane, is to add an extra touch of veracity to my illusion by sprinkling highly toxic Caesium 137, all over this site. You'll open those drums,' he paused and pointed out two yellow drums some distance away from us, 'and you'll dump the Caesium on the tracks and the soil, not on the cones. Get it?'

'Yes,' I grunted.

'When you've done that and incidentally sustained a lethal dose of radiation, you will light the bonfire with that oxy-acetylene torch. It starts with a simple click.'

'Think of everything, don't you?'

'Boss, we've got to get moving,' Lansdale interjected.

'One more moment only, Sergeant, the man must understand his role.'

'Gawd, Boss!' Lansdale growled.

'Now, Cunane, don't get any ideas of escaping. The good sergeant will have a rifle trained on you the whole time and there are still twelve of my contractors available.'

He glanced to his right. I followed his gaze. There were two of the contractors some distance away from us. They were in ordinary clothes not radiation kit. The Nomex uniforms had been discarded.

'I see.'

'As soon as you save your family by taking the lids off the drums your own death is certain, a very painful death. Complete all your tasks to the sergeant's satisfaction and you'll be found dead and regarded as a jihadi martyr whose comrades mercifully sent him to his virgins with a bullet.'

I recognised his obvious lie. There'd be no merciful bullet. Exposure to high level radioactive material would kill me quickly which suited the plan better.

'Very well thought out, Hudson-Piggott,' I said sarcastically, 'but what's all this nonsense in aid of?'

He changed. All the assumed amiability disappeared.

'What it's in aid of, as you put it, is the freeing of this country from the terrorist threat we've lived under since 9/11. Our growing and aggressive Muslim population will get the blame when half of England falls under a radioactive cloud. They will be deported or will voluntarily renounce Islam and we will win the so-called war on terror or do you want your children to live under threat for the rest of their lives?'

I couldn't hold my tongue.

'I want my children to grow up in the tolerant country they were born in,' I snapped.

He scowled; his lips formed a thin white line and he pulled out his gun.

I drew in a breath and flinched for the bullet. My last thought was of Jan as I'd seen her at Topfield on Monday, all pregnant and lovely.

Then instead of pulling the trigger he laughed and holstered his gun.

404

'Nice try Cunane. I can see there's much more to you than I thought. If I'd shot you now we'd have had to force one of the contractors to die of radiation poisoning and I don't think they're up for that.'

He turned to Lansdale.

'Enough of this,' he said. 'I'm going to round up the men. You get Cunane into his Afghan kit and supervise him. Molly, you come with me.'

'A word, sir,' Claverhouse said.

She took Hudson-Piggott's arm and they stepped away from Lansdale for a moment. After a brief conversation she came back towards us.

'Molly stays, Sergeant, apparently she doesn't trust you not to find a reason to kill the annoying Mr Cunane as soon as I'm out of sight.'

Lansdale pulled a face and spat on the ground.

'All the same to me, Boss,' he said.

Hudson-Piggott strode away with his curious duck like gait.

Claverhouse spoke to Lansdale. 'What can he do? His hands and feet are tied. The man's a bungling amateur.'

'Who you've taken a fancy to,' Lansdale said under his breath, 'f**king stuck up bitch.'

The strong south westerly was blowing straight past us into the huge stack so it must lie on a SW/NE axis like a cannon aimed for the destruction of a vast swath of territory.

I shuddered.

There were enough tyres and shredded rubber to burn for days or weeks especially as the fire fighters wouldn't be able to approach the blaze due to the Caesium 137 scattered everywhere. I'd mocked but Hudson-Piggott's plan would succeed. It hit me how right Lew was to want him killed immediately.

'I need him on his feet to look into his eyes,' Claverhouse said.

'So you can peer into his bonny blue eyes for one last time?' Lansdale taunted.

'Arsehole!' she snapped. 'We may have to kill people but you needn't enjoy it so much.'

Lansdale laughed and turned to the sack of clothes. He plucked out a turban and jammed it on my head.

'Who's a pretty boy, then?' he mocked.

He pulled out the long shirt and baggy trousers. He flung the trousers at me. 'Get your jim-jams on then, beddie-bye time soon.'

'How can I get these on when I'm tied hand and foot?' I replied.

'Hey beautiful, cut him free while I cover him,' he ordered Claverhouse.

'Lansdale, you moron, am I supposed to bite through his cuffs with my teeth? You took my knife when you disarmed me for security reasons, remember?'

'Oh yeah gorgeous, so I did,' he said with a sneer. 'I wonder why? You may have taken in the Boss with your smarmy ways but I know what you really thought of dear old Ricky boy even if he doesn't.'

'Bastard,' Claverhouse said coldly.

He laughed again but fumbled in a pouch that was secured by a sling over his shoulder and pulled out a knife.

'Please try something,' he said, holding it to my throat. 'Just make one little move. Lift your legs up.'

'I can't, I'm too stiff,' I said.

'Move!' he threatened.

'I can't,' I said pathetically. 'My legs have gone numb. I've been tied up for hours.'

'You stand well clear,' he said to Claverhouse.

She moved back.

Moving awkwardly in his NBC suit he knelt at my feet and studied my bindings.

'What's this,' he exclaimed as soon as he laid a hand on the plastic cuff and discovered it wasn't fastened to anything. He leaned forward to ram his knife into my throat at the same instant as my blade slipped under his ribs. The force of his movement aided my thrust. His eyes bulged. I pushed my knife forward and upwards and I felt the beating of his heart stop as my knife penetrated it.

He tried to shout something but no sound emerged. His eyes rolled and he went limp.

I started to push him off me. Blood splattered my shirt but didn't gush in torrents.

'Hold him upright,' Claverhouse ordered, 'don't let them see what you've done.'

From the point of view of the contractors to our right and left Lansdale was positioned above me. They observed curiously.

Claverhouse ripped the semi-automatic out of Lansdale's holster. That was the signal for the contractors to pull out their own weapons and rush towards us. Claverhouse went on one knee and shot them all with cold deliberation and frightening accuracy. They tumbled down like so many skittles and lay twitching on the rough ground. The surrounding rubber muffled the shots.

The MI5 agent took charge at once and I wasn't about to start arguing with her. She had the gun in her hand.

'Get into the shirt and trousers! If they see you they've got to think you're carrying out the plan.'

I obeyed, pulling the long shirt over my turban. It covered up the blood stains. My sole remaining shoe was tangled up in the sacking and on the theory that one shoe was better than no shoe I started fumbling for it.

She pulled my hands away.

'Dave! There's no time for that. We've got to get rid of the Caesium or Hudson-Piggott will start all over again.'

'Get rid of it?' I repeated stupidly, 'but it'll kill us. Those drums will leak as soon as we move them.'

'No, they aren't oil drums. They're lead lined stainless steel cylinders and are impact proof against being hit by a locomotive.'

I was about to say, *'This is where we came in,'* thinking about the security van at Manchester Airport until I remembered it was Clint who'd saved our bacon then. I shut up and looked around. It was my first proper inspection of the site. Beyond the cones of shredded rubber there were acres and acres of car tyres. I revised my estimate of how long this fire would burn from weeks to months, years even?

To my left, beyond the dead contractors, the ground fell away sharply. We were in a secluded valley somewhere in the foothills of the Pennines. There wasn't a single house in view. I ran forward, pausing only to pick up a contractor's automatic. There was a steep hill. The tyre dump was on a sort of plateau with hills on three sides.

I ran back. My bare feet were bleeding but it seemed a small sacrifice after what I'd been through.

Claverhouse was removing her radiation suit which I took as a good sign.

'We can push them down there,' I told her. 'They'll roll for half a mile.'

And that's what we did.

The radiation containers were sealed but had screw tops designed to be opened by machines. There was an oddly shaped spanner intended for manual removal of the lids. I slung it high among the tyres. Then we rolled the cylinders and they went bouncing down the slope, gathering speed before disappearing into bushes in the distance.

Hudson-Piggott wouldn't find them in a hurry.

'Now the oxy-acetylene torch,' Claverhouse said urgently. As she spoke a contractor incautiously poked his head round a pile of tyres. She shot him almost as a reflex action. Her accuracy was frightening.

'Dave, get the oxy torch and dump it somewhere where they won't find it in a hurry,' she ordered without turning a hair.

I dragged it over to a loose pile of tyres and heaved some on top to cover it.

When I returned Claverhouse, and I still didn't think of her as Molly, was standing by Appleyard's body. She'd covered him with her discarded radiation suit. Her face was red and she'd been crying but I wasn't feeling compassionate.

'I want some answers,' I said bluntly.

'There are answers but they're not for you,' she said.

I tried a different tack.

'What was Rick Appleyard to you?'

'We were lovers. I was bringing Rick round to my point of view about Hudson-Piggott. The trouble is Rick was so terribly loyal to the service. He found it next to impossible to believe anything bad about a senior man or even that there was a plot. You were helpful in that. He was coming to see things my way but then he had to go running to

Hudson-Piggott when Lansdale was sent for him, the idiot.'

'Oh,' I muttered, not much wiser. 'So who is Hudson-Piggott?'

She paused for a moment considering and then looked down at Appleyard.

'Oh, what does it matter anyway? The point is Dave, as long as he's still alive you're in danger so you deserve the truth.'

'Who is he?'

'He's the Prime Minister's confidential adviser on the security services. He has the Prime Minister's ear and, as the heads of all the other services don't, that means he's effectively in charge of MI5, MI6, Defence Intelligence and all the other secret odds and sods in Whitehall. All that, and he has a whopping big budget to bring about change.'

'No one can say he hasn't been trying.'

She frowned.

'You really are too flippant, Dave. My boss, Sir Freddy Jones, hates him and doesn't trust him an inch which is why I was tasked to get close and report as soon as he made a slip. But I wasn't able to. That rat you stuck Rick's knife in watched me like a hawk. When he accidentally killed the two Ms in the course of removing you, Hudson-Piggott used their deaths to his advantage. He discredited Rick. The man was running his own parallel service. Now we know why.'

'But he's finished now?'

'Who's to say? Hudson-Piggott's a master at blaming other people and coming up smelling of roses.'

'Which other people will he blame for this?' I said, suddenly nervous.

'I don't know . . . you, me, someone we don't know, but he's certain to have a Plan B.'

'Oh, my God!'

'Come on Dave, you've survived being a thorn in his side six days. You'll just have to go on a bit longer. I think he's near the end of his rope now.'

'You think? Thanks a bunch.'

She shrugged. Then she startled me by taking out the semi-automatic. She didn't use it on me. Instead she carefully wiped her prints

409

off it, clamped it in Lansdale's dead fingers and fired it.

'Spent a lot of time in the SAS Killing House, did Ian Lansdale. He was nearly as good a shot as me so a bit of misdirection is in order,' she said. 'Now whoever cleans up this mess might just think dear dead Ian was the shooter.'

'Great,' I muttered.

'Right, Dave, I don't know about you but I'm out of here. It's better if we split up.'

'Are you sure?' I asked, aware that she was the only person on the planet who could testify to my non-involvement.

'Yes, there are still contractors about so be careful. Your best bet may be to lie low somewhere until the police get here.'

'Will they get here?'

'They will when I reach a phone. One of Hudson-Piggott's security precautions was to confiscate all our phones.'

'But . . .'

'Listen Dave, we have five minutes at best before Hudson-Piggott decides Lansdale isn't coming and starts wondering why there isn't a fire, so move it.'

'What about all these?' I asked indicating the six bodies.

'Clean up squad for Rick and Lansdale. The birds and foxes can have the rest as far as I'm concerned. They're just scum.'

Then as good as her word she began running in the direction of the slope we'd sent the Caesium cylinders down. She disappeared.

The thought in my mind was treachery, her treachery to me.

'Job done, Ms Claverhouse' I said to myself. There wasn't going to be a nuclear disaster here but the odds on me avoiding a personal disaster weren't high.

As for Hudson-Piggott's nasty plan, his contractors would have a hell of a time trying to set the damp wood on fire without the oxy torch and even if they succeeded there'd be no Caesium panic now. The hospital waste was barely radioactive at all.

I hovered indecisively for a moment. My feet hurt like hell. There was no way I'd be able to hide from anyone with a trail of bloody footprints following me. I went back to Lansdale's sack. I shook it and surprise, surprise, a pair of serviceable sandals fell out.

I put them on and cast an eye round the scene. There were stiffs everywhere. It was a battlefield. Appleyard, Lansdale, four contractors; but the number was incomplete. I had to add Hudson-Piggott to the total or my own and my family's lives were still in jeopardy. That bastard had killed Uncle Lew and his friend Pickering, blown up my house and murdered most of my friends. Forget about his insane plot against the country, I owed Hudson-Piggott cartloads of payback.

There was another thing. Hanging around here until the boys in blue arrived didn't feel like a very happening sort of thing as far as I was concerned. My knowledge of police procedure told me they'd arrest me on sight and hold me indefinitely. I mean, what was there here?

Dave Cunane + dead bodies = Arrest for murder.

I had no guarantee that Claverhouse would even phone the police. Who was to say what explanation Sir Freddie Jones would think up? Damaging admissions leading to a major scandal involving his service would be low on his shopping list.

Following Claverhouse's lead, I wiped my prints off the knife handle sticking out of Lansdale's chest and collected up all physical traces of my presence in this charnel house. Grabbing Lansdale's sack I stowed away my shoe and the plastic cuffs. After a second's thought I added the sacking I'd been wrapped in. It was bound to have my DNA on it. For good measure I crammed the turban and the baggy pants in as well. I tucked the long shirt into my trousers and set off in the direction Hudson-Piggott had disappeared in.

I was fairly happy about the Caesium drums and the oxy cylinders. I'd wrapped my hands in sacking before I touched them. The only other incriminating thing was that blasted spanner. My prints were on it. It had fallen deep into the tyre mountain. I could only hope it stayed lost.

I was cautious. I peered round every intersection but saw no one.

I argued to myself that the last contractor Claverhouse shot must have been sent back to collect her. Had there been another with him who reported back? Did Claverhouse know Hudson-Piggott would be on his toes as soon as he heard Lansdale was dead? I tried to stop hypothesising before I became paranoid.

I soon passed through Hudson-Piggott's Alps to an older part of the site.

There were yet more piles of salvaged material of every imaginable type but to my right there was a distant building. It was some sort of ramshackle site office.

Was there a telephone?

I approached by an indirect route and entered the heaps of junk. The lane or aisle I was in consisted of architectural salvage, pallet loads of used bricks, chimneys, slates and stone slabs. Paddy Cunane would have been in bliss wandering round here but I used it to cover my stealthy approach to the office.

This place was enormous. Where were the workers? Where were the operators of those shredding machines and conveyor belts? My final observation point was behind a pallet of old yellow bricks. I tried to still my noisy breathing. I was about forty yards from the office. I now saw that the office stood alongside what was probably the only entrance to the site. That was how they controlled these sites, wasn't it . . . a single gate to check whatever was coming in or out.

I crawled through piles of squared timbers, floorboards, building stone, architectural features, mouldings, bumpers, radiators, and hubcaps and after five minutes came out diagonally opposite the entrance of this maze of jumble. There was no sign of life.

I scratched my head and told myself to be cautious.

The place was deserted or was it? There were sounds coming from outside, shouts and revving engines.

The entrance was a gap in the junk heaps wide enough for two trucks to come through abreast. There was a heavy steel and chain link gate which was now open and beyond that a second, much flimsier, wooden gate.

A small watchman's hut stood to one side of the site office I'd noticed before. A rusty weighbridge occupied a space in front of the office. There were no telephone wires visible anywhere. A lot of these small businesses had abandoned landlines.

I stared at the tiny hut until my eyes ached. Was someone

waiting in there to shoot me when I showed myself?

Keeping low and ready to run if necessary I made my way into the wide gap. I saw the two vans disappearing down the rutted lane. I was alone.

I just had time to read the small sign set high up in a tree before I loped off after them. It read:

PATEL WASTE MANAGEMENT
ABDUL K. PATEL PROPRIETOR
WASTE RECYCLING AND DISPOSAL
CAR PARTS AND DEMOLISHING
HOSPITAL WASTE A SPECIALITY
FORMERLY TRADING AS
LOCHHEAD & SONS

There was a mobile number but it had been painted out.

I wondered if Abdul K. Patel had ever existed outside of Hudson-Piggott's diseased imagination.

42

Saturday: 7 a.m.

The track downhill had been paved at one time but now it was deeply rutted. It was a pleasant country lane leading to moorland but had subsided into rural squalor. Overgrown hedges and trees on either side were clogged with paper and rubbish and it was almost impassable. There were old ruts and fresh ruts. My guess was that the fresh ones were made when the 'hospital waste' was trucked in from the warehouse in Manchester.

I'd been puzzled by the absence of a labour force.

They weren't absent. Hudson-Piggott's 'workers' were in the two vans slowly bumping along the track ahead of me. What could be simpler than importing a group of contractors from a former Yugoslavian republic disguised as labourers?

The vans weren't gaining on me. The track was so bad that they had to keep stopping and slowing while I ploughed on. The danger was that I'd get too close. I kept in the shade of the encroaching hedge.

I passed a sign saying Private Road – Keep Out. A steel barrier lay at the side.

Eventually the vans reached civilisation in the form of scattered houses and a paved road and they speeded up.

I kept going. I knew that the house with the garden shed couldn't be far away.

The vans were almost out of sight when they turned down a side street.

I stepped up my pace. I hadn't eaten for hours and my stomach was rumbling but the prospect of catching up with Hudson-Piggott was food enough. I was a little too eager. When I reached the bend they'd disappeared round both vans suddenly zoomed out past me and accelerated away at a speed I couldn't hope to match.

I flung myself back into a privet hedge but I needn't have bothered. They weren't interested in me. I untangled myself and watched them vanish into traffic at a busy intersection in the distance.

Suddenly I was too tired even to curse. I squatted on the kerb.

I must have stayed where I was for ten minutes until I shook off the lethargy.

The house with the nasty pond and the garden shed must be nearby.

I needed to retrieve my other shoe. I didn't want to leave it like Cinderella's slipper for some forensic investigator to trace my DNA.

That is assuming there'd ever be an investigation.

I recalled the way Morgan and Myers' deaths and the helicopter crash had been sanitised. Hudson-Piggott was free and was probably already spinning some yarn to the Prime Minister about how he'd broken the vicious Moloch Plot by Moslem terrorists. The dead contractors would become jihadis, Appleyard and Lansdale the brave MI5 men who'd given their lives to defeat them.

That's how I'd do it and I'm not even a practised liar or a PR man.

Yeah, there were some awkward details to explain . . . Claverhouse in particular . . . but they'd work round them.

I needed to think about myself now. I could get Jan and the kids away to a country where MI5's arm wouldn't reach. It couldn't be any of the English speaking countries; Australia, New Zealand, Canada, and certainly not the United States. Argentina or Brazil would be the best choices. The children were young enough to pick up the language.

I headed off down the short cul-de-sac. The sound of my sandals slapping the flagged pavement was the only noise. Maybe this was a retreat for zombies.

It was certainly very private. The houses all had hedges or towering Leylandii in front but at the end there was one with genuinely massive and well tended yew hedges. They were tall even by 'Golden Triangle' privacy standards, ten or twelve feet. Whoever lived there wanted seclusion. Was it one of the Lochheads, perhaps understandably nervous about reaction after his family had despoiled the moorland?

416

The wrought iron gate was open but as I entered I came to a sudden stop.

A pair of legs was poking out from under the hedge. They were visible from the street.

Scarcely daring to breathe I parted the foliage to see the face. It was one of the contractors. He had a neat round hole between his eyes. I dropped my bag and fumbled in my pocket for the semi-automatic. I chambered a bullet.

Was it possible?

I crept forward. The well screened drive curved towards an open parking area in front of the large stone-built modern house. There was another body lying face down.

It wasn't Hudson-Piggott.

A black, top of the range, Jaguar was parked by the entrance porch. Its boot was open. I moved closer, hugging the wall, close enough to identify it as the type of vehicle used by the Prime Minister. It was an XJ Sentinel with a five litre V8 engine and enough armour plate to stop a rocket or a bullet. They're specially made for the Government at over three hundred K a whack. The days when PMs came into work on the Tube are long gone.

How poor Clint would have loved to see it. He'd have rattled off all the specs for me.

Then I shivered as if cold fingers were stroking my spine.

So Hudson-Piggott was high enough in the Government pecking order to rate a high security vehicle. How long would it take him to squash an annoying little bug like me now that he wasn't also organising a coup d'état?

There was the sound of someone running downstairs.

I pressed myself into the corner formed by the porch and the wall.

Hudson-Piggott emerged. He was wearing the same brown Huntsman suit he'd been wearing when I first met him. There was a small suitcase in his left hand and a semi-automatic in his right. I guessed he had it in case his contractors came back. There must have been a rift; perhaps they didn't like leaving so many bodies behind.

He slung the case into the boot and moved to the driver's door still retaining the pistol in his right hand, cautious bastard that he was.

I was on him in a flash, pressing the muzzle of my gun into his head.

'Cunane,' he said, 'how very unsurprising. My mistake all along has been to underestimate you. I should have moved heaven and earth to eliminate you on the very first day.'

'Move away from the car,' I ordered.

He stepped back two paces.

'Shut the door with your foot.'

He complied. I knew he was calculating how to deal with an amateur like me who was breaking rule number one in taking a prisoner at gunpoint by standing too close. I had the drop on him but only just.

'We can still work something out you know. After all, with your inheritance you're virtually one of us now. I can get your son down for Eton with a click of my finger. Name it, a title, whatever you want and it's yours.'

'Keep moving,' I ordered.

I shifted position from his left side to his right but I could tell he was tensing to whirl and shoot me. He must have thought I was crazy not to have disarmed him.

He moved at my direction but now only needed to flick his hand up and I'd be dead.

I leaned forward and shot him in the right temple at close range.

He went down face first and sprawled on the macadam drive, quite dead. His rimless specs slipped off his nose. There was powder stippling round the hole in his right temple. A gaping exit wound on the other side marked where the slug had passed through his evil brain. His own gun was still clutched tightly in his right hand and no suicide could ever look more convincing.

I stood and drew several deep breaths.

This is where some killers get caught. They forget a tiny unconsidered detail and the whole thing unravels. No unconsidered detail was ever going to unravel for me.

The fatal bullet: that could be it, my own fatal error.

If it was found they'd quickly discover that Hudson-Piggott wasn't killed with his own gun.

I stood close to the position I'd killed him from. My eyes scanned the wall. The bullet hadn't struck the car. I wondered by how much the bullet would be slowed by the journey through a human skull. Very little, I decided. I was patient. I kept looking; the possibility of years in prison riveted my attention to that wall.

Finally I spotted it.

It had struck the brickwork on the porch and ricocheted into the thick mortar between the stone courses on the main wall. It must have lost energy after the first strike because I was able to pull it out from the dense lime mortar with my fingers. I rubbed the spot until it didn't stand out.

I wasn't satisfied.

There had to be more.

What was so important to Hudson-Piggott that he had to come back here and change into his suit? There was the car but he could have sent someone for it. It had to be something else. It was Plan B. There must be information he didn't want to leave lying about; a laptop, a tablet, files. It had to be in the case.

The boot wasn't locked. I took the case out. There was a laptop inside. I propped it by the Jag and dashed to the garden shed. Satisfyingly, my shoe was there in plain view just where I'd kicked it off.

I wasted time putting my own shoes on. I left the shed and then paused. Something had caught my eye. I went back. The jacket I'd been wearing when they picked me up was hanging from a nail behind the door. How could I have missed it? It had my wallet and my ID in it. I put it on.

I picked up the case and set off down the road. I still had no idea where I was. The 'zombie' cul-de-sac, which was actually called Acheron Close, Tameside, was appropriately silent. It was still early and observation cuts both ways. If you surround your property with privets and Leylandii so people can't see in, it follows that you can't see out. All the bedroom curtains were still drawn.

I reached the main road and caught a bus into Manchester. I was home free.

Home free except that Clint and Bren and his oppos were dead. That was far, far worse than the prospect of telling Jan that we were homeless.

When I reached Piccadilly Gardens I was still unsure what to do. I bought a prepaid mobile at an all night shop in the station and phoned Jan.

She picked up immediately.

I barely had time to croak 'hello' before she spoke.

'Dave! You're alive, oh thank God, thank God!'

'A devout atheist thanking God,' I commented, 'that's a turn-up.'

'Oh, don't you go on. I've had your mother on continually threatening to start a novena, whatever that is, for your survival and Bren's got half the police force out scouring the whole of Greater Manchester for you. I honestly think they're expecting to find your body but I never lost faith in you. How did you get away?'

'That's a long story. Tell me about Bren.'

'No you first.'

'I can't. A phone's a radio, remember?'

'You are so infuriating at times Dave.'

'Sorry.'

There was a brief pause.

'When you were kidnapped one of Bren's men was grazed in the arm, nothing serious.'

'But they fired hundreds of bullets, I heard them.'

'Mainly into the air or at Bren's vehicle, apparently.'

'But they killed Clint.'

'Wrong again, Dave. His back and chest are badly bruised but he's fine. He's with those two new assistants you recruited.'

'Tony and Lee.'

'Yes, listen Dave, is it all sorted now? Can we come home?'

'It's all sorted Jan but . . .'

'Dave, I know about Topfield. By 'come home' I mean come back to you. I don't care about the house. I'll live in a squat in Miles Platting as long as it's with you.'

420

Afterword

Hudson-Piggott's laptop was doubly protected by an impenetrable password and encrypted text. However Tony Nolan made cracking it a personal challenge. He worked on it in intervals while running Pimpernel Investigations so progress was slow even for the reconditioned brain. Still, Tony has more time on his hands now that Lee is attending a sort of boarding school/boot camp for young adults in an attempt to repair the defects of his education.

I believe Tony hired time on an American supercomputer to crack the encryption. He said he'd crack it and crack it he did.

It was from Tony that I finally gleaned a few more details of the fate Hudson-Piggott had been planning for us all.

MOLOCH, actually called *Operation Restore*, was originally timed so that the radiation would begin hitting the ground just when afternoon prayers were taking place in the mosques of Northern England. In the ensuing panic it was hoped, and no doubt arranged, that there would be 'spontaneous' attacks on the Muslim community: the long dreaded 'backlash'.

The full awfulness of his plan comes out best in one page of notes among the many pages of his 'operational plans'.

The De Facto Civil Disorder Planning Group

A group of senior civil servants, security officials and police began planning what would happen if there is a major breakdown in civil order in this country following a period of sustained Islamic terrorism. Incidents triggering this would be nuclear bomb in major city, dirty bomb, poisoned reservoir, massive armed attack on civilians at say football match, assault on and assassination of several members of Royal family and/or government at once.

Their final recommendations were

1) Suspension of Parliament. Interim rule by a special troika of soldier, security man, politician. Suspension of constitution.

2) Emergency Powers Act enabling detention without trial of

Other 'Dave Cunane' books in sequence

Red for Rachel

Nine Lives

The Reluctant Investigator: shortlisted for the CWA Gold Dagger

Kingdom Gone

Boiling Point

Above Suspicion

Raised in Silence

Other Frank LeanNovels

Irish Jack's Women: a murder investigation by renowned English railway engineer **Joseph Locke** during the Irish Famine. One of Dave Cunane's ancestors is involved in a minor role.

Asking For It: pathologist **Professor Jack Preston** removes murderers before they provide him with victims to investigate

Murder in a Hollywood Motorhome: an improvisational murder mystery play for 12 actors

Children's Books

Haunted High School Series: children's fantasy involving 'special powers'. A boy stumbles on a long forgotten 'force of nature' with the power of speech. This invisible being decides that the boy, Peter Scattergood, is an ideal candidate for reform in preparation for some special task the purpose of which it doesn't yet know!

   (1) *Peter Scattergood and the Panic Horn*

   (2) *Peter Scattergood and the Owl King*

   (3) *Peter Scattergood and the Dark Force*

Cover Photo Manchester Town Hall from Brazennose Street ©
Frank Lean

17342541R00238

Printed in Great Britain
by Amazon